Cici's journal

LOST
AND
FOUND

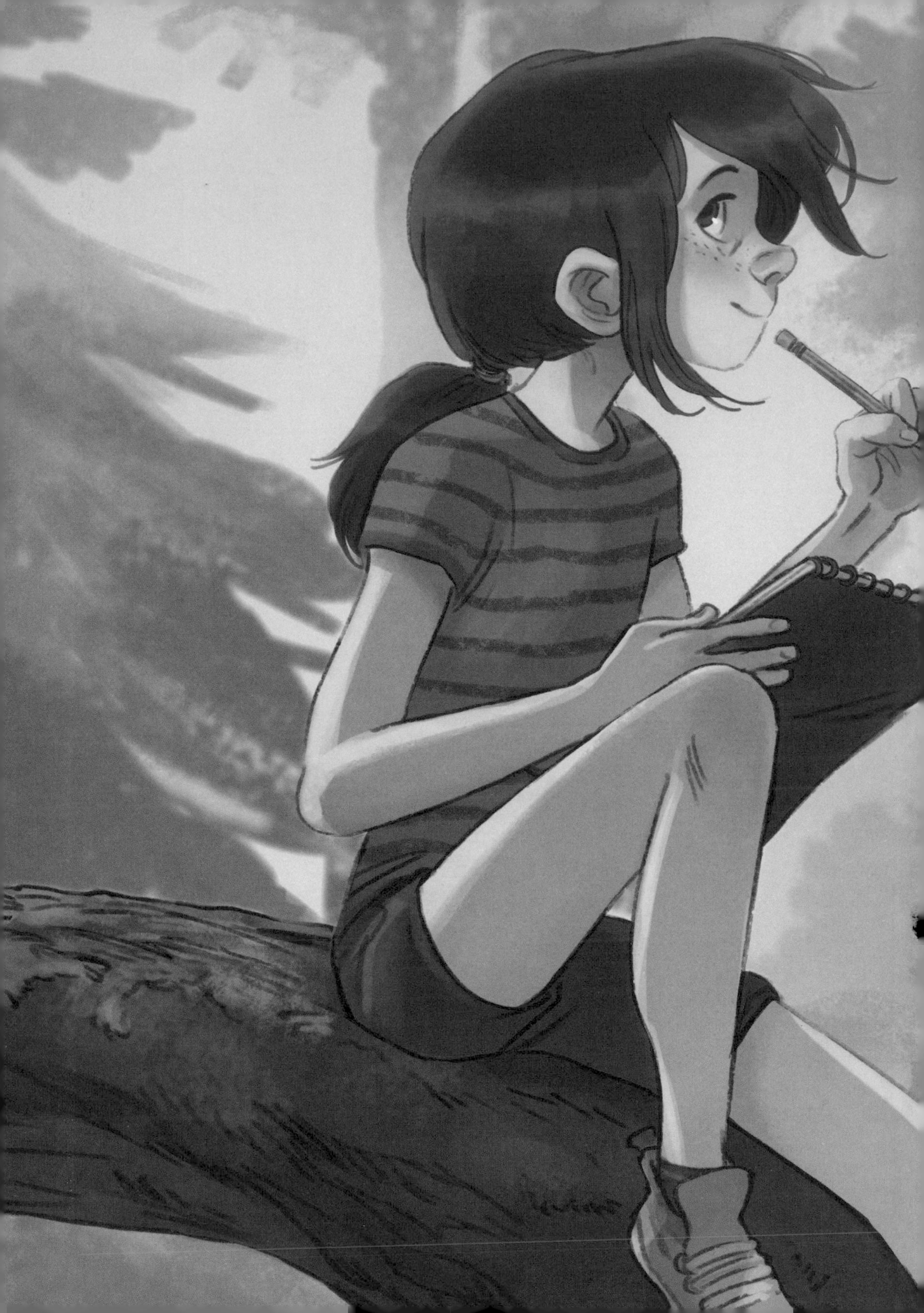

Cici's journal

LOST
AND
FOUND

Joris Chamblain
Aurélie Neyret

:01

First Second

New York

First Second

Published by First Second
First Second is an imprint of Roaring Brook Press,
a division of Holtzbrinck Publishing Holdings Limited Partnership
120 Broadway, New York, NY 10271
firstsecondbooks.com
mackids.com

Translation by Anne and Owen Smith
English translation © 2021 by First Second

Library of Congress Control Number: 2020919585

Our books may be purchased in bulk for promotional, educational, or business use.
Please contact your local bookseller or the Macmillan Corporate and Premium Sales Department at
(800) 221-7945 ext. 5442 or by email at MacmillanSpecialMarkets@macmillan.com.

Originally published in 2014 in French by Éditions Soleil, in the Metamorphose collection
directed by Barbara Canepa and Clotilde Vu, as *Les Carnets de Cerise,*
Tome 3: Le Dernier des Cinq Trésors, in 2016 as *Les Carnets de Cerise, Tome 4: La Déesse sans visage,*
and in 2017 as *Les Carnets de Cerise, Tome 5: Des premières neiges aux perséides*
French edition © 2014, 2016, 2017 by Éditions Soleil/ Chamblain/ Neyret
First American edition, 2021
Cover design by Kirk Benshoff
Interior book design by Molly Johanson and Laura Berry
Edited by Calista Brill and Alex Lu
Printed in China by RR Donnelley Asia Printing Solutions Ltd., Dongguan City,
Guangdong Province

ISBN 978-1-250-76340-2   (paperback)
1 3 5 7 9 10 8 6 4 2

ISBN 978-1-250-76339-6   (hardcover)
1 3 5 7 9 10 8 6 4 2

Don't miss your next favorite book from First Second!
For the latest updates go to firstsecondnewsletter.com and sign up for our enewsletter.

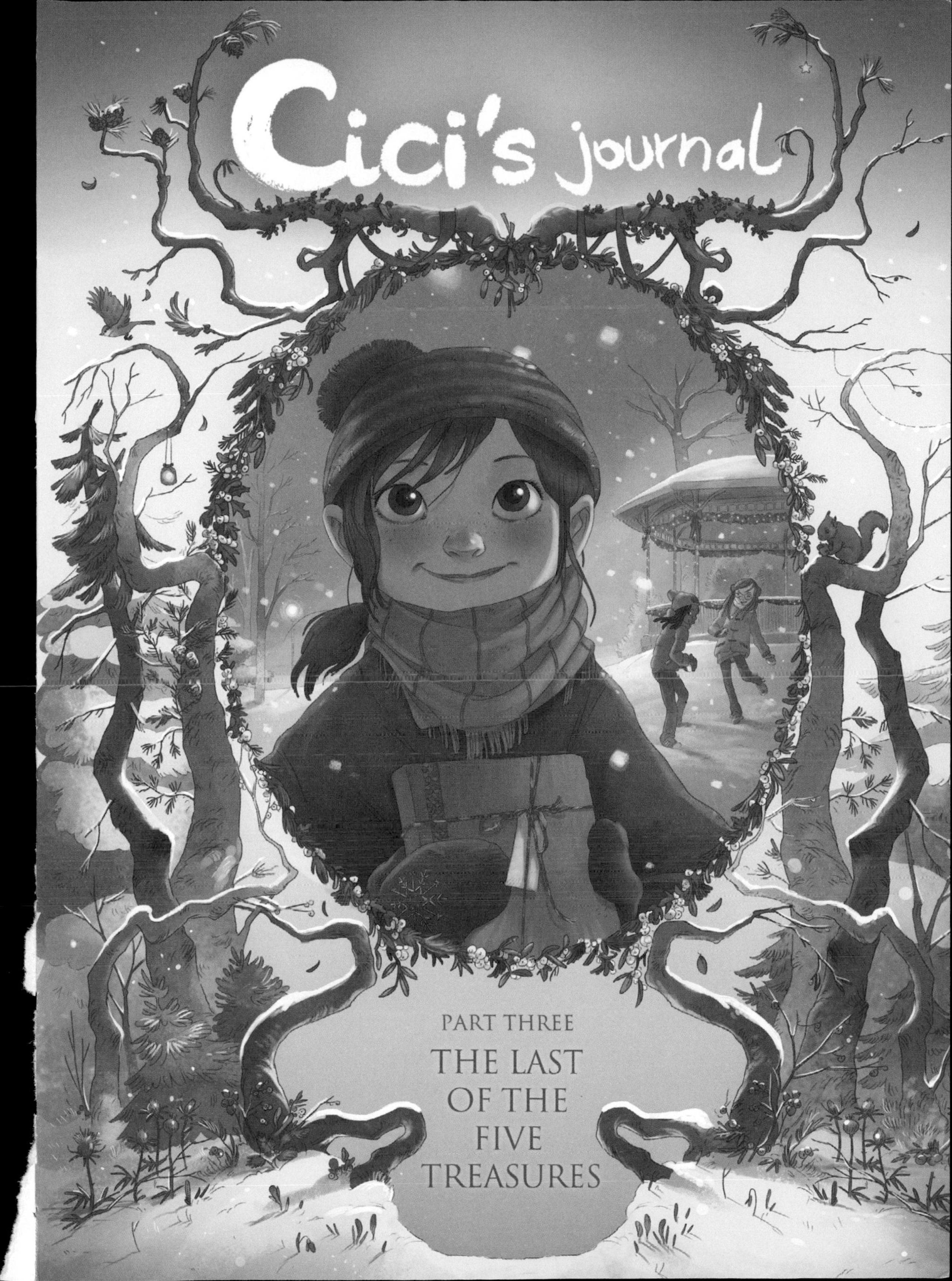
Cici's journal
PART THREE
THE LAST
OF THE
FIVE
TREASURES

For my grandfather Jo, who would have loved this winter story . . .
Thanks to my family, for the wonderful holiday times we've spent together . . .
which have undoubtedly breathed life into the colors of these pages.
Thanks to Joris, for the snow and for this beautiful adventure, as well as to our fairies:
Barbara, Clotilde, and Adeline, for their support.
Thanks to Cédric, Clément, Guillaume, Jérémie, Line, Nico, Romain,
Victoria, and Federico, for their magnificent input.
Finally, thanks to Nico for his help and encouragement,
and thanks for being my lifelong teammate;
your love is what gives me strength.

Aurélie

I dedicate this graphic novel:
—to all the magical family Christmases that brightened my childhood;
—to the tales my parents would tell me every night before I fell asleep;
—to the little fairy who, on the morning of the first day, leaned on my cradle to offer me a wish;
—I thank Agnès D. and Manon F. for their valuable musical assistance,
as well as Marjorie C. for the recipes . . . and all the rest.

Joris

Dear Santa Claus,

It's Cici! You know—that girl who meddles in other people's lives . . . It's been a long time since I sent you a letter. I guess it's because I've gotten bigger—I don't believe in the Tooth Fairy anymore either . . .

Even so, I felt like writing to you this morning, just like when I was little! Christmas Day is coming soon and I want to keep believing in the magic of the holidays. More importantly, I need your help. This year, I want to find a unique present for my mom. She usually likes whatever I give her, but this time, I would like to get her something special that really touches her heart. And I'm running out of time!

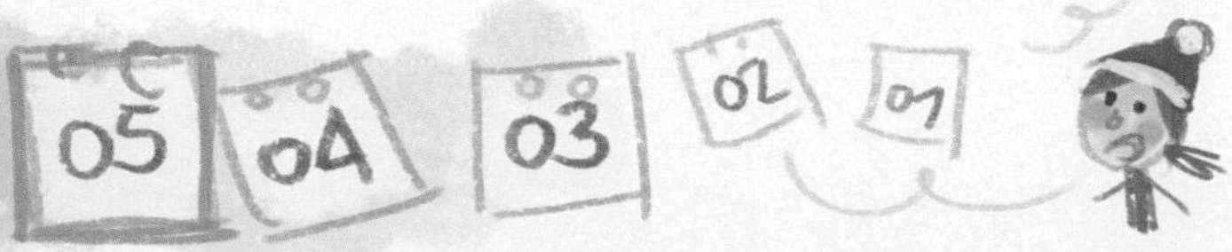
05
04
03
02
01

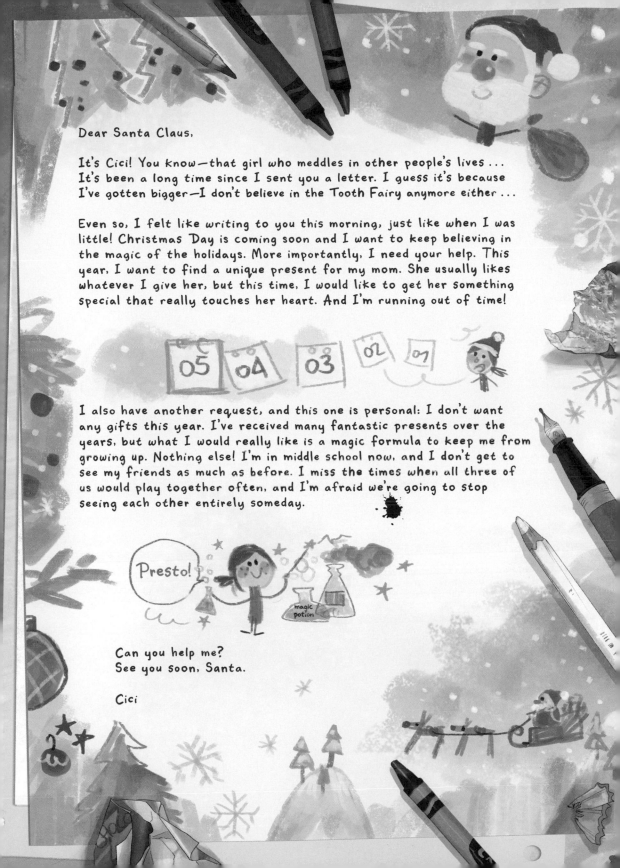

I also have another request, and this one is personal: I don't want any gifts this year. I've received many fantastic presents over the years, but what I would really like is a magic formula to keep me from growing up. Nothing else! I'm in middle school now, and I don't get to see my friends as much as before. I miss the times when all three of us would play together often, and I'm afraid we're going to stop seeing each other entirely someday.

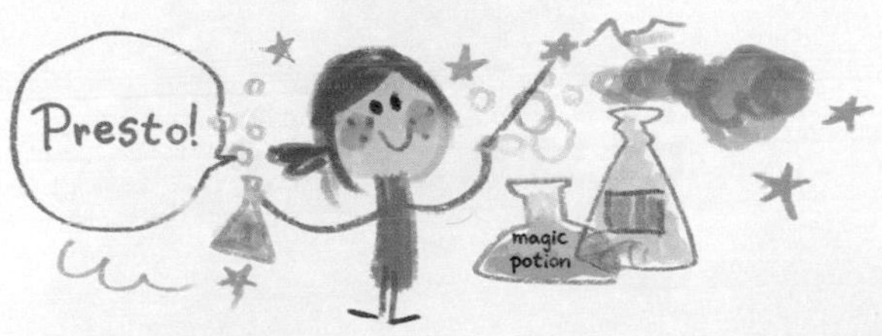
Presto!
magic potion

Can you help me?
See you soon, Santa.

Cici

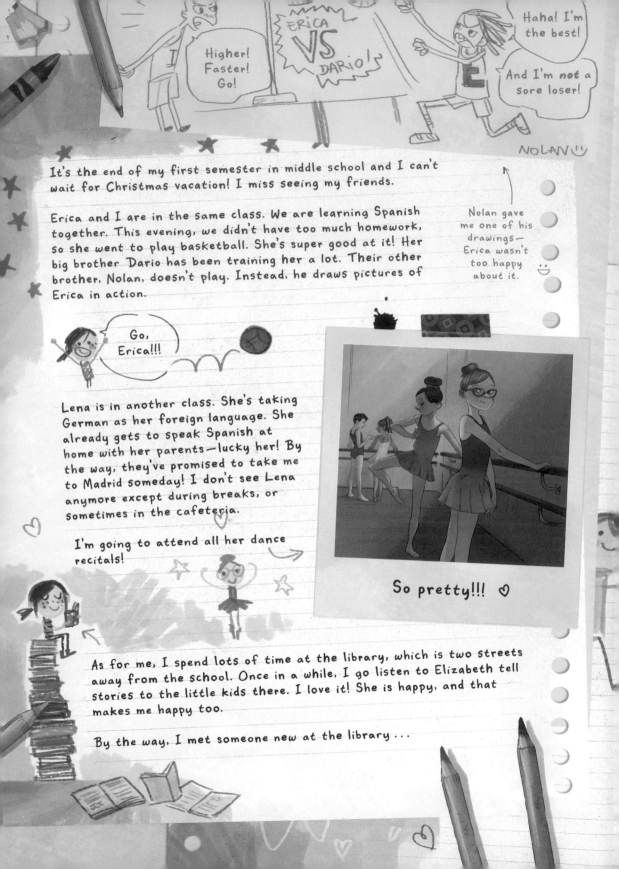

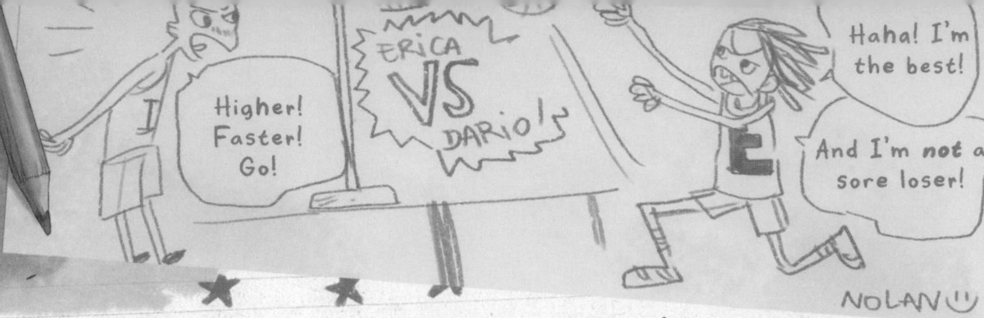
Higher! Faster! Go!
ERICA VS DARIO!
Haha! I'm the best!
And I'm **not** a sore loser!
NOLAN

It's the end of my first semester in middle school and I can't wait for Christmas vacation! I miss seeing my friends.

Nolan gave me one of his drawings—Erica wasn't too happy about it.

Erica and I are in the same class. We are learning Spanish together. This evening, we didn't have too much homework, so she went to play basketball. She's super good at it! Her big brother Dario has been training her a lot. Their other brother, Nolan, doesn't play. Instead, he draws pictures of Erica in action.

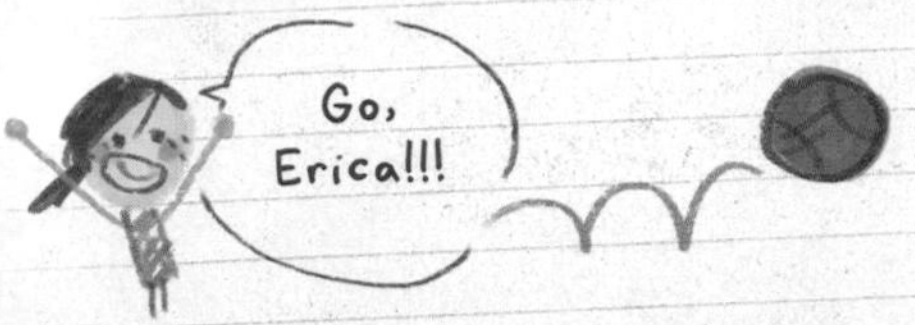
Go, Erica!!!

Lena is in another class. She's taking German as her foreign language. She already gets to speak Spanish at home with her parents—lucky her! By the way, they've promised to take me to Madrid someday! I don't see Lena anymore except during breaks, or sometimes in the cafeteria.

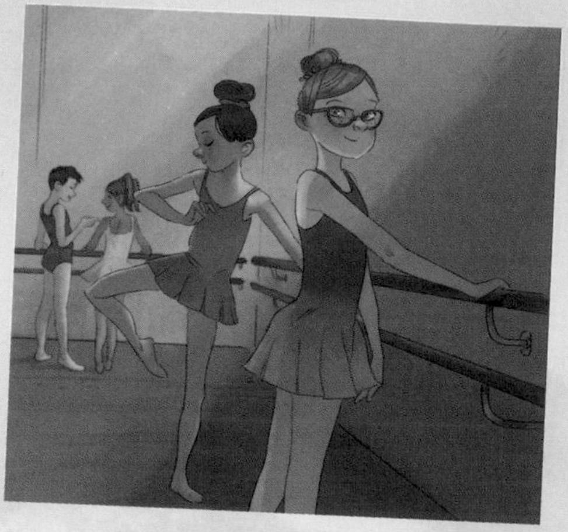

So pretty!!!

I'm going to attend all her dance recitals!

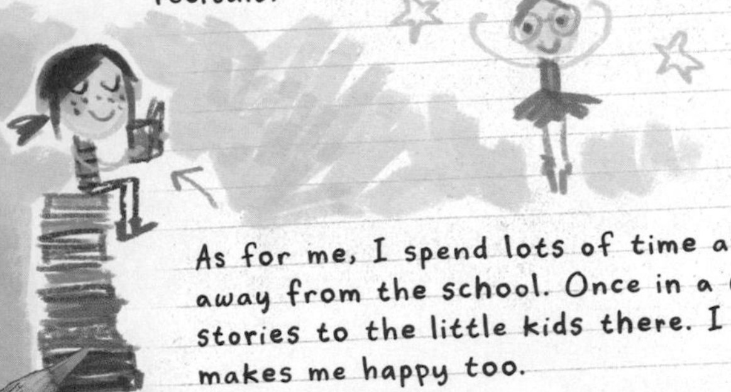

As for me, I spend lots of time at the library, which is two streets away from the school. Once in a while, I go listen to Elizabeth tell stories to the little kids there. I love it! She is happy, and that makes me happy too.

By the way, I met someone new at the library . . .

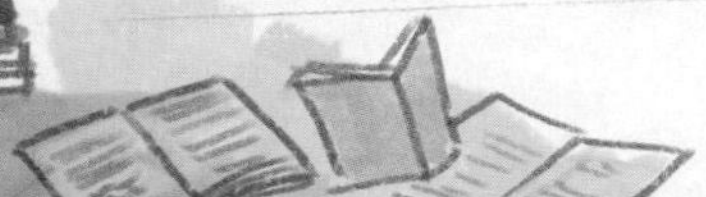

I knew that a bookbinder came to the library from time to time to repair books and to hold creative workshops for children, but I had never met her. The girls and I got to know her during fall break ...

Look what I made! (during one of the workshops)

Here's Sandra! She's super nice. We see each other all the time and have discovered that we have a lot in common:

-Her favorite book is Robert Stevenson's "Treasure Island."
-When she buys a new book, the first thing she does is smell it.
-She loves to watch people on the street.
-She loves peace and quiet—and secrets too.

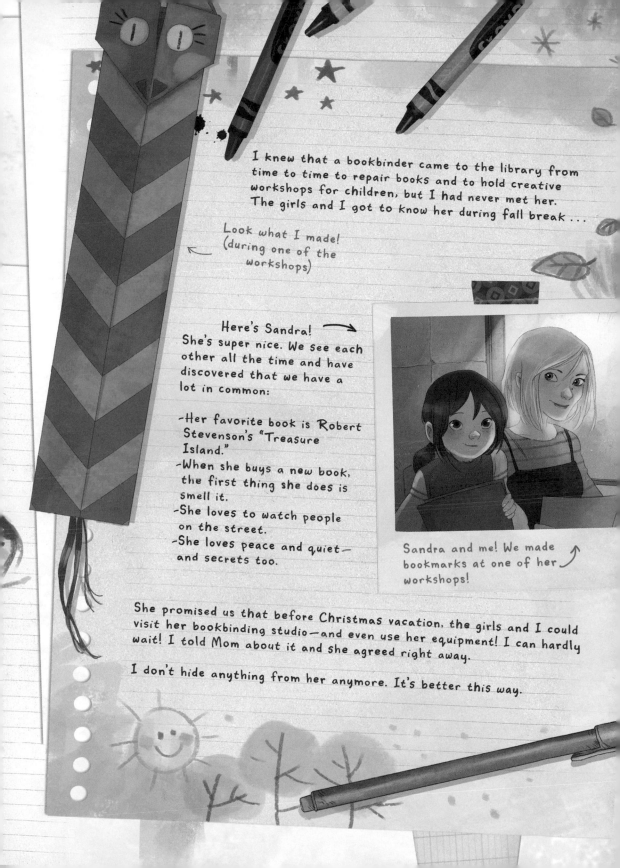

Sandra and me! We made bookmarks at one of her workshops!

She promised us that before Christmas vacation, the girls and I could visit her bookbinding studio—and even use her equipment! I can hardly wait! I told Mom about it and she agreed right away.

I don't hide anything from her anymore. It's better this way.

Here we are at the beginning of December. The first snowflakes are starting to fall. I'm going to be sure to put on my snow gear. I'm not going to catch the flu this year!

A knit hat with a pom-pom.

2 heavy wool sweaters over an undershirt.

A super long scarf that I can wrap around myself plenty of times.

Mittens knitted by Grandma.

My cape! I feel invincible wearing a cape! And it keeps me warm.

Tights under a nice warm skirt.

Heavy striped socks. (My favorite!)

Boots (which are starting to get a little small).

Last weekend, there was a lot of snow! We made a big snowman at the foot of our treehouse. I told the girls about the letter I had just written to Santa Claus. Lena told me that she knew a very good way to stop us from growing up—the three of us are going on another investigation!

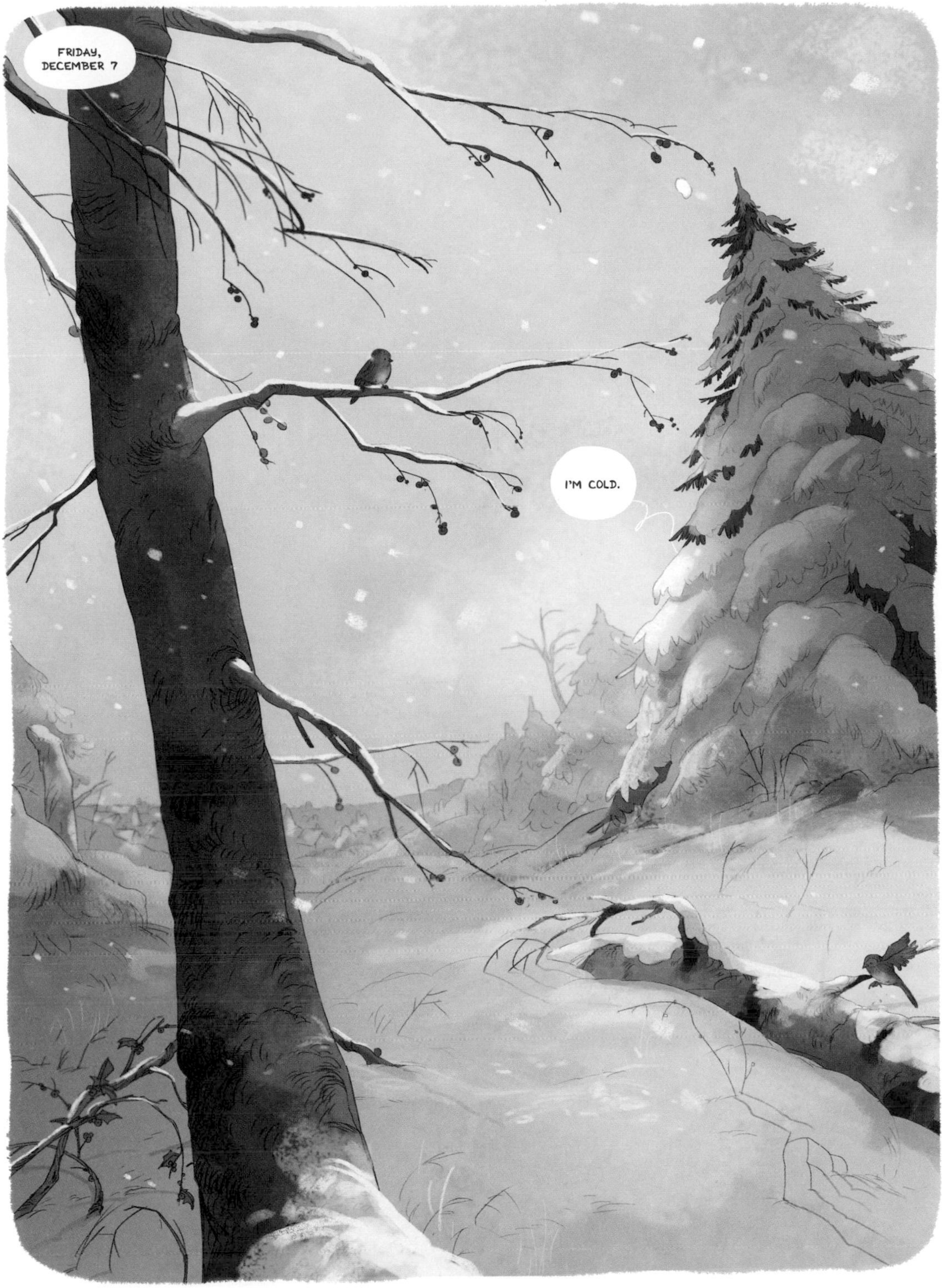
FRIDAY,
DECEMBER 7
I'M COLD.

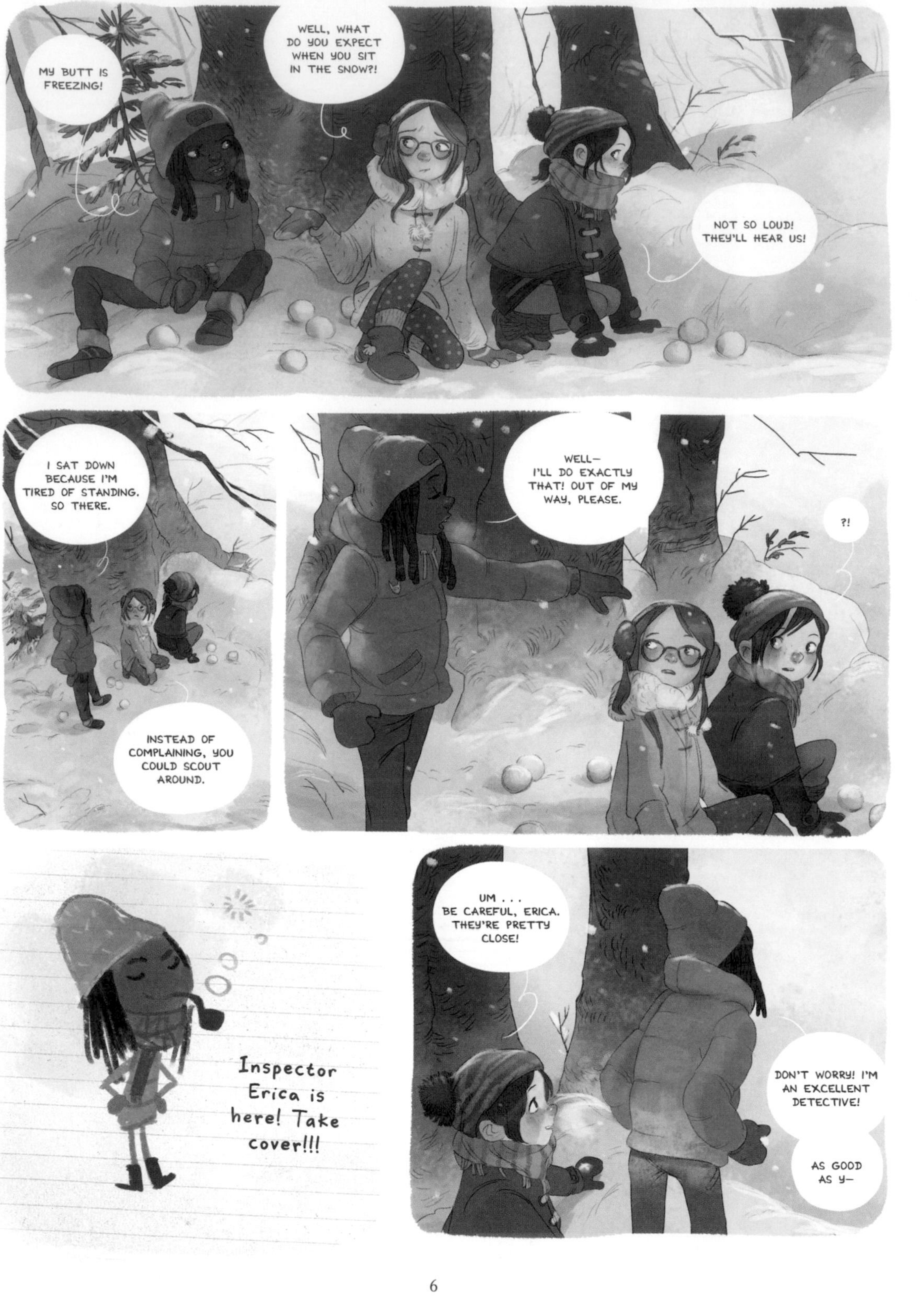
MY BUTT IS FREEZING!
WELL, WHAT DO YOU EXPECT WHEN YOU SIT IN THE SNOW?!
NOT SO LOUD! THEY'LL HEAR US!
I SAT DOWN BECAUSE I'M TIRED OF STANDING. SO THERE.
INSTEAD OF COMPLAINING, YOU COULD SCOUT AROUND.
WELL— I'LL DO EXACTLY THAT! OUT OF MY WAY, PLEASE.
?!
Inspector Erica is here! Take cover!!!
UM . . . BE CAREFUL, ERICA. THEY'RE PRETTY CLOSE!
DON'T WORRY! I'M AN EXCELLENT DETECTIVE!
AS GOOD AS Y—

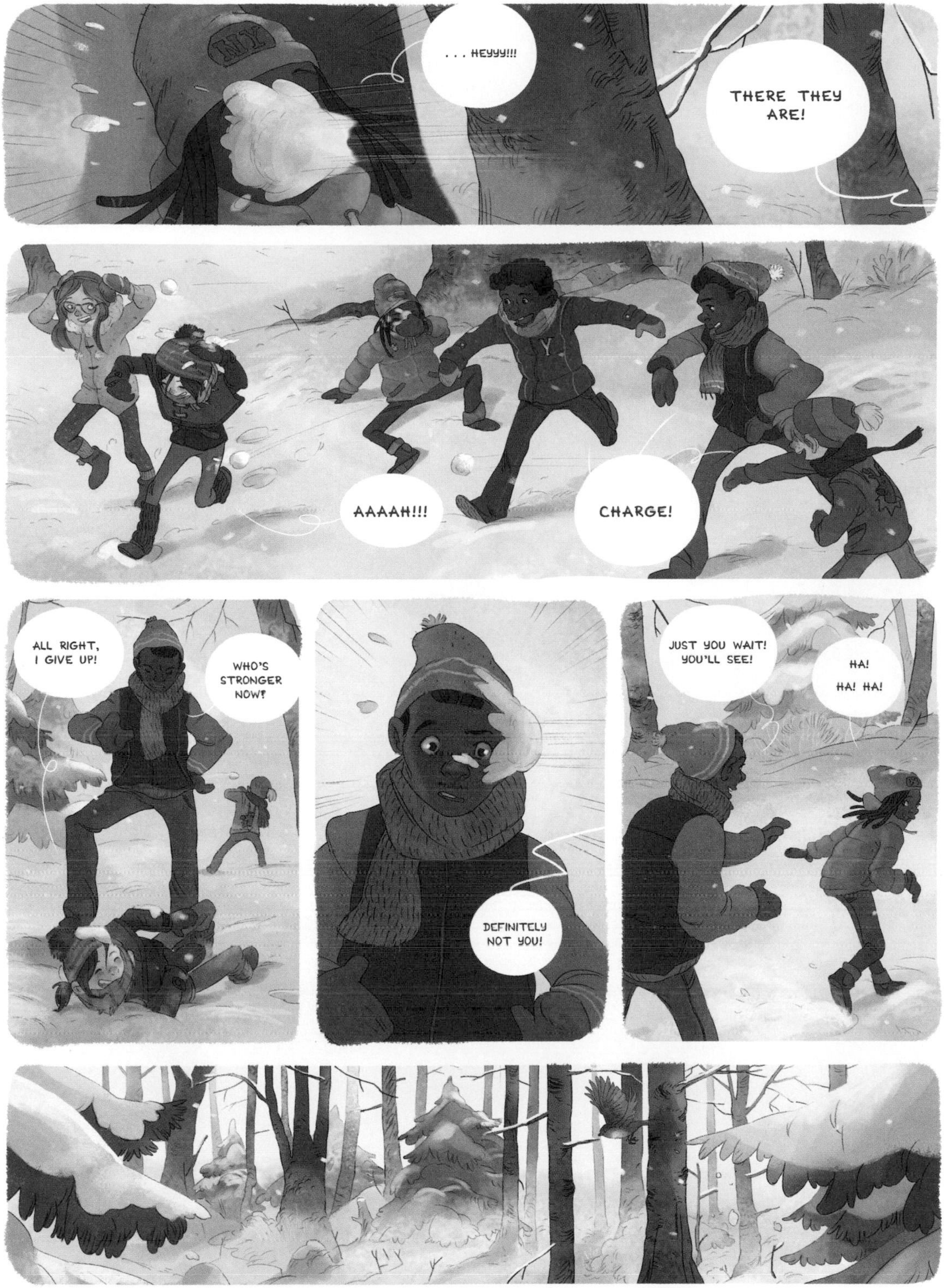

. . . HEYYY!!!
THERE THEY ARE!
AAAAH!!!
CHARGE!
ALL RIGHT, I GIVE UP!
WHO'S STRONGER NOW?
DEFINITELY NOT YOU!
JUST YOU WAIT! YOU'LL SEE!
HA! HA! HA!

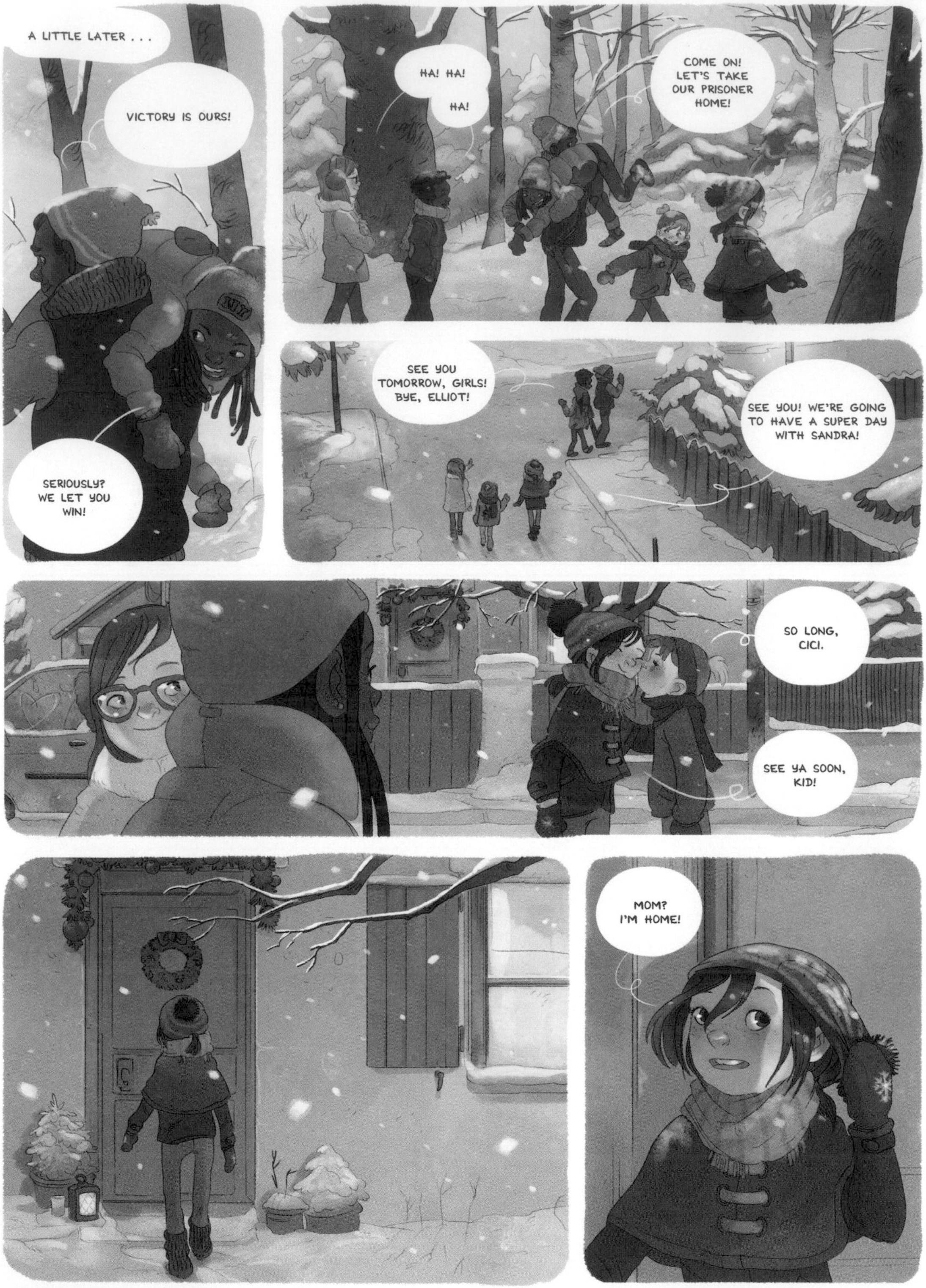
A LITTLE LATER . . .
VICTORY IS OURS!
SERIOUSLY? WE LET YOU WIN!
HA! HA!
HA!
COME ON! LET'S TAKE OUR PRISONER HOME!
SEE YOU TOMORROW, GIRLS! BYE, ELLIOT!
SEE YOU! WE'RE GOING TO HAVE A SUPER DAY WITH SANDRA!
SO LONG, CICI.
SEE YA SOON, KID!
MOM? I'M HOME!

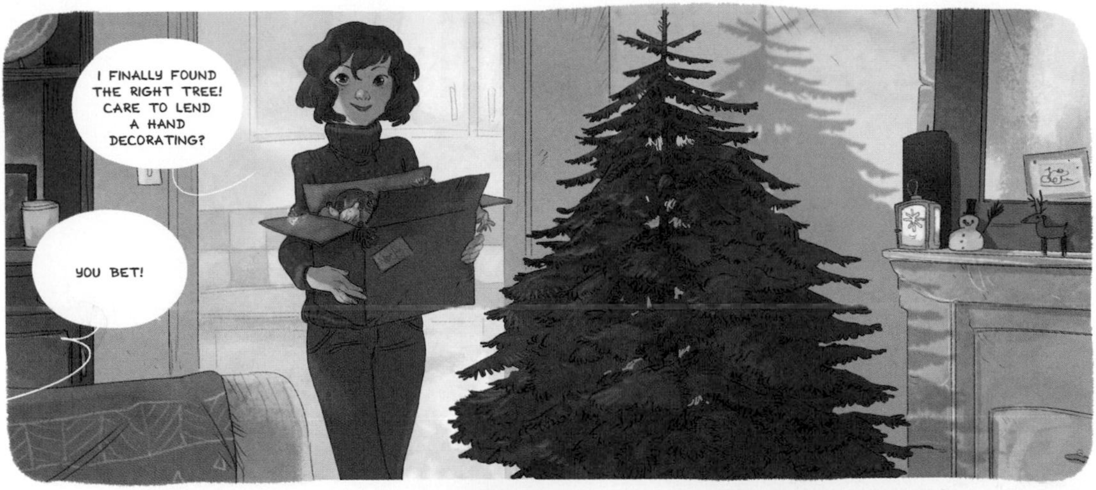
I FINALLY FOUND THE RIGHT TREE! CARE TO LEND A HAND DECORATING?
YOU BET!

This is my favorite part of Christmas . . .

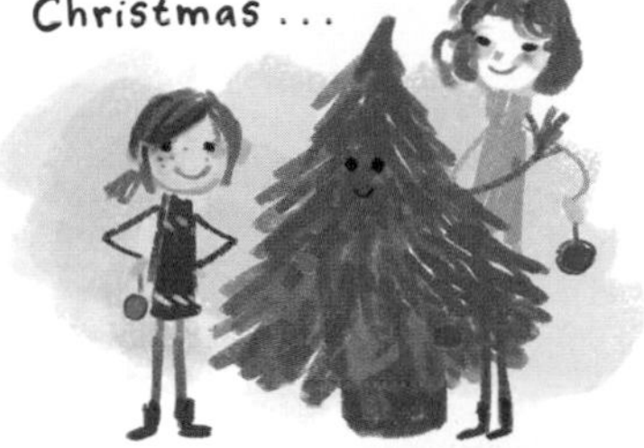

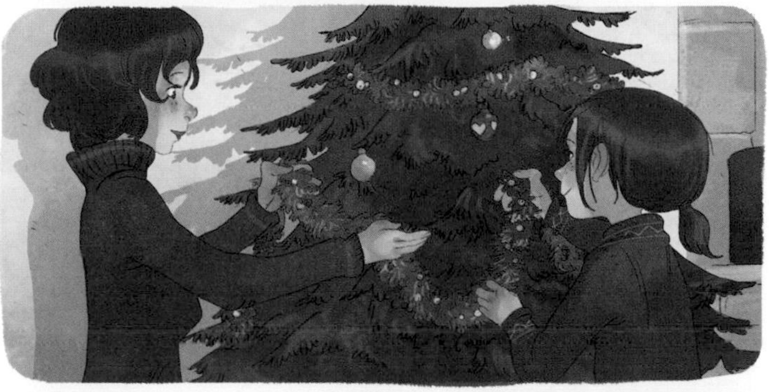

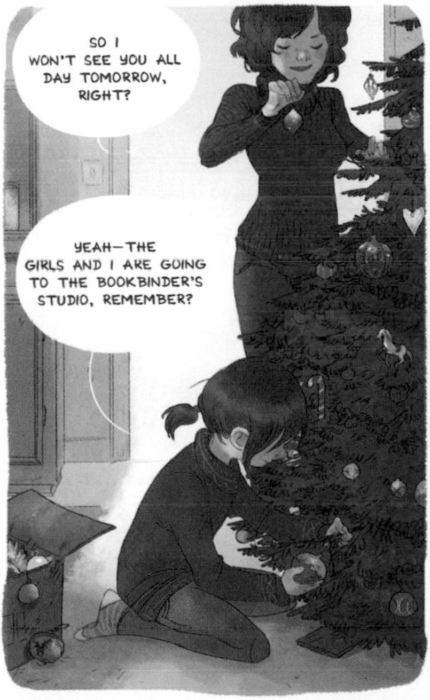
SO I WON'T SEE YOU ALL DAY TOMORROW, RIGHT?
YEAH—THE GIRLS AND I ARE GOING TO THE BOOKBINDER'S STUDIO, REMEMBER?

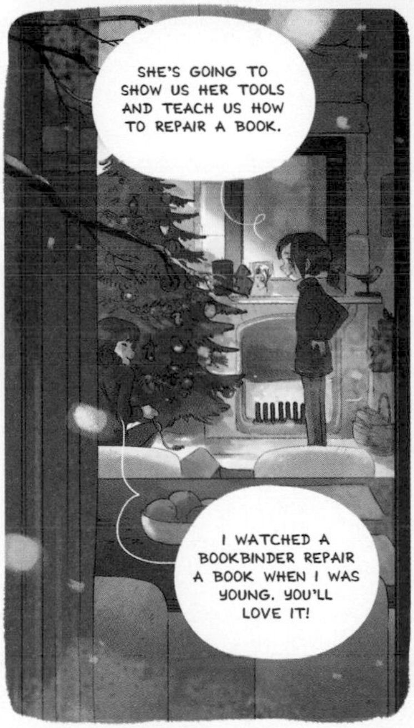
SHE'S GOING TO SHOW US HER TOOLS AND TEACH US HOW TO REPAIR A BOOK.
I WATCHED A BOOKBINDER REPAIR A BOOK WHEN I WAS YOUNG. YOU'LL LOVE IT!

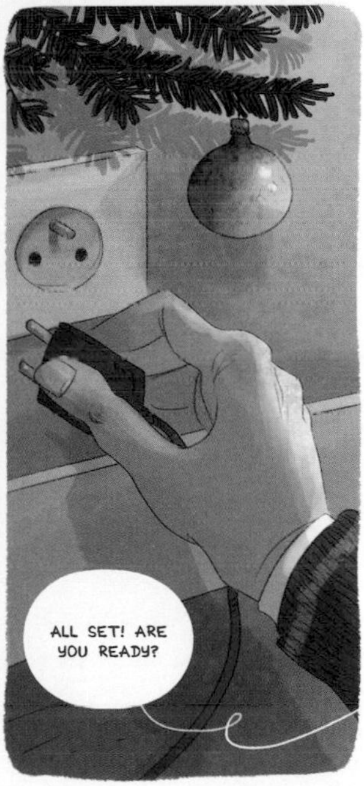
ALL SET! ARE YOU READY?

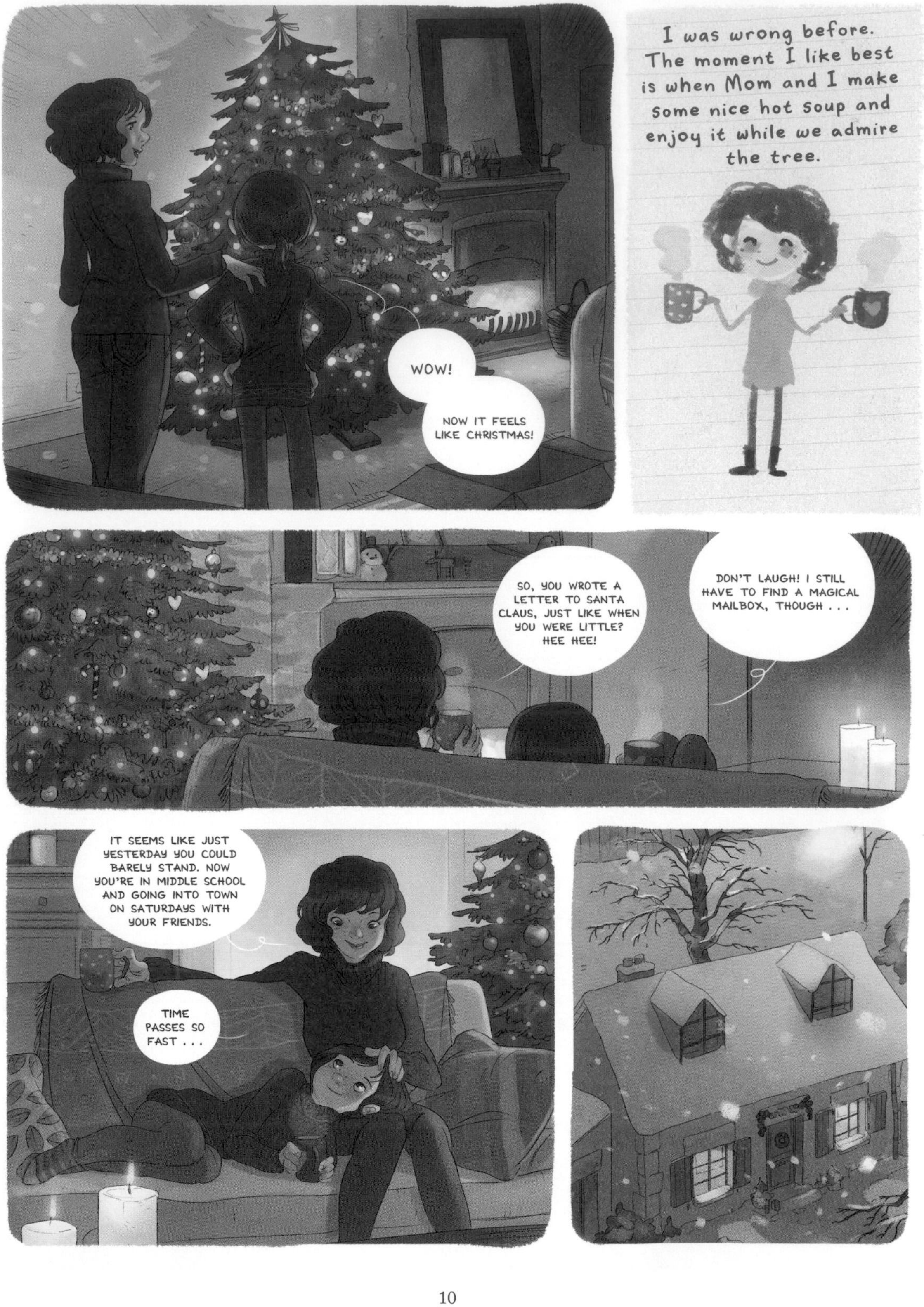
WOW!
NOW IT FEELS LIKE CHRISTMAS!
I was wrong before. The moment I like best is when Mom and I make some nice hot soup and enjoy it while we admire the tree.
SO, YOU WROTE A LETTER TO SANTA CLAUS, JUST LIKE WHEN YOU WERE LITTLE? HEE HEE!
DON'T LAUGH! I STILL HAVE TO FIND A MAGICAL MAILBOX, THOUGH . . .
IT SEEMS LIKE JUST YESTERDAY YOU COULD BARELY STAND. NOW YOU'RE IN MIDDLE SCHOOL AND GOING INTO TOWN ON SATURDAYS WITH YOUR FRIENDS.
TIME PASSES SO FAST . . .

SATURDAY, DECEMBER 8
SEE YOU TONIGHT, MOM! AND THANKS!
THANKS, MS. ARMAND!
SEE YOU LATER, GIRLS!
PFFFT . . . FOUR INCHES OF SNOW AND THE BUSES STOP RUNNING!
FOR REAL! IT'S A GOOD THING MOM WAS AVAILABLE!
SANDRA ISN'T HERE YET.
PHARMACY
Book-binding Studio
CHRISTMAS MARKET
HELLO, GIRLS!
SORRY I'M LATE. FOUR INCHES OF SNOW AND THE BUSES STOP RUNNING!
HA! HA! HA!
OH . . . WHAT DID I SAY?!
COME ON, LET'S ENTER MY CAVE . . .

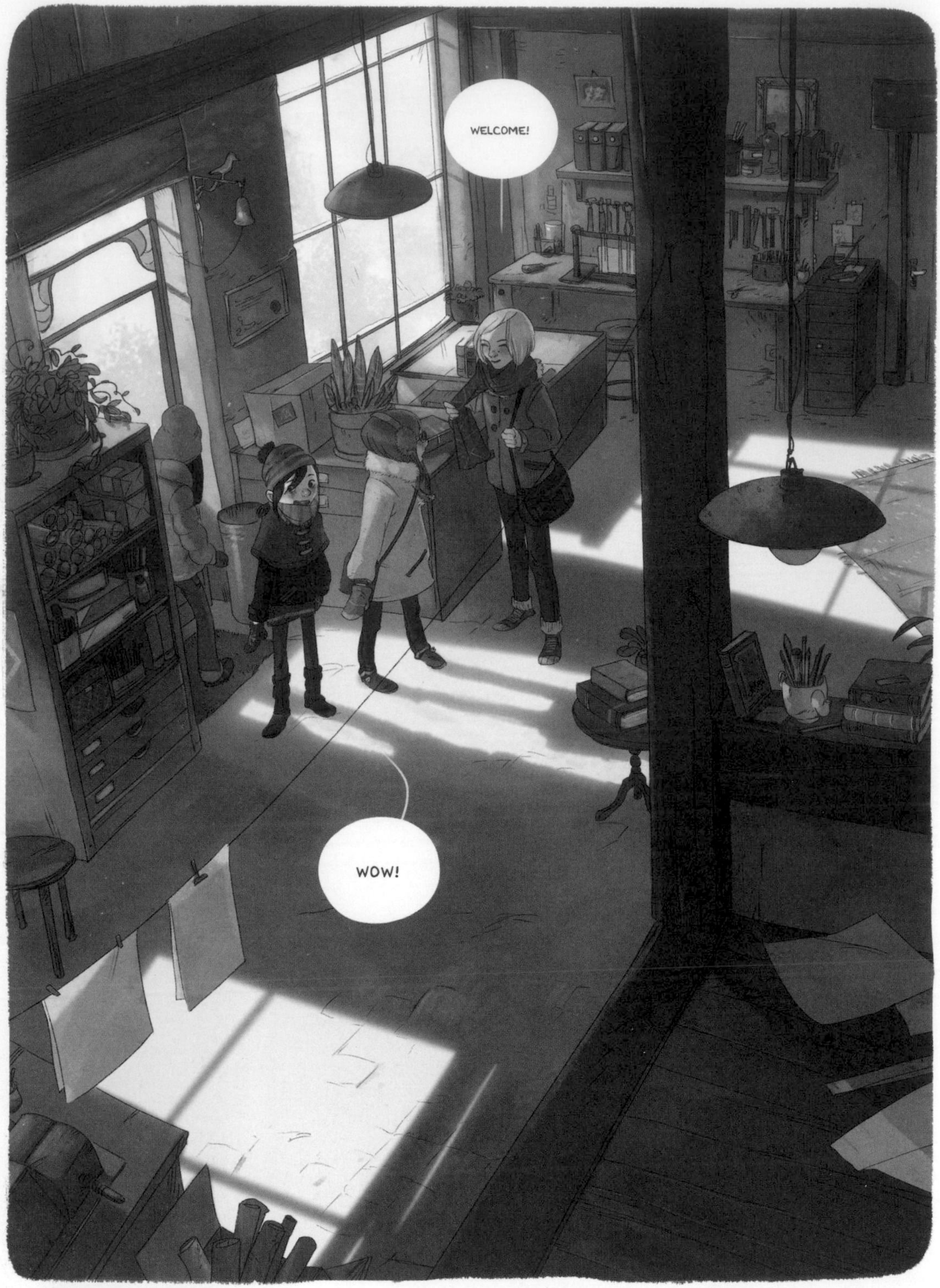
WELCOME!
WOW!

IMPRESSIVE! WHAT A MACHINE!

HEE HEE! IT'S A BOOK PRESS. TO RESTORE BOOKS CORRECTLY, IT'S IMPORTANT TO BE FAMILIAR WITH OLD-FASHIONED BOOKMAKING TECHNIQUES!

IN FACT, THERE ARE STRICT INTERNATIONAL GUIDELINES WE HAVE TO FOLLOW.

MY FATHER PURCHASED THIS PRESS FROM A PRINTER'S SHOP. HIGH-QUALITY EQUIPMENT LIKE THIS ALLOWS US TO RESTORE A WORK TO ITS ORIGINAL APPEARANCE AS FAITHFULLY AS POSSIBLE.

THERE'S AN INCREDIBLE *FEELING* TO THIS STUDIO . . .

IT'S MAGICAL . . .

I'M THRILLED THAT YOU LIKE IT!

BUT THERE'S NO CHRISTMAS TREE—NOT EVEN A SMALL ONE.

UM, NO . . . I'VE NEVER LIKED THEM MUCH. BESIDES, IT . . . WOULD TAKE UP TOO MUCH SPACE.

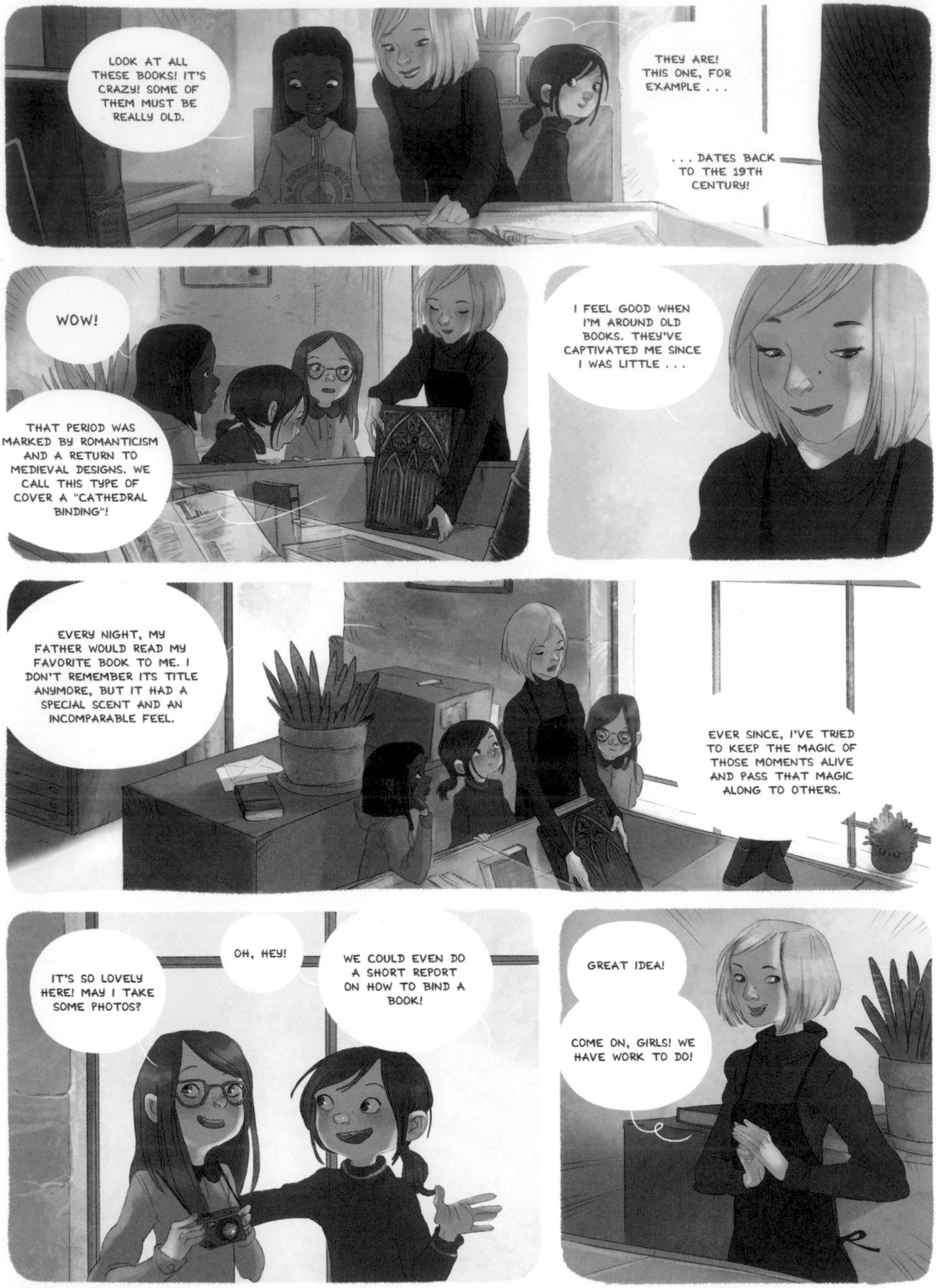
LOOK AT ALL THESE BOOKS! IT'S CRAZY! SOME OF THEM MUST BE REALLY OLD.
THEY ARE! THIS ONE, FOR EXAMPLE . . .
. . . DATES BACK TO THE 19TH CENTURY!
WOW!
THAT PERIOD WAS MARKED BY ROMANTICISM AND A RETURN TO MEDIEVAL DESIGNS. WE CALL THIS TYPE OF COVER A "CATHEDRAL BINDING"!
I FEEL GOOD WHEN I'M AROUND OLD BOOKS. THEY'VE CAPTIVATED ME SINCE I WAS LITTLE . . .
EVERY NIGHT, MY FATHER WOULD READ MY FAVORITE BOOK TO ME. I DON'T REMEMBER ITS TITLE ANYMORE, BUT IT HAD A SPECIAL SCENT AND AN INCOMPARABLE FEEL.
EVER SINCE, I'VE TRIED TO KEEP THE MAGIC OF THOSE MOMENTS ALIVE AND PASS THAT MAGIC ALONG TO OTHERS.
IT'S SO LOVELY HERE! MAY I TAKE SOME PHOTOS?
OH, HEY!
WE COULD EVEN DO A SHORT REPORT ON HOW TO BIND A BOOK!
GREAT IDEA!
COME ON, GIRLS! WE HAVE WORK TO DO!

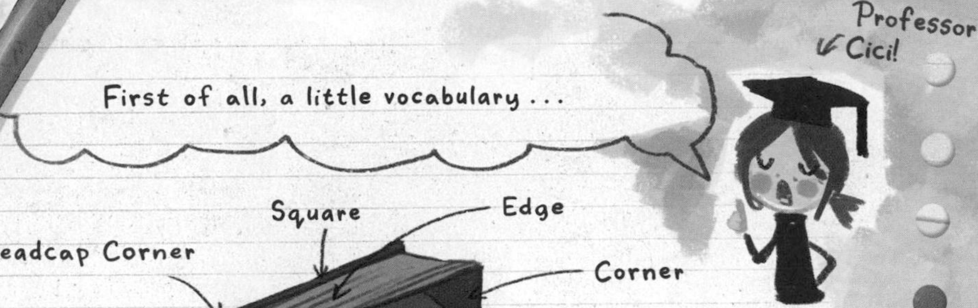
First of all, a little vocabulary . . .
Professor Cici!

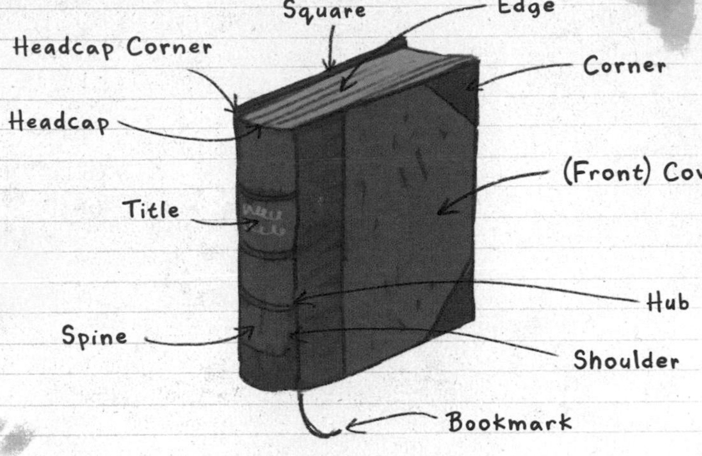
Square
Edge
Headcap Corner
Corner
Headcap
(Front) Cover
Title
Hub
Spine
Shoulder
Bookmark

Next, let me show you how to restore a book!
First, the original book must be unstitched by taking a scalpel and cutting all the quires* apart.

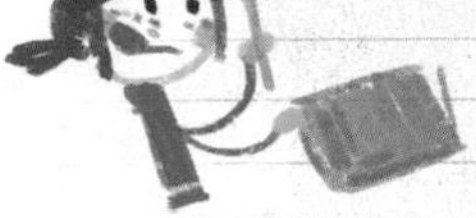

*Quires are sheets of paper that are folded to make the pages of a book! Cool, huh?

Then, all the quires are placed into a nipping press. (We get to compress them by pushing down from the top! Awesome!)

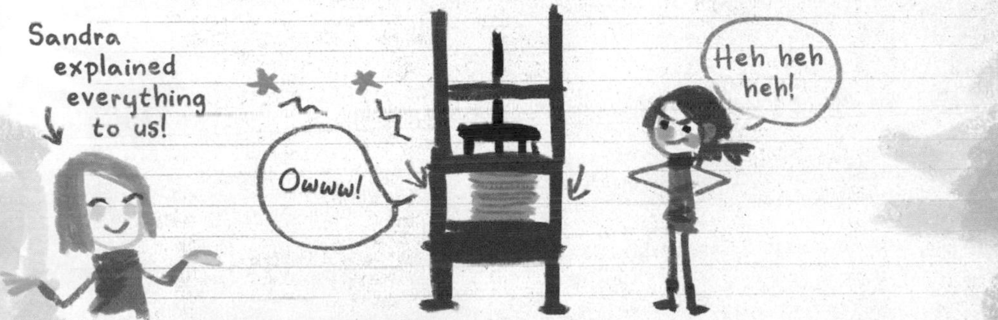
Sandra explained everything to us!
Owww!
Heh heh heh!

After making sure the quires are in order, there's the sawbinding process (all these words are so strange!). We make incisions—you know, cuts—on the back of the pages while they are held in a vise.

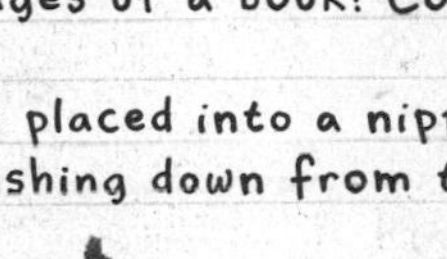
chop chop

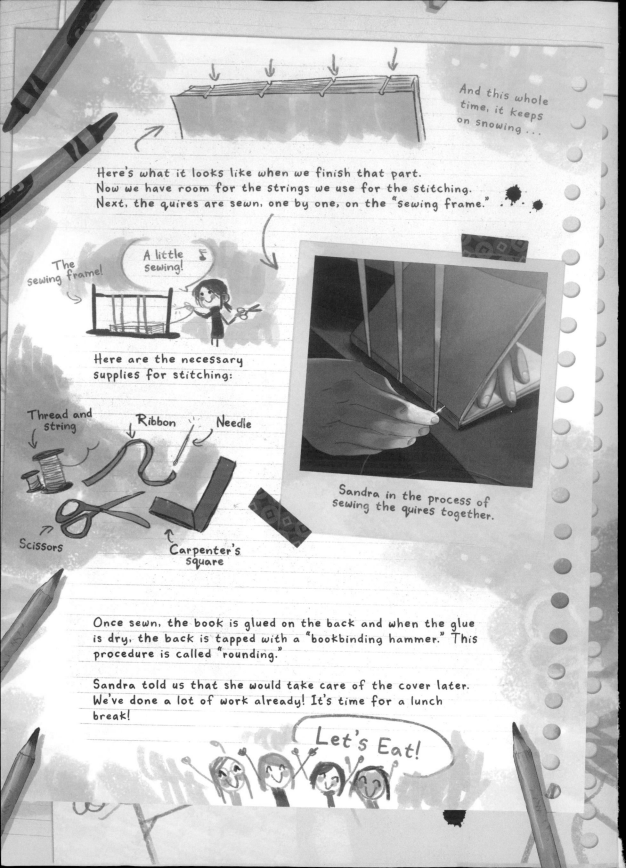

And this whole time, it keeps on snowing . . .

Here's what it looks like when we finish that part.
Now we have room for the strings we use for the stitching.
Next, the quires are sewn, one by one, on the "sewing frame."

The sewing frame!

A little sewing!

Here are the necessary supplies for stitching:

Thread and string

Ribbon

Needle

Scissors

Carpenter's square

Sandra in the process of sewing the quires together.

Once sewn, the book is glued on the back and when the glue is dry, the back is tapped with a "bookbinding hammer." This procedure is called "rounding."

Sandra told us that she would take care of the cover later. We've done a lot of work already! It's time for a lunch break!

Let's Eat!

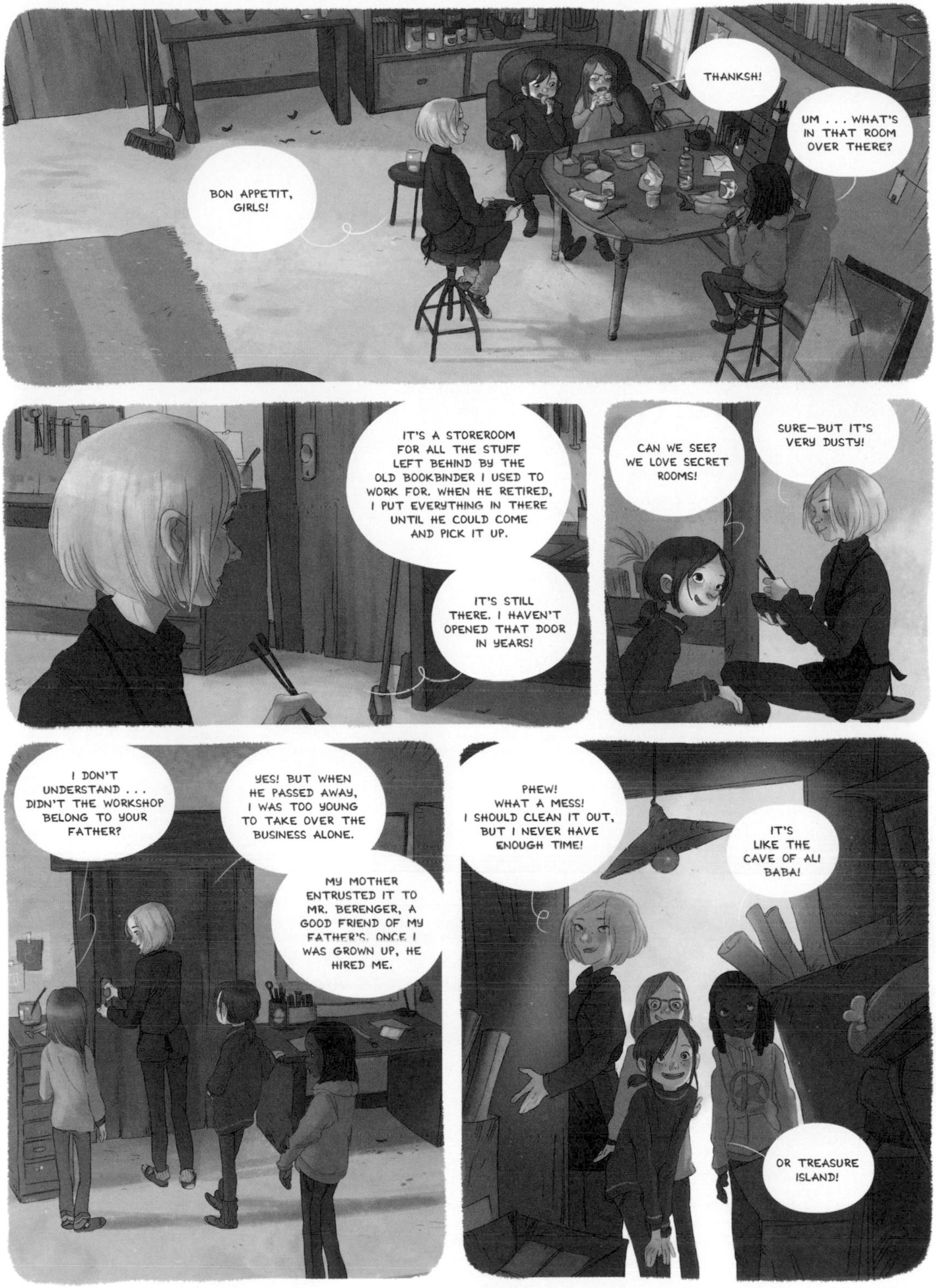
BON APPETIT, GIRLS!
THANKSH!
UM . . . WHAT'S IN THAT ROOM OVER THERE?
IT'S A STOREROOM FOR ALL THE STUFF LEFT BEHIND BY THE OLD BOOKBINDER I USED TO WORK FOR. WHEN HE RETIRED, I PUT EVERYTHING IN THERE UNTIL HE COULD COME AND PICK IT UP.
IT'S STILL THERE. I HAVEN'T OPENED THAT DOOR IN YEARS!
CAN WE SEE? WE LOVE SECRET ROOMS!
SURE—BUT IT'S VERY DUSTY!
I DON'T UNDERSTAND . . . DIDN'T THE WORKSHOP BELONG TO YOUR FATHER?
YES! BUT WHEN HE PASSED AWAY, I WAS TOO YOUNG TO TAKE OVER THE BUSINESS ALONE.
MY MOTHER ENTRUSTED IT TO MR. BERENGER, A GOOD FRIEND OF MY FATHER'S. ONCE I WAS GROWN UP, HE HIRED ME.
PHEW! WHAT A MESS! I SHOULD CLEAN IT OUT, BUT I NEVER HAVE ENOUGH TIME!
IT'S LIKE THE CAVE OF ALI BABA!
OR TREASURE ISLAND!

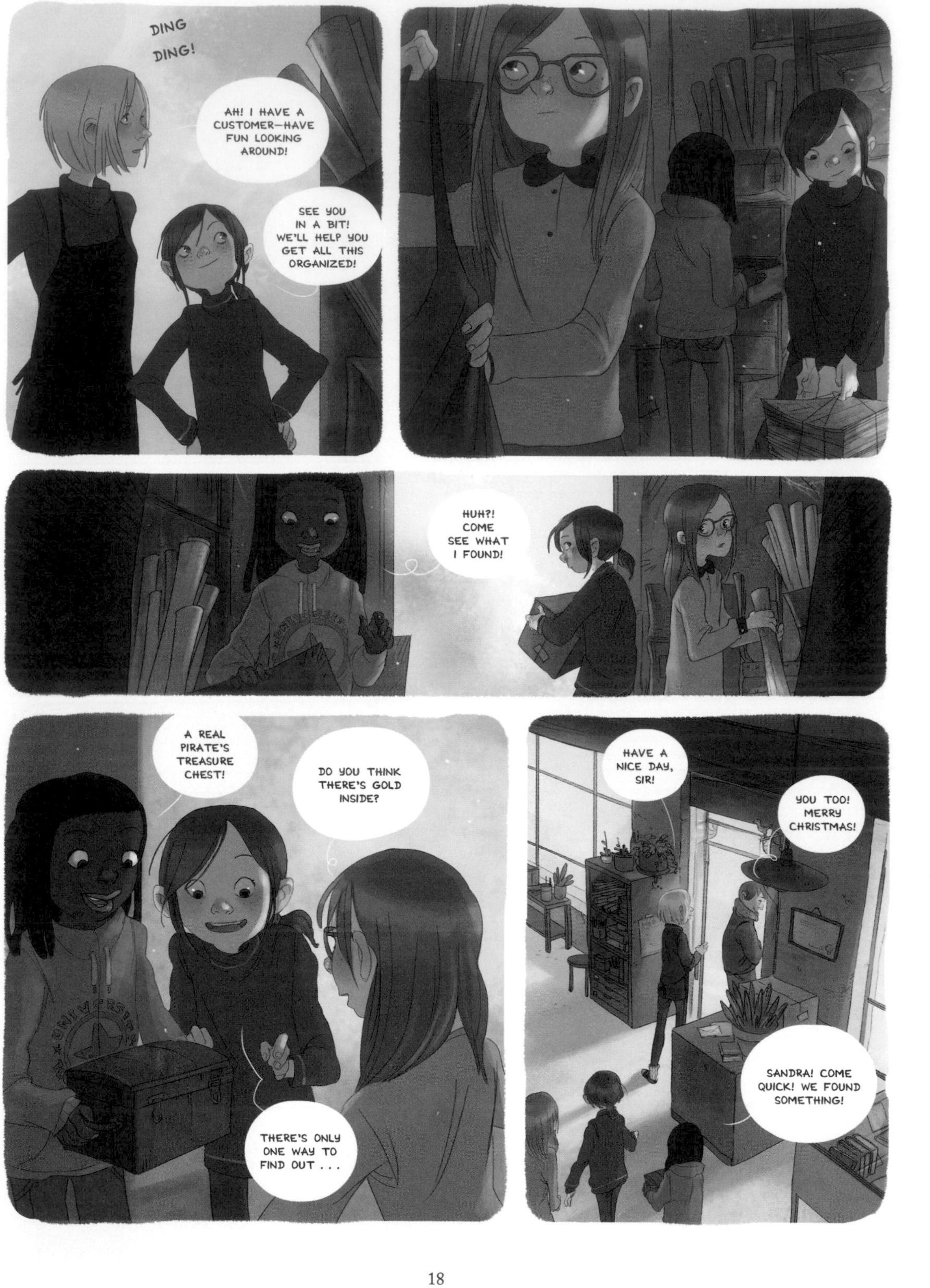
DING
DING!
AH! I HAVE A CUSTOMER—HAVE FUN LOOKING AROUND!
SEE YOU IN A BIT! WE'LL HELP YOU GET ALL THIS ORGANIZED!
HUH?! COME SEE WHAT I FOUND!
A REAL PIRATE'S TREASURE CHEST!
DO YOU THINK THERE'S GOLD INSIDE?
THERE'S ONLY ONE WAY TO FIND OUT . . .
HAVE A NICE DAY, SIR!
YOU TOO! MERRY CHRISTMAS!
SANDRA! COME QUICK! WE FOUND SOMETHING!

WHAT A NICE BOX! I DON'T REMEMBER EVER SEEING IT BEFORE. THEN AGAIN—I'VE NEVER HAD A GOOD MEMORY . . .

IT'S SO PRETTY. I DON'T THINK WE SHOULD RISK DAMAGING IT BY FORCING IT OPEN.

WELL, IT'S NOT LOCKED . . .

GO AHEAD— OPEN IT!

. . . SHEET MUSIC?

THEY'RE MAGNIFICENT!

THE CHEST IS FULL OF THEM!

THEY MUST BE FROM AN OLD BOOK THAT MR. BERENGER FORGOT TO REPAIR . . .

I'D LIKE TO DO IT. MAY I REPAIR THIS BOOK?

WITH PLEASURE! BUT I DON'T KNOW IF WE'LL BE ABLE TO LOCATE ITS ORIGINAL OWNER.

WAIT . . . THERE'S SOMETHING ELSE. LOOK!

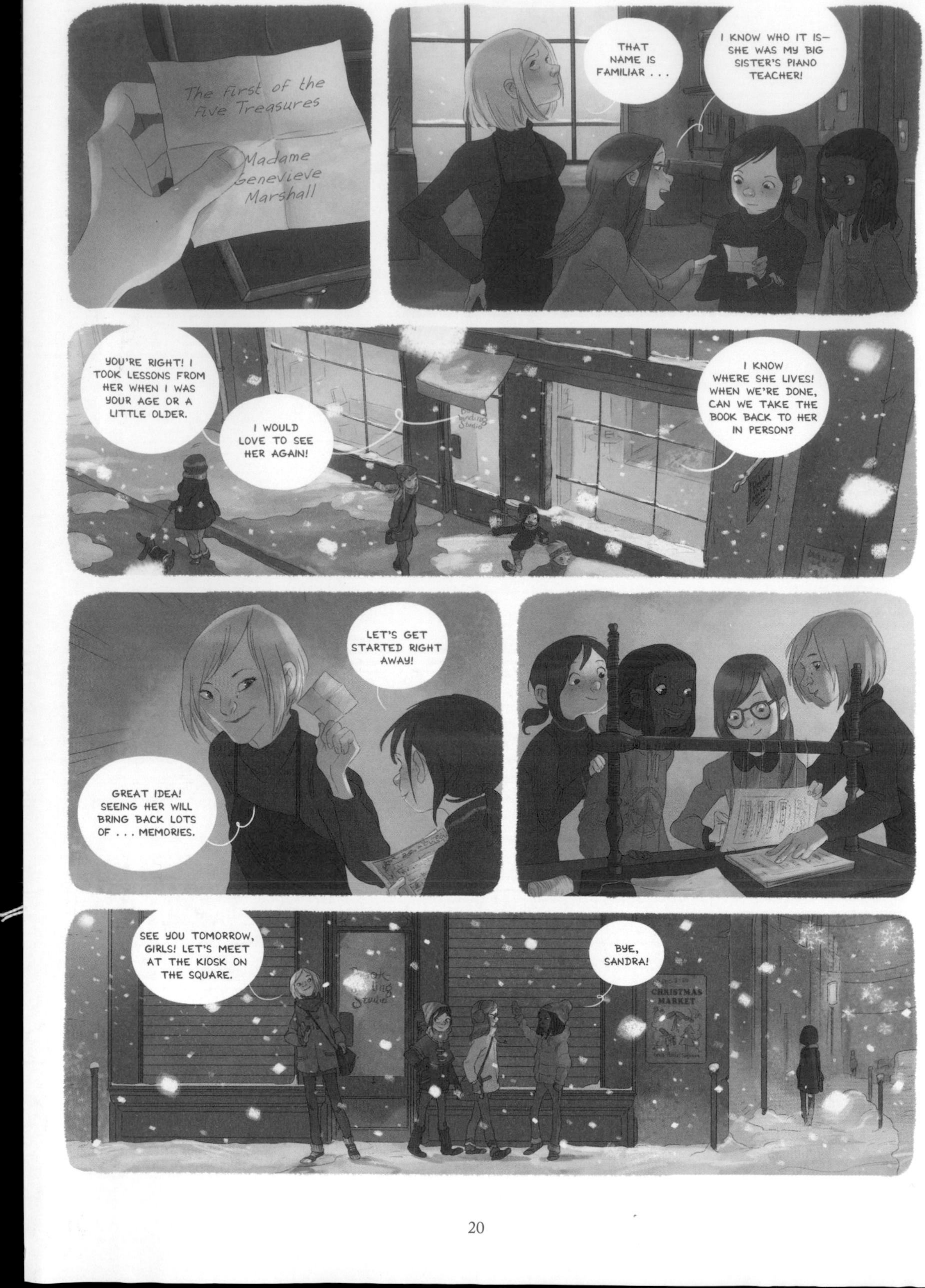
The First of the Five Treasures
Madame Genevieve Marshall
THAT NAME IS FAMILIAR . . .
I KNOW WHO IT IS— SHE WAS MY BIG SISTER'S PIANO TEACHER!
YOU'RE RIGHT! I TOOK LESSONS FROM HER WHEN I WAS YOUR AGE OR A LITTLE OLDER.
I WOULD LOVE TO SEE HER AGAIN!
I KNOW WHERE SHE LIVES! WHEN WE'RE DONE, CAN WE TAKE THE BOOK BACK TO HER IN PERSON?
LET'S GET STARTED RIGHT AWAY!
GREAT IDEA! SEEING HER WILL BRING BACK LOTS OF . . . MEMORIES.
SEE YOU TOMORROW, GIRLS! LET'S MEET AT THE KIOSK ON THE SQUARE.
BYE, SANDRA!
CHRISTMAS MARKET

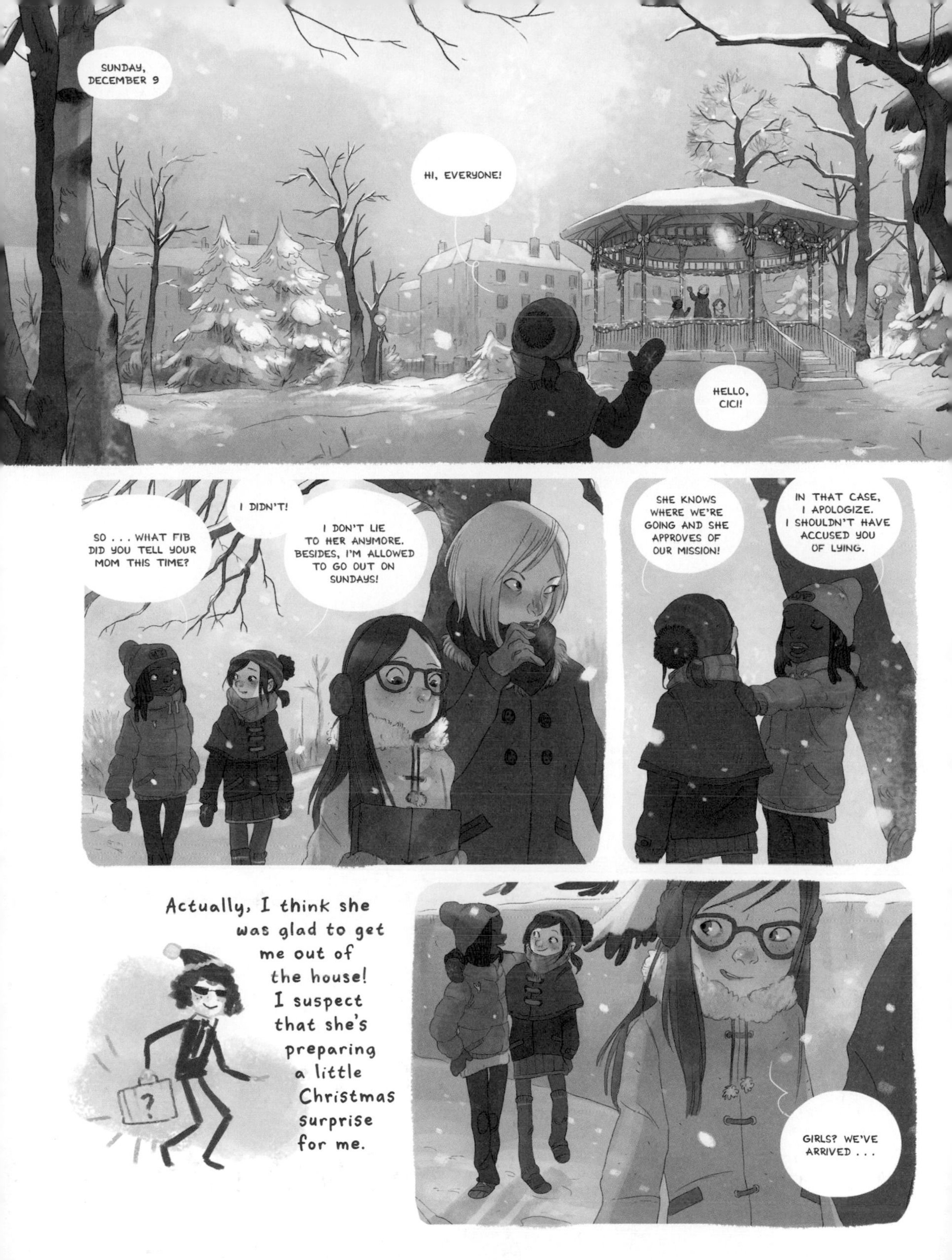
SUNDAY, DECEMBER 9
HI, EVERYONE!
HELLO, CICI!
SO . . . WHAT FIB DID YOU TELL YOUR MOM THIS TIME?
I DIDN'T!
I DON'T LIE TO HER ANYMORE. BESIDES, I'M ALLOWED TO GO OUT ON SUNDAYS!
SHE KNOWS WHERE WE'RE GOING AND SHE APPROVES OF OUR MISSION!
IN THAT CASE, I APOLOGIZE. I SHOULDN'T HAVE ACCUSED YOU OF LYING.
Actually, I think she was glad to get me out of the house! I suspect that she's preparing a little Christmas surprise for me.
?
GIRLS? WE'VE ARRIVED . . .

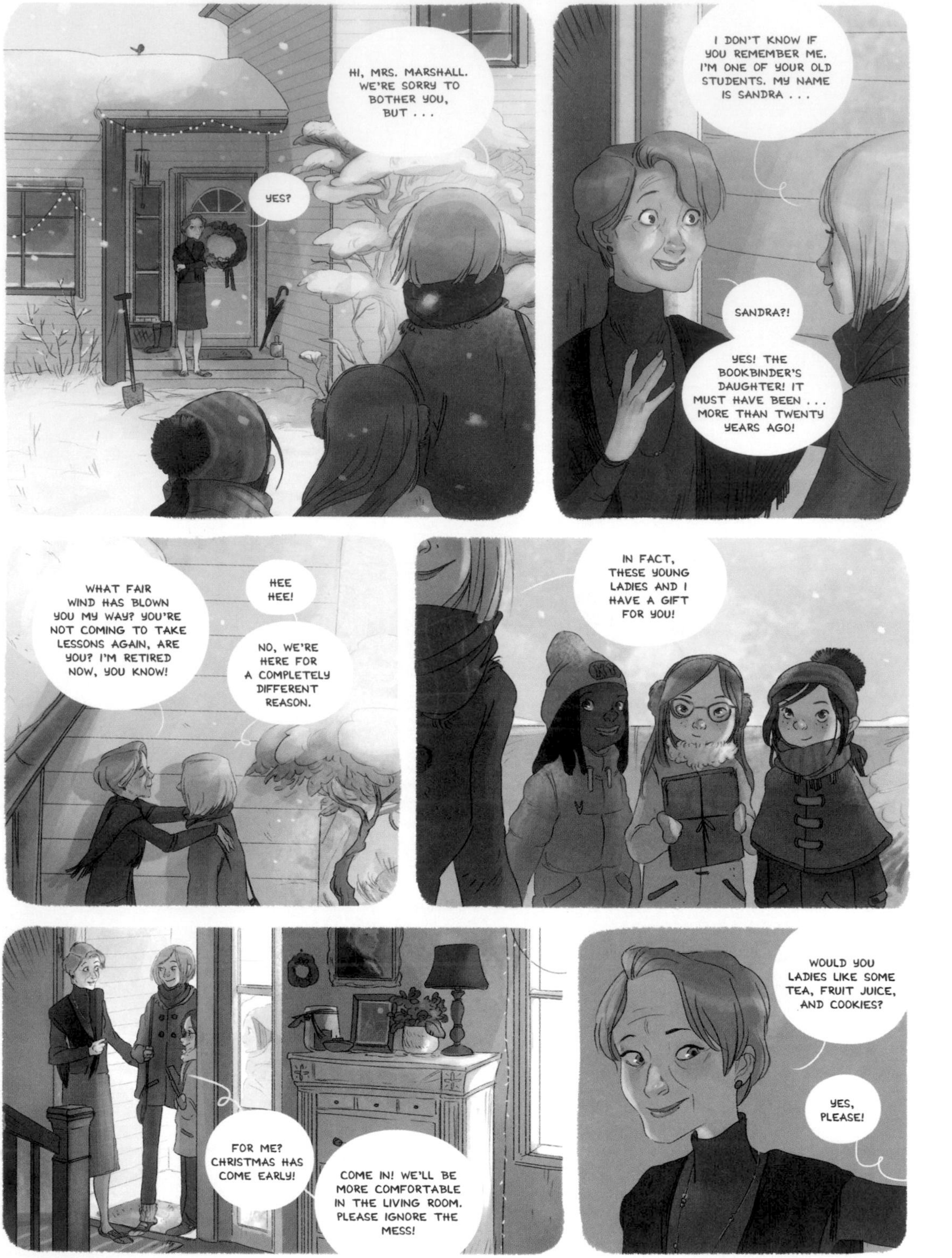
HI, MRS. MARSHALL. WE'RE SORRY TO BOTHER YOU, BUT . . .
YES?
I DON'T KNOW IF YOU REMEMBER ME. I'M ONE OF YOUR OLD STUDENTS. MY NAME IS SANDRA . . .
SANDRA?!
YES! THE BOOKBINDER'S DAUGHTER! IT MUST HAVE BEEN . . . MORE THAN TWENTY YEARS AGO!
WHAT FAIR WIND HAS BLOWN YOU MY WAY? YOU'RE NOT COMING TO TAKE LESSONS AGAIN, ARE YOU? I'M RETIRED NOW, YOU KNOW!
HEE HEE!
NO, WE'RE HERE FOR A COMPLETELY DIFFERENT REASON.
IN FACT, THESE YOUNG LADIES AND I HAVE A GIFT FOR YOU!
FOR ME? CHRISTMAS HAS COME EARLY!
COME IN! WE'LL BE MORE COMFORTABLE IN THE LIVING ROOM. PLEASE IGNORE THE MESS!
WOULD YOU LADIES LIKE SOME TEA, FRUIT JUICE, AND COOKIES?
YES, PLEASE!

A LITTLE LATER . . .

OH MY GOODNESS! I NEVER THOUGHT I'D SEE THESE AGAIN!

THEY'RE VERY OLD AND VALUABLE!

WE FOUND THEM IN AN OLD CHEST. THEY MUST HAVE BEEN HIDDEN THERE FOR A LONG TIME . . .

I REBOUND THEM WITH GREAT CARE!

AND I ADDED A COVER WORTHY OF THE CONTENTS!

ALL THESE OLD MELODIES . . . DO YOU REMEMBER? YOU ALWAYS GOT STUCK ON THE SAME NOTE.

I'M AFRAID I DON'T!

DO YOU STILL HAVE PROBLEMS WITH YOUR MEMORY?

I'M A BIT BETTER NOW. I'M STILL WORKING HARD TO BUILD IT UP.

IT WAS DR. CLERGUE WHO THOUGHT THAT MUSIC LESSONS MIGHT HELP SHARPEN YOUR MEMORY. YOU MADE ENORMOUS PROGRESS! I WAS VERY PROUD OF YOU.

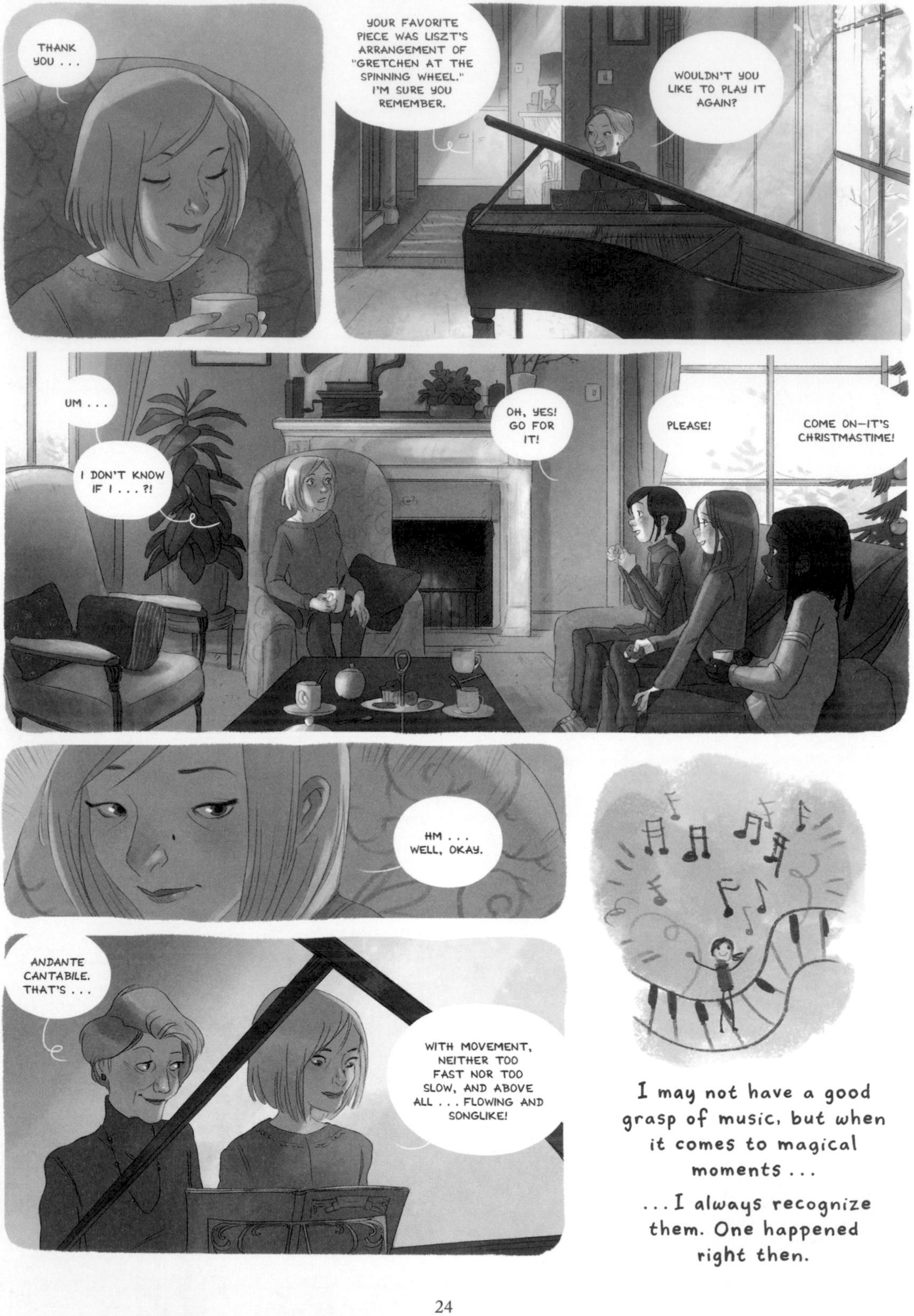
THANK YOU . . .
YOUR FAVORITE PIECE WAS LISZT'S ARRANGEMENT OF "GRETCHEN AT THE SPINNING WHEEL." I'M SURE YOU REMEMBER.
WOULDN'T YOU LIKE TO PLAY IT AGAIN?
UM . . .
I DON'T KNOW IF I . . . ?!
OH, YES! GO FOR IT!
PLEASE!
COME ON—IT'S CHRISTMASTIME!
HM . . . WELL, OKAY.
ANDANTE CANTABILE. THAT'S . . .
WITH MOVEMENT, NEITHER TOO FAST NOR TOO SLOW, AND ABOVE ALL . . . FLOWING AND SONGLIKE!
I may not have a good grasp of music, but when it comes to magical moments . . .
. . . I always recognize them. One happened right then.

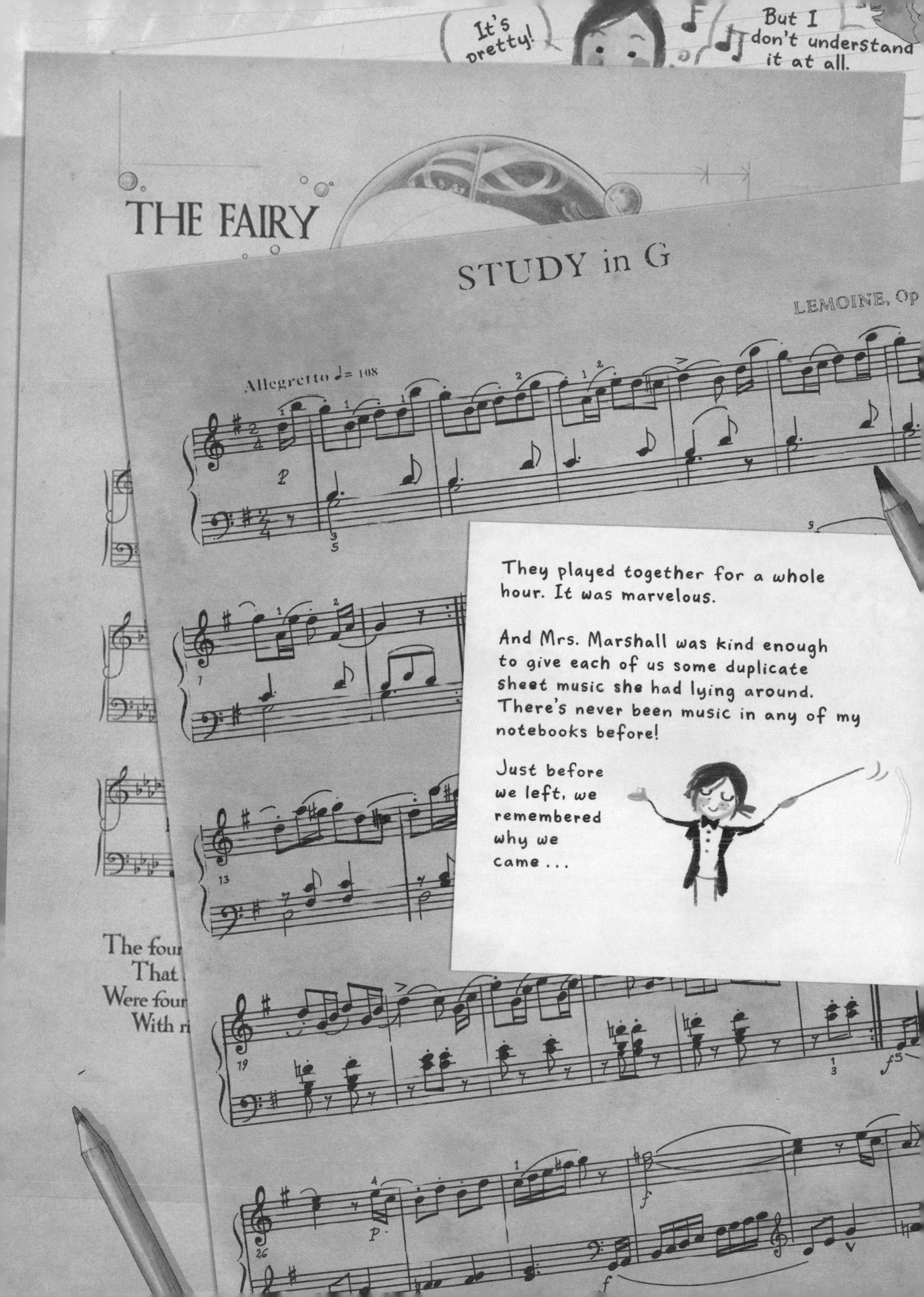
It's pretty!
But I don't understand it at all.
THE FAIRY
STUDY in G
LEMOINE, Op
Allegretto ♩= 108
The four
That
Were four
With ri

They played together for a whole hour. It was marvelous.

And Mrs. Marshall was kind enough to give each of us some duplicate sheet music she had lying around. There's never been music in any of my notebooks before!

Just before we left, we remembered why we came . . .

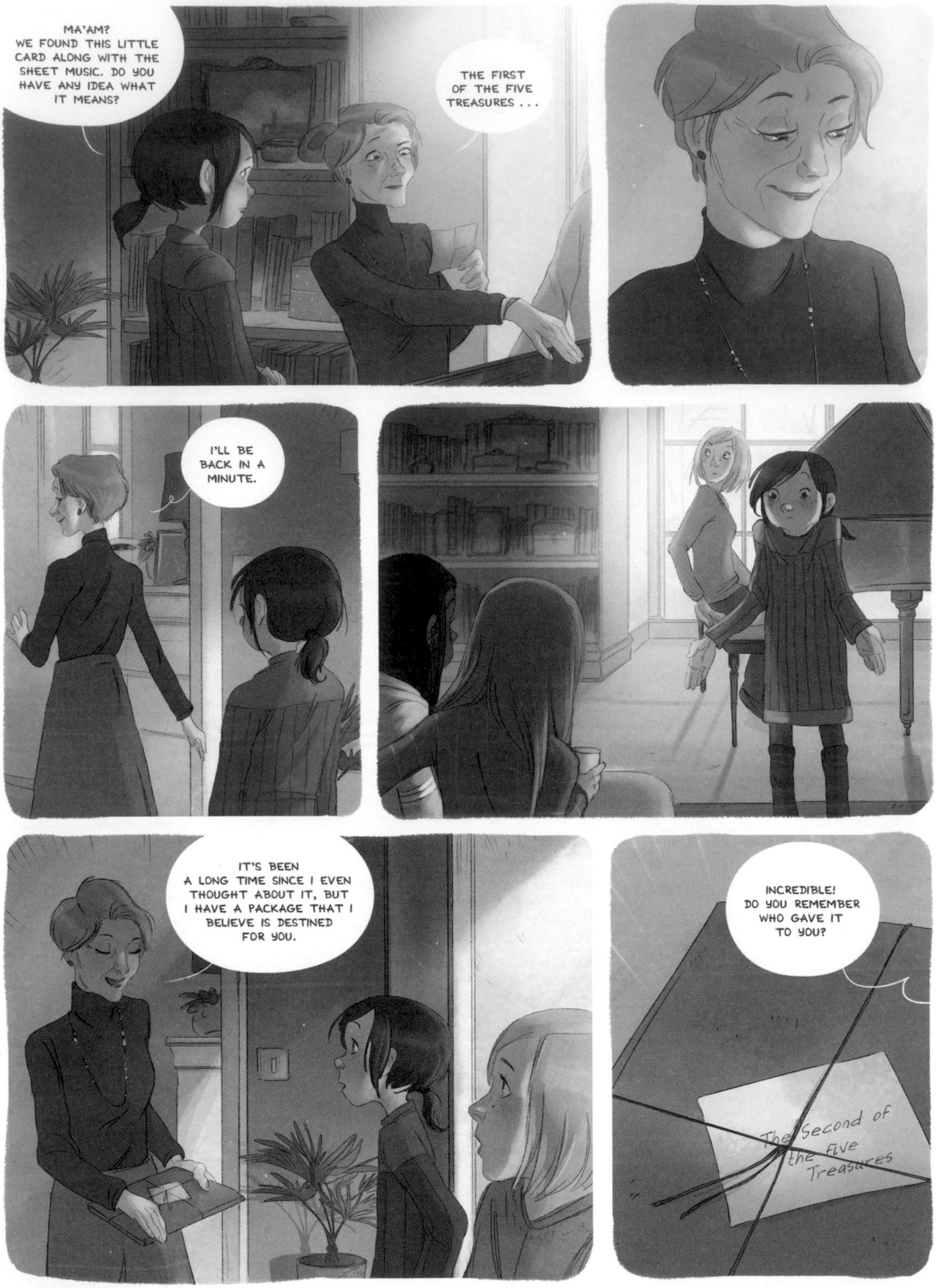
MA'AM? WE FOUND THIS LITTLE CARD ALONG WITH THE SHEET MUSIC. DO YOU HAVE ANY IDEA WHAT IT MEANS?
THE FIRST OF THE FIVE TREASURES . . .
I'LL BE BACK IN A MINUTE.
IT'S BEEN A LONG TIME SINCE I EVEN THOUGHT ABOUT IT, BUT I HAVE A PACKAGE THAT I BELIEVE IS DESTINED FOR YOU.
INCREDIBLE! DO YOU REMEMBER WHO GAVE IT TO YOU?
The Second of the Five Treasures

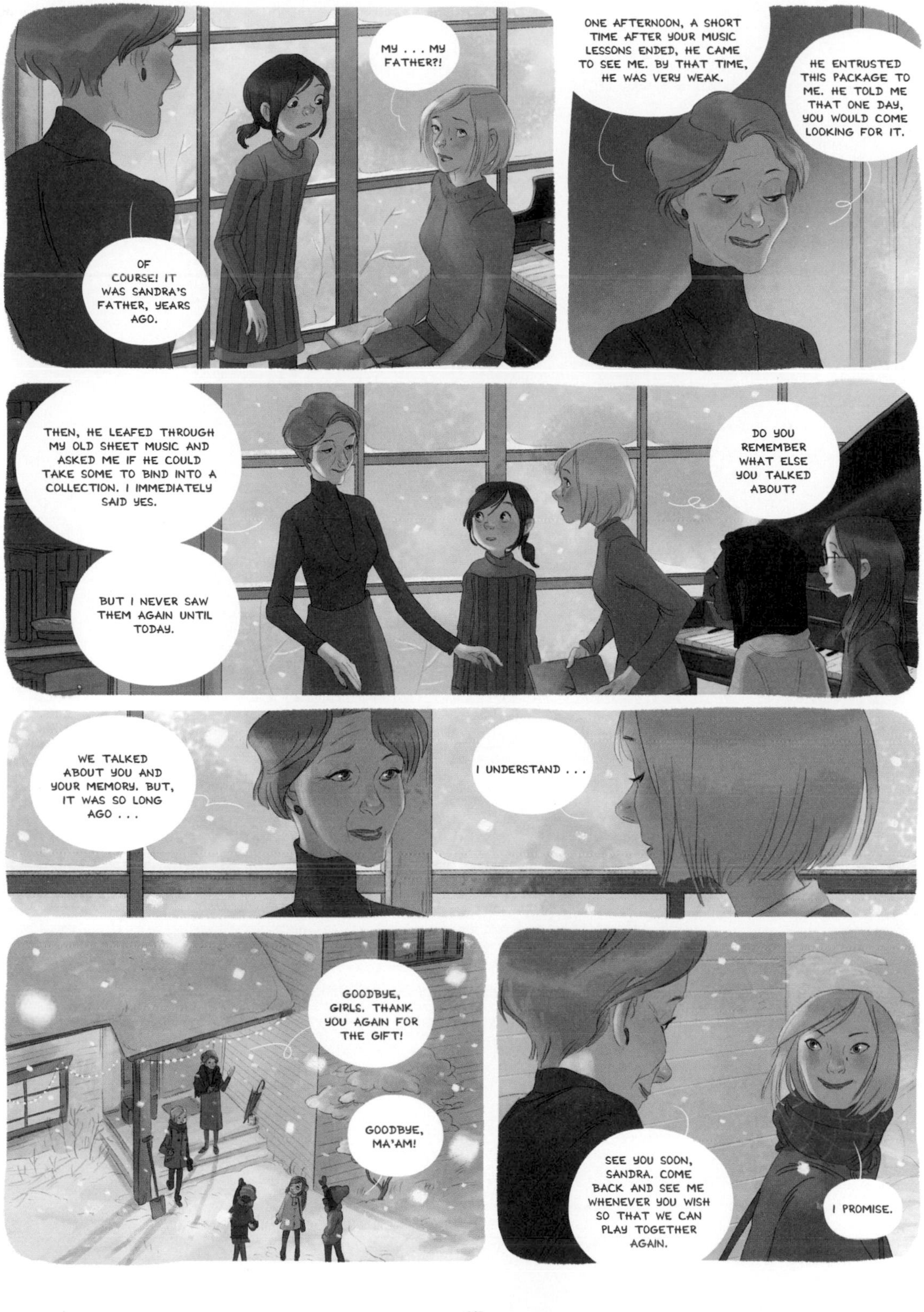
MY . . . MY FATHER?!
OF COURSE! IT WAS SANDRA'S FATHER, YEARS AGO.
ONE AFTERNOON, A SHORT TIME AFTER YOUR MUSIC LESSONS ENDED, HE CAME TO SEE ME. BY THAT TIME, HE WAS VERY WEAK.
HE ENTRUSTED THIS PACKAGE TO ME. HE TOLD ME THAT ONE DAY, YOU WOULD COME LOOKING FOR IT.
THEN, HE LEAFED THROUGH MY OLD SHEET MUSIC AND ASKED ME IF HE COULD TAKE SOME TO BIND INTO A COLLECTION. I IMMEDIATELY SAID YES.
BUT I NEVER SAW THEM AGAIN UNTIL TODAY.
DO YOU REMEMBER WHAT ELSE YOU TALKED ABOUT?
WE TALKED ABOUT YOU AND YOUR MEMORY. BUT, IT WAS SO LONG AGO . . .
I UNDERSTAND . . .
GOODBYE, GIRLS. THANK YOU AGAIN FOR THE GIFT!
GOODBYE, MA'AM!
SEE YOU SOON, SANDRA. COME BACK AND SEE ME WHENEVER YOU WISH SO THAT WE CAN PLAY TOGETHER AGAIN.
I PROMISE.

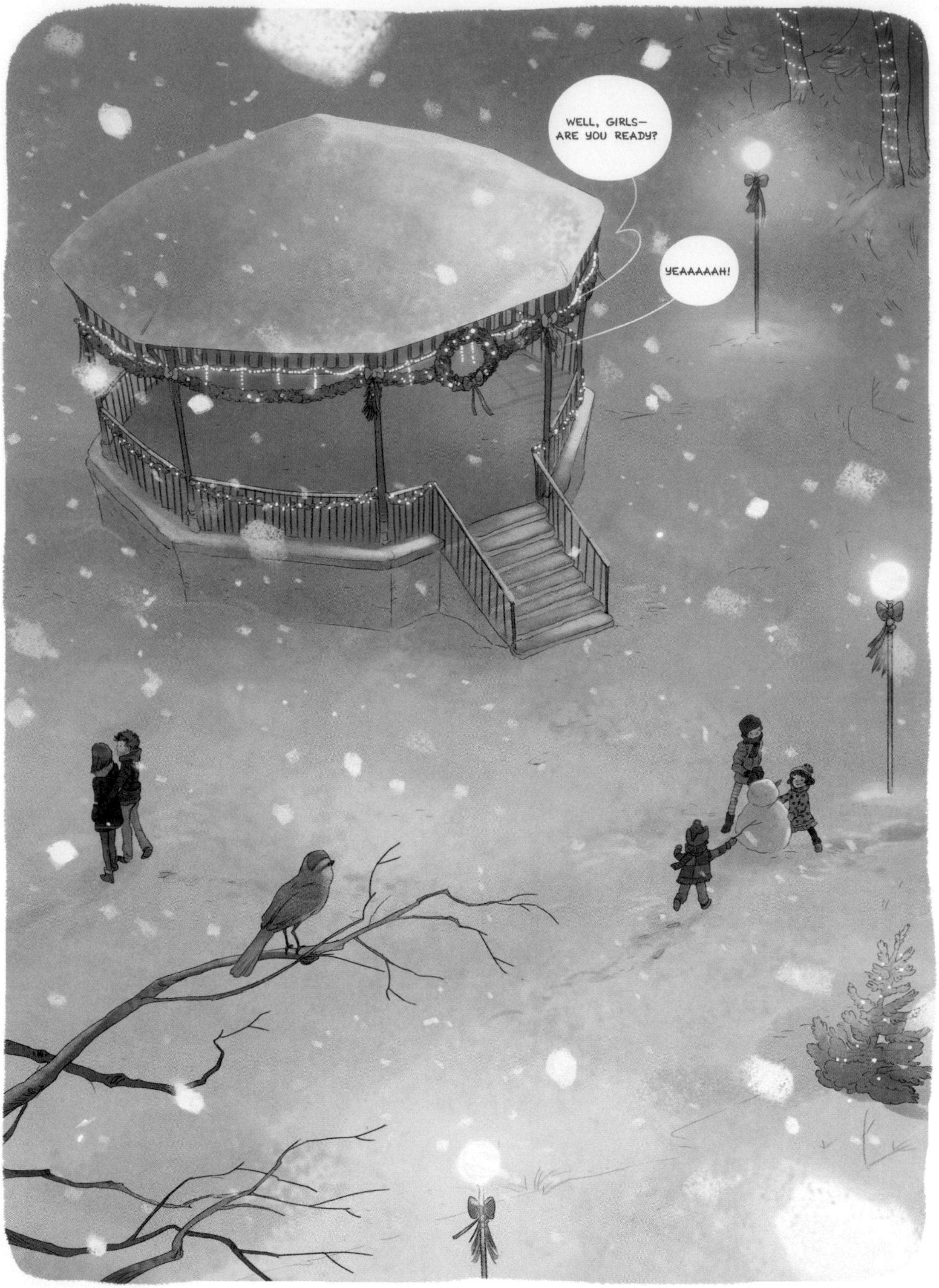
WELL, GIRLS—
ARE YOU READY?
YEAAAAAH!

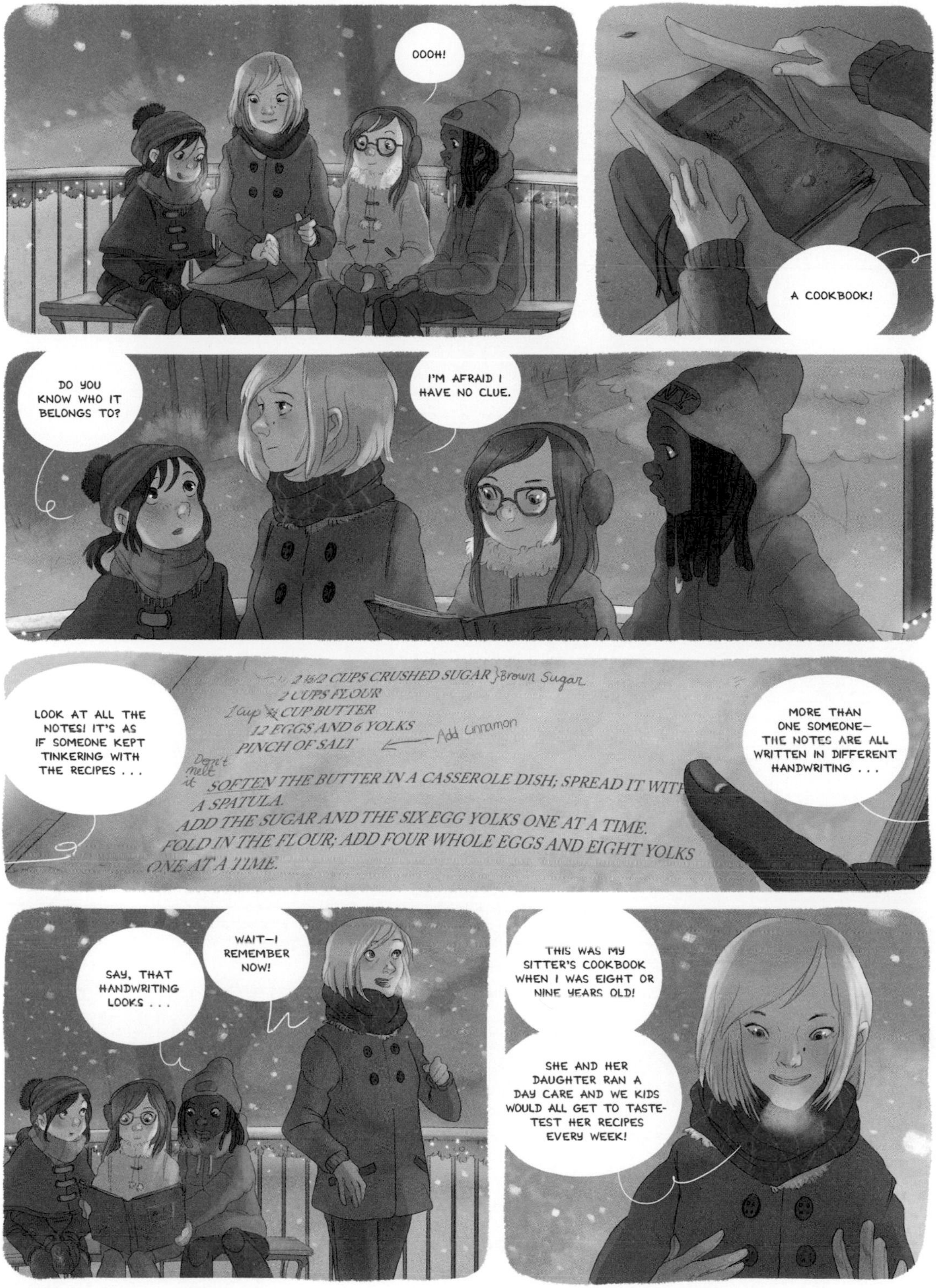
OOOH!
A COOKBOOK!
DO YOU KNOW WHO IT BELONGS TO?
I'M AFRAID I HAVE NO CLUE.
LOOK AT ALL THE NOTES! IT'S AS IF SOMEONE KEPT TINKERING WITH THE RECIPES . . .
2 1/2 CUPS CRUSHED SUGAR
Brown Sugar
2 CUPS FLOUR
1 cup
CUP BUTTER
12 EGGS AND 6 YOLKS
PINCH OF SALT
Add Cinnamon
Don't melt it
SOFTEN THE BUTTER IN A CASSEROLE DISH; SPREAD IT WITH A SPATULA.
ADD THE SUGAR AND THE SIX EGG YOLKS ONE AT A TIME.
FOLD IN THE FLOUR; ADD FOUR WHOLE EGGS AND EIGHT YOLKS ONE AT A TIME.
MORE THAN ONE SOMEONE—THE NOTES ARE ALL WRITTEN IN DIFFERENT HANDWRITING . . .
SAY, THAT HANDWRITING LOOKS . . .
WAIT—I REMEMBER NOW!
THIS WAS MY SITTER'S COOKBOOK WHEN I WAS EIGHT OR NINE YEARS OLD!
SHE AND HER DAUGHTER RAN A DAY CARE AND WE KIDS WOULD ALL GET TO TASTE-TEST HER RECIPES EVERY WEEK!

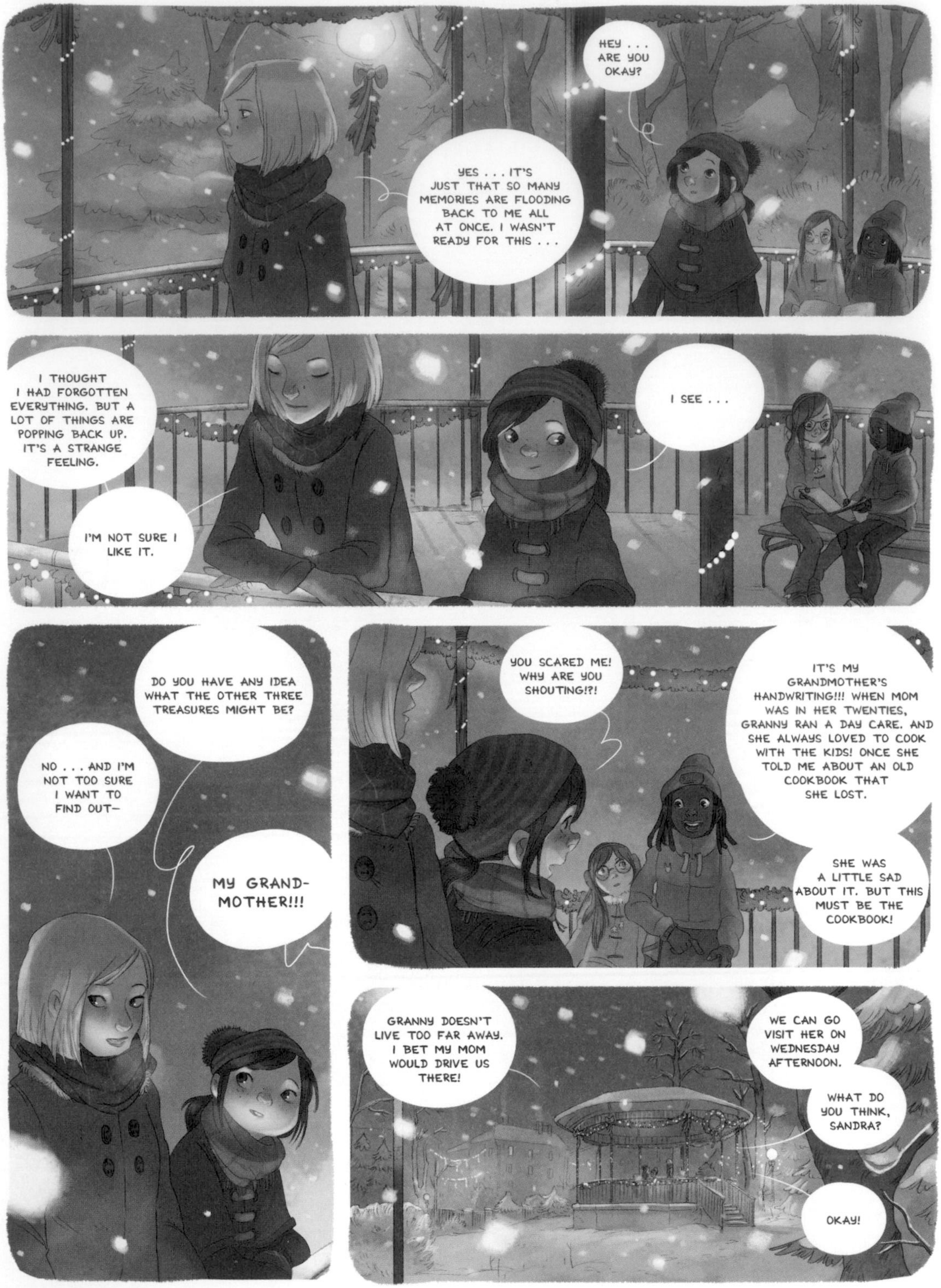
HEY . . . ARE YOU OKAY?
YES . . . IT'S JUST THAT SO MANY MEMORIES ARE FLOODING BACK TO ME ALL AT ONCE. I WASN'T READY FOR THIS . . .
I THOUGHT I HAD FORGOTTEN EVERYTHING. BUT A LOT OF THINGS ARE POPPING BACK UP. IT'S A STRANGE FEELING.
I'M NOT SURE I LIKE IT.
I SEE . . .
DO YOU HAVE ANY IDEA WHAT THE OTHER THREE TREASURES MIGHT BE?
NO . . . AND I'M NOT TOO SURE I WANT TO FIND OUT—
MY GRAND-MOTHER!!!
YOU SCARED ME! WHY ARE YOU SHOUTING!?!
IT'S MY GRANDMOTHER'S HANDWRITING!!! WHEN MOM WAS IN HER TWENTIES, GRANNY RAN A DAY CARE. AND SHE ALWAYS LOVED TO COOK WITH THE KIDS! ONCE SHE TOLD ME ABOUT AN OLD COOKBOOK THAT SHE LOST.
SHE WAS A LITTLE SAD ABOUT IT. BUT THIS MUST BE THE COOKBOOK!
GRANNY DOESN'T LIVE TOO FAR AWAY. I BET MY MOM WOULD DRIVE US THERE!
WE CAN GO VISIT HER ON WEDNESDAY AFTERNOON.
WHAT DO YOU THINK, SANDRA?
OKAY!

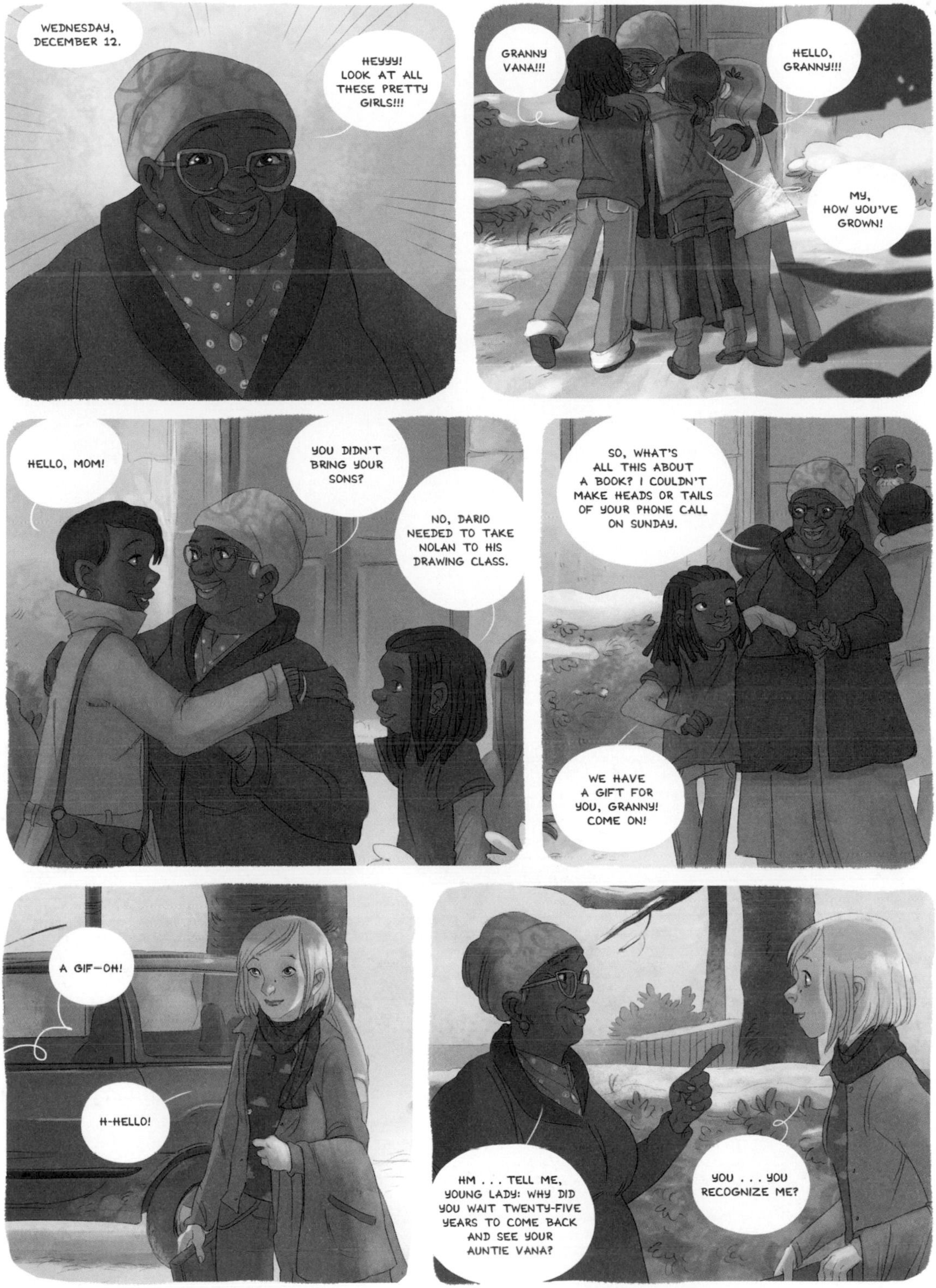
WEDNESDAY, DECEMBER 12.
HEYYY! LOOK AT ALL THESE PRETTY GIRLS!!!
GRANNY VANA!!!
HELLO, GRANNY!!!
MY, HOW YOU'VE GROWN!
HELLO, MOM!
YOU DIDN'T BRING YOUR SONS?
NO, DARIO NEEDED TO TAKE NOLAN TO HIS DRAWING CLASS.
SO, WHAT'S ALL THIS ABOUT A BOOK? I COULDN'T MAKE HEADS OR TAILS OF YOUR PHONE CALL ON SUNDAY.
WE HAVE A GIFT FOR YOU, GRANNY! COME ON!
A GIF—OH!
H-HELLO!
HM . . . TELL ME, YOUNG LADY: WHY DID YOU WAIT TWENTY-FIVE YEARS TO COME BACK AND SEE YOUR AUNTIE VANA?
YOU . . . YOU RECOGNIZE ME?

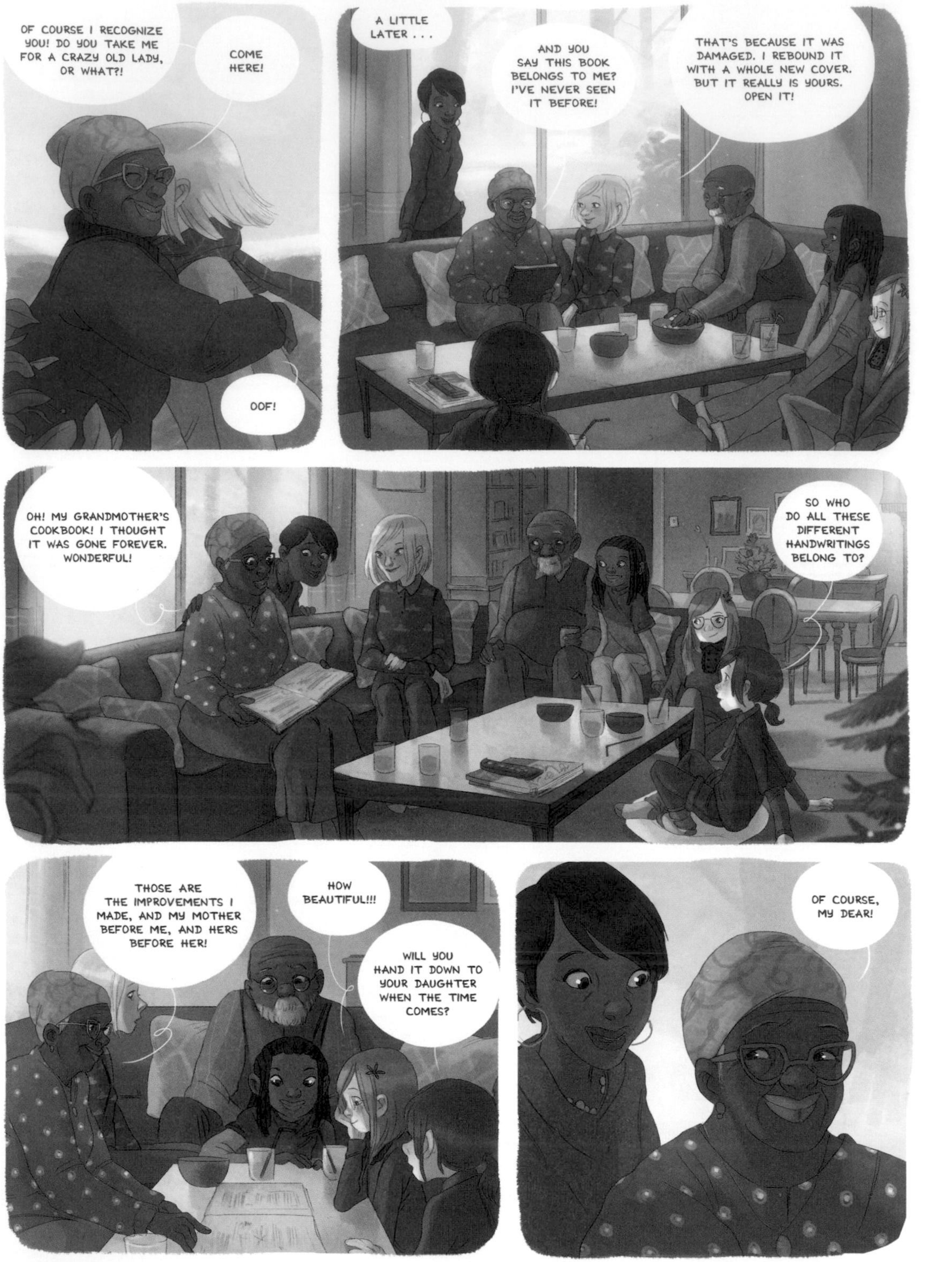
OF COURSE I RECOGNIZE YOU! DO YOU TAKE ME FOR A CRAZY OLD LADY, OR WHAT?!
COME HERE!
OOF!
A LITTLE LATER . . .
AND YOU SAY THIS BOOK BELONGS TO ME? I'VE NEVER SEEN IT BEFORE!
THAT'S BECAUSE IT WAS DAMAGED. I REBOUND IT WITH A WHOLE NEW COVER. BUT IT REALLY IS YOURS. OPEN IT!
OH! MY GRANDMOTHER'S COOKBOOK! I THOUGHT IT WAS GONE FOREVER. WONDERFUL!
SO WHO DO ALL THESE DIFFERENT HANDWRITINGS BELONG TO?
THOSE ARE THE IMPROVEMENTS I MADE, AND MY MOTHER BEFORE ME, AND HERS BEFORE HER!
HOW BEAUTIFUL!!!
WILL YOU HAND IT DOWN TO YOUR DAUGHTER WHEN THE TIME COMES?
OF COURSE, MY DEAR!

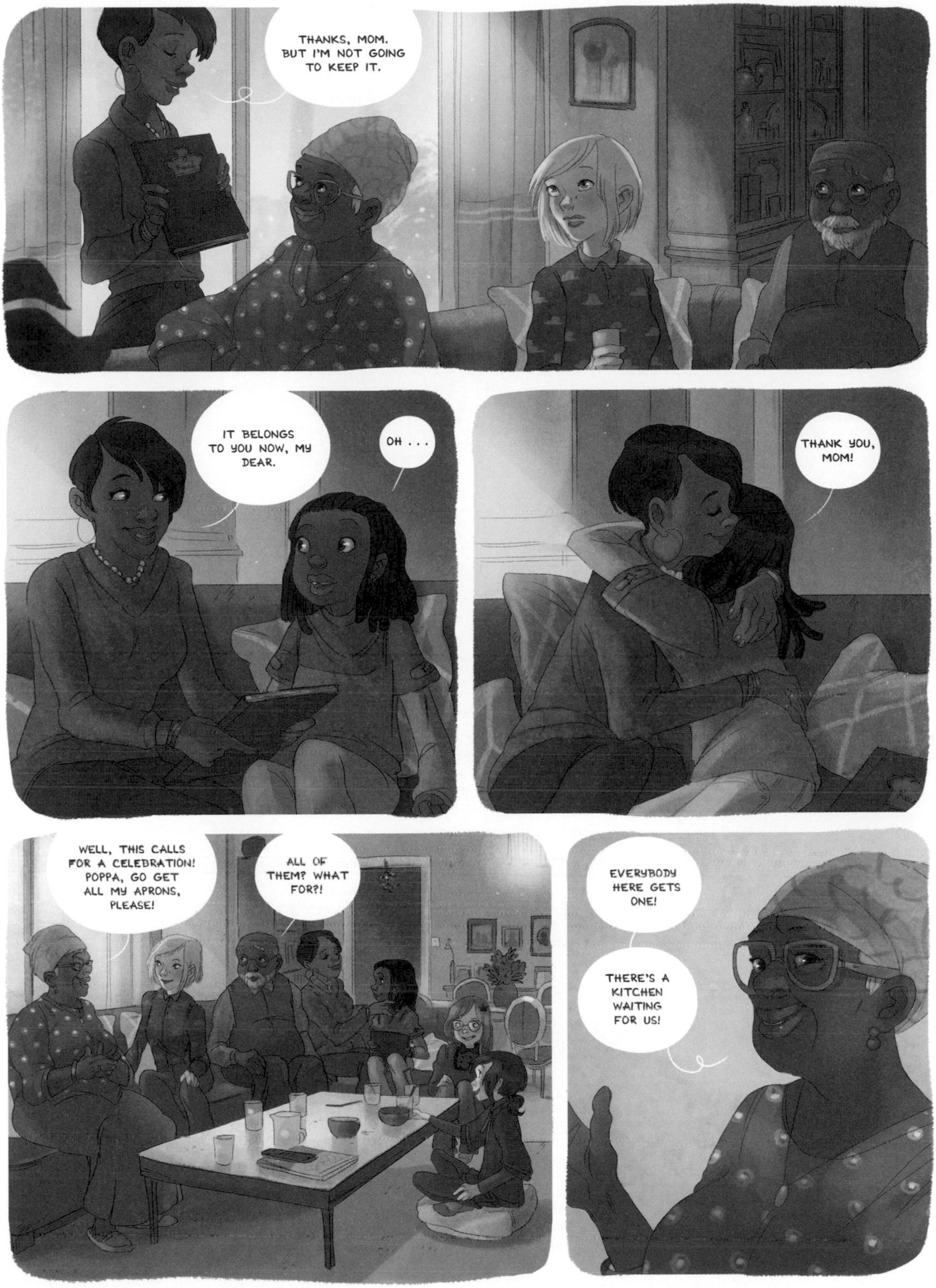
THANKS, MOM. BUT I'M NOT GOING TO KEEP IT.
IT BELONGS TO YOU NOW, MY DEAR.
OH . . .
THANK YOU, MOM!
WELL, THIS CALLS FOR A CELEBRATION! POPPA, GO GET ALL MY APRONS, PLEASE!
ALL OF THEM? WHAT FOR?!
EVERYBODY HERE GETS ONE!
THERE'S A KITCHEN WAITING FOR US!

Today was so much fun! Erica's granny is kind and
full of laughs. We had a great time!

CHOCOLATE CHIP
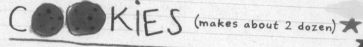
C**OO**KIES (makes about 2 dozen) ★

Half a bag of dark chocolate chips (or more, to taste)
-1 tsp cinnamon
-1/3 cup butter, softened
-5/8 cup brown sugar
-3/4 cup flour
-1 egg
-1 tbsp milk
-1 tsp baking powder

Preheat the oven to 410 degrees.
Put the butter in a large bowl. Add the sugar and cinnamon,
then mix well. Add the egg. Stir again. Fold in flour using a
wooden spatula. Or with your fingers—it's more fun!

Add baking powder, then chocolate chips and milk.
Cover a cookie sheet with parchment paper. Form the dough
into balls and put them on the paper; flatten them to a
thickness of about a third of an inch. Bake twelve minutes.

Erica's granny once
made Halloween
cookies by adding
orange food coloring
to the dough and
putting extra
chocolate bits on top
to make a pumpkin
face. Too funny!

Boo!

Shortbread cookies

-2 cups flour
-1/2 cup soft butter
-5/8 cup brown sugar
-1 tsp cinnamon
-Pinch salt
-Yolk of 1 egg

Preheat oven to 350 degrees.

Mix the softened butter, flour, salt, cinnamon, and sugar.
Work the dough with fingertips until it has a sandy texture.

Be careful not to work the dough too long or the cookies will be too hard!

Add the yolk of an egg; form dough into ball. Wrap the ball of dough in plastic wrap and let rest in a cool place for at least 30 minutes. Once the dough has rested, roll it out and use cookie cutters (or a glass) to cut out shapes.

We made Christmas trees and stars!

Bake ten minutes.

To make the cookies turn out golden, you can brush them with egg yolk before cooking—it's prettier!

Afterward, Granny Vana made icing and we decorated the cookies!

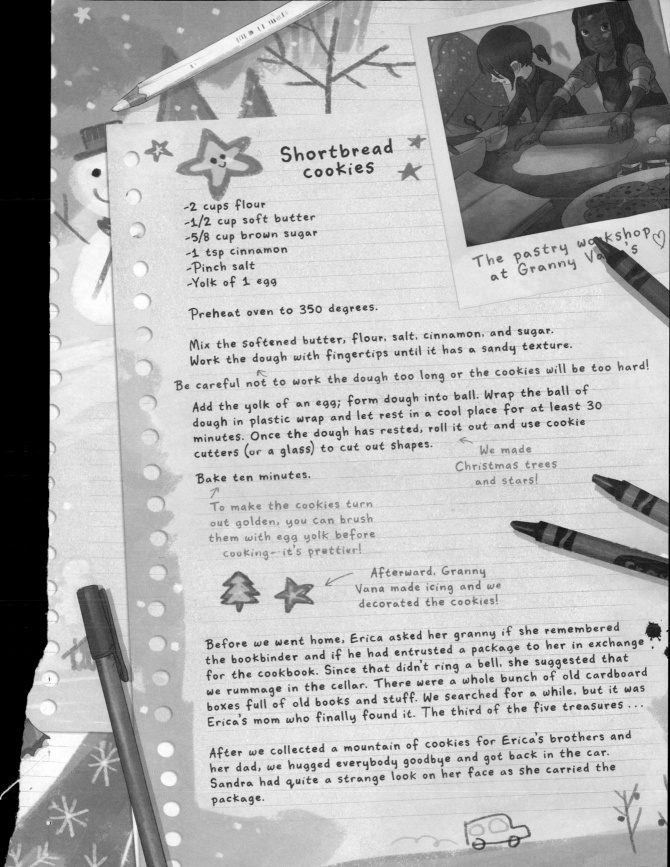

The pastry workshop at Granny Vana's

Before we went home, Erica asked her granny if she remembered the bookbinder and if he had entrusted a package to her in exchange for the cookbook. Since that didn't ring a bell, she suggested that we rummage in the cellar. There were a whole bunch of old cardboard boxes full of old books and stuff. We searched for a while, but it was Erica's mom who finally found it. The third of the five treasures . . .

After we collected a mountain of cookies for Erica's brothers and her dad, we hugged everybody goodbye and got back in the car. Sandra had quite a strange look on her face as she carried the package.

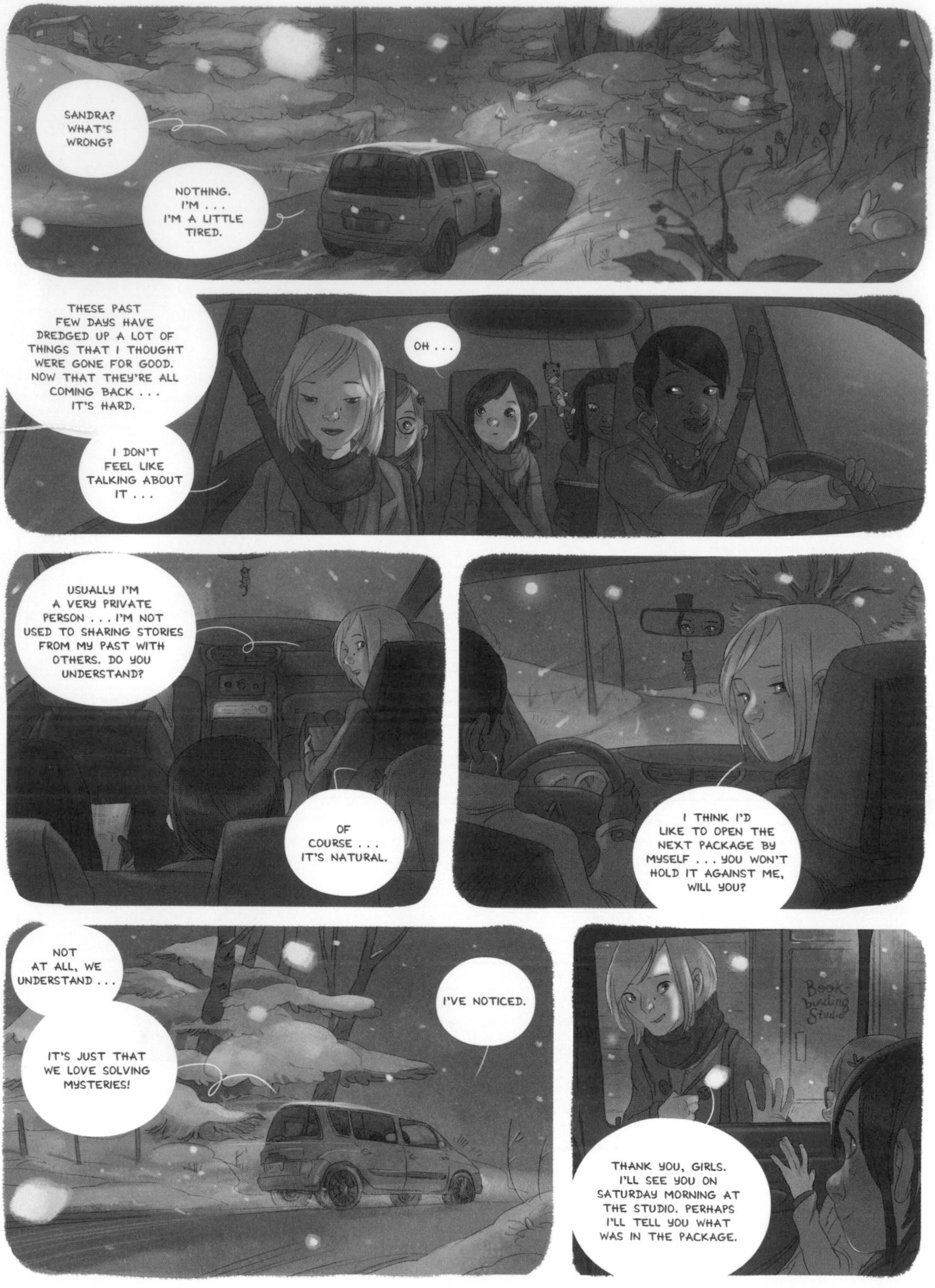
SANDRA? WHAT'S WRONG?
NOTHING. I'M . . . I'M A LITTLE TIRED.
THESE PAST FEW DAYS HAVE DREDGED UP A LOT OF THINGS THAT I THOUGHT WERE GONE FOR GOOD. NOW THAT THEY'RE ALL COMING BACK . . . IT'S HARD.
OH . . .
I DON'T FEEL LIKE TALKING ABOUT IT . . .
USUALLY I'M A VERY PRIVATE PERSON . . . I'M NOT USED TO SHARING STORIES FROM MY PAST WITH OTHERS. DO YOU UNDERSTAND?
OF COURSE . . . IT'S NATURAL.
I THINK I'D LIKE TO OPEN THE NEXT PACKAGE BY MYSELF . . . YOU WON'T HOLD IT AGAINST ME, WILL YOU?
NOT AT ALL, WE UNDERSTAND . . .
IT'S JUST THAT WE LOVE SOLVING MYSTERIES!
I'VE NOTICED.
Book-binding Studio
THANK YOU, GIRLS. I'LL SEE YOU ON SATURDAY MORNING AT THE STUDIO. PERHAPS I'LL TELL YOU WHAT WAS IN THE PACKAGE.

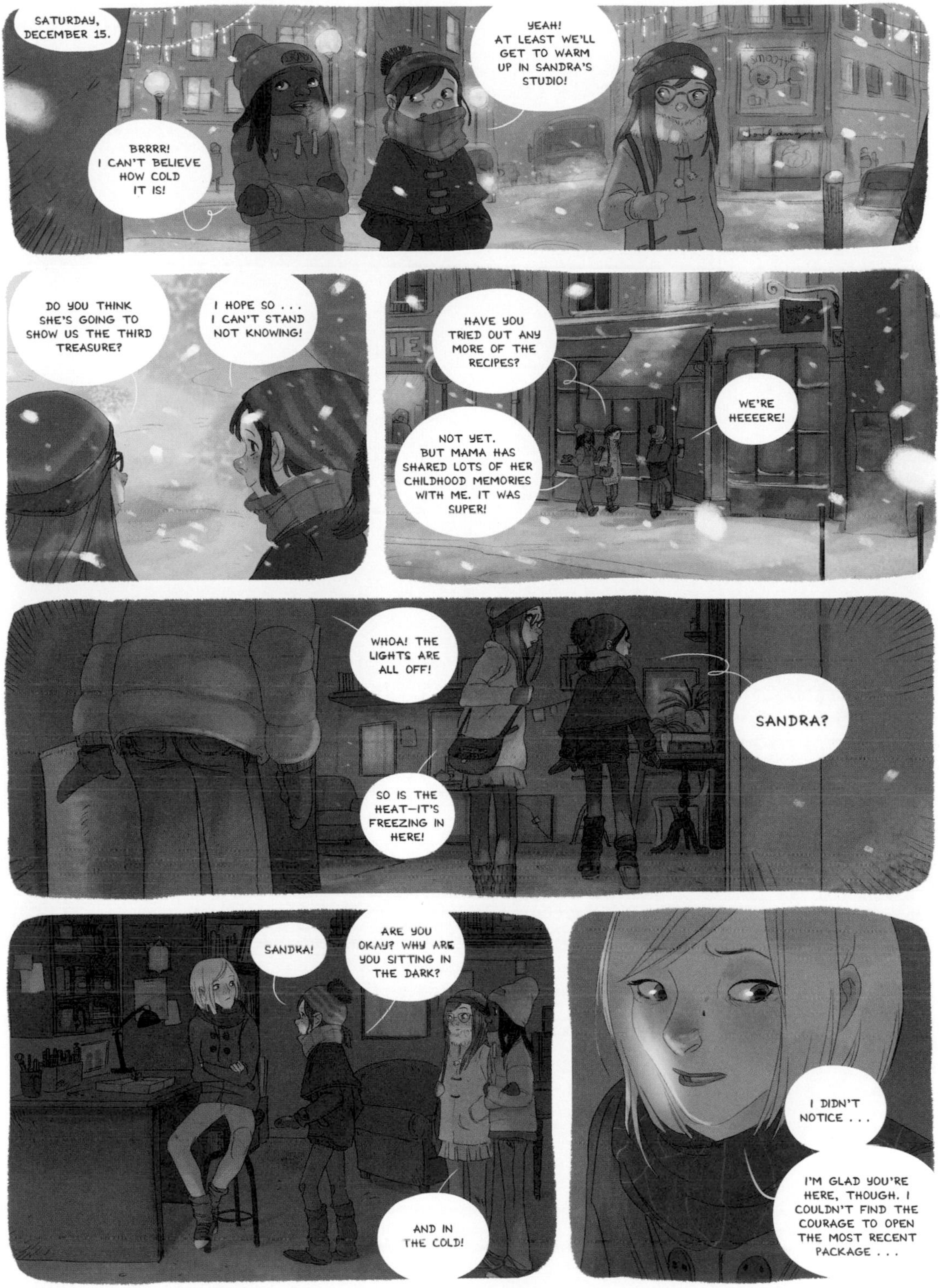
SATURDAY, DECEMBER 15.
BRRRR! I CAN'T BELIEVE HOW COLD IT IS!
YEAH! AT LEAST WE'LL GET TO WARM UP IN SANDRA'S STUDIO!
DO YOU THINK SHE'S GOING TO SHOW US THE THIRD TREASURE?
I HOPE SO . . . I CAN'T STAND NOT KNOWING!
HAVE YOU TRIED OUT ANY MORE OF THE RECIPES?
NOT YET. BUT MAMA HAS SHARED LOTS OF HER CHILDHOOD MEMORIES WITH ME. IT WAS SUPER!
WE'RE HEEEERE!
WHOA! THE LIGHTS ARE ALL OFF!
SO IS THE HEAT—IT'S FREEZING IN HERE!
SANDRA?
SANDRA!
ARE YOU OKAY? WHY ARE YOU SITTING IN THE DARK?
AND IN THE COLD!
I DIDN'T NOTICE . . .
I'M GLAD YOU'RE HERE, THOUGH. I COULDN'T FIND THE COURAGE TO OPEN THE MOST RECENT PACKAGE . . .

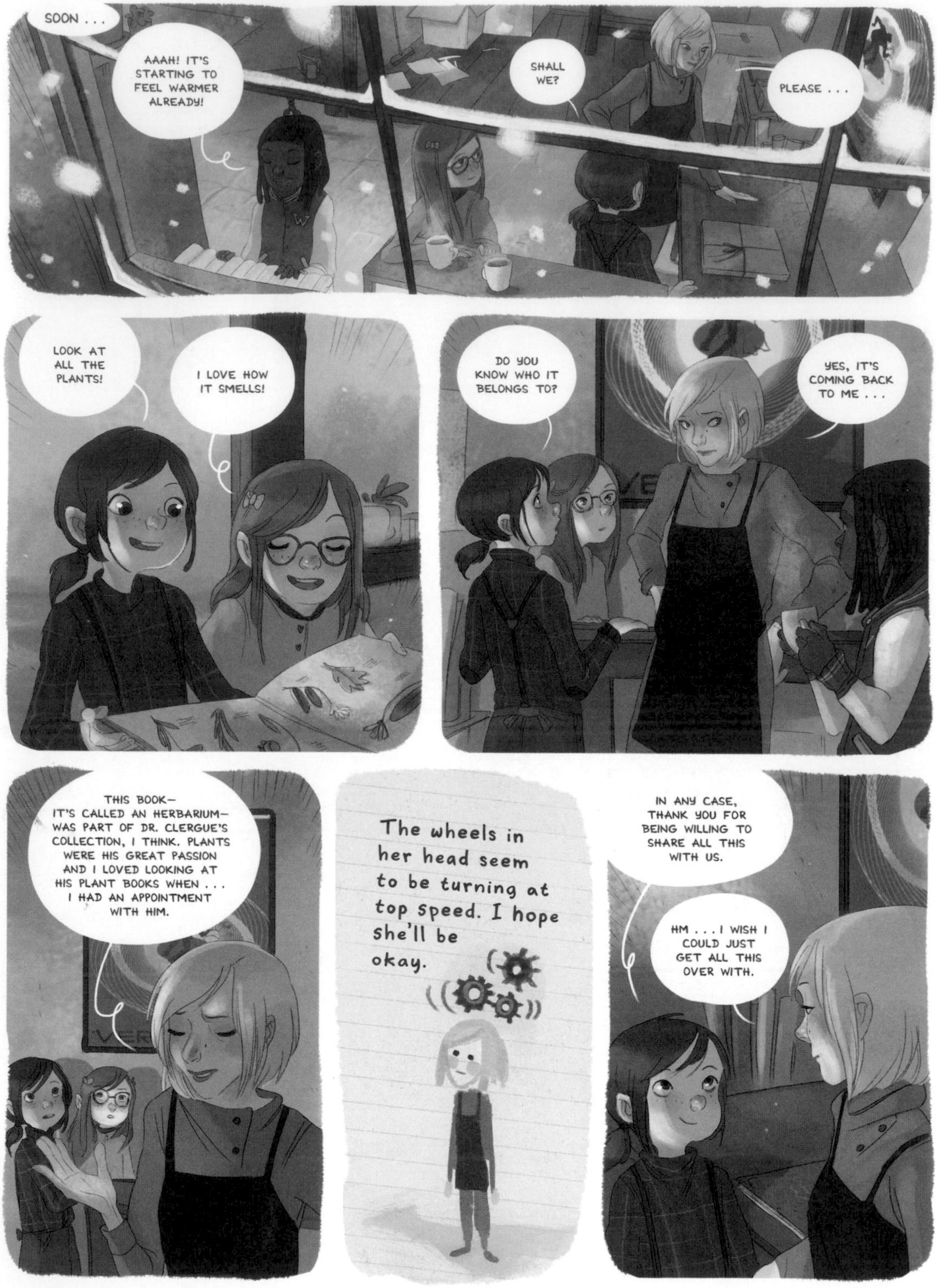
SOON . . .
AAAH! IT'S STARTING TO FEEL WARMER ALREADY!
SHALL WE?
PLEASE . . .
LOOK AT ALL THE PLANTS!
I LOVE HOW IT SMELLS!
DO YOU KNOW WHO IT BELONGS TO?
YES, IT'S COMING BACK TO ME . . .
THIS BOOK— IT'S CALLED AN HERBARIUM— WAS PART OF DR. CLERGUE'S COLLECTION, I THINK. PLANTS WERE HIS GREAT PASSION AND I LOVED LOOKING AT HIS PLANT BOOKS WHEN . . . I HAD AN APPOINTMENT WITH HIM.
The wheels in her head seem to be turning at top speed. I hope she'll be okay.
IN ANY CASE, THANK YOU FOR BEING WILLING TO SHARE ALL THIS WITH US.
HM . . . I WISH I COULD JUST GET ALL THIS OVER WITH.

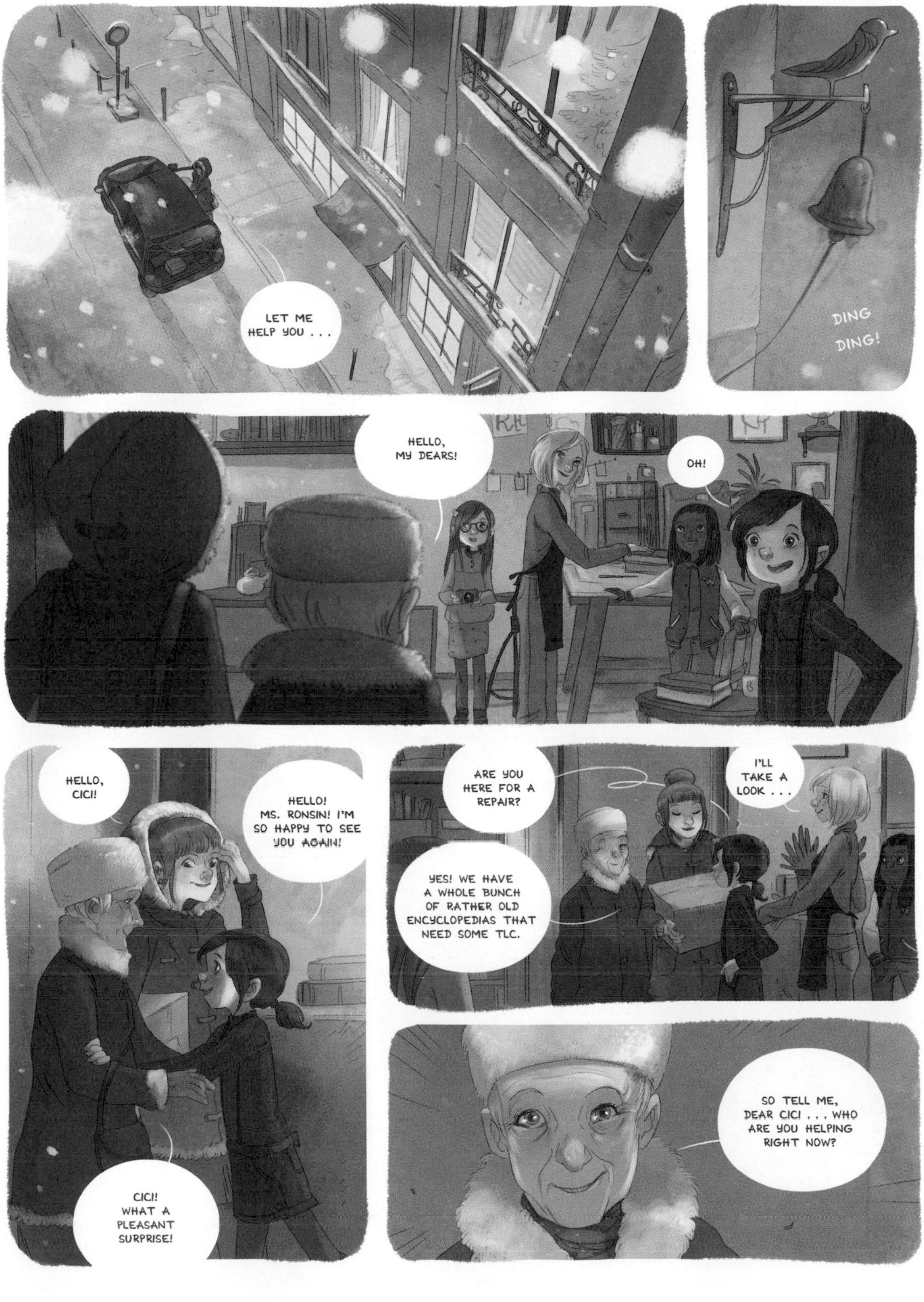
LET ME HELP YOU . . .
DING DING!
HELLO, MY DEARS!
OH!
HELLO, CICI!
HELLO! MS. RONSIN! I'M SO HAPPY TO SEE YOU AGAIN!
CICI! WHAT A PLEASANT SURPRISE!
ARE YOU HERE FOR A REPAIR?
YES! WE HAVE A WHOLE BUNCH OF RATHER OLD ENCYCLOPEDIAS THAT NEED SOME TLC.
I'LL TAKE A LOOK . . .
SO TELL ME, DEAR CICI . . . WHO ARE YOU HELPING RIGHT NOW?

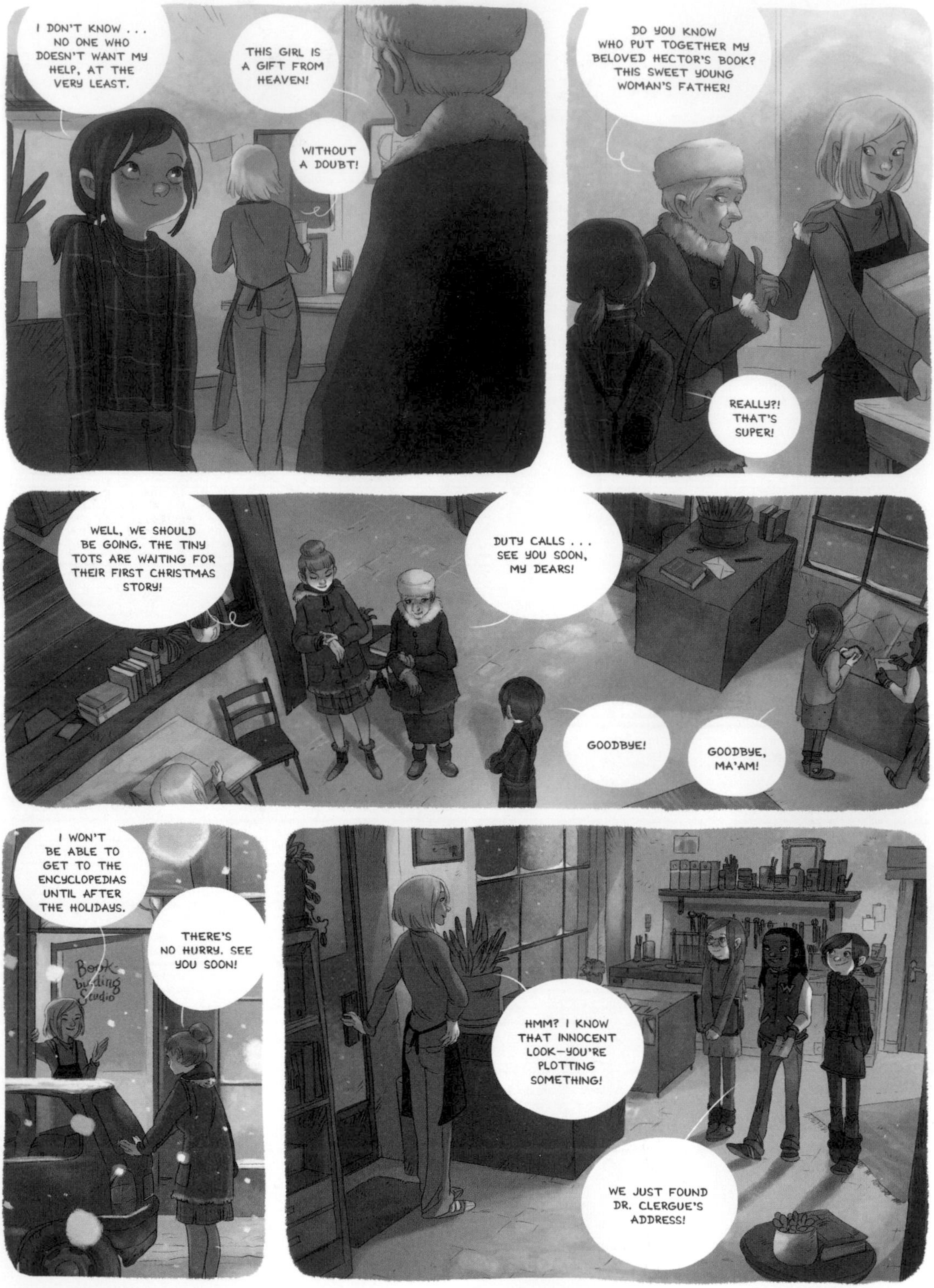
I DON'T KNOW . . . NO ONE WHO DOESN'T WANT MY HELP, AT THE VERY LEAST.
THIS GIRL IS A GIFT FROM HEAVEN!
WITHOUT A DOUBT!
DO YOU KNOW WHO PUT TOGETHER MY BELOVED HECTOR'S BOOK? THIS SWEET YOUNG WOMAN'S FATHER!
REALLY?! THAT'S SUPER!
WELL, WE SHOULD BE GOING. THE TINY TOTS ARE WAITING FOR THEIR FIRST CHRISTMAS STORY!
DUTY CALLS . . . SEE YOU SOON, MY DEARS!
GOODBYE!
GOODBYE, MA'AM!
I WON'T BE ABLE TO GET TO THE ENCYCLOPEDIAS UNTIL AFTER THE HOLIDAYS.
Book-binding Studio
THERE'S NO HURRY. SEE YOU SOON!
HMM? I KNOW THAT INNOCENT LOOK—YOU'RE PLOTTING SOMETHING!
WE JUST FOUND DR. CLERGUE'S ADDRESS!

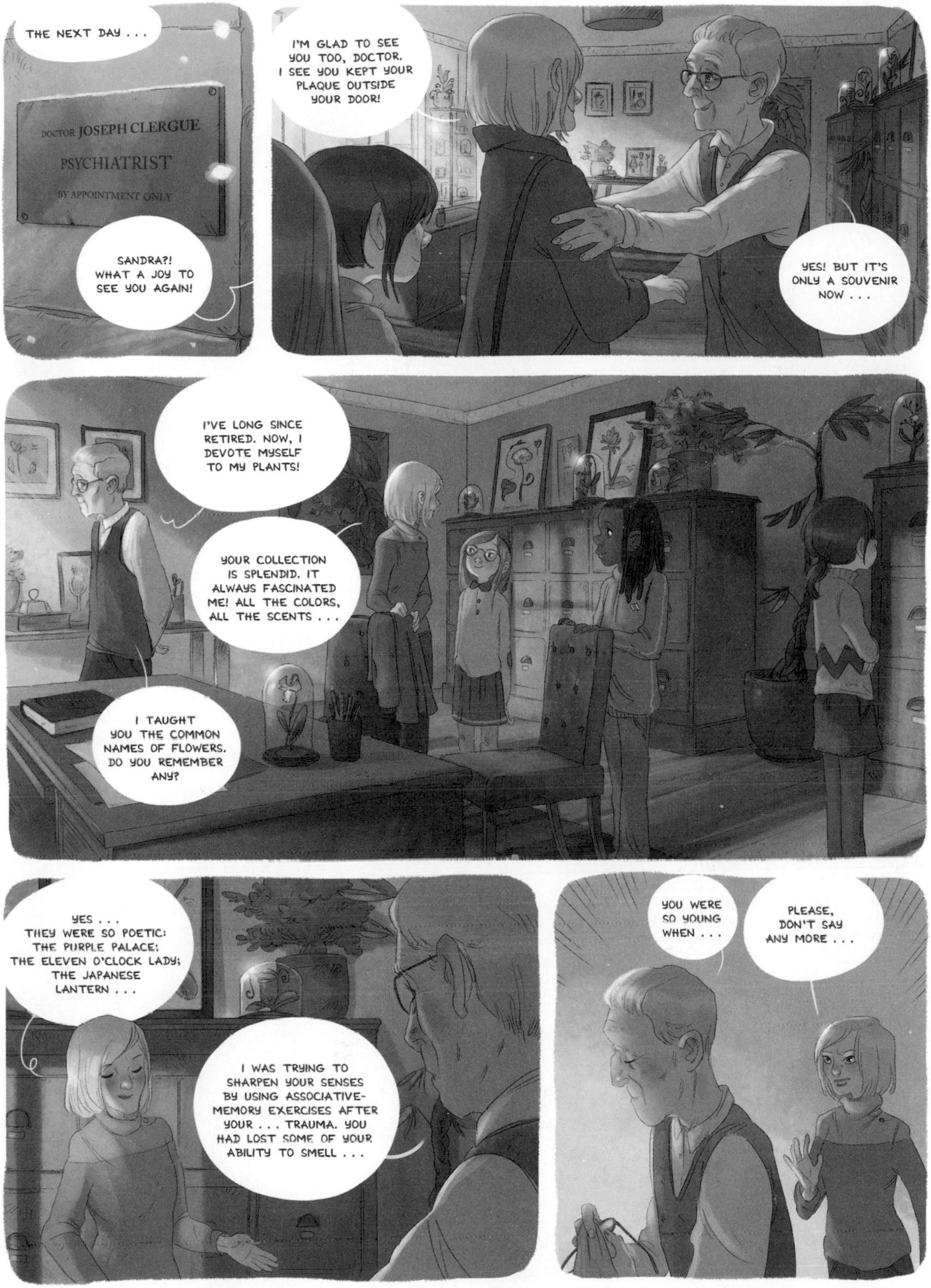
THE NEXT DAY . . .
DOCTOR JOSEPH CLERGUE
PSYCHIATRIST
BY APPOINTMENT ONLY
SANDRA?! WHAT A JOY TO SEE YOU AGAIN!
I'M GLAD TO SEE YOU TOO, DOCTOR. I SEE YOU KEPT YOUR PLAQUE OUTSIDE YOUR DOOR!
YES! BUT IT'S ONLY A SOUVENIR NOW . . .
I'VE LONG SINCE RETIRED. NOW, I DEVOTE MYSELF TO MY PLANTS!
YOUR COLLECTION IS SPLENDID. IT ALWAYS FASCINATED ME! ALL THE COLORS, ALL THE SCENTS . . .
I TAUGHT YOU THE COMMON NAMES OF FLOWERS. DO YOU REMEMBER ANY?
YES . . . THEY WERE SO POETIC: THE PURPLE PALACE; THE ELEVEN O'CLOCK LADY; THE JAPANESE LANTERN . . .
I WAS TRYING TO SHARPEN YOUR SENSES BY USING ASSOCIATIVE-MEMORY EXERCISES AFTER YOUR . . . TRAUMA. YOU HAD LOST SOME OF YOUR ABILITY TO SMELL . . .
YOU WERE SO YOUNG WHEN . . .
PLEASE, DON'T SAY ANY MORE . . .

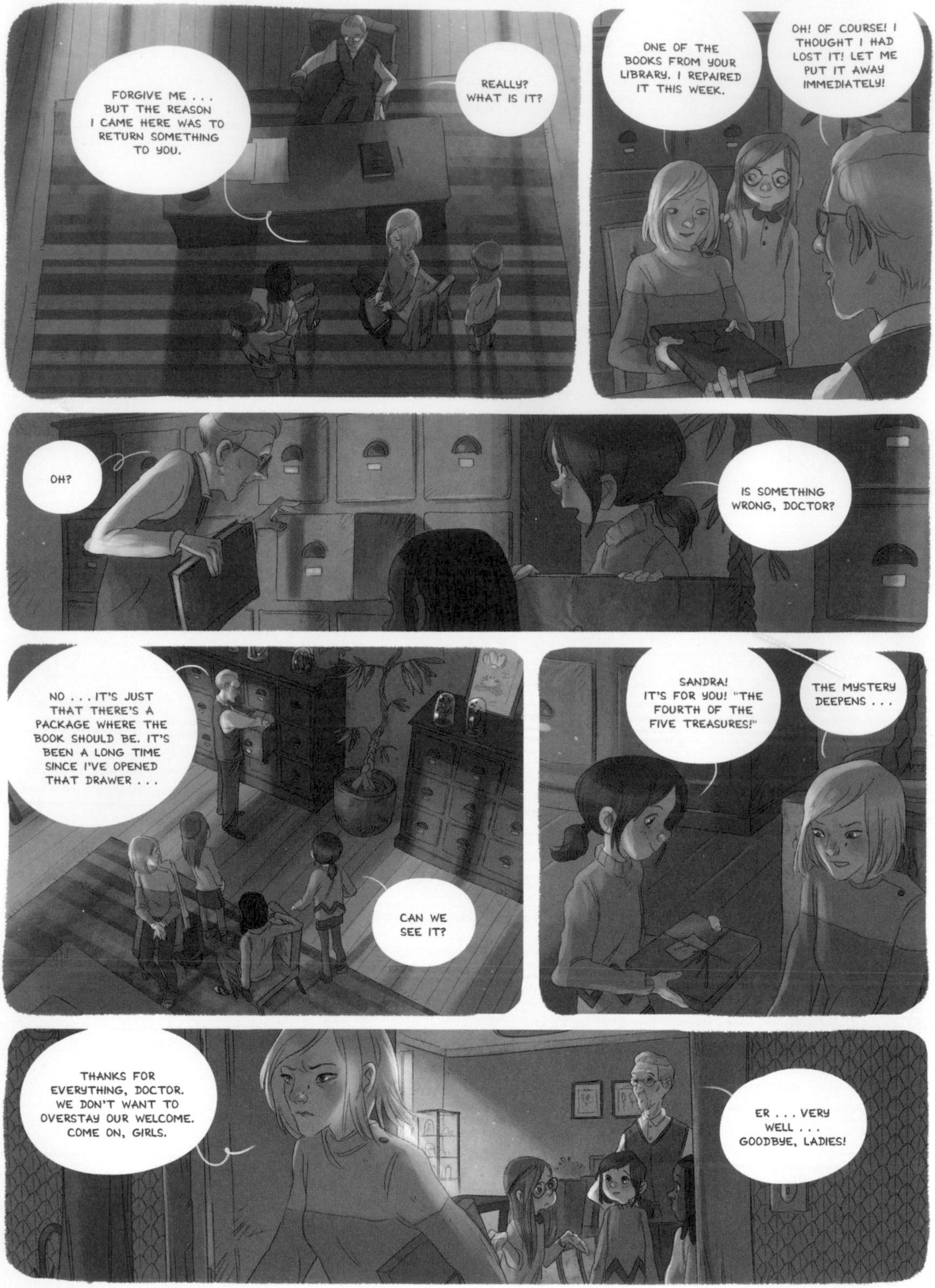
FORGIVE ME . . . BUT THE REASON I CAME HERE WAS TO RETURN SOMETHING TO YOU.
REALLY? WHAT IS IT?
ONE OF THE BOOKS FROM YOUR LIBRARY. I REPAIRED IT THIS WEEK.
OH! OF COURSE! I THOUGHT I HAD LOST IT! LET ME PUT IT AWAY IMMEDIATELY!
OH?
IS SOMETHING WRONG, DOCTOR?
NO . . . IT'S JUST THAT THERE'S A PACKAGE WHERE THE BOOK SHOULD BE. IT'S BEEN A LONG TIME SINCE I'VE OPENED THAT DRAWER . . .
CAN WE SEE IT?
SANDRA! IT'S FOR YOU! "THE FOURTH OF THE FIVE TREASURES!"
THE MYSTERY DEEPENS . . .
THANKS FOR EVERYTHING, DOCTOR. WE DON'T WANT TO OVERSTAY OUR WELCOME. COME ON, GIRLS.
ER . . . VERY WELL . . . GOODBYE, LADIES!

gentiana
acaulis

trifolium
alpestre

Isopyrum
thalictroides

Walk in the
Alps 1983

Before we left, Dr. Clergue kindly offered us some loose pages from one of his old plant books.

They're super! These pages make me want to create an herbarium of my own and learn the common names for flowers! There are lots of books about plants at the library— I can borrow some.

After gathering the pages, we caught up with Sandra and we all left without another word. It was pretty tense...

As soon as Dr. Clergue said the word "trauma," Sandra became angry. But at whom? Angry at Dr. Clergue—or at herself? I don't know. In any case, it's clear that she doesn't want to talk about her memory problems. But she seems to be tormented by something.

She and I seem more and more alike...

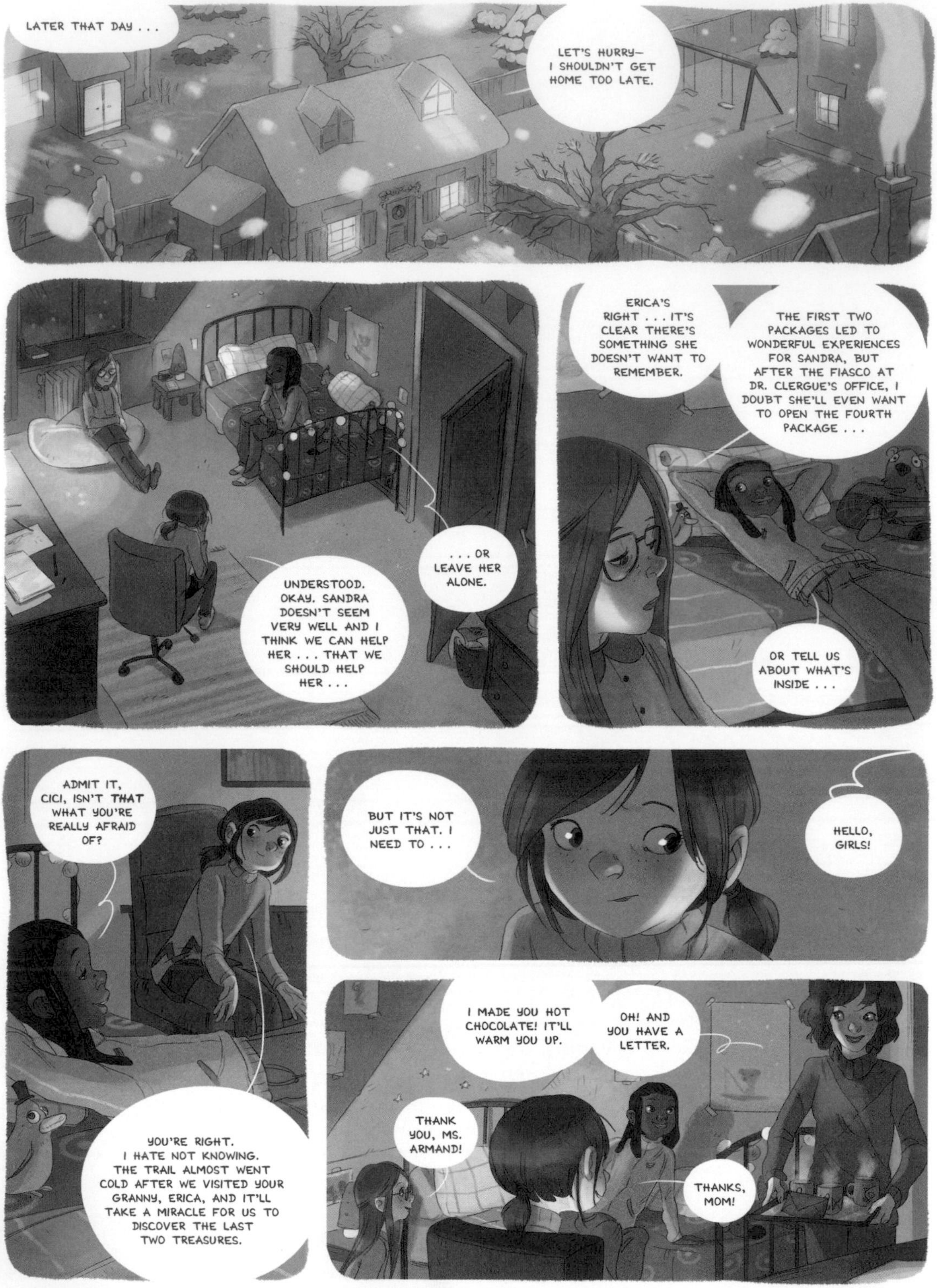
LATER THAT DAY . . .
LET'S HURRY— I SHOULDN'T GET HOME TOO LATE.
UNDERSTOOD. OKAY. SANDRA DOESN'T SEEM VERY WELL AND I THINK WE CAN HELP HER . . . THAT WE SHOULD HELP HER . . .
. . . OR LEAVE HER ALONE.
ERICA'S RIGHT . . . IT'S CLEAR THERE'S SOMETHING SHE DOESN'T WANT TO REMEMBER.
THE FIRST TWO PACKAGES LED TO WONDERFUL EXPERIENCES FOR SANDRA, BUT AFTER THE FIASCO AT DR. CLERGUE'S OFFICE, I DOUBT SHE'LL EVEN WANT TO OPEN THE FOURTH PACKAGE . . .
OR TELL US ABOUT WHAT'S INSIDE . . .
ADMIT IT, CICI, ISN'T THAT WHAT YOU'RE REALLY AFRAID OF?
YOU'RE RIGHT. I HATE NOT KNOWING. THE TRAIL ALMOST WENT COLD AFTER WE VISITED YOUR GRANNY, ERICA, AND IT'LL TAKE A MIRACLE FOR US TO DISCOVER THE LAST TWO TREASURES.
BUT IT'S NOT JUST THAT. I NEED TO . . .
HELLO, GIRLS!
I MADE YOU HOT CHOCOLATE! IT'LL WARM YOU UP.
OH! AND YOU HAVE A LETTER.
THANK YOU, MS. ARMAND!
THANKS, MOM!

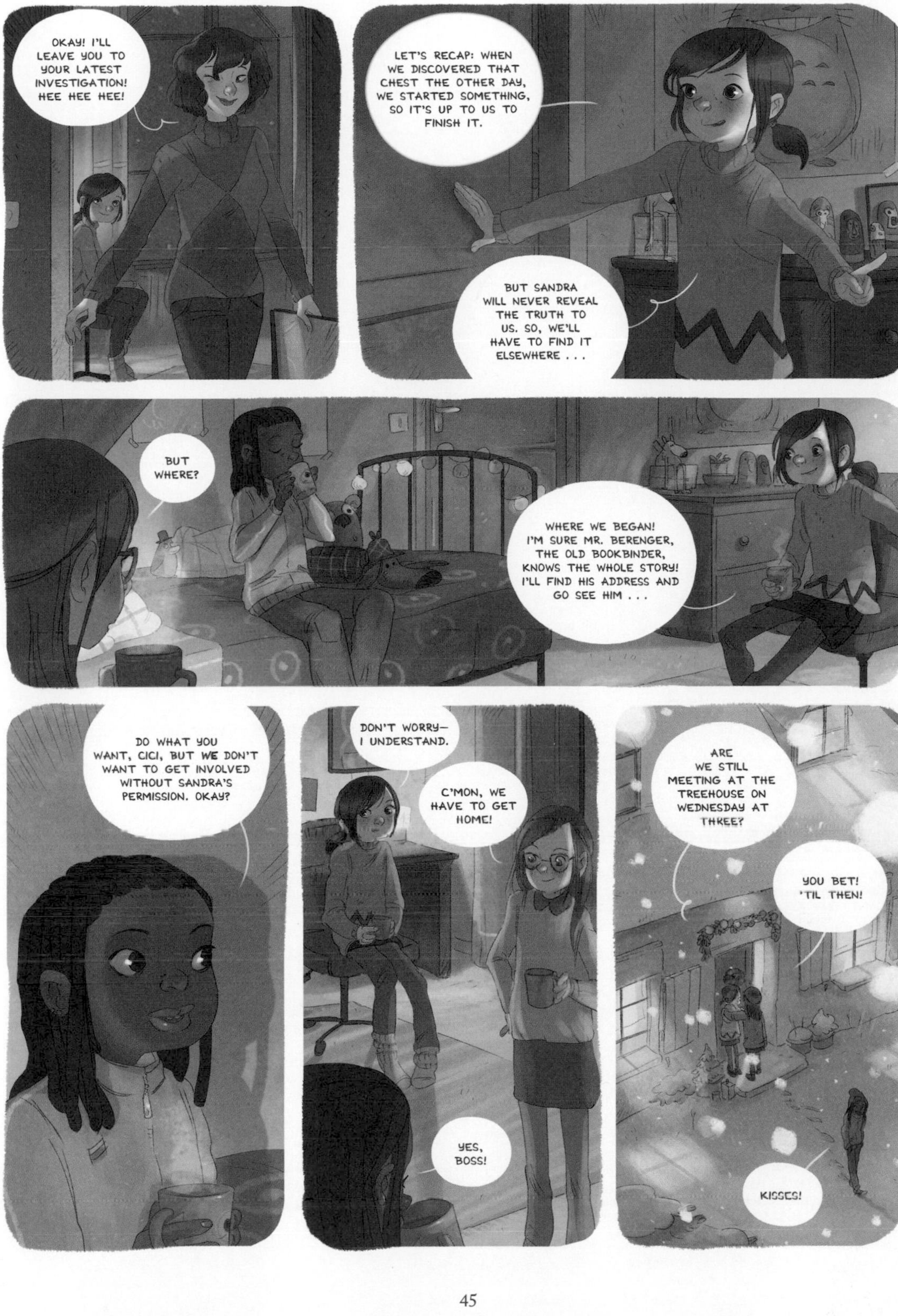
OKAY! I'LL LEAVE YOU TO YOUR LATEST INVESTIGATION! HEE HEE HEE!
LET'S RECAP: WHEN WE DISCOVERED THAT CHEST THE OTHER DAY, WE STARTED SOMETHING, SO IT'S UP TO US TO FINISH IT.
BUT SANDRA WILL NEVER REVEAL THE TRUTH TO US. SO, WE'LL HAVE TO FIND IT ELSEWHERE . . .
BUT WHERE?
WHERE WE BEGAN! I'M SURE MR. BERENGER, THE OLD BOOKBINDER, KNOWS THE WHOLE STORY! I'LL FIND HIS ADDRESS AND GO SEE HIM . . .
DO WHAT YOU WANT, CICI, BUT WE DON'T WANT TO GET INVOLVED WITHOUT SANDRA'S PERMISSION. OKAY?
DON'T WORRY— I UNDERSTAND.
C'MON, WE HAVE TO GET HOME!
YES, BOSS!
ARE WE STILL MEETING AT THE TREEHOUSE ON WEDNESDAY AT THREE?
YOU BET! 'TIL THEN!
KISSES!

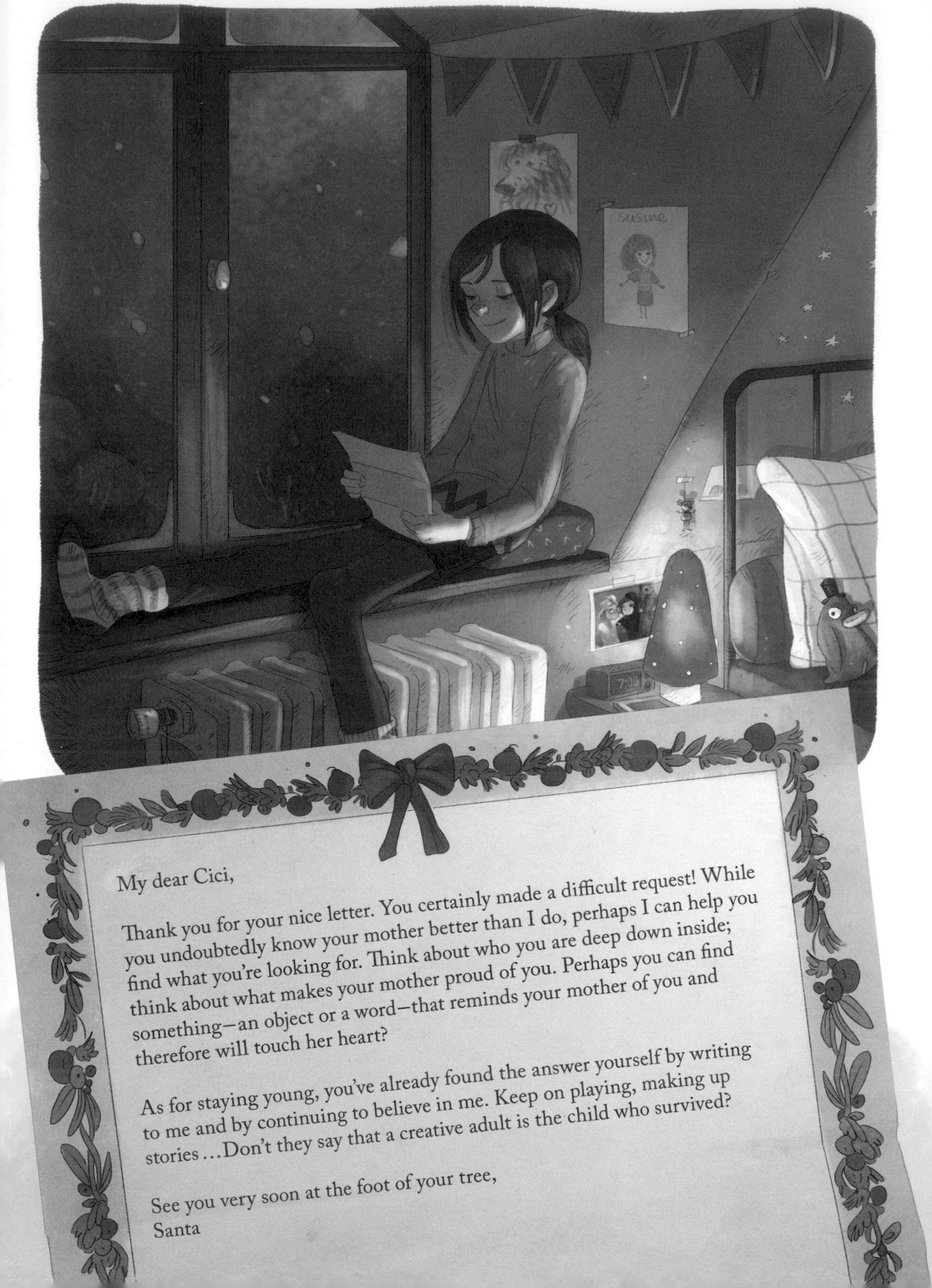
Susine
7:00

My dear Cici,

Thank you for your nice letter. You certainly made a difficult request! While you undoubtedly know your mother better than I do, perhaps I can help you find what you're looking for. Think about who you are deep down inside; think about what makes your mother proud of you. Perhaps you can find something—an object or a word—that reminds your mother of you and therefore will touch her heart?

As for staying young, you've already found the answer yourself by writing to me and by continuing to believe in me. Keep on playing, making up stories . . . Don't they say that a creative adult is the child who survived?

See you very soon at the foot of your tree,
Santa

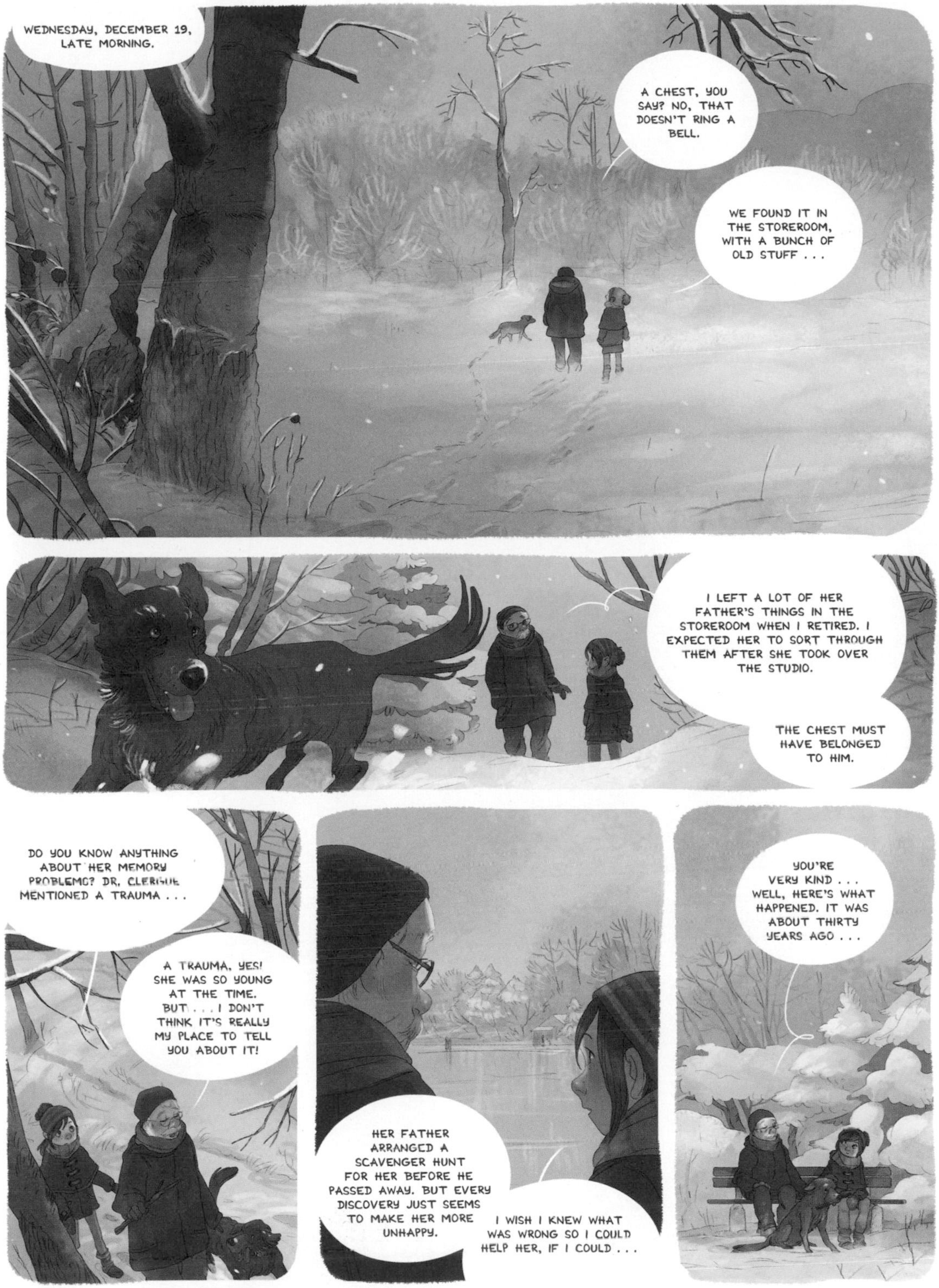
WEDNESDAY, DECEMBER 19, LATE MORNING.
A CHEST, YOU SAY? NO, THAT DOESN'T RING A BELL.
WE FOUND IT IN THE STOREROOM, WITH A BUNCH OF OLD STUFF . . .
I LEFT A LOT OF HER FATHER'S THINGS IN THE STOREROOM WHEN I RETIRED. I EXPECTED HER TO SORT THROUGH THEM AFTER SHE TOOK OVER THE STUDIO.
THE CHEST MUST HAVE BELONGED TO HIM.
DO YOU KNOW ANYTHING ABOUT HER MEMORY PROBLEMS? DR. CLERGUE MENTIONED A TRAUMA . . .
A TRAUMA, YES! SHE WAS SO YOUNG AT THE TIME. BUT . . . I DON'T THINK IT'S REALLY MY PLACE TO TELL YOU ABOUT IT!
HER FATHER ARRANGED A SCAVENGER HUNT FOR HER BEFORE HE PASSED AWAY. BUT EVERY DISCOVERY JUST SEEMS TO MAKE HER MORE UNHAPPY.
I WISH I KNEW WHAT WAS WRONG SO I COULD HELP HER, IF I COULD . . .
YOU'RE VERY KIND . . . WELL, HERE'S WHAT HAPPENED. IT WAS ABOUT THIRTY YEARS AGO . . .

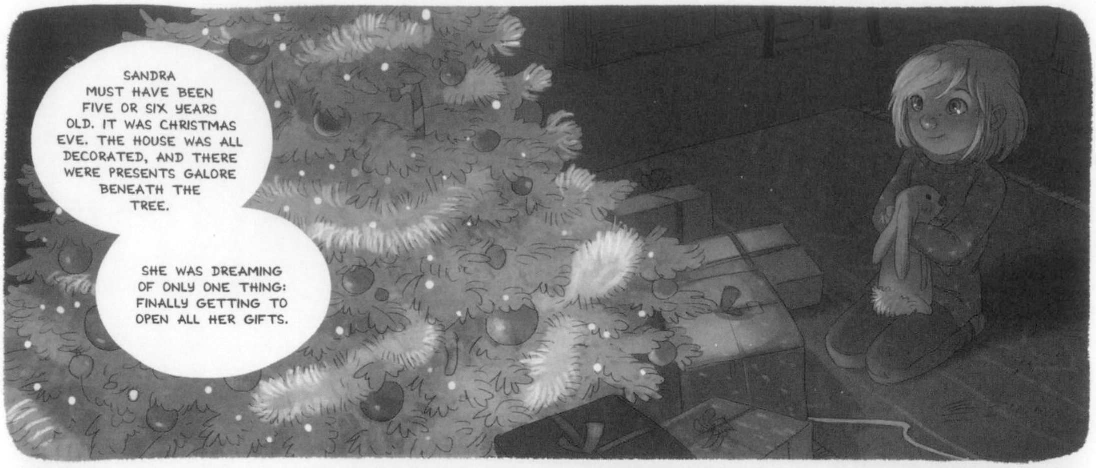
SANDRA MUST HAVE BEEN FIVE OR SIX YEARS OLD. IT WAS CHRISTMAS EVE. THE HOUSE WAS ALL DECORATED, AND THERE WERE PRESENTS GALORE BENEATH THE TREE.
SHE WAS DREAMING OF ONLY ONE THING: FINALLY GETTING TO OPEN ALL HER GIFTS.

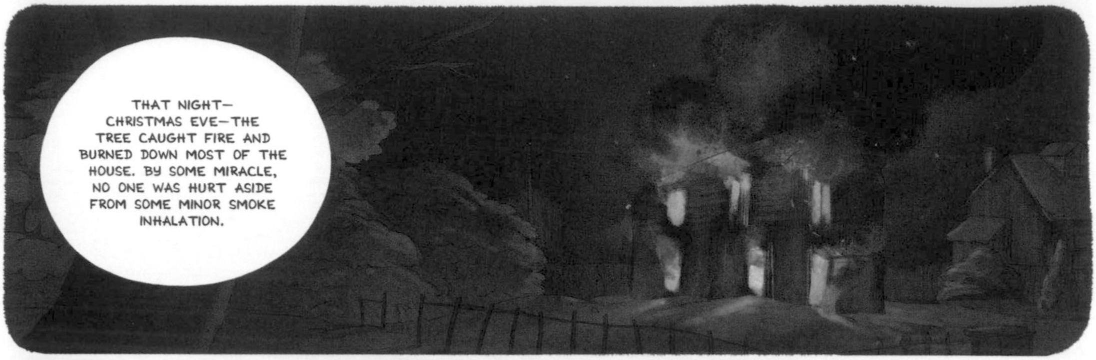
THAT NIGHT—CHRISTMAS EVE—THE TREE CAUGHT FIRE AND BURNED DOWN MOST OF THE HOUSE. BY SOME MIRACLE, NO ONE WAS HURT ASIDE FROM SOME MINOR SMOKE INHALATION.

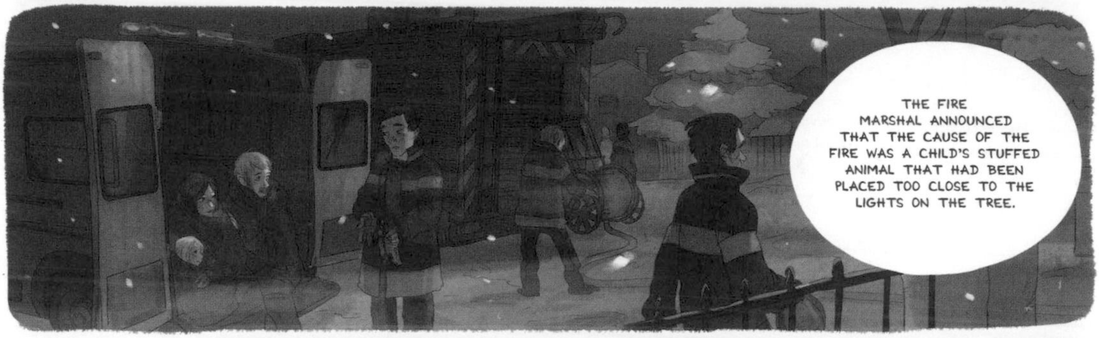
THE FIRE MARSHAL ANNOUNCED THAT THE CAUSE OF THE FIRE WAS A CHILD'S STUFFED ANIMAL THAT HAD BEEN PLACED TOO CLOSE TO THE LIGHTS ON THE TREE.

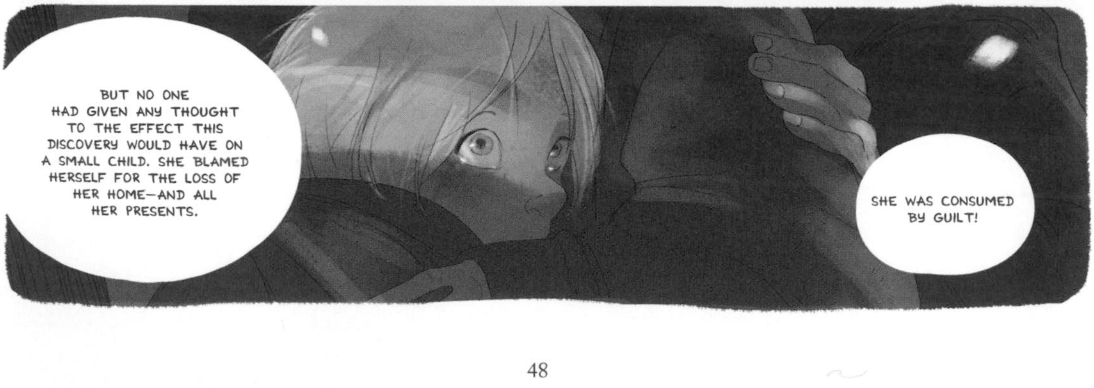
BUT NO ONE HAD GIVEN ANY THOUGHT TO THE EFFECT THIS DISCOVERY WOULD HAVE ON A SMALL CHILD. SHE BLAMED HERSELF FOR THE LOSS OF HER HOME—AND ALL HER PRESENTS.
SHE WAS CONSUMED BY GUILT!

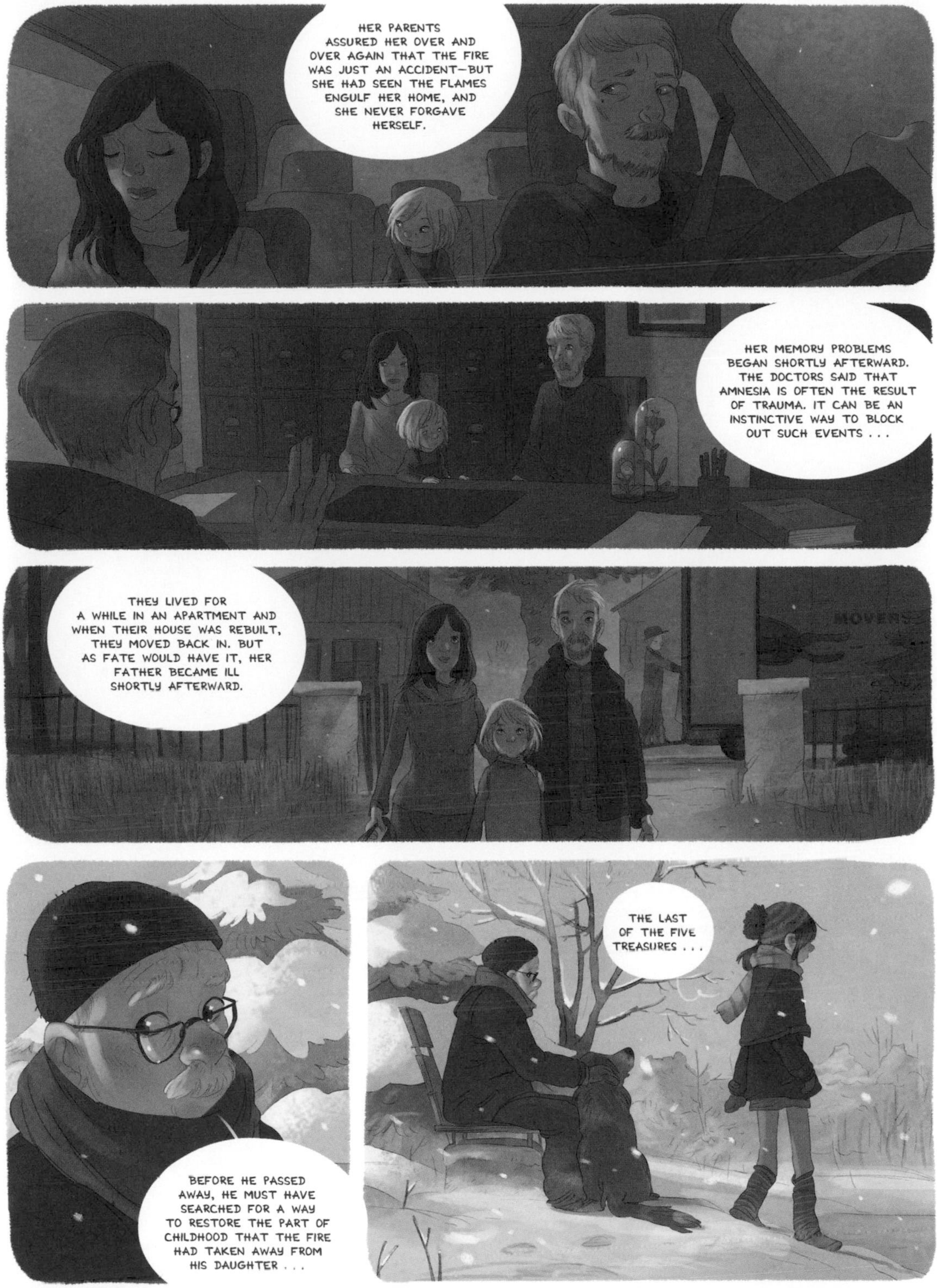
HER PARENTS ASSURED HER OVER AND OVER AGAIN THAT THE FIRE WAS JUST AN ACCIDENT—BUT SHE HAD SEEN THE FLAMES ENGULF HER HOME, AND SHE NEVER FORGAVE HERSELF.
HER MEMORY PROBLEMS BEGAN SHORTLY AFTERWARD. THE DOCTORS SAID THAT AMNESIA IS OFTEN THE RESULT OF TRAUMA. IT CAN BE AN INSTINCTIVE WAY TO BLOCK OUT SUCH EVENTS . . .
THEY LIVED FOR A WHILE IN AN APARTMENT AND WHEN THEIR HOUSE WAS REBUILT, THEY MOVED BACK IN. BUT AS FATE WOULD HAVE IT, HER FATHER BECAME ILL SHORTLY AFTERWARD.
BEFORE HE PASSED AWAY, HE MUST HAVE SEARCHED FOR A WAY TO RESTORE THE PART OF CHILDHOOD THAT THE FIRE HAD TAKEN AWAY FROM HIS DAUGHTER . . .
THE LAST OF THE FIVE TREASURES . . .

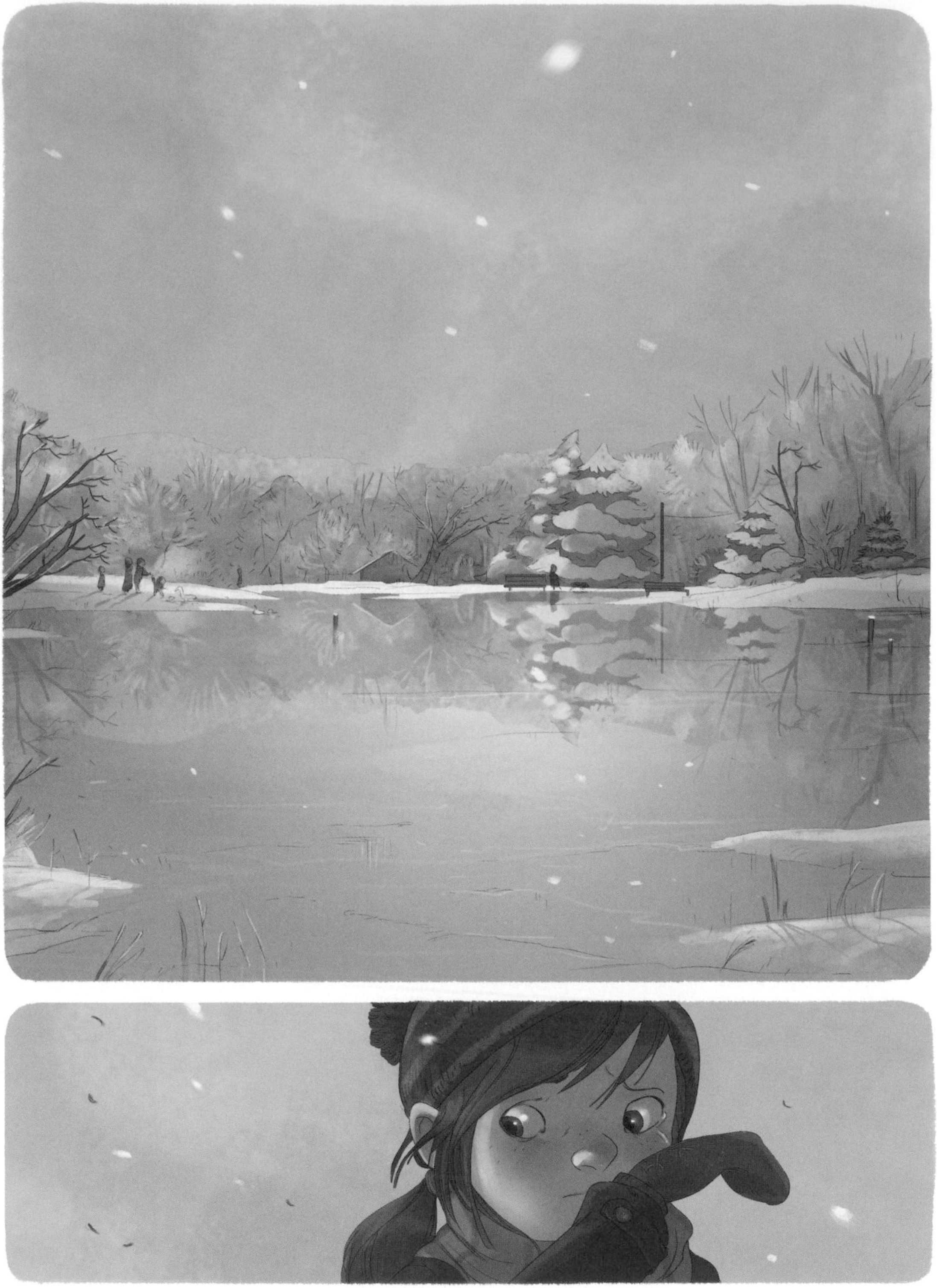

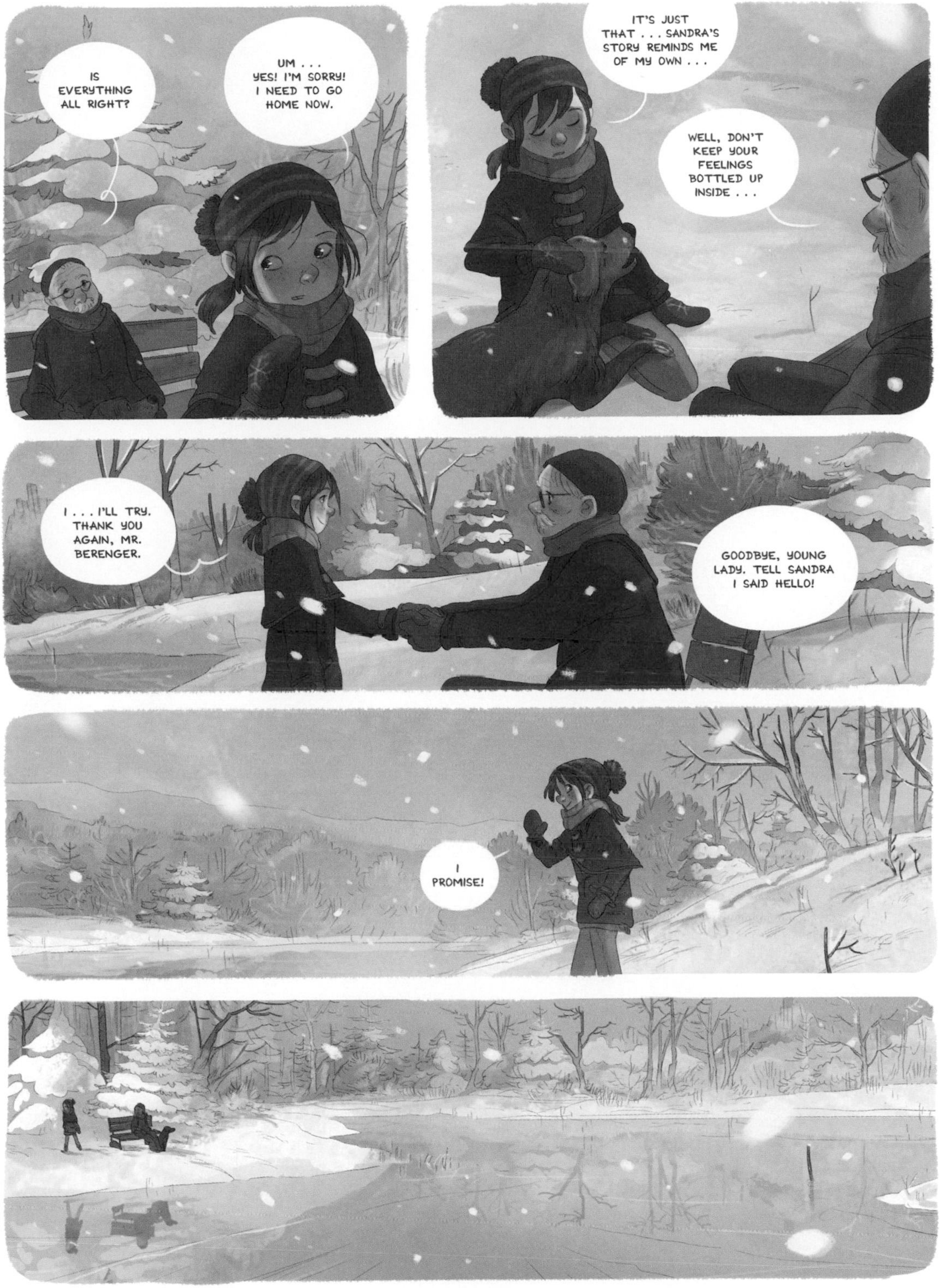
IS EVERYTHING ALL RIGHT?
UM . . . YES! I'M SORRY! I NEED TO GO HOME NOW.
IT'S JUST THAT . . . SANDRA'S STORY REMINDS ME OF MY OWN . . .
WELL, DON'T KEEP YOUR FEELINGS BOTTLED UP INSIDE . . .
I . . . I'LL TRY. THANK YOU AGAIN, MR. BERENGER.
GOODBYE, YOUNG LADY. TELL SANDRA I SAID HELLO!
I PROMISE!

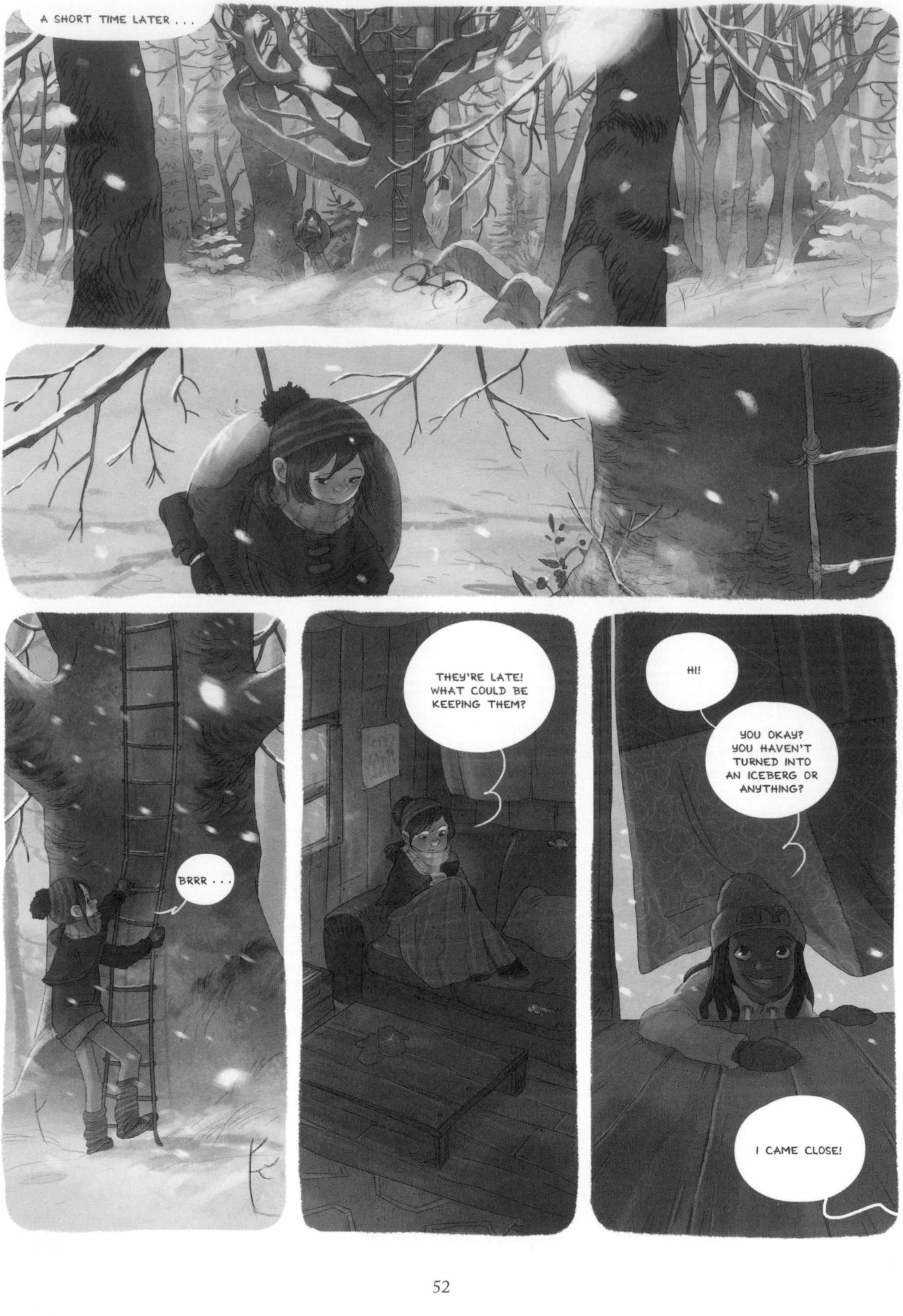
A SHORT TIME LATER . . .
BRRR . . .
THEY'RE LATE! WHAT COULD BE KEEPING THEM?
HI!
YOU OKAY? YOU HAVEN'T TURNED INTO AN ICEBERG OR ANYTHING?
I CAME CLOSE!

NOPE! THERE WAS A SLIGHT . . . COMPLICATION.

DID YOU GET LOST IN THE SNOW OR WHAT?

HEY, THERE! THANKS, ERICA.

WHAT DO YOU MEAN?

HELLO, CICI.

SO THIS IS THE FAMOUS TREEHOUSE! IT'S GREAT!

WHAT ON EARTH ARE YOU DOING HERE?!

WELL, IT'S ABOUT THE FOURTH TREASURE . . .

PREPARE FOR A SURPRISE!

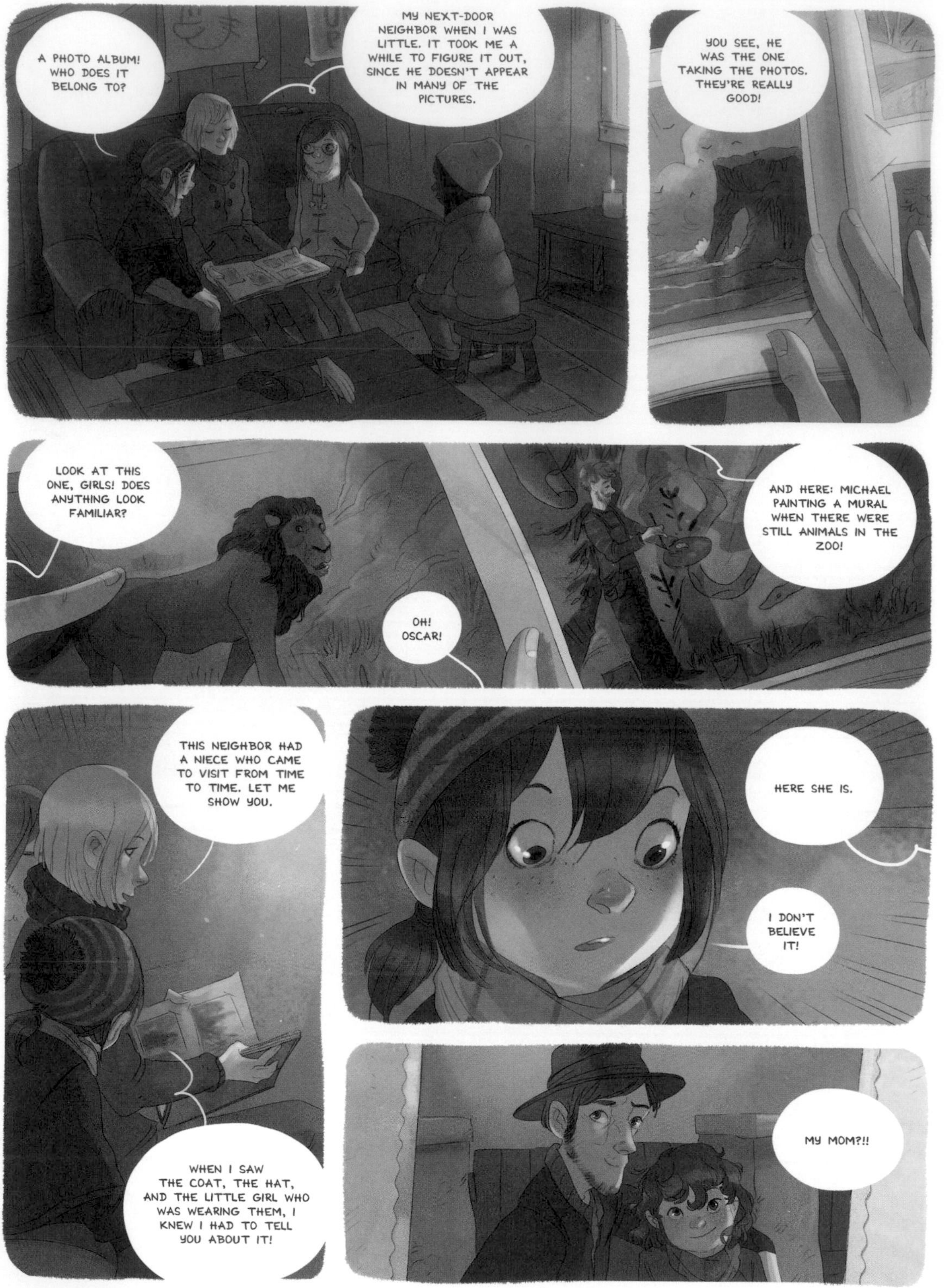
A PHOTO ALBUM! WHO DOES IT BELONG TO?
MY NEXT-DOOR NEIGHBOR WHEN I WAS LITTLE. IT TOOK ME A WHILE TO FIGURE IT OUT, SINCE HE DOESN'T APPEAR IN MANY OF THE PICTURES.
YOU SEE, HE WAS THE ONE TAKING THE PHOTOS. THEY'RE REALLY GOOD!
LOOK AT THIS ONE, GIRLS! DOES ANYTHING LOOK FAMILIAR?
OH! OSCAR!
AND HERE: MICHAEL PAINTING A MURAL WHEN THERE WERE STILL ANIMALS IN THE ZOO!
THIS NEIGHBOR HAD A NIECE WHO CAME TO VISIT FROM TIME TO TIME. LET ME SHOW YOU.
WHEN I SAW THE COAT, THE HAT, AND THE LITTLE GIRL WHO WAS WEARING THEM, I KNEW I HAD TO TELL YOU ABOUT IT!
HERE SHE IS.
I DON'T BELIEVE IT!
MY MOM?!!

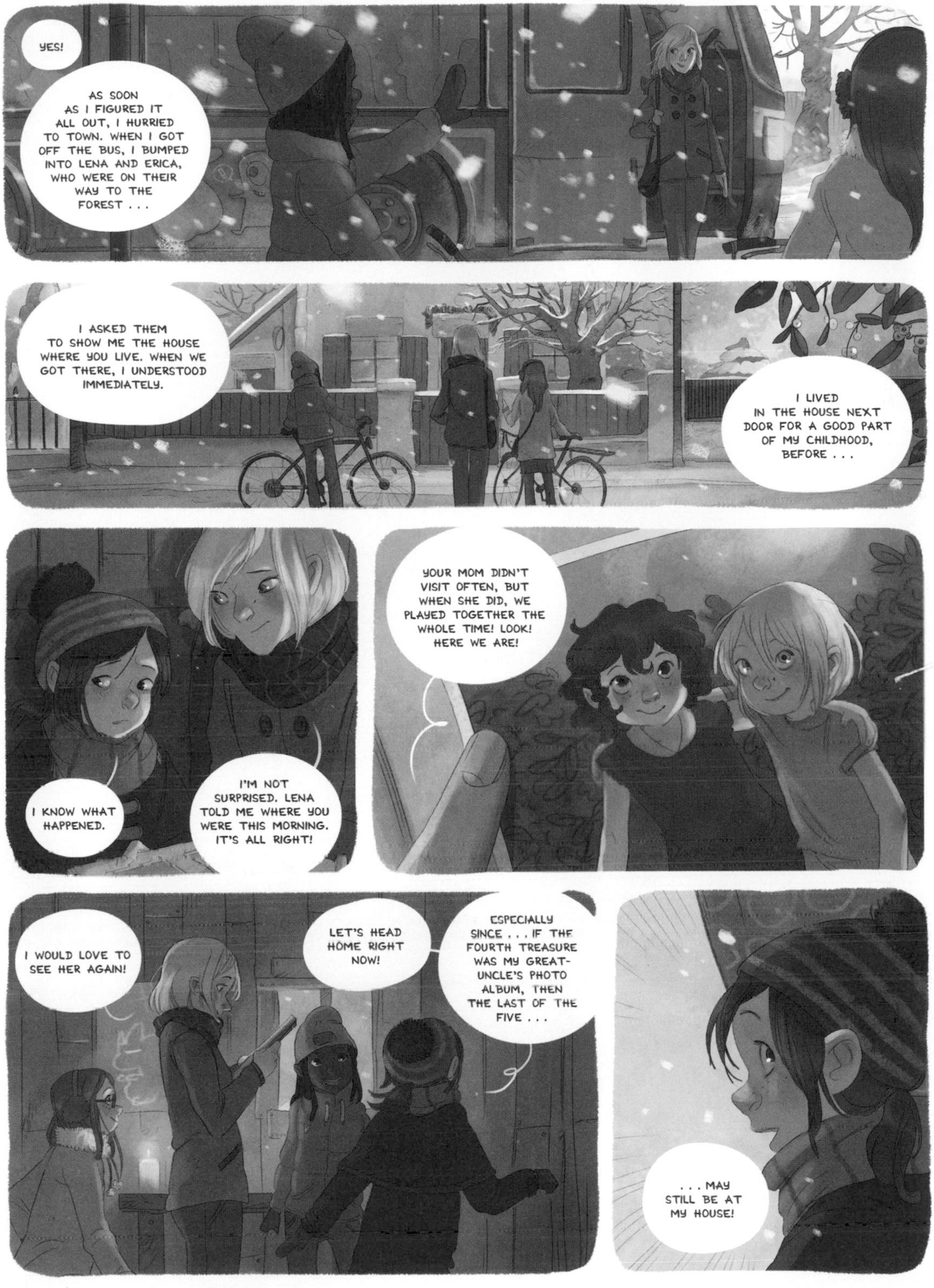
YES!
AS SOON AS I FIGURED IT ALL OUT, I HURRIED TO TOWN. WHEN I GOT OFF THE BUS, I BUMPED INTO LENA AND ERICA, WHO WERE ON THEIR WAY TO THE FOREST . . .
I ASKED THEM TO SHOW ME THE HOUSE WHERE YOU LIVE. WHEN WE GOT THERE, I UNDERSTOOD IMMEDIATELY.
I LIVED IN THE HOUSE NEXT DOOR FOR A GOOD PART OF MY CHILDHOOD, BEFORE . . .
I KNOW WHAT HAPPENED.
I'M NOT SURPRISED. LENA TOLD ME WHERE YOU WERE THIS MORNING. IT'S ALL RIGHT!
YOUR MOM DIDN'T VISIT OFTEN, BUT WHEN SHE DID, WE PLAYED TOGETHER THE WHOLE TIME! LOOK! HERE WE ARE!
I WOULD LOVE TO SEE HER AGAIN!
LET'S HEAD HOME RIGHT NOW!
ESPECIALLY SINCE . . . IF THE FOURTH TREASURE WAS MY GREAT-UNCLE'S PHOTO ALBUM, THEN THE LAST OF THE FIVE . . .
. . . MAY STILL BE AT MY HOUSE!

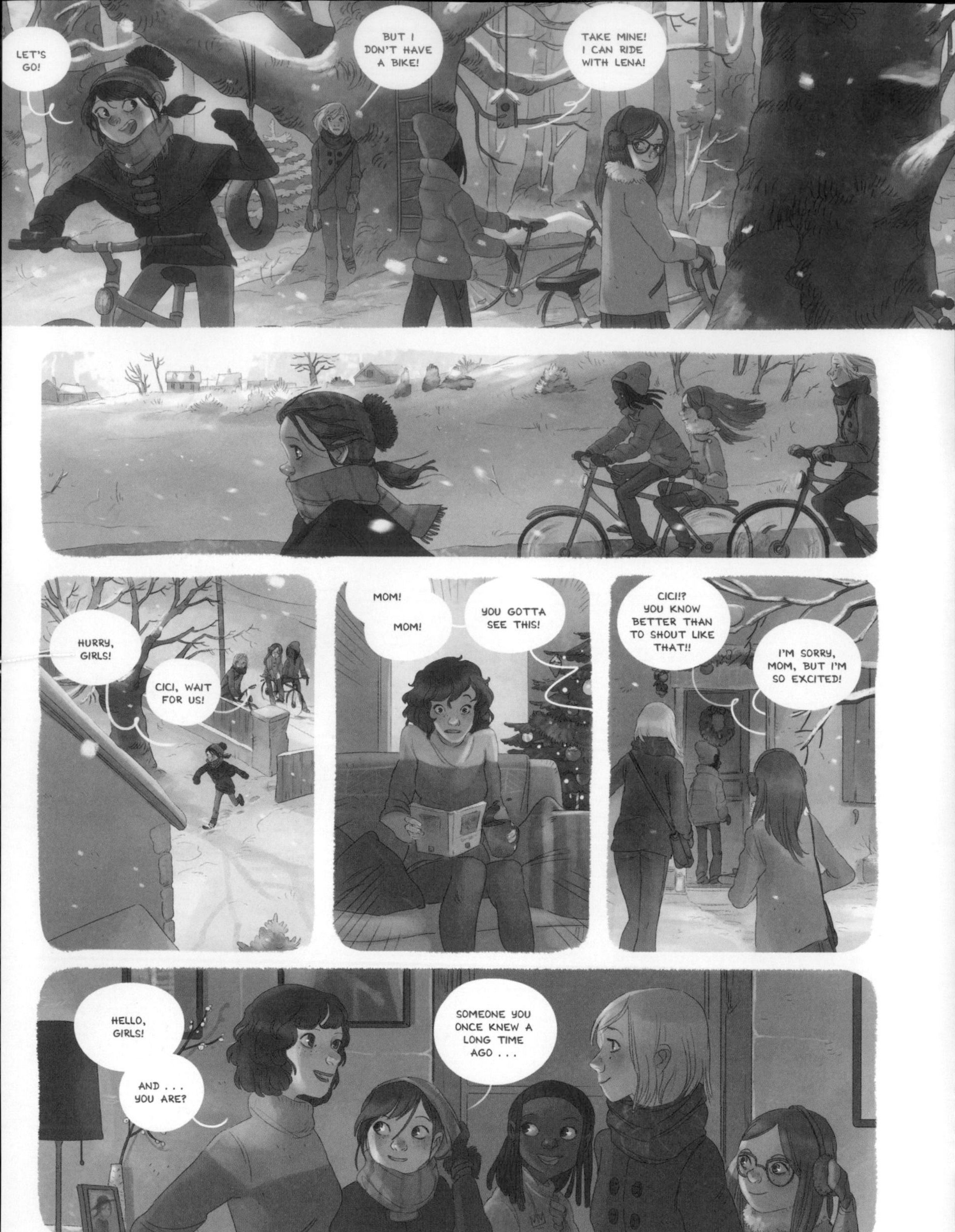
LET'S GO!
BUT I DON'T HAVE A BIKE!
TAKE MINE! I CAN RIDE WITH LENA!
HURRY, GIRLS!
CICI, WAIT FOR US!
MOM!
MOM!
YOU GOTTA SEE THIS!
CICI!? YOU KNOW BETTER THAN TO SHOUT LIKE THAT!!
I'M SORRY, MOM, BUT I'M SO EXCITED!
HELLO, GIRLS!
AND . . . YOU ARE?
SOMEONE YOU ONCE KNEW A LONG TIME AGO . . .

. . . AND THAT'S HOW WE FOUND THE PHOTO ALBUM!

THAT'S . . . INCREDIBLE!!!

ONCE, WHEN I WAS LITTLE, MY UNCLE TOLD ME THAT THE NEIGHBORS' HOUSE HAD BURNED DOWN. I WAS TERRIFIED.

HE SAID EVERYONE WAS OKAY, BUT THAT MY FRIEND WOULD HAVE TO MOVE AWAY . . .

AND NOW HERE SHE IS, RIGHT IN FRONT OF ME, AFTER ALL THESE YEARS! I CAN HARDLY BELIEVE IT!

I'M SO HAPPY!

WE'LL LEAVE YOU TWO TO TALK—WE'RE HEADING UP TO THE ATTIC. WE HAVE A TREASURE TO FIND!

BE CAREFUL UP THERE! DON'T TRIP OVER ANYTHING!

UM . . . DO WE REALLY HAVE TO GO IN THERE?

YES! THAT'S WHERE I FOUND MY HAT AND JACKET! AND, IF I'M NOT MISTAKEN . . .

. . . IT'S ALSO WHERE THE LAST TREASURE IS HIDDEN!

OH NO . . .

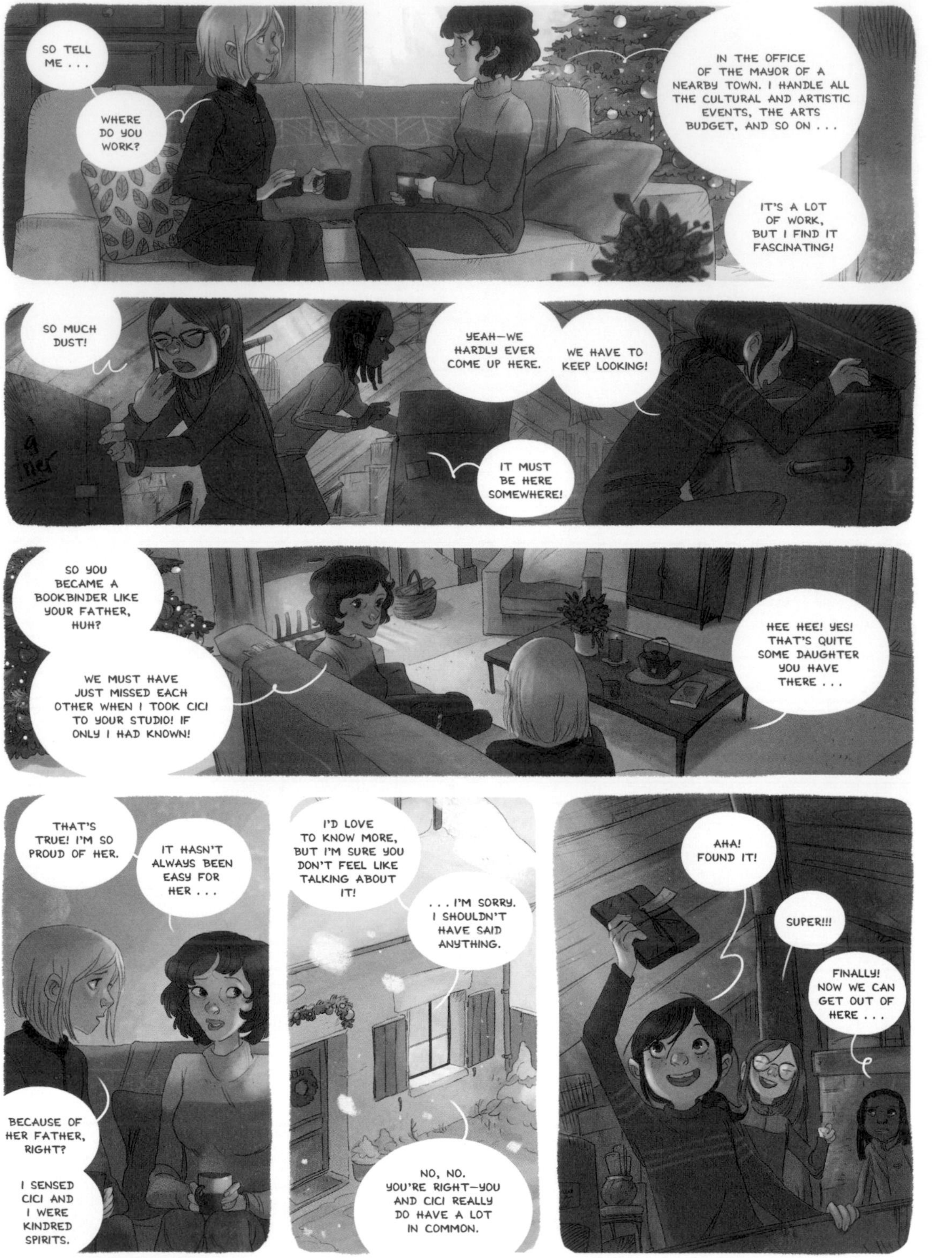
SO TELL ME . . .
WHERE DO YOU WORK?
IN THE OFFICE OF THE MAYOR OF A NEARBY TOWN. I HANDLE ALL THE CULTURAL AND ARTISTIC EVENTS, THE ARTS BUDGET, AND SO ON . . .
IT'S A LOT OF WORK, BUT I FIND IT FASCINATING!
SO MUCH DUST!
YEAH—WE HARDLY EVER COME UP HERE.
WE HAVE TO KEEP LOOKING!
IT MUST BE HERE SOMEWHERE!
SO YOU BECAME A BOOKBINDER LIKE YOUR FATHER, HUH?
WE MUST HAVE JUST MISSED EACH OTHER WHEN I TOOK CICI TO YOUR STUDIO! IF ONLY I HAD KNOWN!
HEE HEE! YES! THAT'S QUITE SOME DAUGHTER YOU HAVE THERE . . .
THAT'S TRUE! I'M SO PROUD OF HER.
IT HASN'T ALWAYS BEEN EASY FOR HER . . .
BECAUSE OF HER FATHER, RIGHT?
I SENSED CICI AND I WERE KINDRED SPIRITS.
I'D LOVE TO KNOW MORE, BUT I'M SURE YOU DON'T FEEL LIKE TALKING ABOUT IT!
. . . I'M SORRY. I SHOULDN'T HAVE SAID ANYTHING.
NO, NO. YOU'RE RIGHT—YOU AND CICI REALLY DO HAVE A LOT IN COMMON.
AHA! FOUND IT!
SUPER!!!
FINALLY! NOW WE CAN GET OUT OF HERE . . .

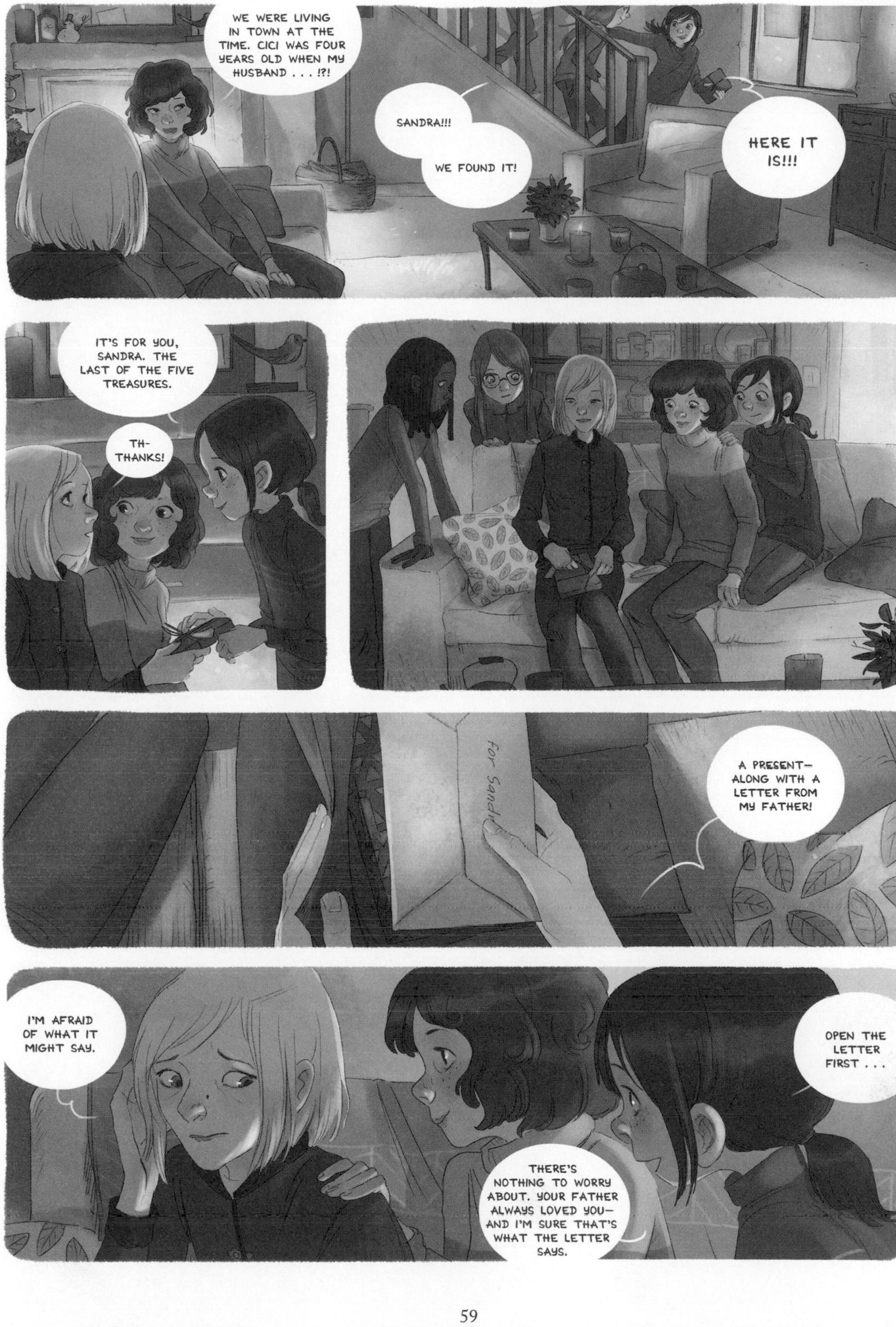
WE WERE LIVING IN TOWN AT THE TIME. CICI WAS FOUR YEARS OLD WHEN MY HUSBAND . . . !?!
SANDRA!!!
WE FOUND IT!
HERE IT IS!!!
IT'S FOR YOU, SANDRA. THE LAST OF THE FIVE TREASURES.
TH-THANKS!
A PRESENT—ALONG WITH A LETTER FROM MY FATHER!
I'M AFRAID OF WHAT IT MIGHT SAY.
THERE'S NOTHING TO WORRY ABOUT. YOUR FATHER ALWAYS LOVED YOU—AND I'M SURE THAT'S WHAT THE LETTER SAYS.
OPEN THE LETTER FIRST . . .

Sandra let me copy the letter so my notebook would be complete.

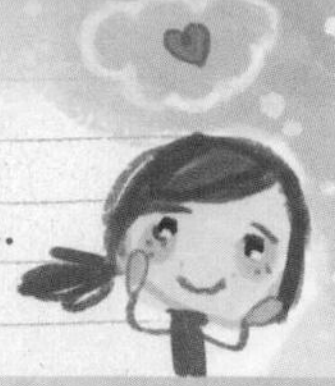

Sweetie,

You've come to the end of the scavenger hunt that I arranged for you. Congratulations!

I hope the wonderful, caring people you have met along the way have brought you much happiness and have shown you that you are surrounded by people who love you.

It was important that you go back to your childhood and revisit that tragic day when the fire carried away our house.

You may not remember, but when you found out the extent of the damage, you uttered two words before fainting:

"My book." That's what you said. Afterward, the amnesia struck and you struggled to regain your memory.

I searched the ash and debris of our house, and I managed to find the book that you treasured so much.

According to Dr. Clergue, seeing how badly your book had been burned would only have reinforced your feelings of guilt and made your condition worse.

So I repaired it and set it aside, waiting for the right moment to return it to you. As I write this letter, you are a happy teenager. You will undoubtedly have become a young woman who is finding her place in life by the time you read this.

So, I offer you the fifth and final treasure you've been searching for. I hope it will finally solve the puzzle of your memory and restore it to wholeness, just as a bookbinder lovingly restores a book.

All my love,

Dad

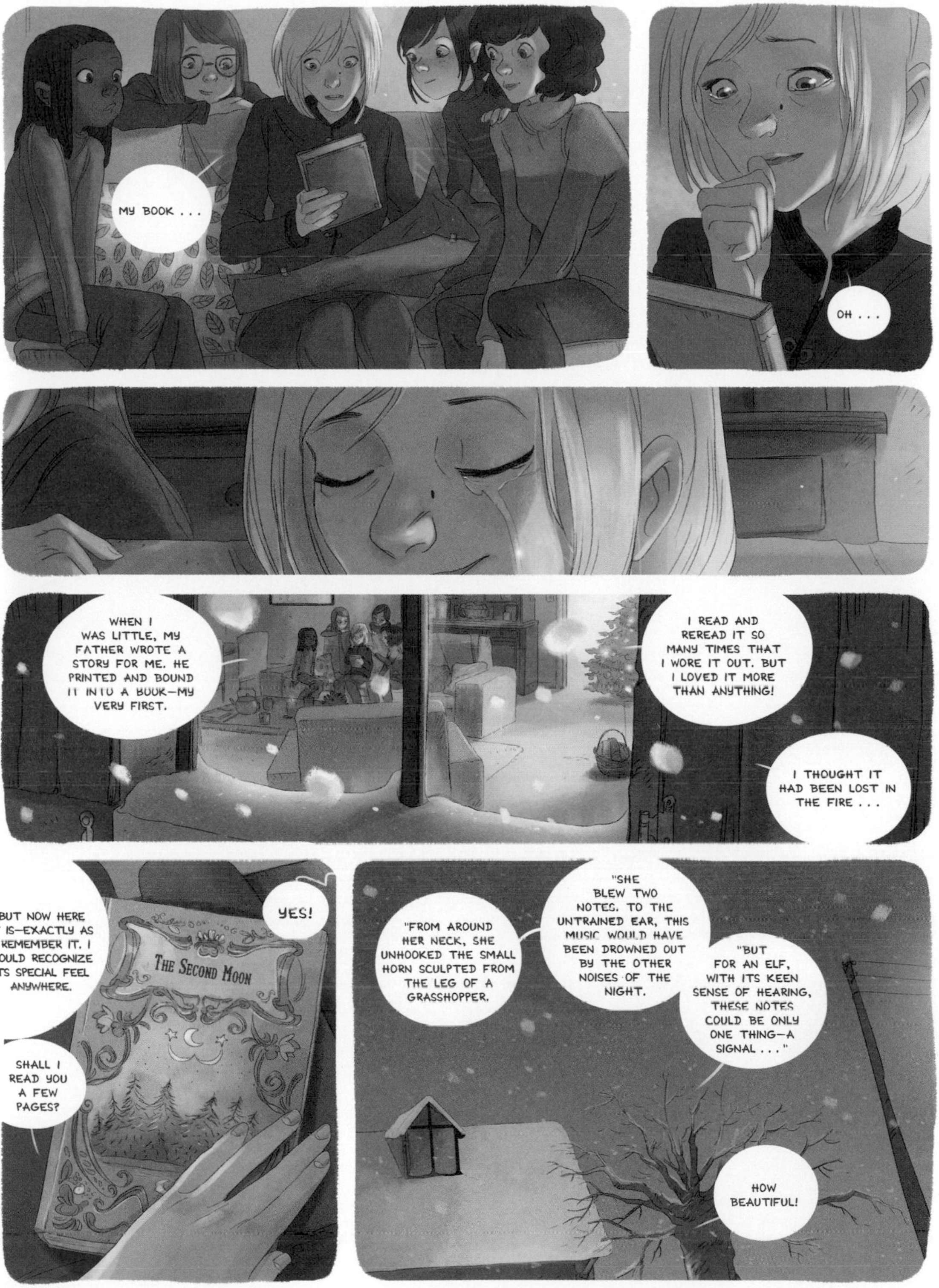
MY BOOK . . .
OH . . .
WHEN I WAS LITTLE, MY FATHER WROTE A STORY FOR ME. HE PRINTED AND BOUND IT INTO A BOOK—MY VERY FIRST.
I READ AND REREAD IT SO MANY TIMES THAT I WORE IT OUT. BUT I LOVED IT MORE THAN ANYTHING!
I THOUGHT IT HAD BEEN LOST IN THE FIRE . . .
BUT NOW HERE IT IS—EXACTLY AS I REMEMBER IT. I WOULD RECOGNIZE ITS SPECIAL FEEL ANYWHERE.
YES!
THE SECOND MOON
SHALL I READ YOU A FEW PAGES?
"FROM AROUND HER NECK, SHE UNHOOKED THE SMALL HORN SCULPTED FROM THE LEG OF A GRASSHOPPER.
"SHE BLEW TWO NOTES. TO THE UNTRAINED EAR, THIS MUSIC WOULD HAVE BEEN DROWNED OUT BY THE OTHER NOISES OF THE NIGHT.
"BUT FOR AN ELF, WITH ITS KEEN SENSE OF HEARING, THESE NOTES COULD BE ONLY ONE THING—A SIGNAL . . ."
HOW BEAUTIFUL!

THANK YOU, CICI. THANK YOU FOR EVERYTHING.

YOU'RE WELCOME . . . BUT I DIDN'T DO IT ALONE!

THAT'S TRUE! WE ALL WANT A HUG!

I CERTAINLY WASN'T GOING TO LEAVE YOU OUT. THANK YOU, ERICA. THANK YOU, LENA.

AHH. I LIKE THIS BETTER.

HA HA HA!

WHEN THE FIRE STARTED, WE HAD TO ESCAPE RIGHT AWAY. I COULDN'T TAKE ANYTHING WITH ME. NOT EVEN MY BOOK.

WHEN I THOUGHT THAT THE FIRE WAS MY FAULT, I FELT UNBEARABLE GUILT. I HAD DESTROYED MY SPECIAL BOND WITH MY DAD.

BUT NOW IT'S REPAIRED.

YOU'RE RIGHT! HE DID A MAGNIFICENT JOB.

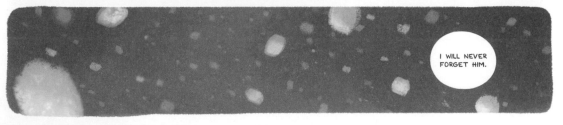

I WILL NEVER FORGET HIM.

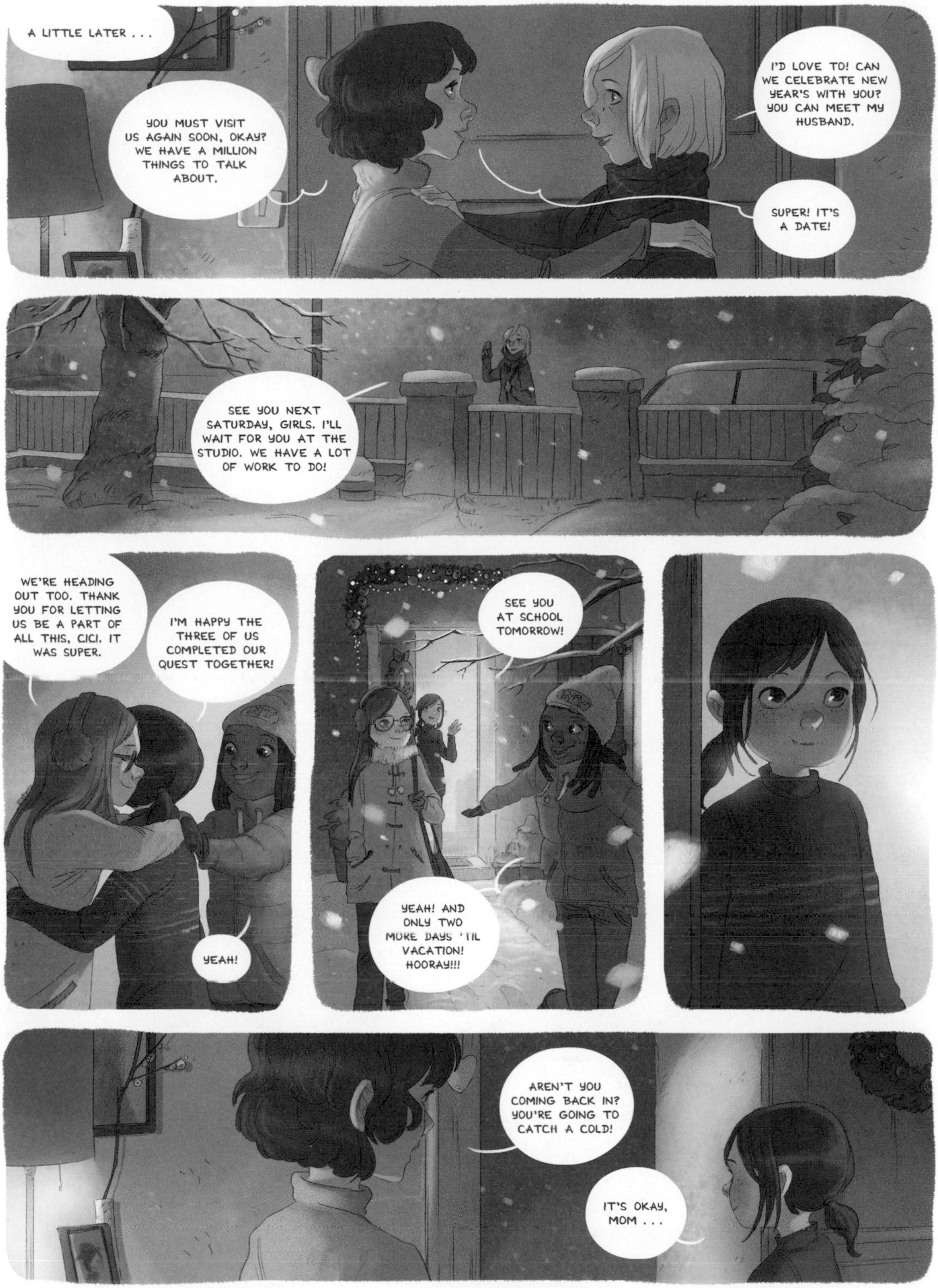
A LITTLE LATER . . .
YOU MUST VISIT US AGAIN SOON, OKAY? WE HAVE A MILLION THINGS TO TALK ABOUT.
I'D LOVE TO! CAN WE CELEBRATE NEW YEAR'S WITH YOU? YOU CAN MEET MY HUSBAND.
SUPER! IT'S A DATE!
SEE YOU NEXT SATURDAY, GIRLS. I'LL WAIT FOR YOU AT THE STUDIO. WE HAVE A LOT OF WORK TO DO!
WE'RE HEADING OUT TOO. THANK YOU FOR LETTING US BE A PART OF ALL THIS, CICI. IT WAS SUPER.
I'M HAPPY THE THREE OF US COMPLETED OUR QUEST TOGETHER!
YEAH!
SEE YOU AT SCHOOL TOMORROW!
YEAH! AND ONLY TWO MORE DAYS 'TIL VACATION! HOORAY!!!
AREN'T YOU COMING BACK IN? YOU'RE GOING TO CATCH A COLD!
IT'S OKAY, MOM . . .

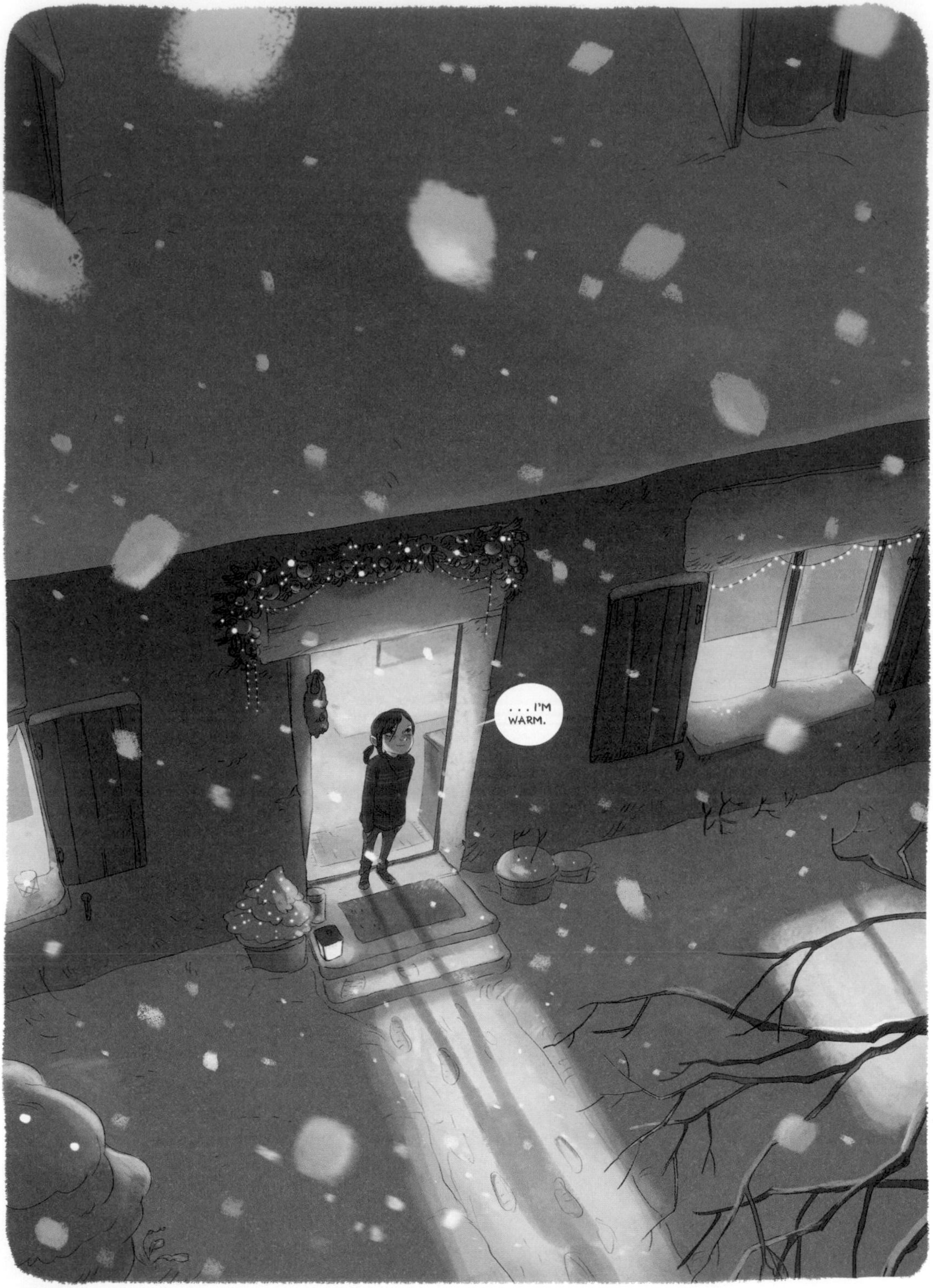
. . . I'M WARM.

It's almost Christmas!!!

I'm so glad I was able to help Sandra; it was a wonderful adventure. I saw her again just after classes ended, and she was different, almost glowing. There was even a little Christmas tree in the window of her workshop! There were no lights on it, but one must be careful around books, after all!

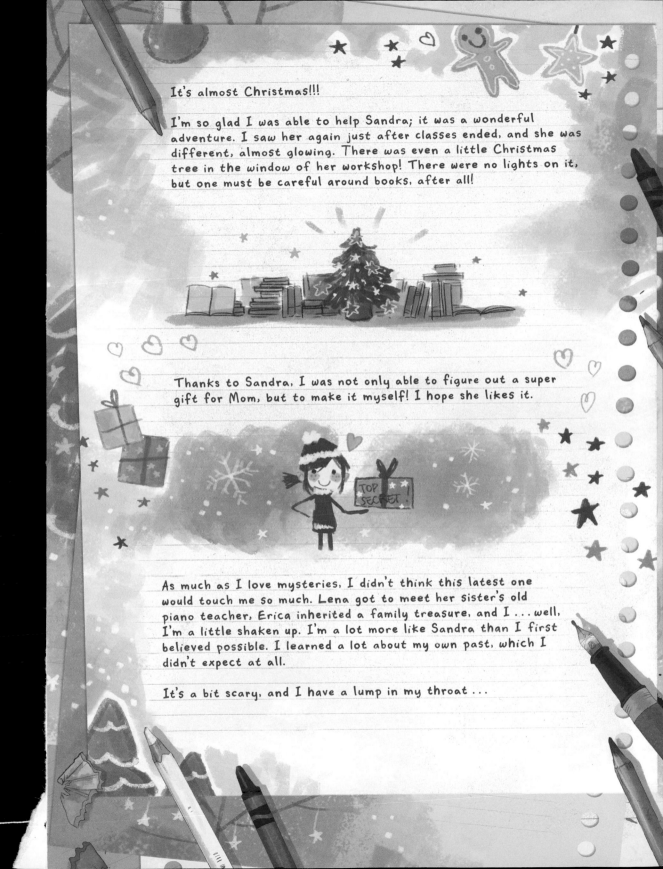

Thanks to Sandra, I was not only able to figure out a super gift for Mom, but to make it myself! I hope she likes it.

As much as I love mysteries, I didn't think this latest one would touch me so much. Lena got to meet her sister's old piano teacher, Erica inherited a family treasure, and I ... well, I'm a little shaken up. I'm a lot more like Sandra than I first believed possible. I learned a lot about my own past, which I didn't expect at all.

It's a bit scary, and I have a lump in my throat ...

Since we're all going to celebrate Christmas with our families, the girls and I went back to our treehouse to exchange presents, first!

For Lena, blue ballerina slippers*! She's wanted a pair for a long time. My mom helped us with that one!

Lena and I gave Erica a jersey, just like the one her favorite basketball player wore.

*From Erica and me!

I got a stuffed lion wearing a little locket. Of course, I named him Oscar after the lion in the zoo! Lena and Erica also gave me a magnificent feather pen. It goes perfectly with the gift I'm going to give Mom!

Tomorrow is Christmas Day. Mom and I share a wonderful little ritual...

...JOLLY OLD ST. NICHOLAS,
LEAN YOUR EAR THIS WAY...

...DON'T YOU TELL A
SINGLE SOUL WHAT I'M
GOING TO SAY...

...CHRISTMAS EVE IS
COMING SOON, NOW YOU
DEAR OLD MAN,

...WHISPER WHAT YOU'LL
BRING TO ME, TELL
ME IF YOU CAN.

WOW!

MERRY
CHRISTMAS,
DARLING!

I can't open any
of my presents
until the end
of the song, so
I have time to
admire the tree.

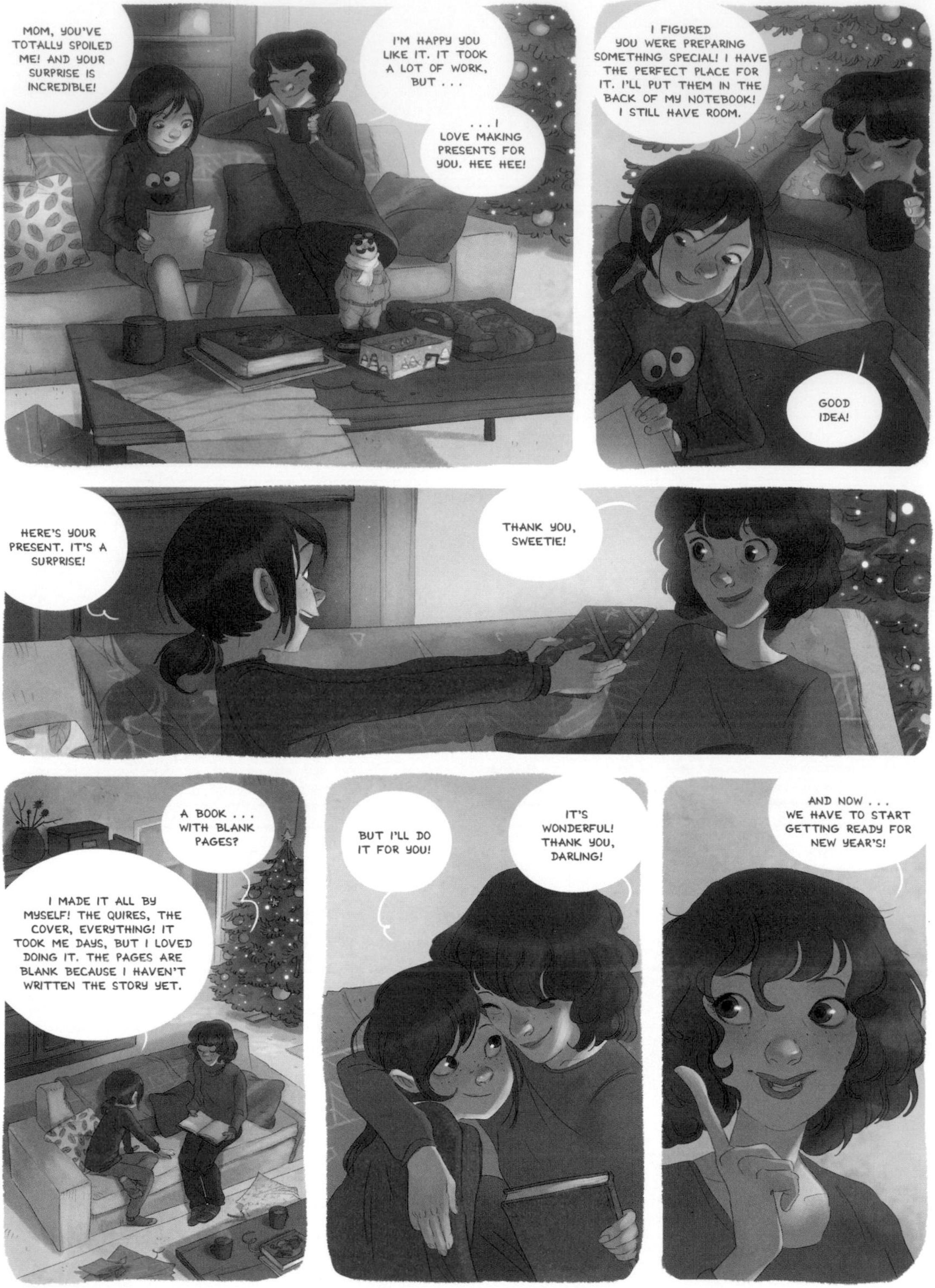
MOM, YOU'VE TOTALLY SPOILED ME! AND YOUR SURPRISE IS INCREDIBLE!
I'M HAPPY YOU LIKE IT. IT TOOK A LOT OF WORK, BUT . . .
. . . I LOVE MAKING PRESENTS FOR YOU. HEE HEE!
I FIGURED YOU WERE PREPARING SOMETHING SPECIAL! I HAVE THE PERFECT PLACE FOR IT. I'LL PUT THEM IN THE BACK OF MY NOTEBOOK! I STILL HAVE ROOM.
GOOD IDEA!
HERE'S YOUR PRESENT. IT'S A SURPRISE!
THANK YOU, SWEETIE!
A BOOK . . . WITH BLANK PAGES?
I MADE IT ALL BY MYSELF! THE QUIRES, THE COVER, EVERYTHING! IT TOOK ME DAYS, BUT I LOVED DOING IT. THE PAGES ARE BLANK BECAUSE I HAVEN'T WRITTEN THE STORY YET.
IT'S WONDERFUL! THANK YOU, DARLING!
BUT I'LL DO IT FOR YOU!
AND NOW . . . WE HAVE TO START GETTING READY FOR NEW YEAR'S!

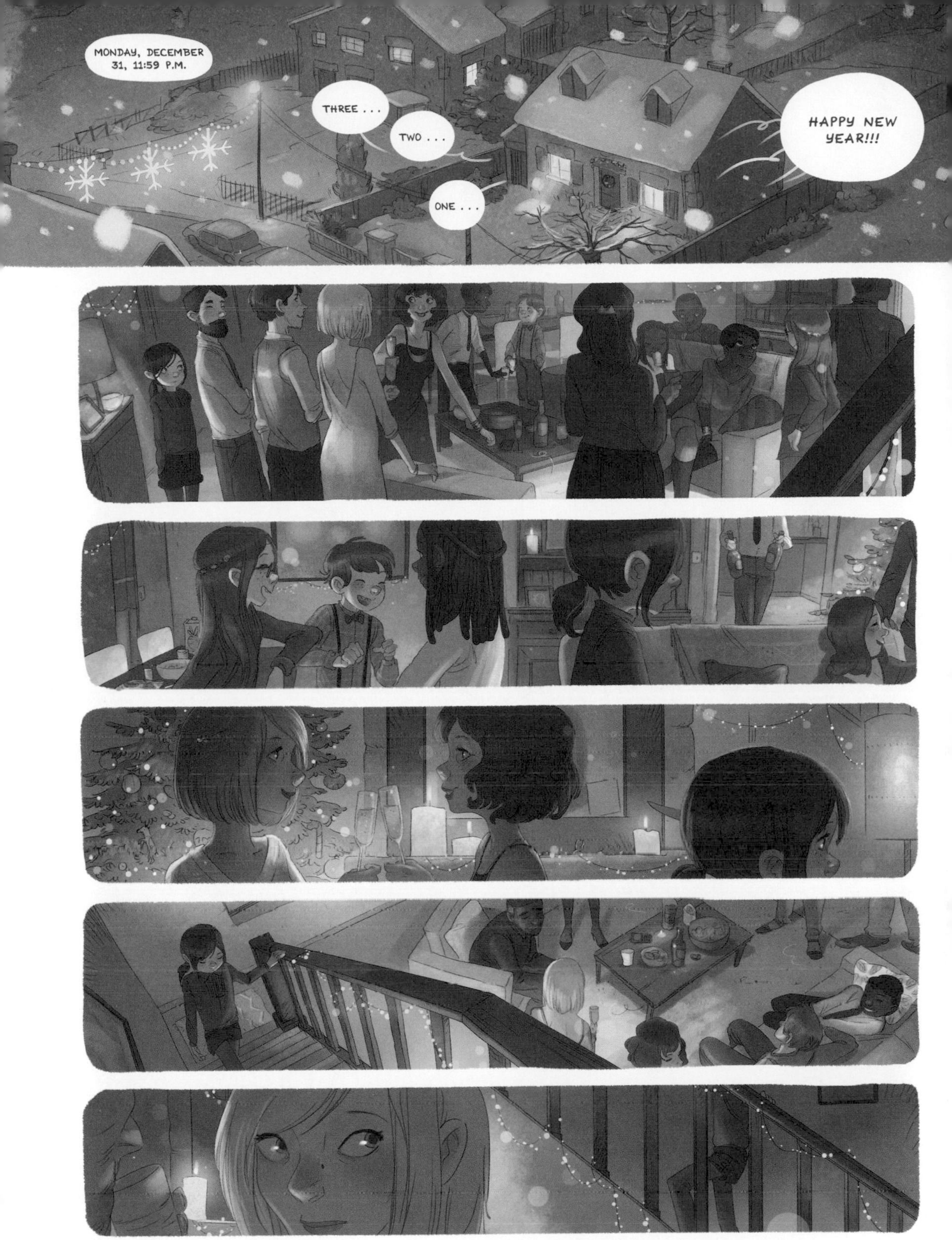
MONDAY, DECEMBER 31, 11:59 P.M.
THREE . . .
TWO . . .
ONE . . .
HAPPY NEW YEAR!!!

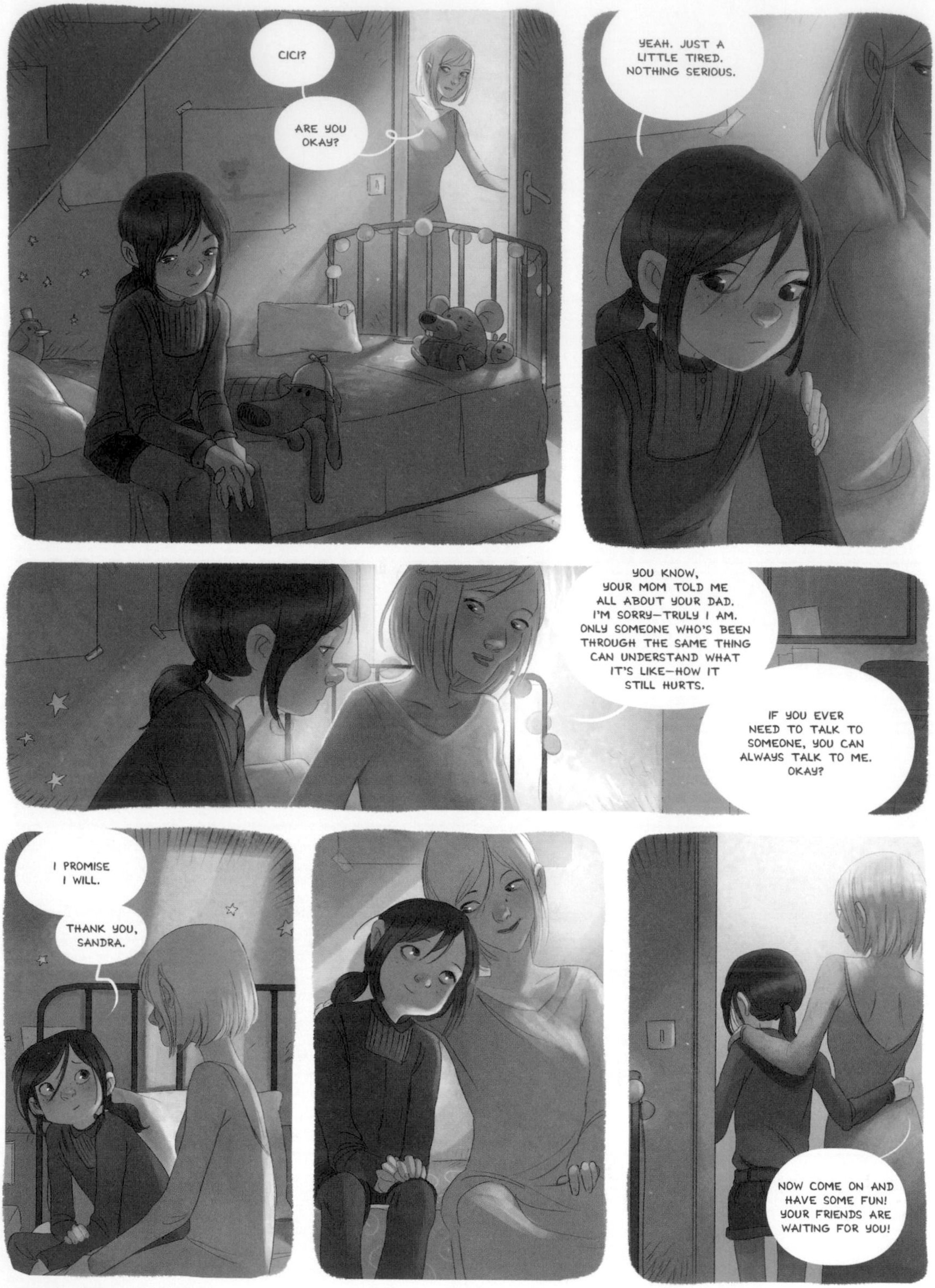
CICI?
ARE YOU OKAY?
YEAH. JUST A LITTLE TIRED. NOTHING SERIOUS.
YOU KNOW, YOUR MOM TOLD ME ALL ABOUT YOUR DAD. I'M SORRY—TRULY I AM. ONLY SOMEONE WHO'S BEEN THROUGH THE SAME THING CAN UNDERSTAND WHAT IT'S LIKE—HOW IT STILL HURTS.
IF YOU EVER NEED TO TALK TO SOMEONE, YOU CAN ALWAYS TALK TO ME. OKAY?
I PROMISE I WILL.
THANK YOU, SANDRA.
NOW COME ON AND HAVE SOME FUN! YOUR FRIENDS ARE WAITING FOR YOU!

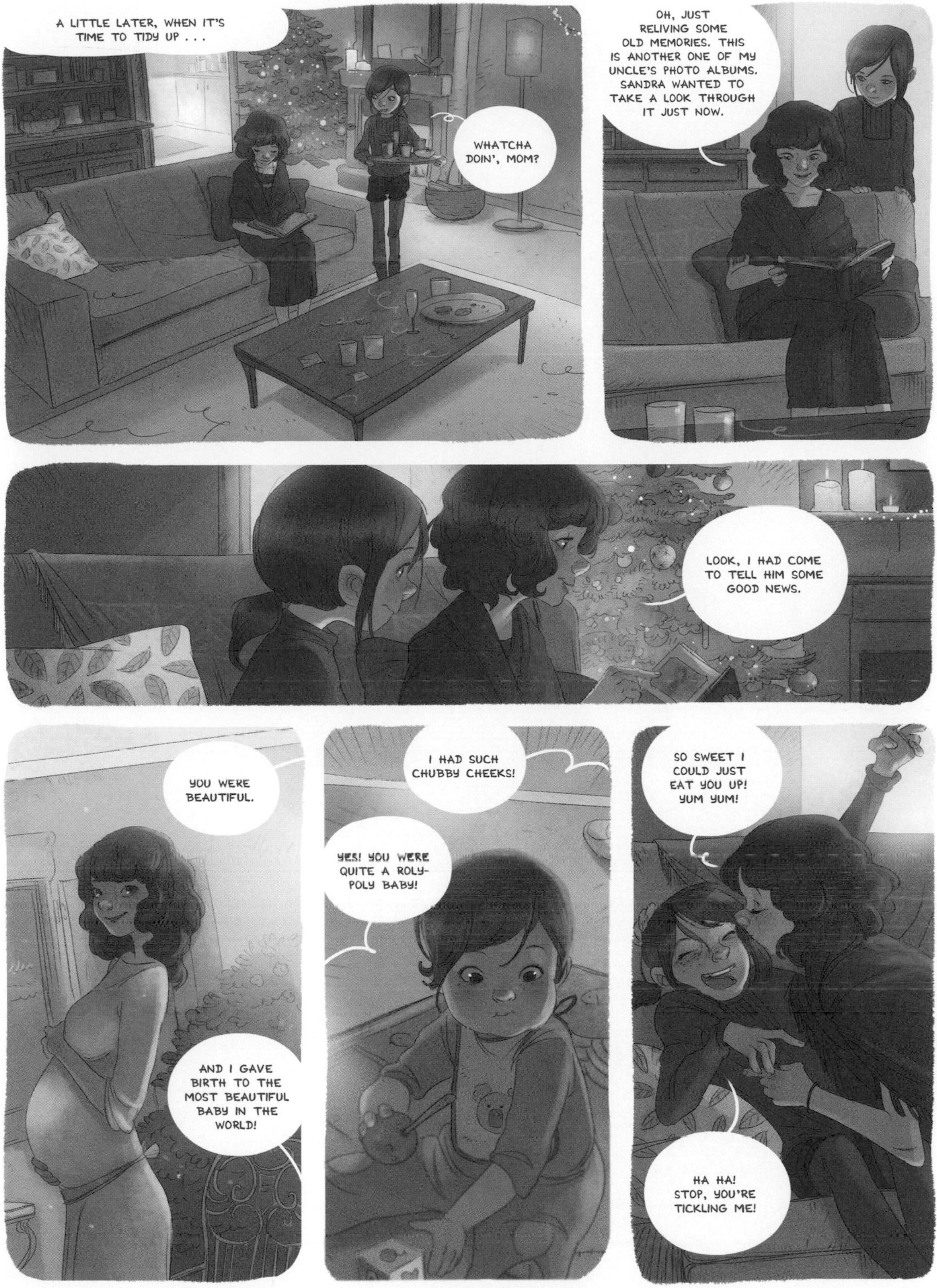
A LITTLE LATER, WHEN IT'S TIME TO TIDY UP . . .
WHATCHA DOIN', MOM?
OH, JUST RELIVING SOME OLD MEMORIES. THIS IS ANOTHER ONE OF MY UNCLE'S PHOTO ALBUMS. SANDRA WANTED TO TAKE A LOOK THROUGH IT JUST NOW.
LOOK, I HAD COME TO TELL HIM SOME GOOD NEWS.
YOU WERE BEAUTIFUL.
AND I GAVE BIRTH TO THE MOST BEAUTIFUL BABY IN THE WORLD!
I HAD SUCH CHUBBY CHEEKS!
YES! YOU WERE QUITE A ROLY-POLY BABY!
SO SWEET I COULD JUST EAT YOU UP! YUM YUM!
HA HA! STOP, YOU'RE TICKLING ME!

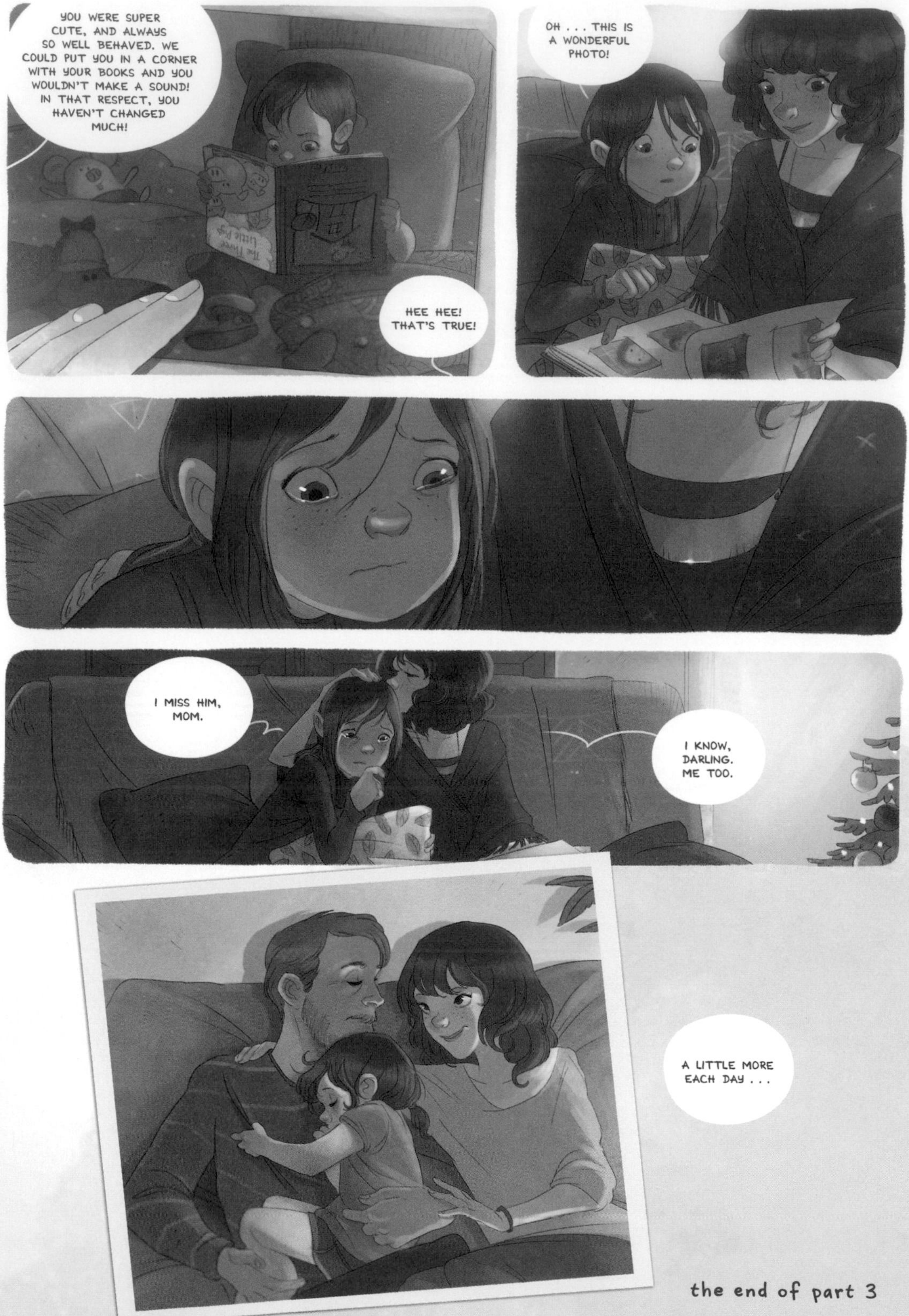
YOU WERE SUPER CUTE, AND ALWAYS SO WELL BEHAVED. WE COULD PUT YOU IN A CORNER WITH YOUR BOOKS AND YOU WOULDN'T MAKE A SOUND! IN THAT RESPECT, YOU HAVEN'T CHANGED MUCH!
The Three Little Pigs
HEE HEE! THAT'S TRUE!
OH . . . THIS IS A WONDERFUL PHOTO!
I MISS HIM, MOM.
I KNOW, DARLING. ME TOO.
A LITTLE MORE EACH DAY . . .

the end of part 3

My little Cici,

It's been more than a year since you made an incredible discovery in an abandoned zoo. Michael's works have been a part of your life ever since— a part of our life, really, and I wanted to offer you a gift in their image: in color and with a soul.

In my work, I meet artists from all walks of life. As I looked at their wonderful art, I began to wonder how each of them might portray you. I shared with them how you have a way of bringing joy into people's lives, and was delighted when nine of them agreed to take their paintbrushes in hand and imagine you and your adventures in their own individual styles.

I hope you enjoy their work as much as I do!

Merry Christmas, darling,
Mom

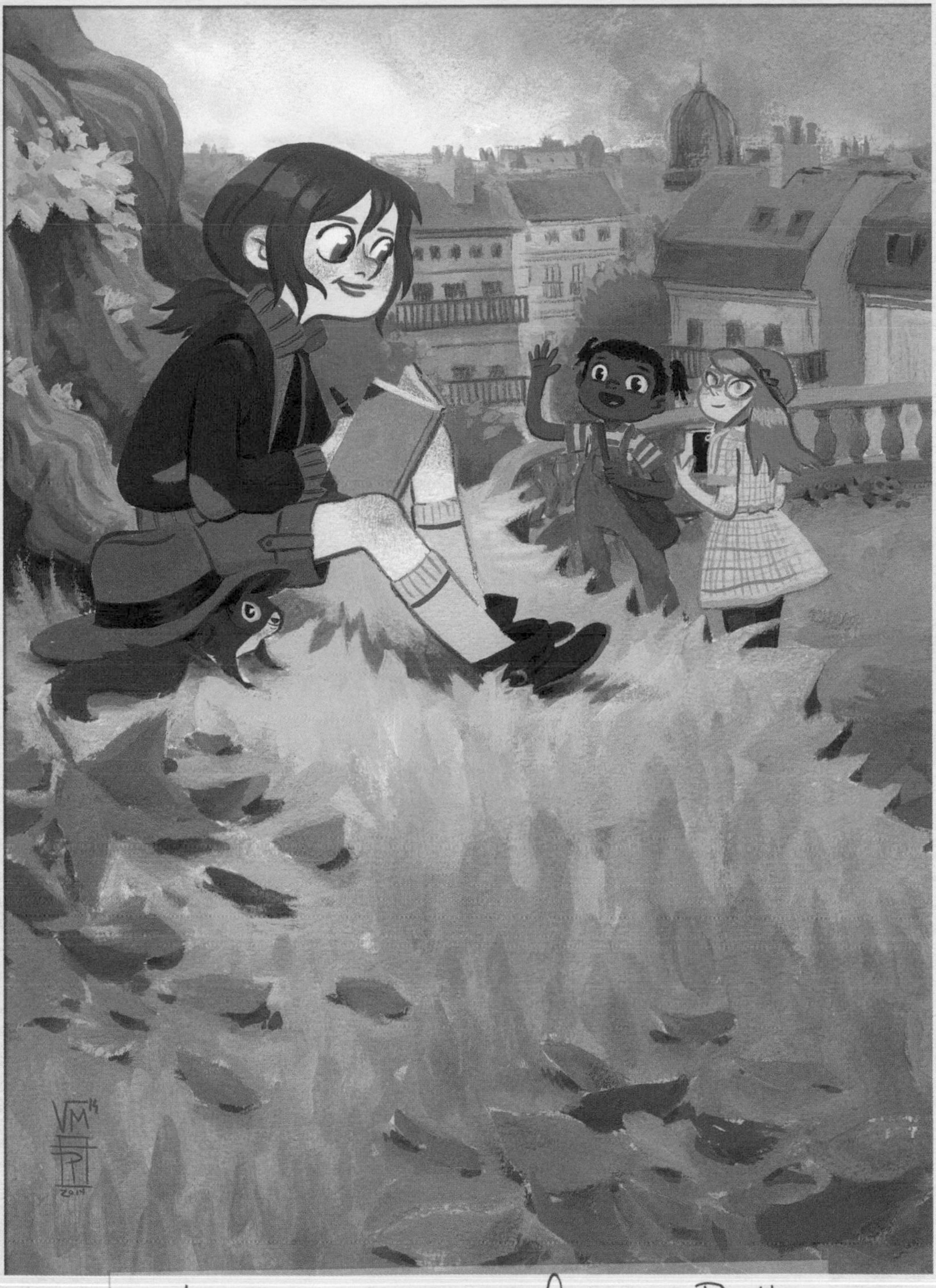

Victoria Maderna and federico Piatti

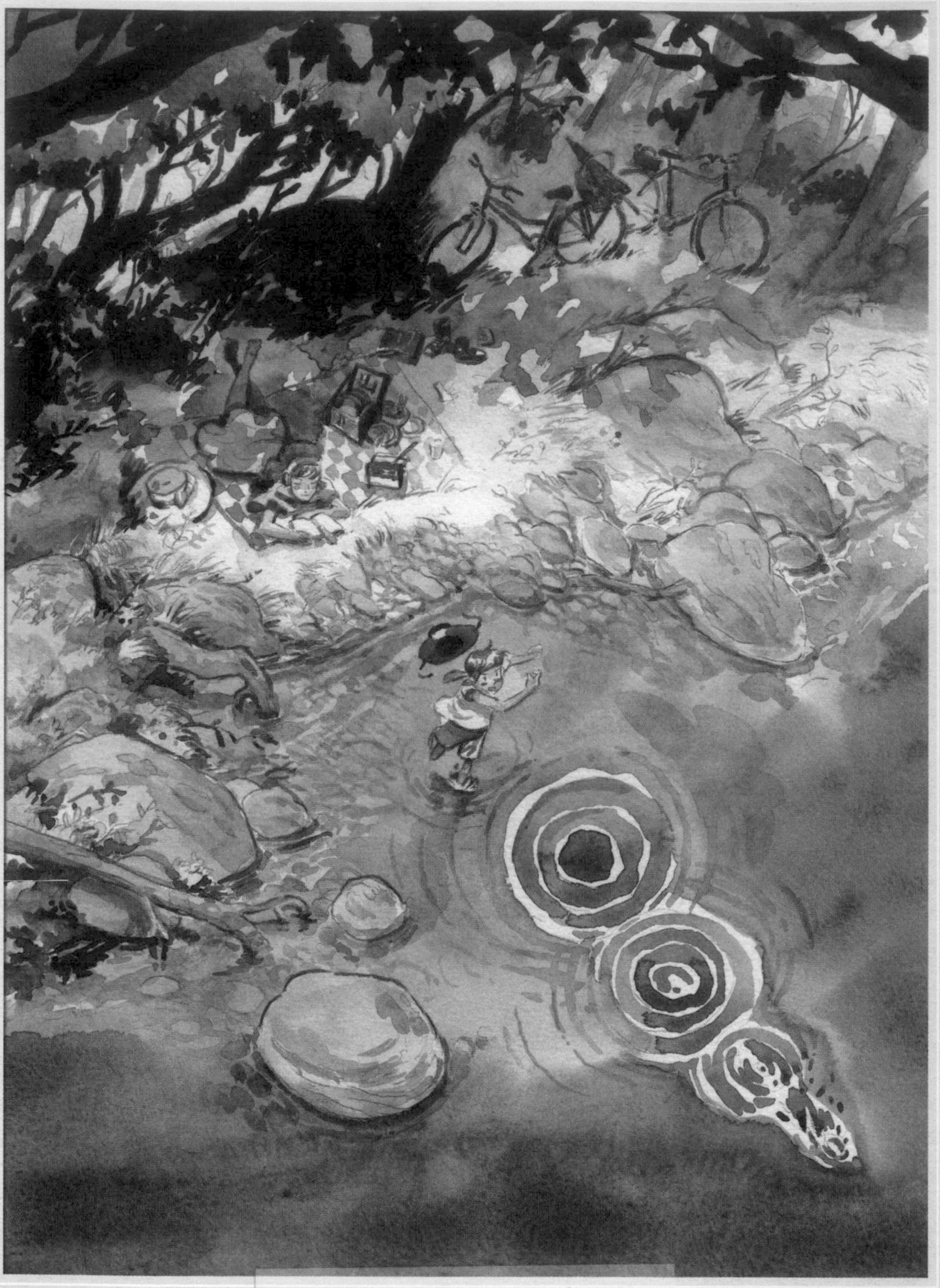

Cédric Babouche

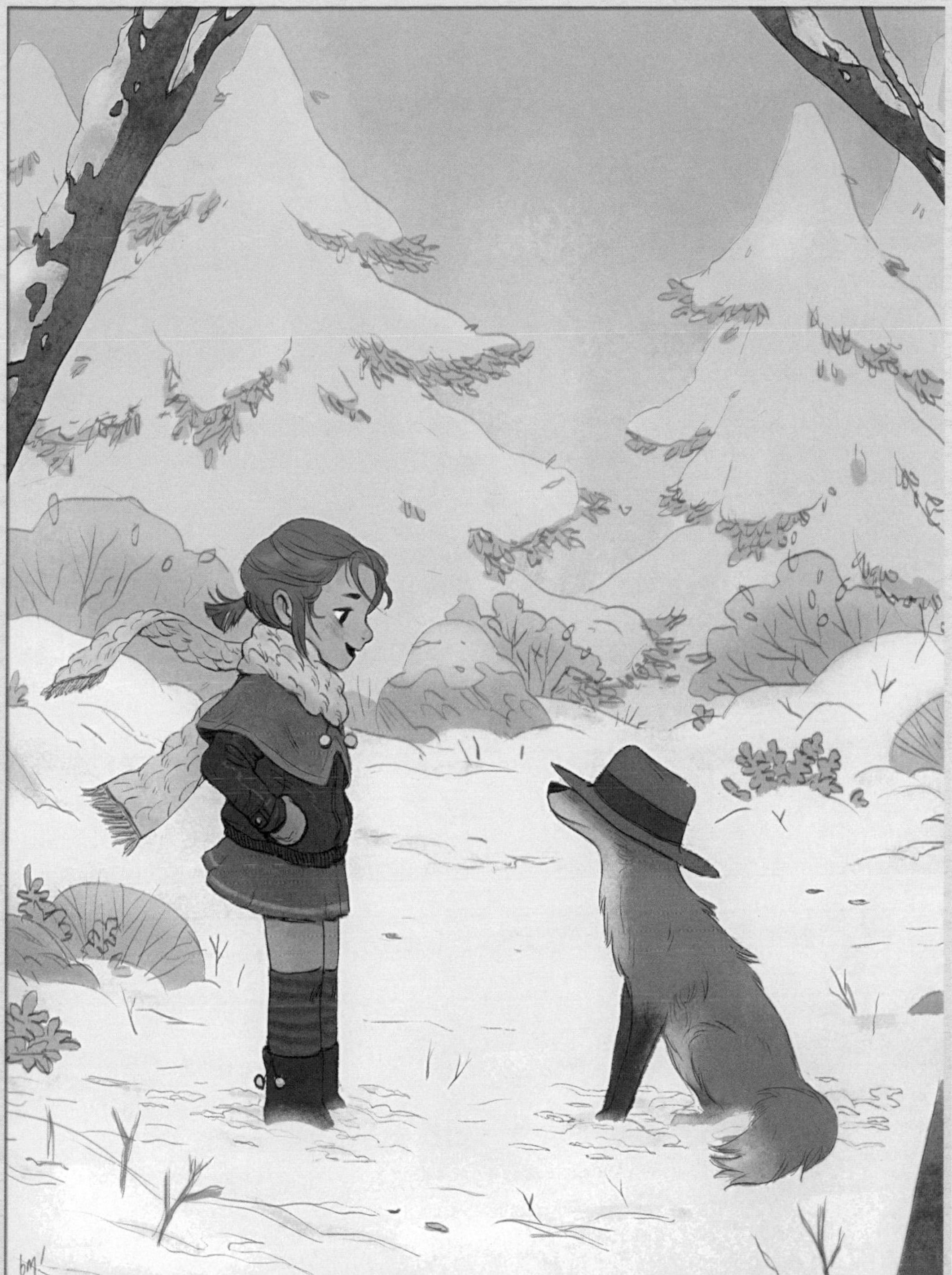

Romain Mennetrier

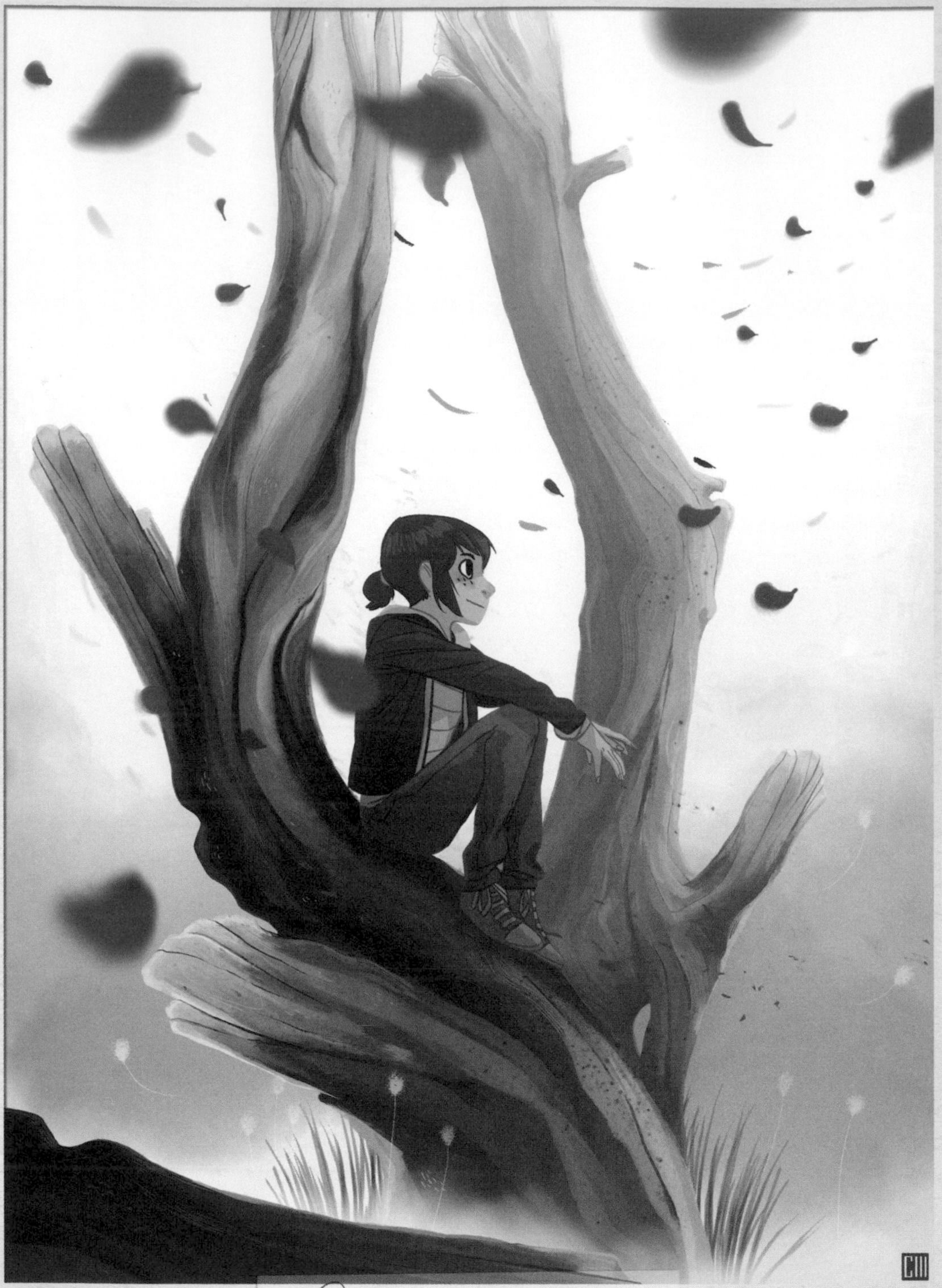

Guillaume Ospital

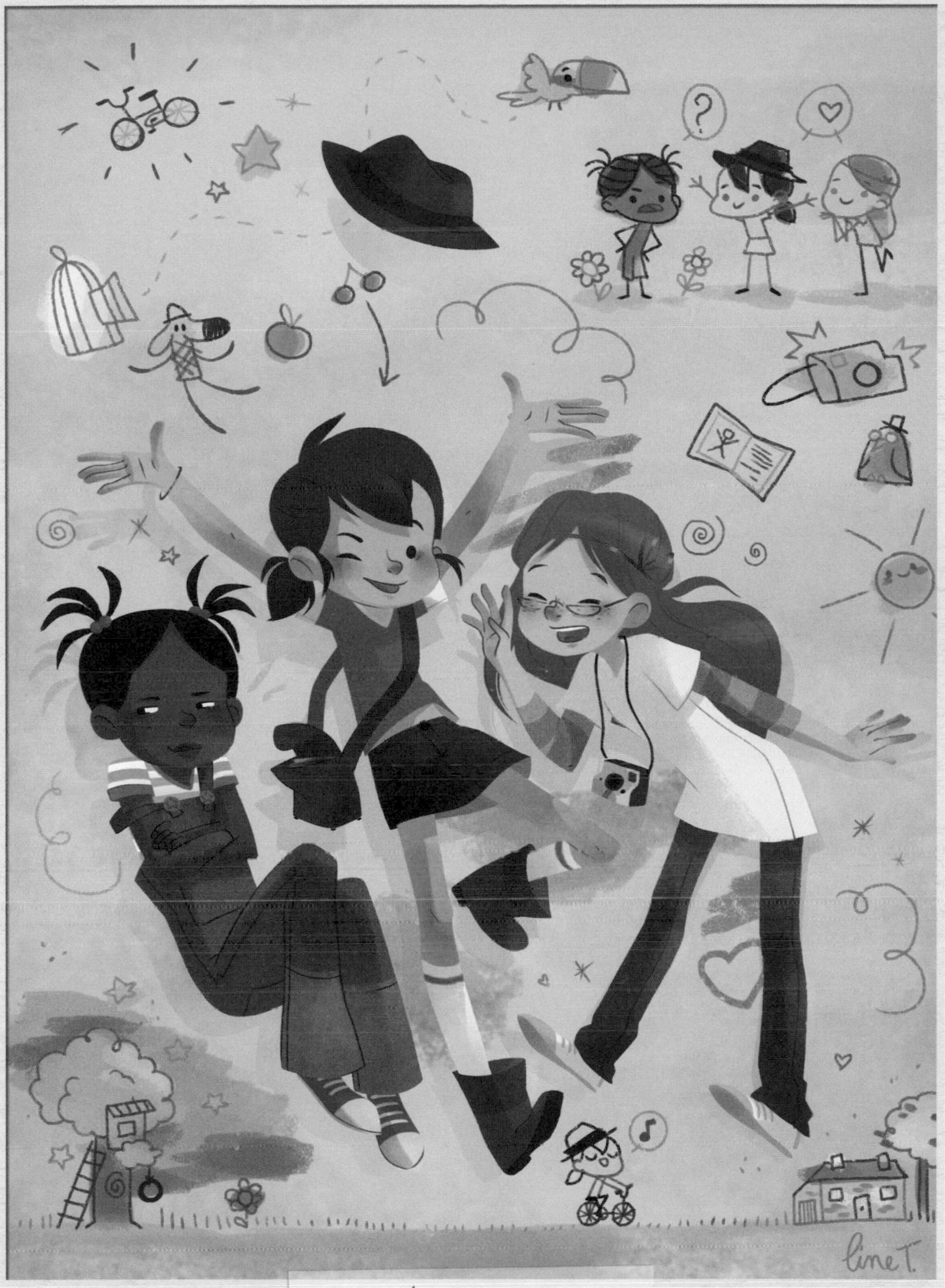
line T.

line T

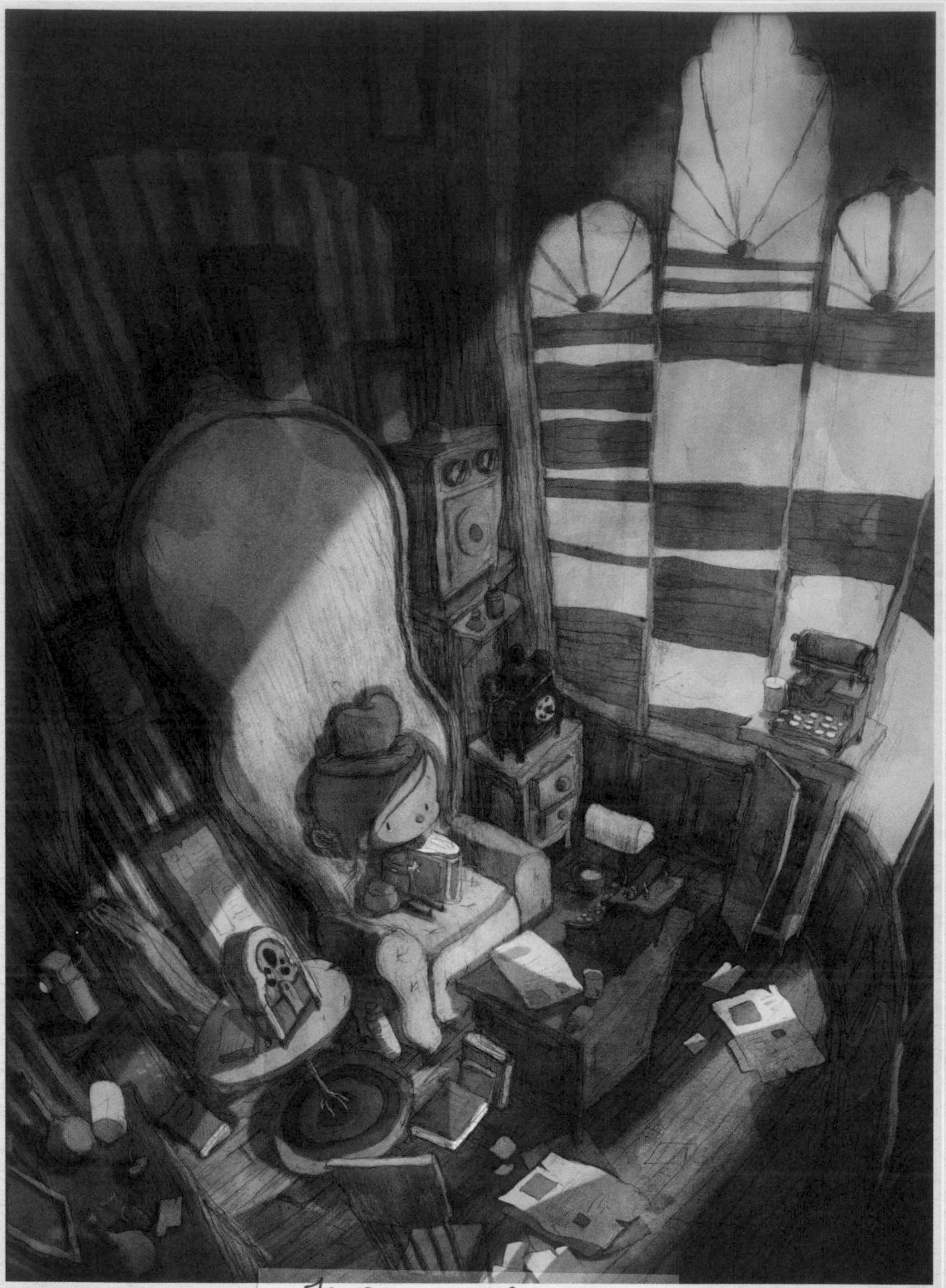

Jérémie Almanza

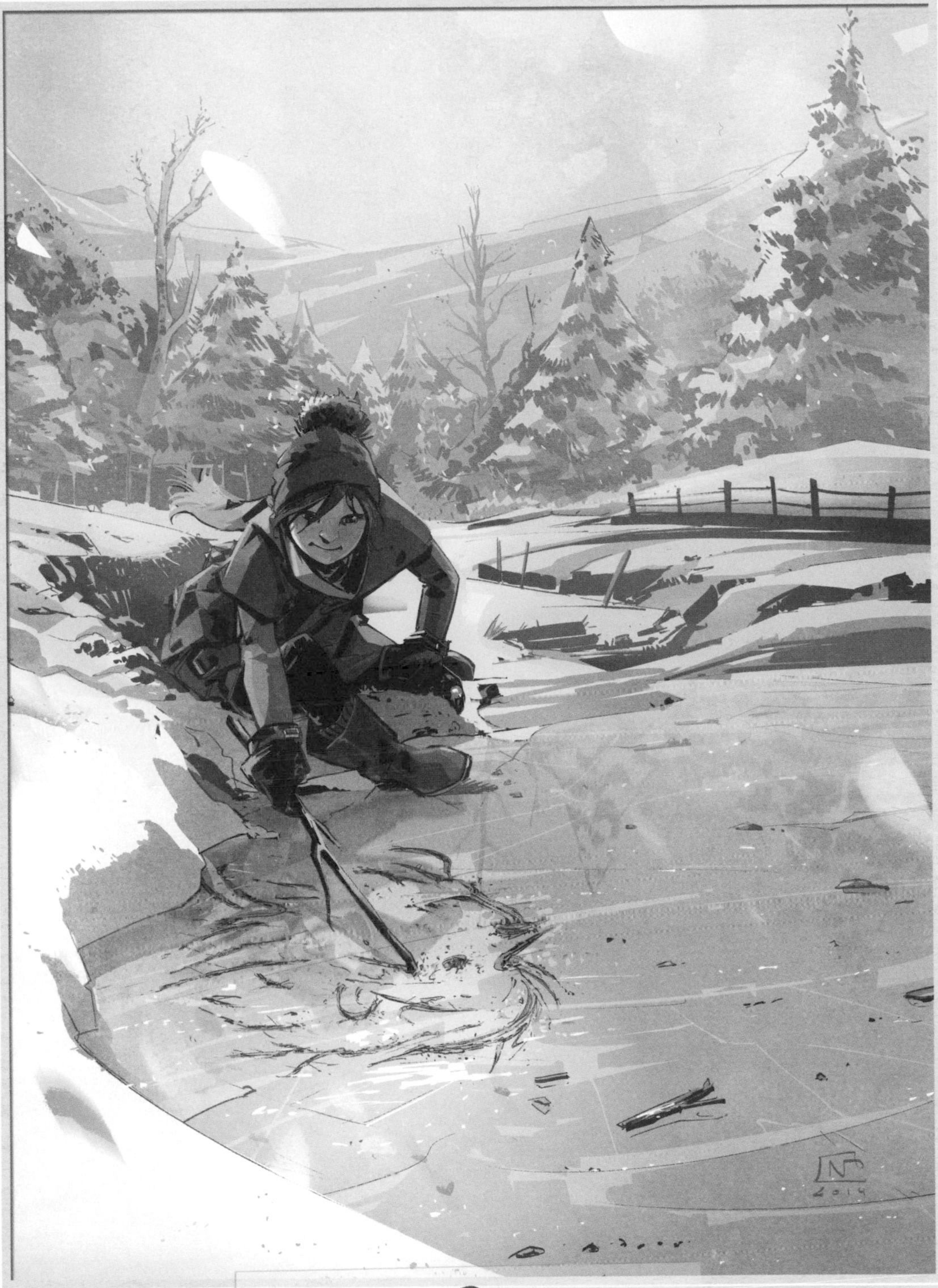

Nicolas Petrimaux

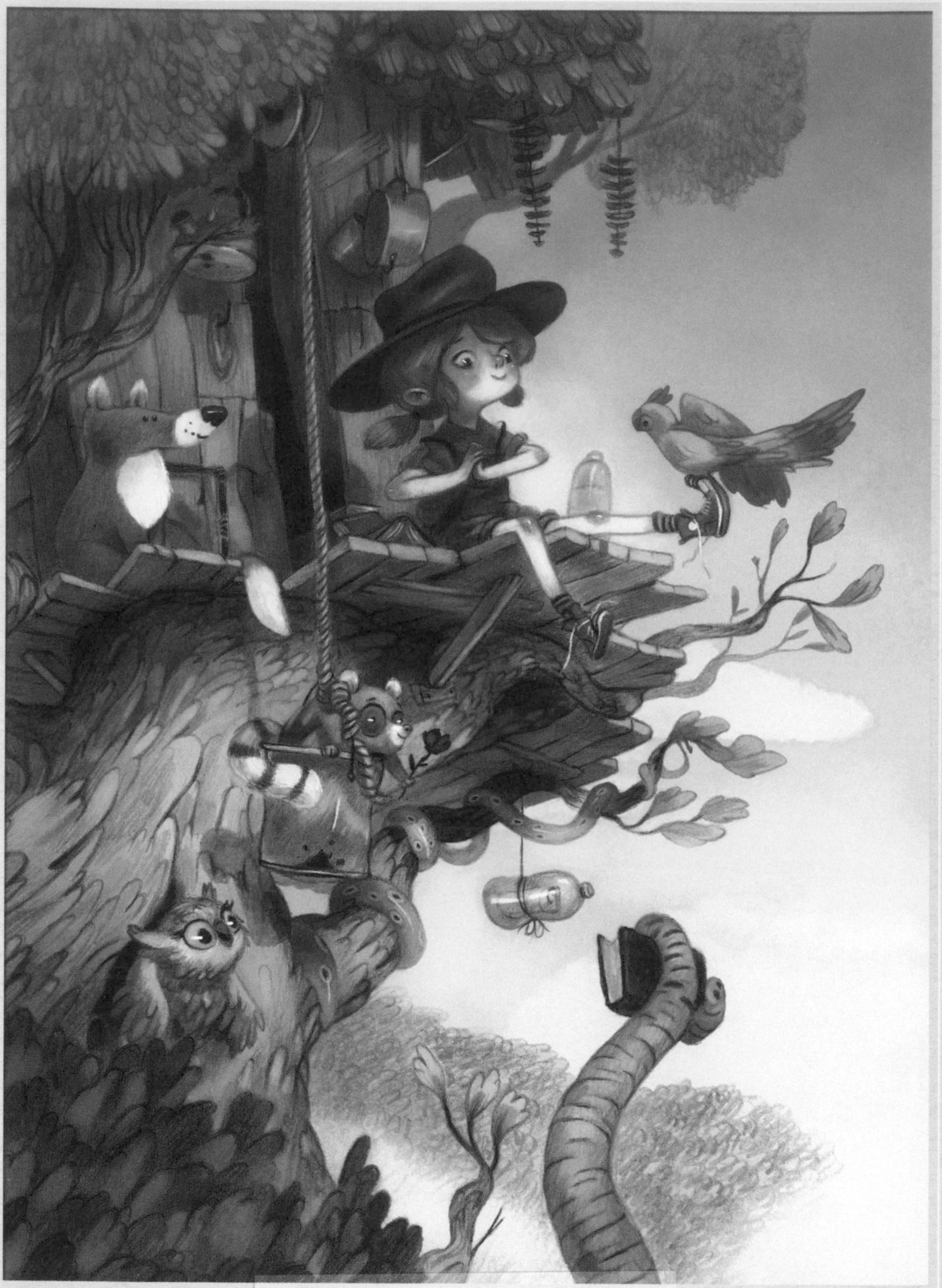

Clément Lefèvre

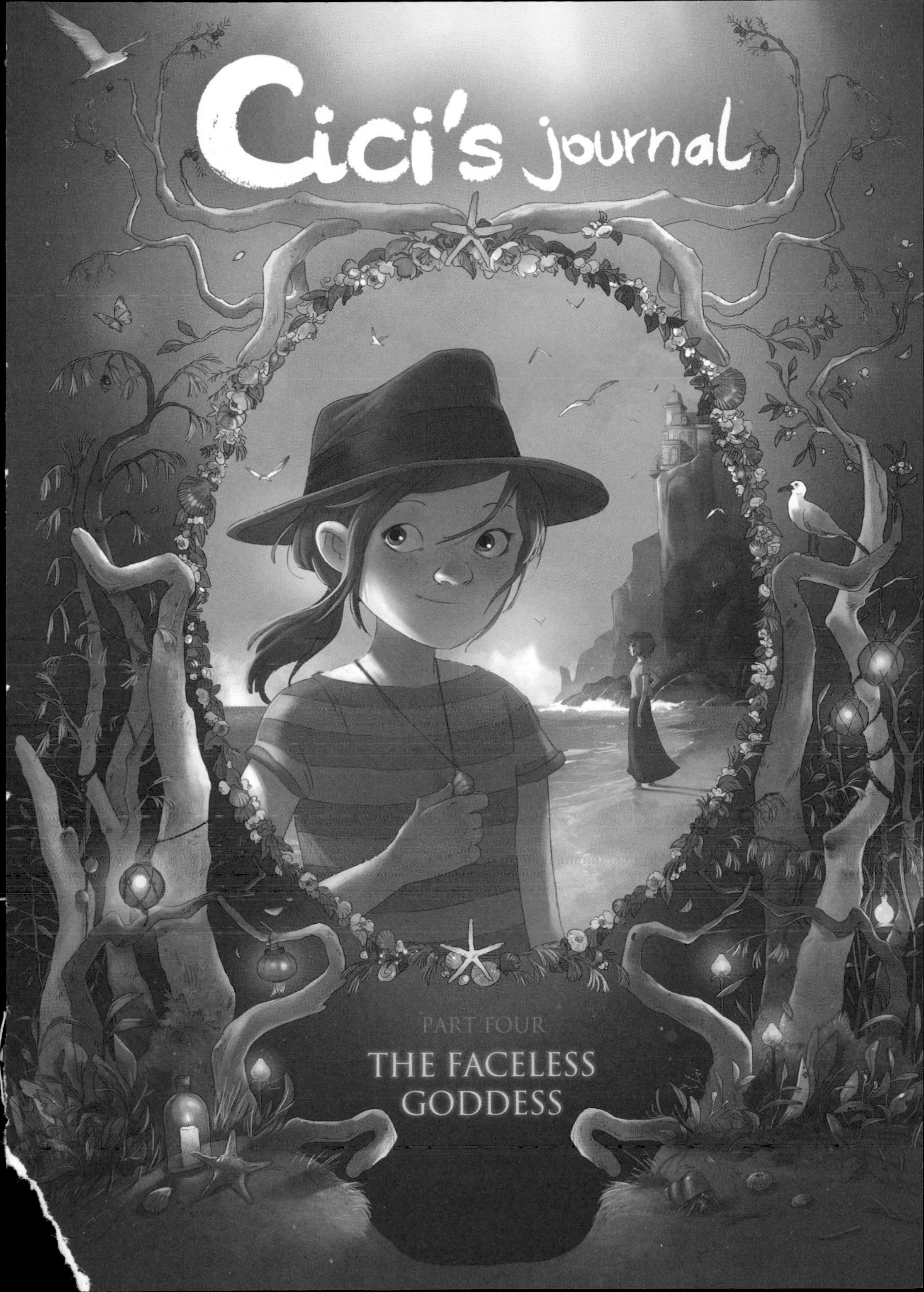
Cici's journal
PART FOUR
THE FACELESS
GODDESS

To Rachel. To our adventures on the beach, here or elsewhere, to seagulls and freedom!
To my dear and loving Nico, thank for you being my companion through winds and tides.
Thanks to Fanny for her invaluable help in the home stretch.
Finally, thanks to our all-star team: Joris, Clotilde, Barbara, Adeline, and Géraldine.

Aurélie

To Bertrand B. I would so have liked to tell you the end of the story …

Joris

Happy Birthday
I wish you a very happy birthday, my darling!
Love,
Mom

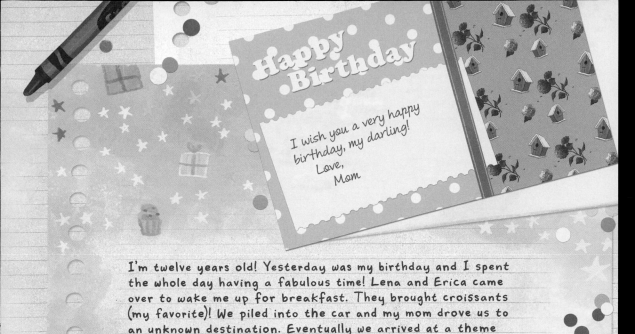

I'm twelve years old! Yesterday was my birthday and I spent the whole day having a fabulous time! Lena and Erica came over to wake me up for breakfast. They brought croissants (my favorite)! We piled into the car and my mom drove us to an unknown destination. Eventually we arrived at a theme park and all my friends were there!

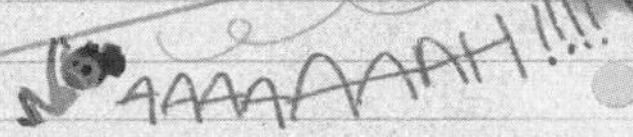

Now I'm a real adventurer!

There was a climbing wall, tree climbing routes, and even a small cave to explore . . . it was brilliant! The final zipline was scary! Erica screamed the whole time—it was so funny!

AAAAAAAH!!!!

Next, we all had a picnic lunch and played games together. When we were done, we drove back home. But the day wasn't over—Granny Vana came, and we organized a cupcake workshop! All five of us stuffed ourselves!

YUM!

The day concluded with a movie and a sleepover at my house. We told loads of stories in my room until the wee hours of the morning!

Lena and Erica gave me a **SUPER** gift! A long time ago, we
played a writing game with Mrs. Flores, and as part of the
game we developed a whole set of character sheets. The three
of us used to watch people from our windows and imagine
their secret stories. Some we kept, and others we gave to Mrs.
Flores. It had been a long time since I had even thought about
those pages, but Lena and Erica collected them all together
and put them into a binder for me. What a surprise!
 I had forgotten how many there were!

↰ My own binder from Sandra's studio!

In the process, Lena found something else: the mini-pages (I'm not
sure if they have a more official name) of the graphic novel that the
three of us had drawn together. It was really funny!

Come to think of it, I'll have a great opportunity to start a new
graphic novel this week!

Next...

Oh no,
the engine
is broken!

cough cough

We can
fix it!

Hey!

Meteor
shower!
Dead ahead!

Let's go!
Hurry!

AAA-AAH!

Mom gave me an incredible present too: We're going away together for a week of vacation!

We're going to stay in a little cottage at the seaside, but since the water is still a little too cold for swimming, Mom came up with another activity . . .

And look what she found—it'll be awesome!

THE

MANSION
OF A HUNDRED MYSTERIES

for the whole family

∼ The Hundred Mysteries ∼

Begin your adventure in the streets of a quaint, but eerie village. Then, travel through the heart of a dense pine forest to a desolate mansion perched on a cliff that overlooks the ocean. A hundred mysteries haunt the house's uncanny corridors and historic rooms, all waiting to be unlocked—by you!

Here, each object is a clue! Can you decipher them?

Lost pirate treasures, cursed tomes, hidden passageways... What secrets will you discover?

Riddles for children and adults.

∼ Entrance Fees / Reservations ∼

	Adult	Student	Children over 10	Childr...
Weekday	$30	$22	$14	Fr...
Weekend	$40	$25	$17	Fr...

Reservations by telephone from June through September 30.

The Mansion of the Hundred Mysteries

Telephone : 03 40 40 79 78
Fax : 03 40 40 79 79
Address : 56, allée du chataigner
56670 LEBRIEC

Open Tuesday to Saturday: 9 a.m. to 8 p.m.
(Late-night events available once per month!)

I can't wait to go there! But before I can leave, I have to solve a riddle of my own: how do I fit everything I want to bring into my suitcase?

Solved it! All packed and ready. I'm really looking forward to this vacation with Mom. A week at the beach will do us good. Do me good. They say that after you come back from a trip, you're no longer the same person you were when you left! We'll see if it's true.

I've been feeling up and down a lot since Christmas. I never thought that helping Sandra rediscover her memories would remind me so much about my own past. Now, it feels like I've swallowed a yo-yo. At least, there's something in my stomach that's bouncing up and down. It doesn't feel good.

Let me see—I'm twelve now. That means I've lived almost eight years without my dad. Now all that's left of him is vague memories. In fact, I can barely remember his face or his voice. At least I have some photos and videos to keep his memory alive.

Daddy, do you want to help me blow out my candles again?

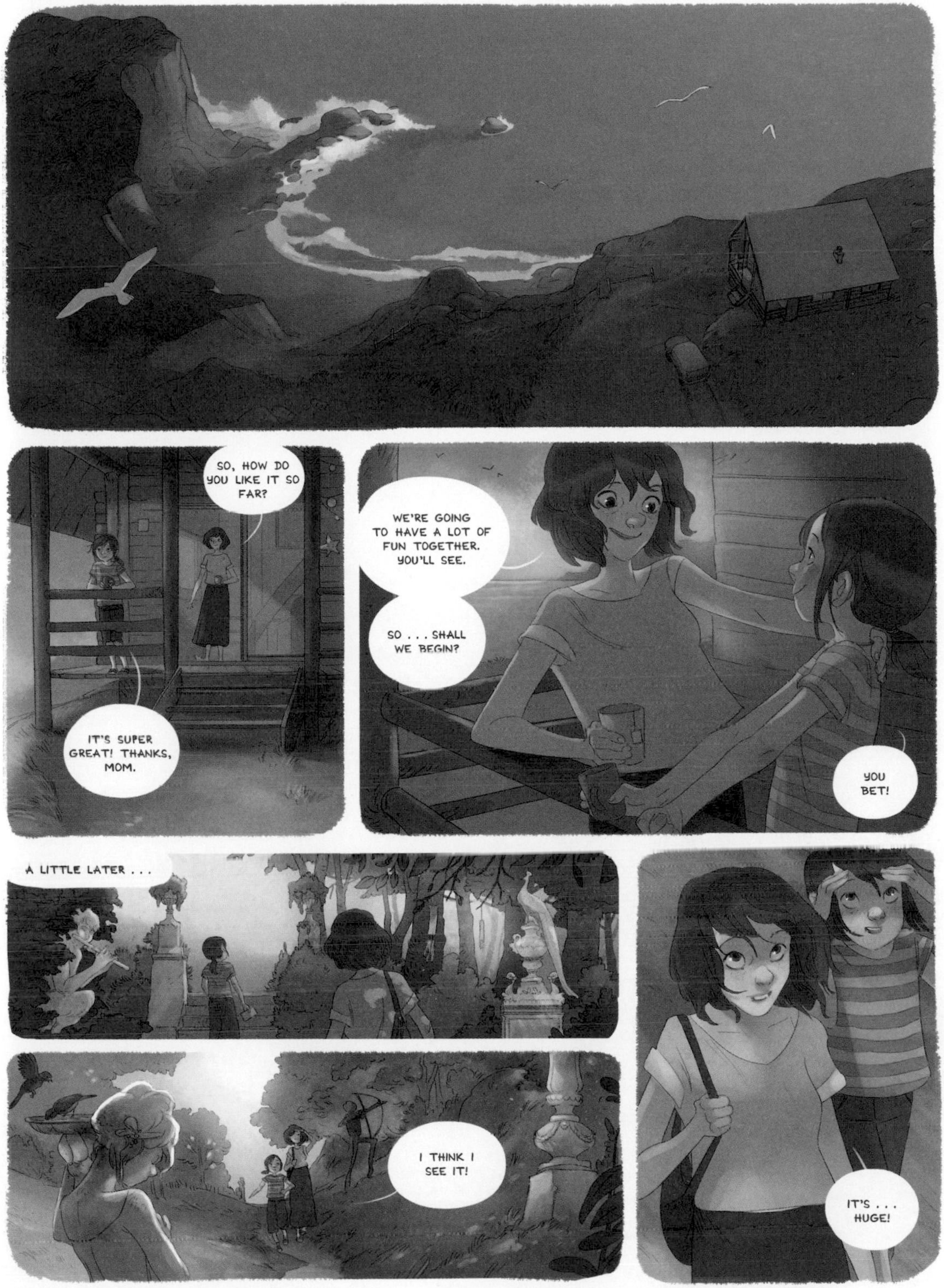

SO, HOW DO YOU LIKE IT SO FAR?
IT'S SUPER GREAT! THANKS, MOM.
WE'RE GOING TO HAVE A LOT OF FUN TOGETHER. YOU'LL SEE.
SO . . . SHALL WE BEGIN?
YOU BET!
A LITTLE LATER . . .
I THINK I SEE IT!
IT'S . . . HUGE!

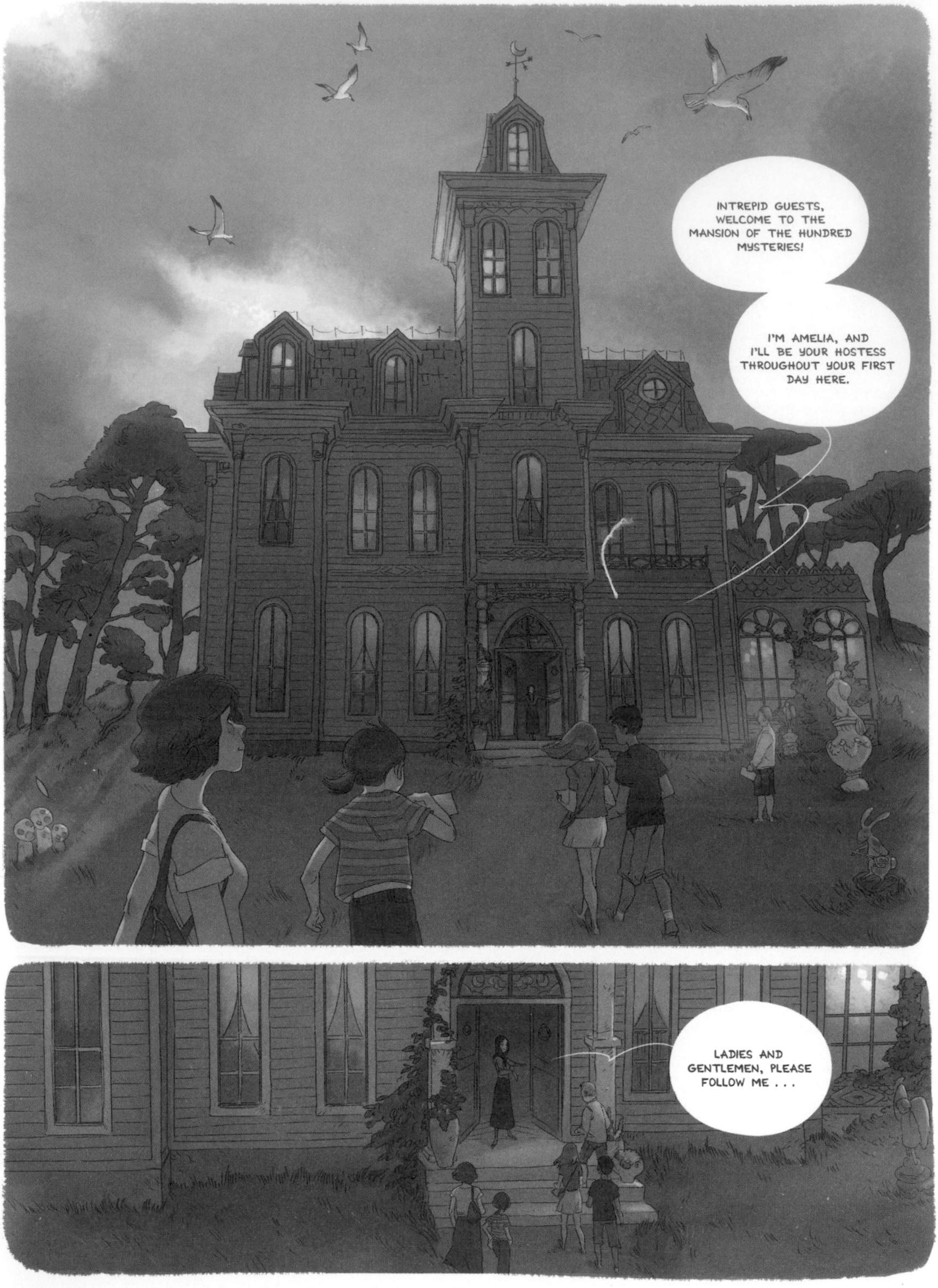
INTREPID GUESTS, WELCOME TO THE MANSION OF THE HUNDRED MYSTERIES!
I'M AMELIA, AND I'LL BE YOUR HOSTESS THROUGHOUT YOUR FIRST DAY HERE.
LADIES AND GENTLEMEN, PLEASE FOLLOW ME . . .

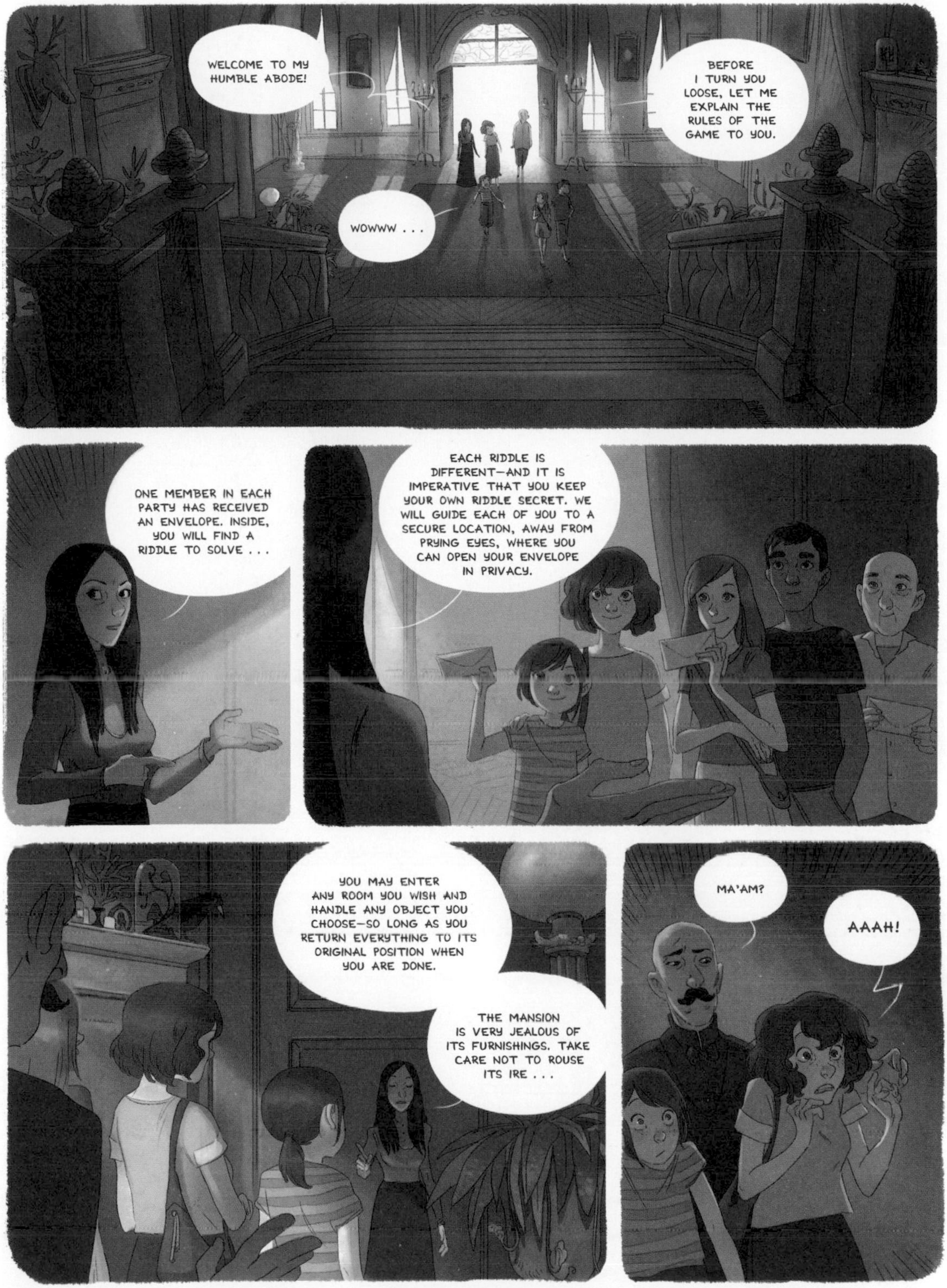

WELCOME TO MY HUMBLE ABODE!
BEFORE I TURN YOU LOOSE, LET ME EXPLAIN THE RULES OF THE GAME TO YOU.
WOWWW . . .
ONE MEMBER IN EACH PARTY HAS RECEIVED AN ENVELOPE. INSIDE, YOU WILL FIND A RIDDLE TO SOLVE . . .
EACH RIDDLE IS DIFFERENT—AND IT IS IMPERATIVE THAT YOU KEEP YOUR OWN RIDDLE SECRET. WE WILL GUIDE EACH OF YOU TO A SECURE LOCATION, AWAY FROM PRYING EYES, WHERE YOU CAN OPEN YOUR ENVELOPE IN PRIVACY.
YOU MAY ENTER ANY ROOM YOU WISH AND HANDLE ANY OBJECT YOU CHOOSE—SO LONG AS YOU RETURN EVERYTHING TO ITS ORIGINAL POSITION WHEN YOU ARE DONE.
THE MANSION IS VERY JEALOUS OF ITS FURNISHINGS. TAKE CARE NOT TO ROUSE ITS IRE . . .
MA'AM?
AAAH!

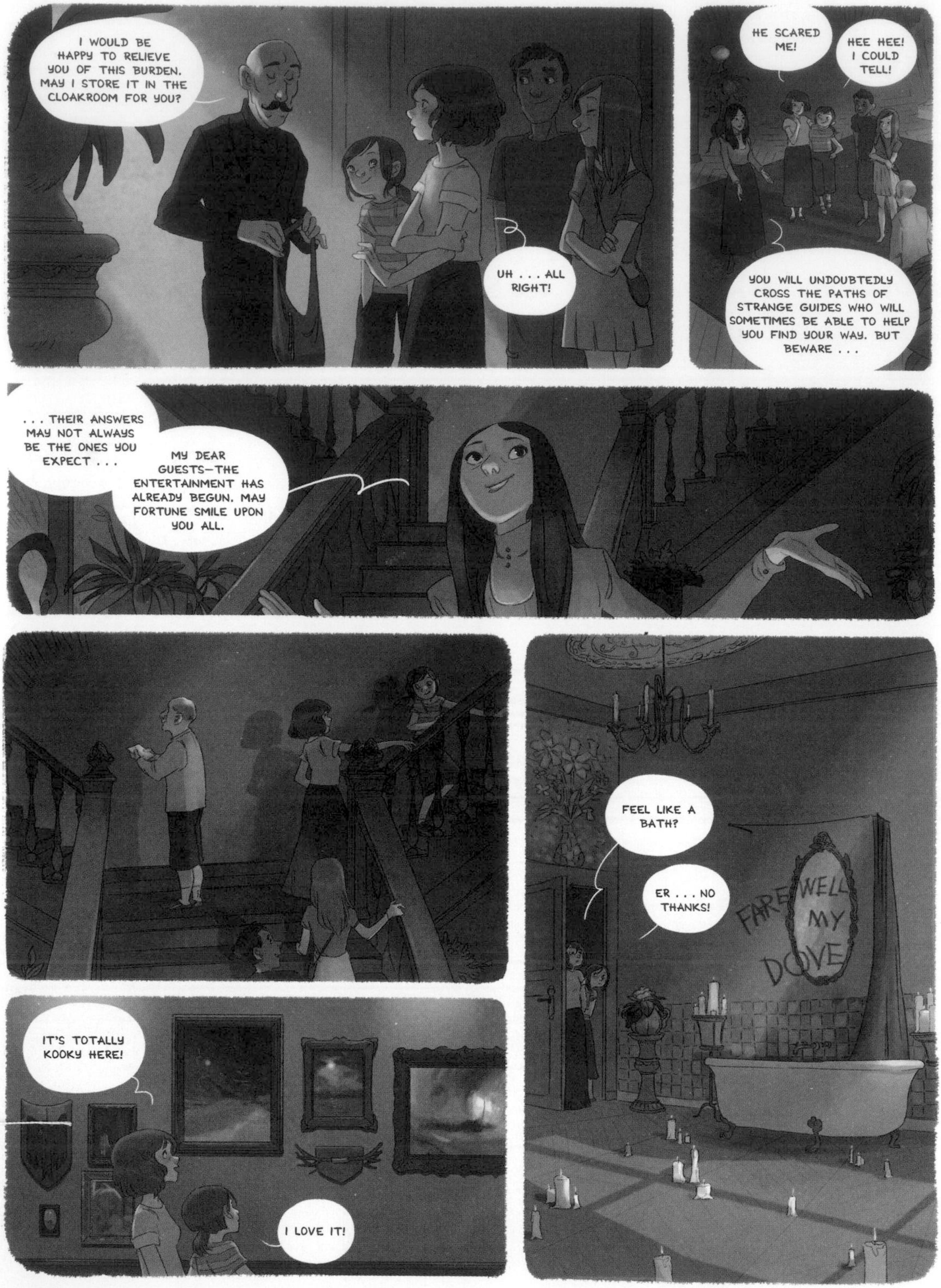
I WOULD BE HAPPY TO RELIEVE YOU OF THIS BURDEN. MAY I STORE IT IN THE CLOAKROOM FOR YOU?
UH . . . ALL RIGHT!
HE SCARED ME!
HEE HEE! I COULD TELL!
YOU WILL UNDOUBTEDLY CROSS THE PATHS OF STRANGE GUIDES WHO WILL SOMETIMES BE ABLE TO HELP YOU FIND YOUR WAY. BUT BEWARE . . .
. . . THEIR ANSWERS MAY NOT ALWAYS BE THE ONES YOU EXPECT . . .
MY DEAR GUESTS—THE ENTERTAINMENT HAS ALREADY BEGUN. MAY FORTUNE SMILE UPON YOU ALL.
IT'S TOTALLY KOOKY HERE!
I LOVE IT!
FEEL LIKE A BATH?
ER . . . NO THANKS!
FAREWELL MY DOVE

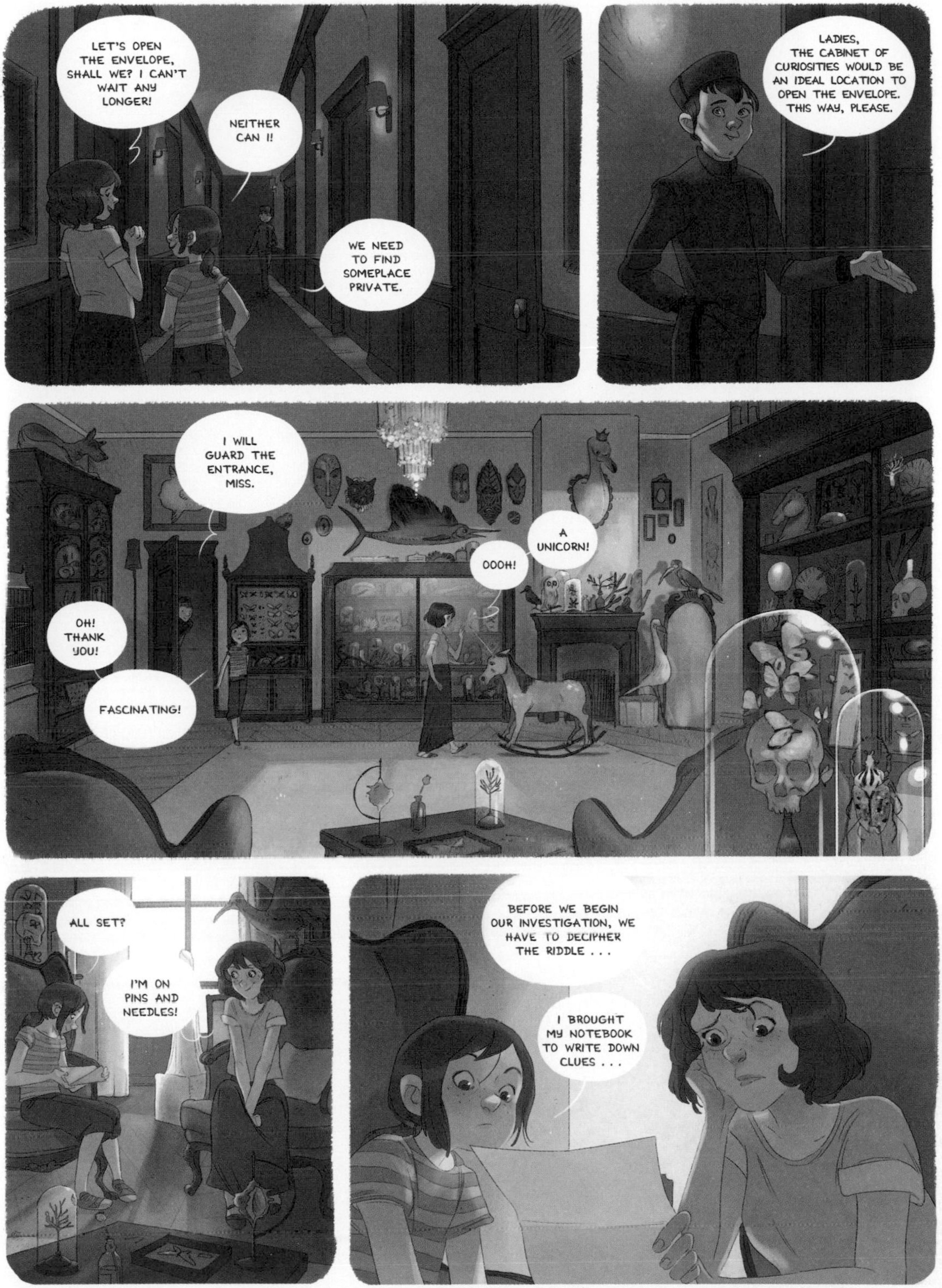
LET'S OPEN THE ENVELOPE, SHALL WE? I CAN'T WAIT ANY LONGER!
NEITHER CAN I!
WE NEED TO FIND SOMEPLACE PRIVATE.
LADIES, THE CABINET OF CURIOSITIES WOULD BE AN IDEAL LOCATION TO OPEN THE ENVELOPE. THIS WAY, PLEASE.
I WILL GUARD THE ENTRANCE, MISS.
OH! THANK YOU!
FASCINATING!
OOOH!
A UNICORN!
ALL SET?
I'M ON PINS AND NEEDLES!
BEFORE WE BEGIN OUR INVESTIGATION, WE HAVE TO DECIPHER THE RIDDLE . . .
I BROUGHT MY NOTEBOOK TO WRITE DOWN CLUES . . .

Happy Hunting!

Mansion of a Hundred Mysteries

When will the Ringmaster fly off to Venus?

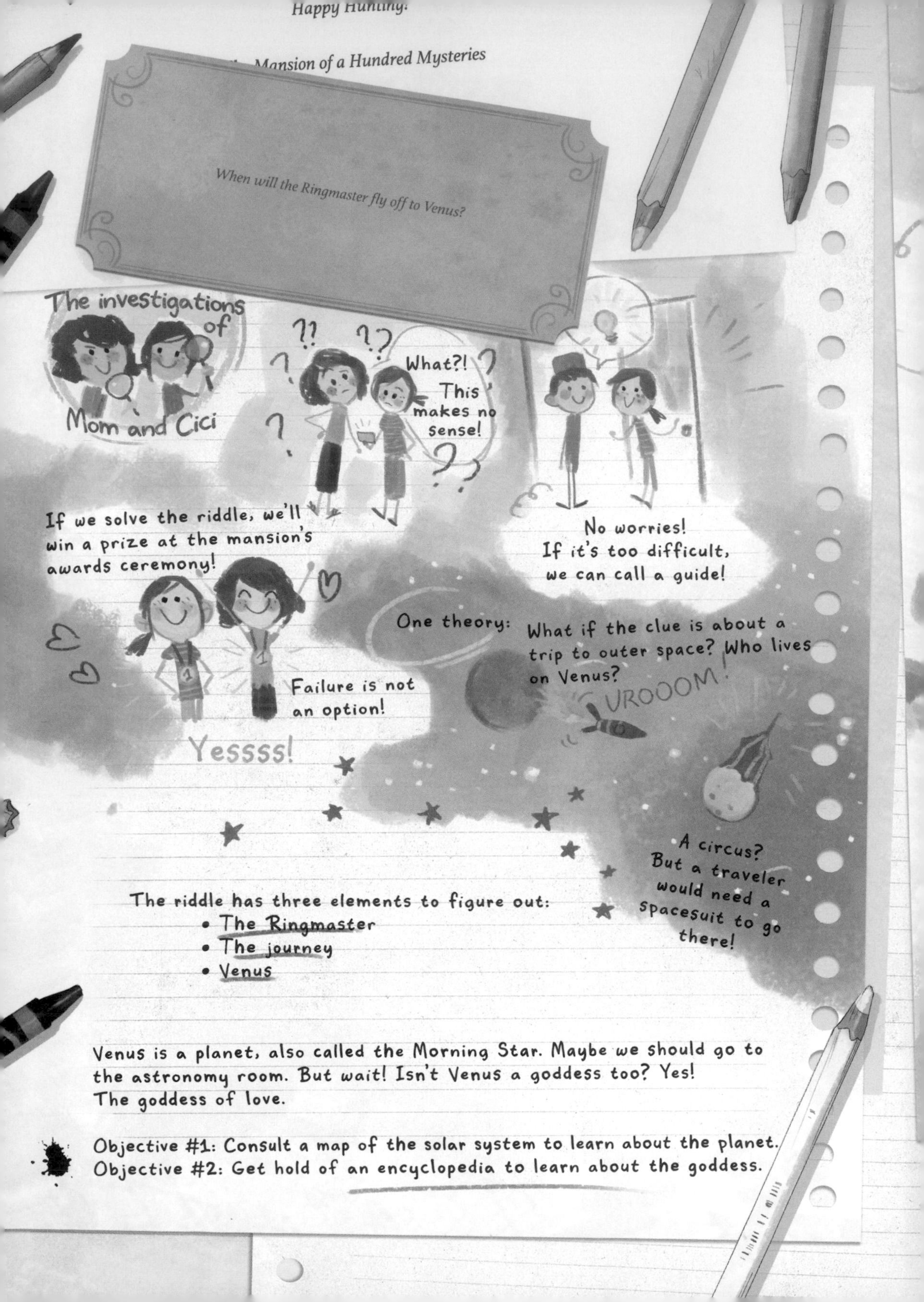
The investigations of Mom and Cici
What?! This makes no sense!
If we solve the riddle, we'll win a prize at the mansion's awards ceremony!
No worries! If it's too difficult, we can call a guide!
One theory:
What if the clue is about a trip to outer space? Who lives on Venus?
VROOOM!
Failure is not an option!
Yessss!
A circus? But a traveler would need a spacesuit to go there!

The riddle has three elements to figure out:

- The Ringmaster
- The journey
- Venus

Venus is a planet, also called the Morning Star. Maybe we should go to the astronomy room. But wait! Isn't Venus a goddess too? Yes! The goddess of love.

Objective #1: Consult a map of the solar system to learn about the planet.
Objective #2: Get hold of an encyclopedia to learn about the goddess.

Thanks to the map, we found the astronomy room.

It was magnificent! And because Lena lent me her camera, we could take pictures!

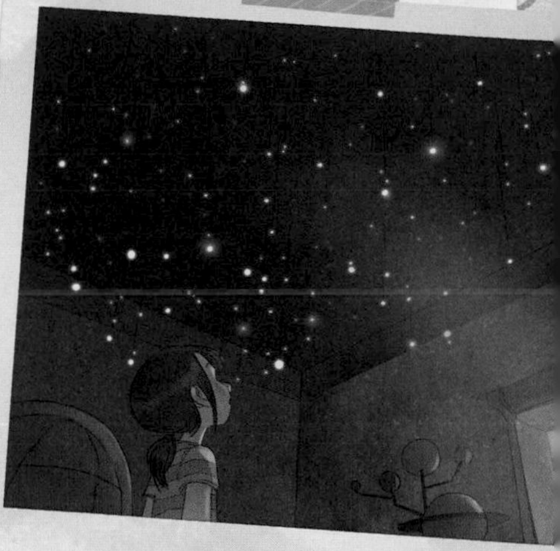

The ceiling was **awesome!!!**

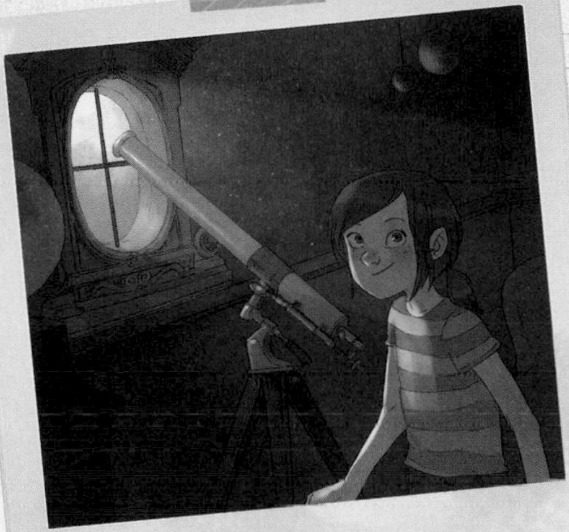

I would have loved to look at the stars, but it wasn't nighttime yet . . .

We examined several books about space.
We also discovered a whole solar system built out of wood and metal, but still—we had no solid lead about Venus.

Before we knew it, it was time for lunch. Mom was worried that the steward wouldn't return her purse, but there was no problem at all.

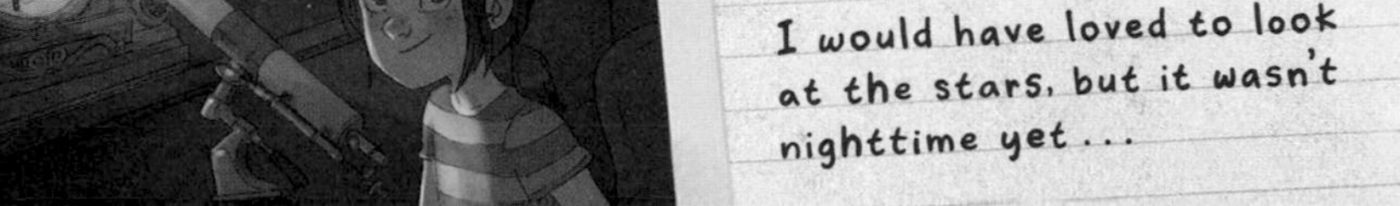
Lunchtime!

There was a boy my age sitting there by himself. His name is Marvin. He's the son of Amelia, the owner of the mansion. He told us about how his parents came up with the idea for the place, and went to bring back some photo albums. He said he'd be right back—I can't wait to look through them!

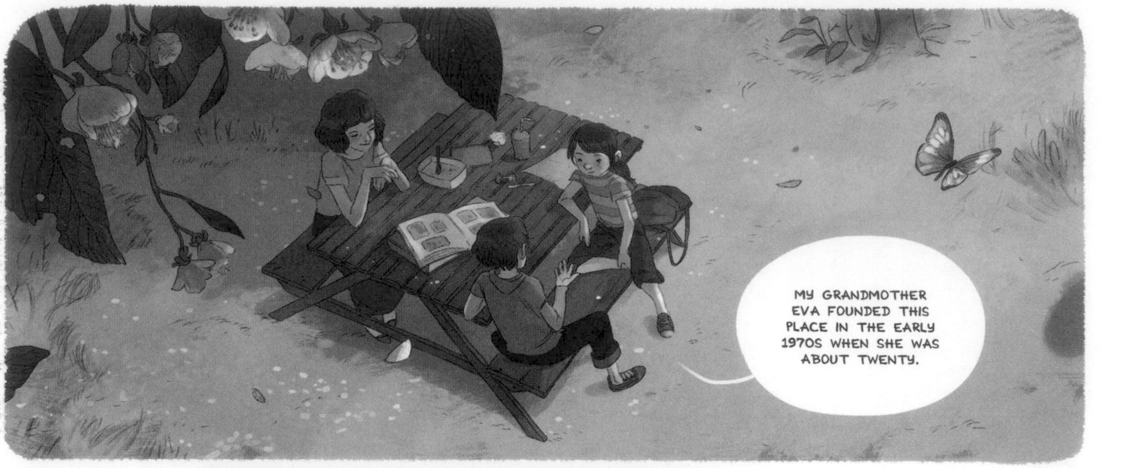
MY GRANDMOTHER EVA FOUNDED THIS PLACE IN THE EARLY 1970S WHEN SHE WAS ABOUT TWENTY.

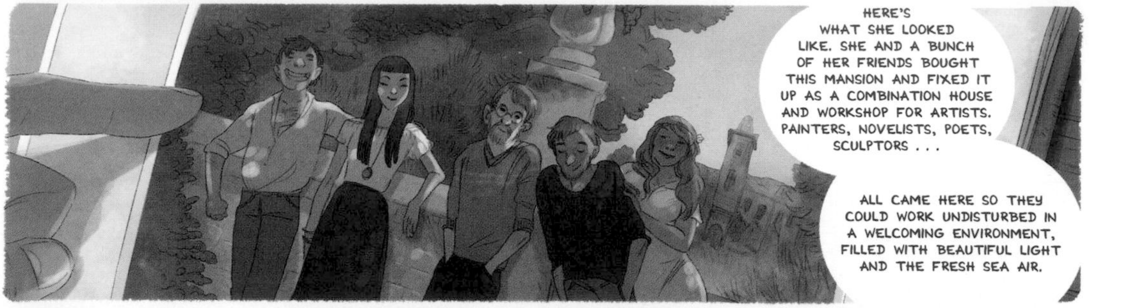
HERE'S WHAT SHE LOOKED LIKE. SHE AND A BUNCH OF HER FRIENDS BOUGHT THIS MANSION AND FIXED IT UP AS A COMBINATION HOUSE AND WORKSHOP FOR ARTISTS. PAINTERS, NOVELISTS, POETS, SCULPTORS . . .
ALL CAME HERE SO THEY COULD WORK UNDISTURBED IN A WELCOMING ENVIRONMENT, FILLED WITH BEAUTIFUL LIGHT AND THE FRESH SEA AIR.

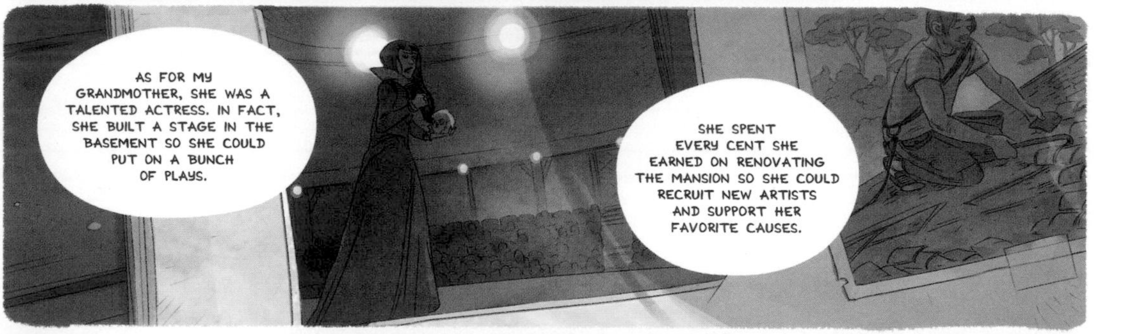
AS FOR MY GRANDMOTHER, SHE WAS A TALENTED ACTRESS. IN FACT, SHE BUILT A STAGE IN THE BASEMENT SO SHE COULD PUT ON A BUNCH OF PLAYS.
SHE SPENT EVERY CENT SHE EARNED ON RENOVATING THE MANSION SO SHE COULD RECRUIT NEW ARTISTS AND SUPPORT HER FAVORITE CAUSES.

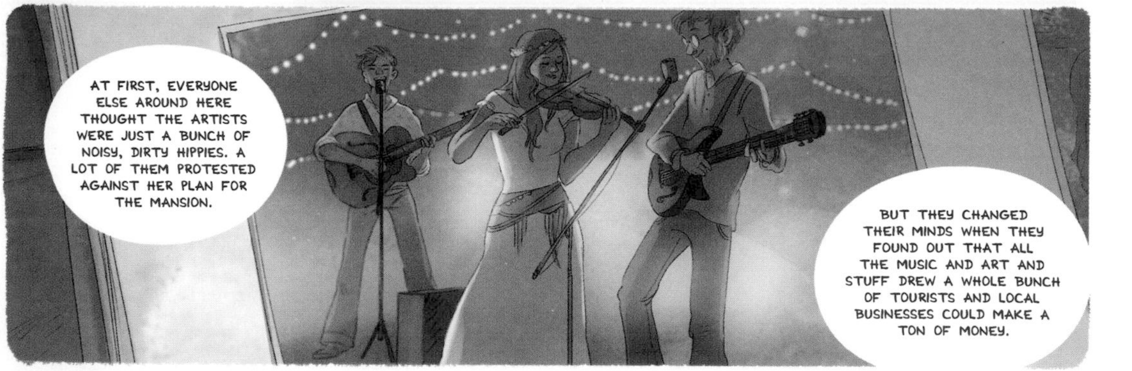
AT FIRST, EVERYONE ELSE AROUND HERE THOUGHT THE ARTISTS WERE JUST A BUNCH OF NOISY, DIRTY HIPPIES. A LOT OF THEM PROTESTED AGAINST HER PLAN FOR THE MANSION.
BUT THEY CHANGED THEIR MINDS WHEN THEY FOUND OUT THAT ALL THE MUSIC AND ART AND STUFF DREW A WHOLE BUNCH OF TOURISTS AND LOCAL BUSINESSES COULD MAKE A TON OF MONEY.

UNFORTUNATELY, THE WHOLE THING LASTED ONLY SIX YEARS OR SO. MY GRANDMOTHER ASKED ALL THE ARTISTS TO MOVE OUT OF THE MANSION AND, A WHILE LATER, SHE LEFT TOO . . .

SHE NEVER EXPLAINED TO ME WHY EVERYTHING FELL APART. I THINK HER PARENTS DISAPPROVED OF HER LIFESTYLE BECAUSE THEY WANTED HER TO FIND A HUSBAND.

SHE MARRIED MY GRANDFATHER SHORTLY AFTERWARD AND HAD MY MOM. BUT THEY GOT DIVORCED A FEW YEARS LATER.

WHEN MY MOM GREW UP, SHE WANTED TO REOPEN THE PLACE. MY GRANDMOTHER HAD ALWAYS REGRETTED HAVING TO SHUT DOWN THE MANSION, AND SO . . .

AFTER MY MOM GOT MARRIED, SHE AND MY DAD DECIDED TO ACTUALLY DO IT. THEY KEPT EVERYTHING THAT THE ARTISTS HAD LEFT BEHIND AND BOUGHT A BUNCH OF OLD STUFF FROM FLEA MARKETS AND ANTIQUE STORES.

THEY HIT ON THE IDEA OF TURNING THE MANSION INTO A TOURIST ATTRACTION WITH RIDDLES FOR THE GUESTS TO SOLVE.

IT'S GOTTEN QUITE POPULAR, AND PEOPLE COME FROM ALL OVER TO HAVE FUN HERE. NOT ALL THE LOCALS LIKE THE CROWDS, BUT THEY'RE HAPPY TO GET THE TOURISTS' MONEY.

I IMAGINE SO!

WOW, WHAT A STORY! THANKS FOR TELLING IT TO US!

NO PROBLEM! IT'S NOT OFTEN THAT I GET TO MEET PEOPLE MY OWN AGE HERE . . .

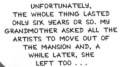

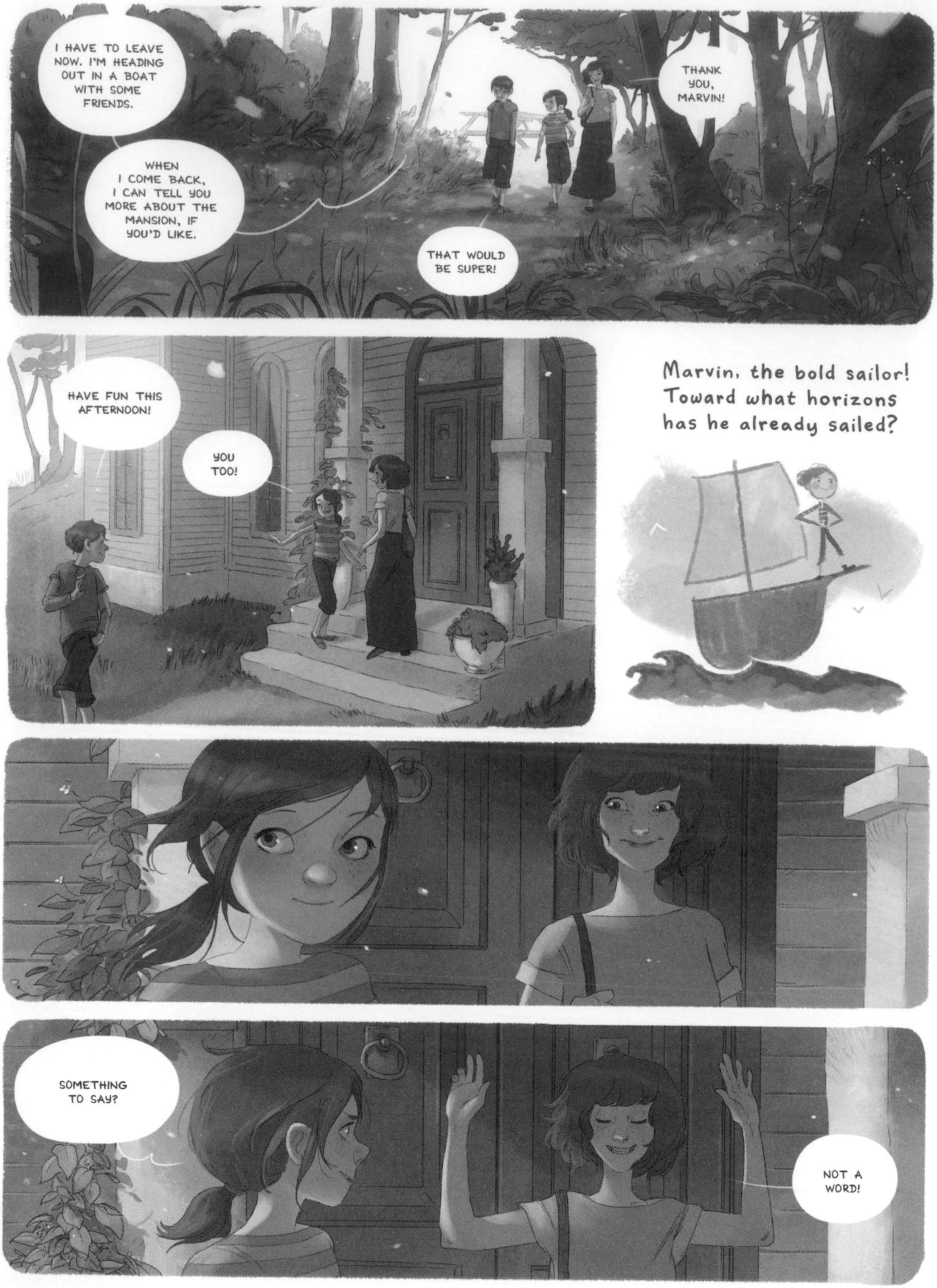
I HAVE TO LEAVE NOW. I'M HEADING OUT IN A BOAT WITH SOME FRIENDS.
WHEN I COME BACK, I CAN TELL YOU MORE ABOUT THE MANSION, IF YOU'D LIKE.
THANK YOU, MARVIN!
THAT WOULD BE SUPER!
HAVE FUN THIS AFTERNOON!
YOU TOO!
Marvin, the bold sailor! Toward what horizons has he already sailed?
SOMETHING TO SAY?
NOT A WORD!

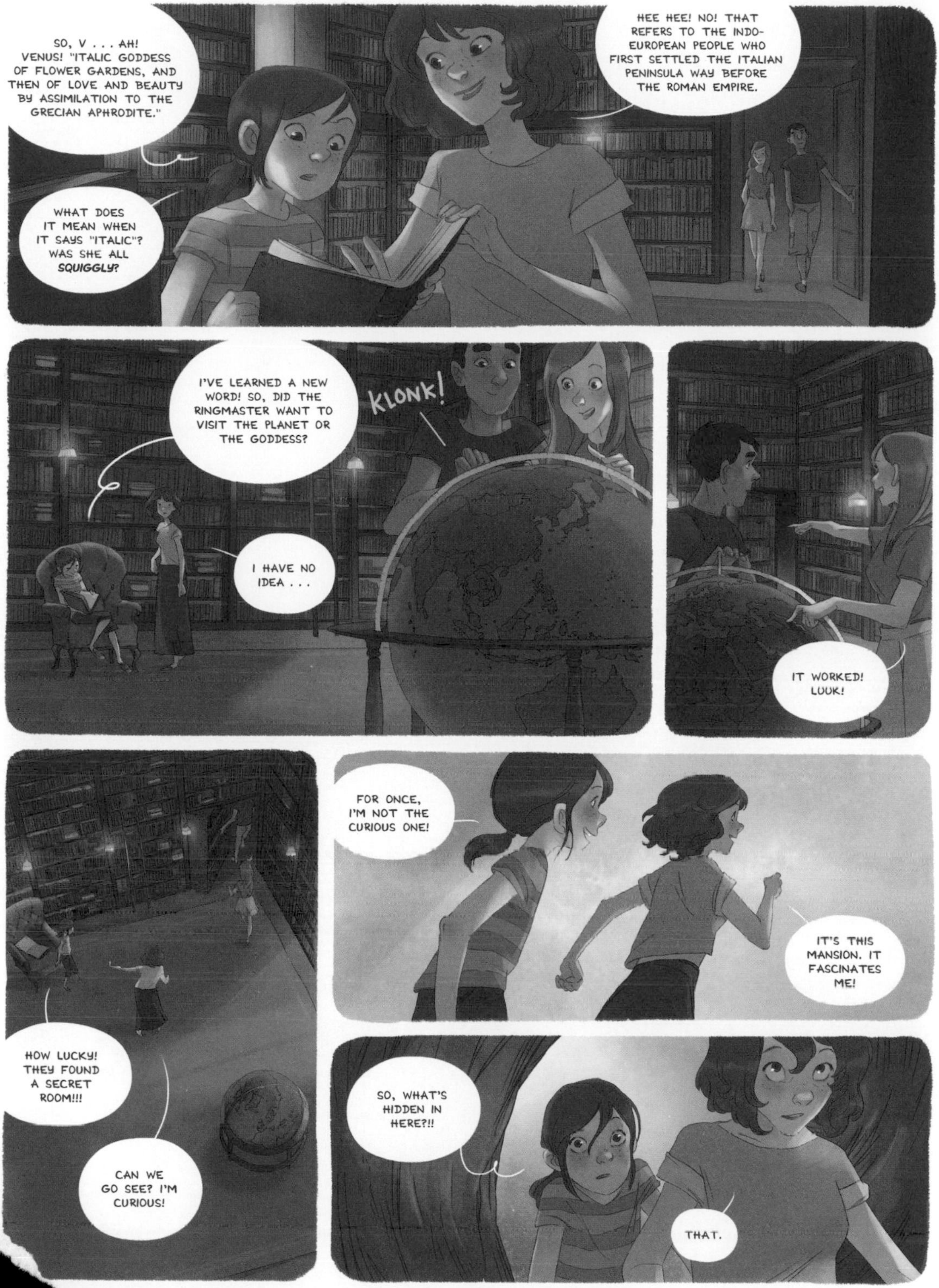
SO, V . . . AH! VENUS! "ITALIC GODDESS OF FLOWER GARDENS, AND THEN OF LOVE AND BEAUTY BY ASSIMILATION TO THE GRECIAN APHRODITE."
HEE HEE! NO! THAT REFERS TO THE INDO-EUROPEAN PEOPLE WHO FIRST SETTLED THE ITALIAN PENINSULA WAY BEFORE THE ROMAN EMPIRE.
WHAT DOES IT MEAN WHEN IT SAYS "ITALIC"? WAS SHE ALL SQUIGGLY?
I'VE LEARNED A NEW WORD! SO, DID THE RINGMASTER WANT TO VISIT THE PLANET OR THE GODDESS?
KLONK!
I HAVE NO IDEA . . .
IT WORKED! LOOK!
HOW LUCKY! THEY FOUND A SECRET ROOM!!!
CAN WE GO SEE? I'M CURIOUS!
FOR ONCE, I'M NOT THE CURIOUS ONE!
IT'S THIS MANSION. IT FASCINATES ME!
SO, WHAT'S HIDDEN IN HERE?!!
THAT.

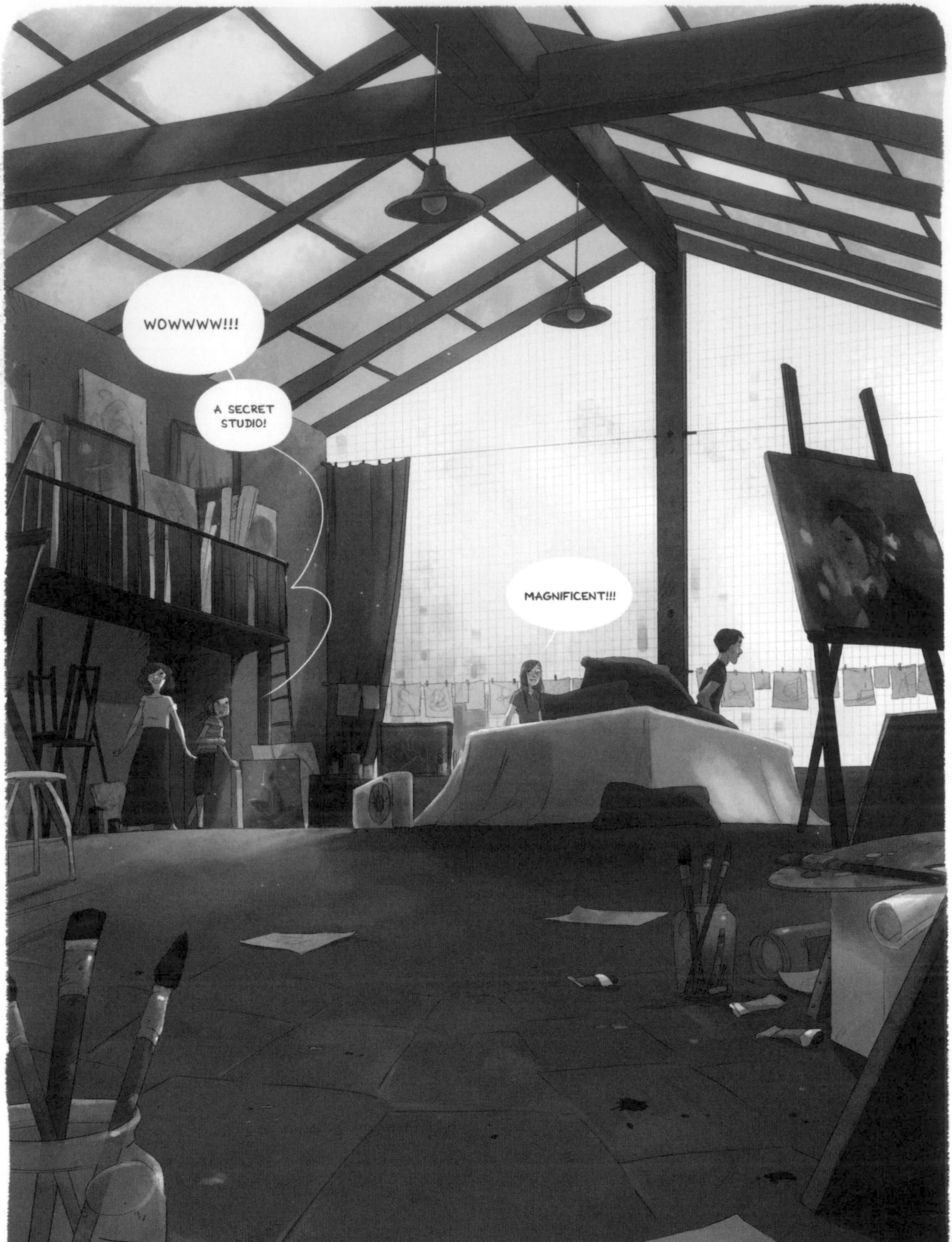
WOWWWW!!!
A SECRET STUDIO!
MAGNIFICENT!!!

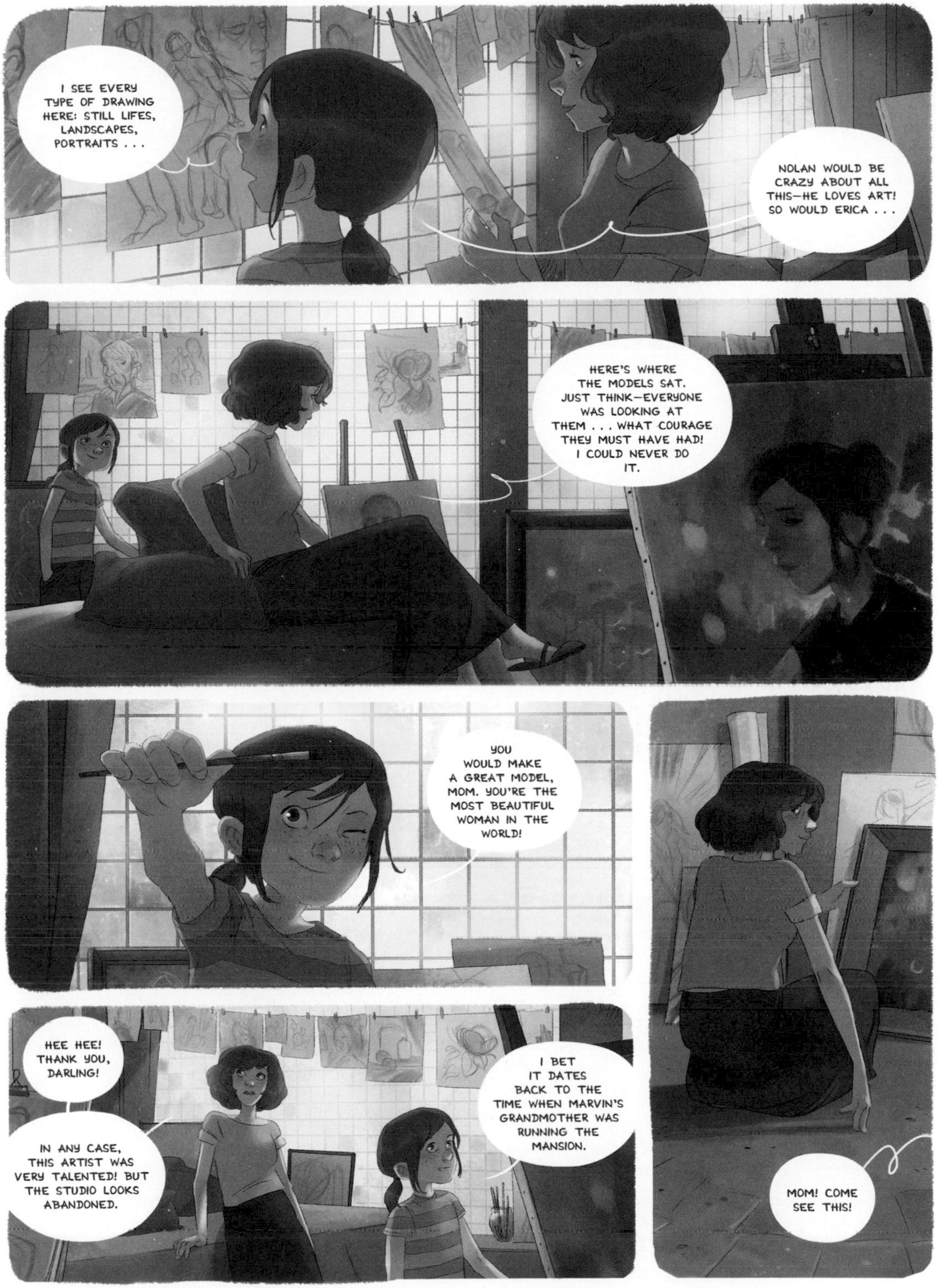
I SEE EVERY TYPE OF DRAWING HERE: STILL LIFES, LANDSCAPES, PORTRAITS . . .
NOLAN WOULD BE CRAZY ABOUT ALL THIS—HE LOVES ART! SO WOULD ERICA . . .
HERE'S WHERE THE MODELS SAT. JUST THINK—EVERYONE WAS LOOKING AT THEM . . . WHAT COURAGE THEY MUST HAVE HAD! I COULD NEVER DO IT.
YOU WOULD MAKE A GREAT MODEL, MOM. YOU'RE THE MOST BEAUTIFUL WOMAN IN THE WORLD!
HEE HEE! THANK YOU, DARLING!
IN ANY CASE, THIS ARTIST WAS VERY TALENTED! BUT THE STUDIO LOOKS ABANDONED.
I BET IT DATES BACK TO THE TIME WHEN MARVIN'S GRANDMOTHER WAS RUNNING THE MANSION.
MOM! COME SEE THIS!

LOVELY!

BUT WHAT A SHAME THAT PART OF IT WAS CUT OUT! SHE MUST HAVE BEEN VERY BEAUTIFUL FOR SOMEONE TO STEAL HER FACE.

LOOK AT THE TITLE!

OH!

LABELLEVÉNUS

WE FOUND HER!

MAYBE THE RINGMASTER ISN'T LOOKING FOR A GODDESS, BUT FOR THE WOMAN IN THIS PAINTING!

SO . . . ARE WE TALKING ABOUT A LOVE STORY?

PERHAPS! THE ONLY WAY WE'LL FIND OUT IS TO KEEP INVESTIGATING.

I hope we discover the missing face!

We took a photo of the painting. Right now it's our only clue.

We kept looking around the mansion until the end of the afternoon.

It's a truly incredible place. The light here is so distinctive!

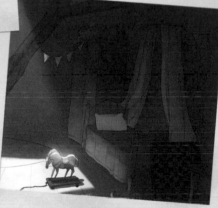

Mom got frightened by a bear that had been stuffed. :(Maybe he ate the missing piece of the painting!

Time passed very quickly. We really enjoyed ourselves—it was brilliant! Mom knows I've been a little depressed since Christmas, and she worked hard to make me forget what happened. I really want to talk with her about it! But whenever I start, I freeze up! Still though, we're spending quality time together, and that's what counts.

After touring the mansion, we went for a walk on the beach and ate at a restaurant. It was awesome! Then we went back to the cottage to rest. It's been a long day! Mom read her book while I drew an account of everything!.

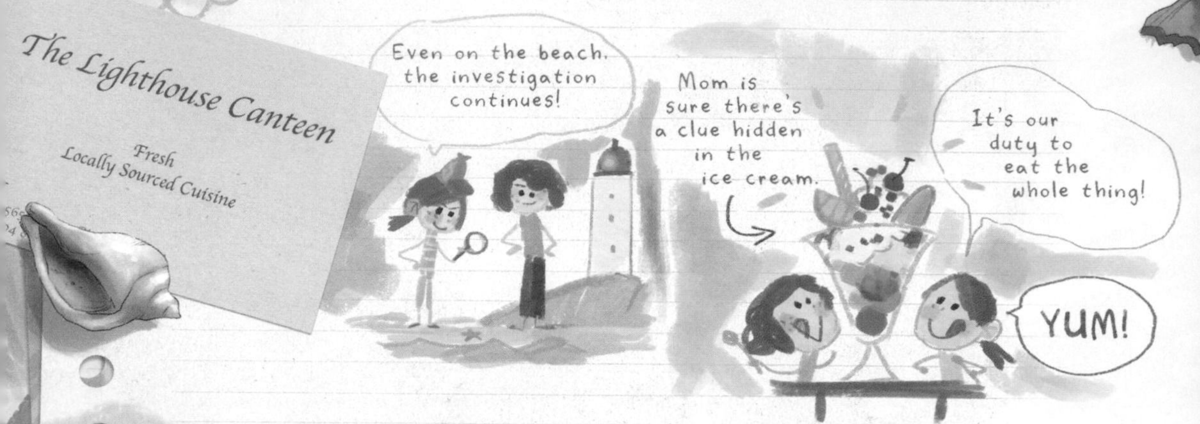

The Lighthouse Canteen
Fresh
Locally Sourced Cuisine
Even on the beach, the investigation continues!
Mom is sure there's a clue hidden in the ice cream.
It's our duty to eat the whole thing!
YUM!

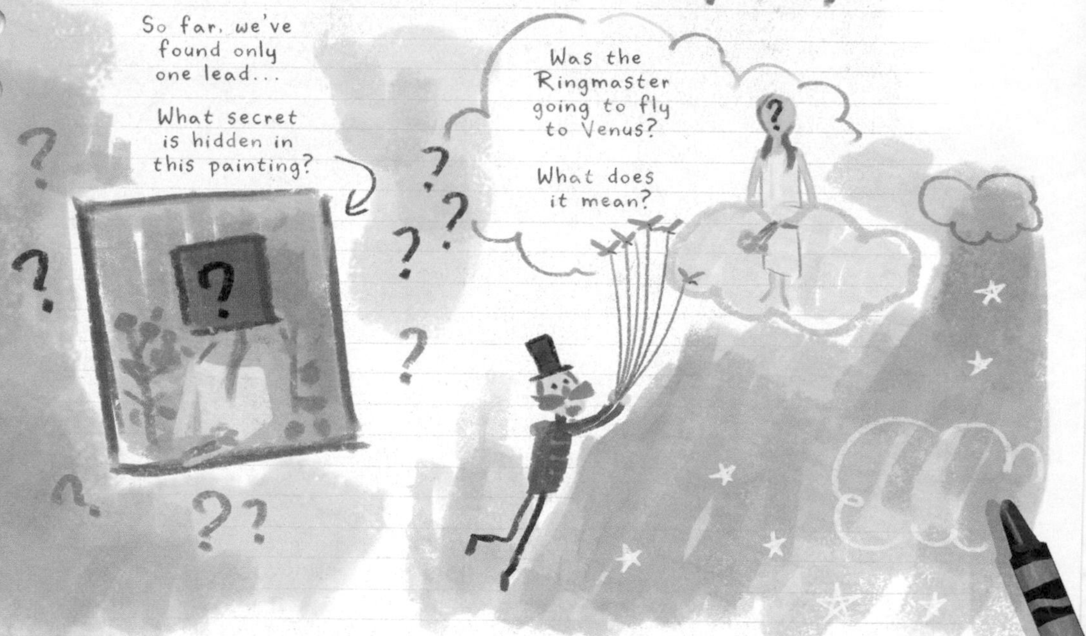

So far, we've found only one lead...
What secret is hidden in this painting?
Was the Ringmaster going to fly to Venus?
What does it mean?

Tomorrow we plan to visit the village. The brochure from the mansion says that certain shops there can help solve the riddles. I can't wait to go! And so we'll take a stroll around the harbor—that's gonna be super!

THE NEXT DAY . . .
souvenirs
MMM . . . SMELL THE FRESH SEA AIR!
Flowers
I LOVE THE FRAGRANCE OF THE FLOWERS HERE TOO!
ULYSSES WOULD LOVE THESE ARRANGEMENTS.
Art Gallery
LOOK HERE, CICI!
DOESN'T IT REMIND YOU OF OUR PAINTING?
YOU'RE RIGHT!! THIS ONE'S BY THE SAME PAINTER!
EXCUSE ME, SIR. CAN YOU TELL ME WHO PAINTED THESE PICTURES?
I'M VERY SORRY, LADIES, BUT THE ARTIST WISHES TO REMAIN ANONYMOUS.
JUST OUR LUCK!
So who are you, "mystery painter"?

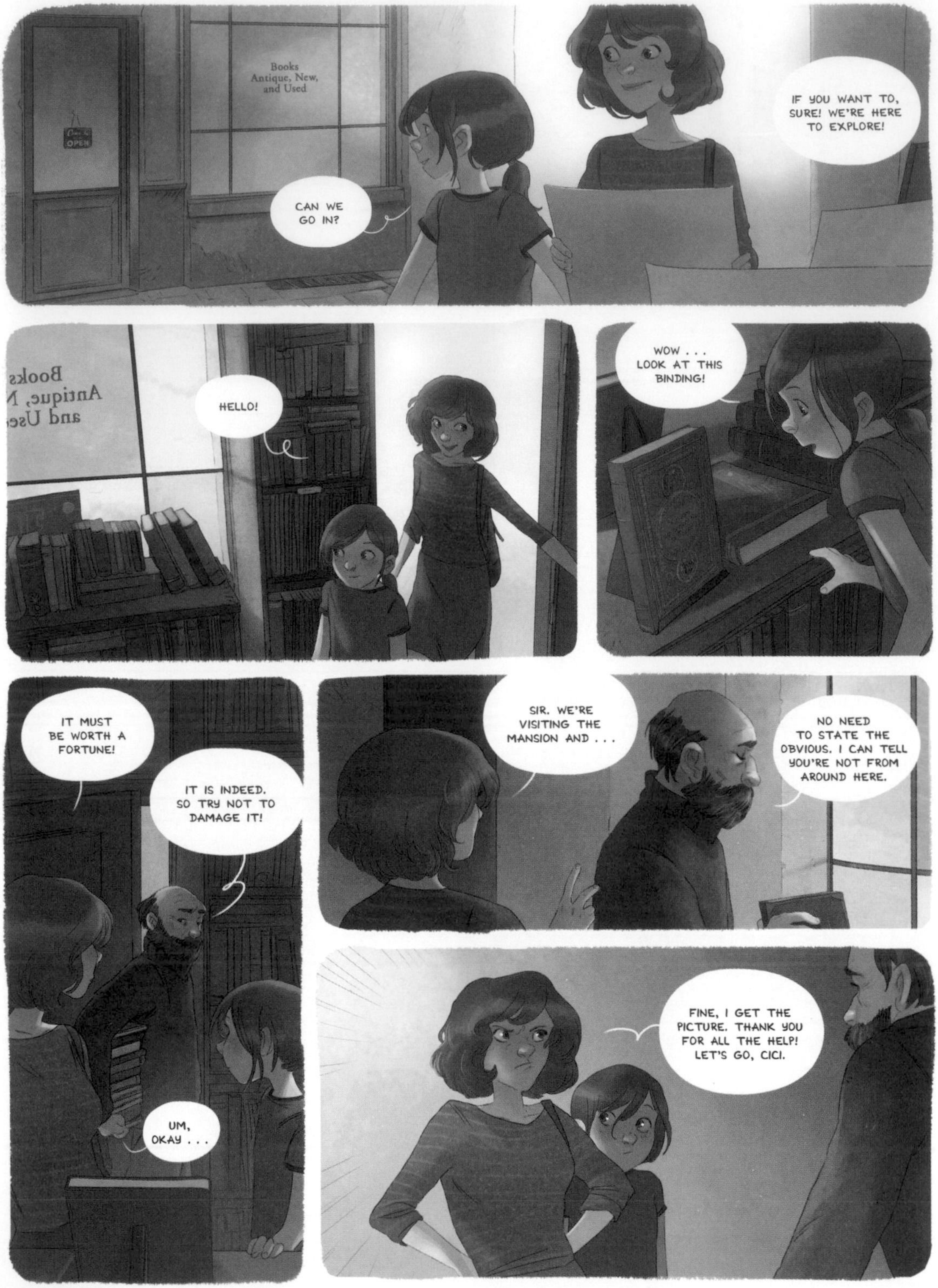

Books
Antique, New,
and Used
OPEN
CAN WE GO IN?
IF YOU WANT TO, SURE! WE'RE HERE TO EXPLORE!
HELLO!
WOW . . . LOOK AT THIS BINDING!
IT MUST BE WORTH A FORTUNE!
IT IS INDEED. SO TRY NOT TO DAMAGE IT!
UM, OKAY . . .
SIR. WE'RE VISITING THE MANSION AND . . .
NO NEED TO STATE THE OBVIOUS. I CAN TELL YOU'RE NOT FROM AROUND HERE.
FINE, I GET THE PICTURE. THANK YOU FOR ALL THE HELP! LET'S GO, CICI.

A LITTLE BIT LATER . . .

HONESTLY! HOW RUDE! WHAT'S UP WITH HIM?!

HEY! CICI! DOWN HERE!

MARVIN!

LET ME GUESS . . . DID YOU GO INTO THE BOOKSTORE? I BET YOU GOT A COLD RECEPTION. MR. GEORGES DOESN'T LIKE TOURISTS.

WE NOTICED! HE MUST NOT SELL MANY BOOKS.

SO YOU KNOW HIM?

EVERYONE AROUND HERE KNOWS HIM! HE'S AN OLD SOURPUSS—HE'S ALSO ANTHONY'S GREAT-UNCLE. HE SPENDS HIS TIME SHUT UP IN HIS OLD BOOKSTORE, STARING OUT THE WINDOW AND CURSING AT EVERYONE HE SEES.

After that, Marvin offered to take us on a little boat ride around the harbor. I accepted, but Mom said she needed to stock up on supplies before the big storm arrived.

We told her we had no idea what she meant and she just laughed . . .

She left me strict orders to always wear my life jacket and to return before 7:00.

THESE ARE MY FRIENDS! GWEN, HER BIG BROTHER YANNICK, AND ANTHONY. THIS IS CICI, THE ONE I TOLD YOU ABOUT YESTERDAY!

HI, EVERYONE!

HI, CICI!

WHAT DID YOUR MOM MEAN BY A BIG STORM?

NOT A CLUE! SHE'LL TELL ME WHAT SHE MEANT LATER.

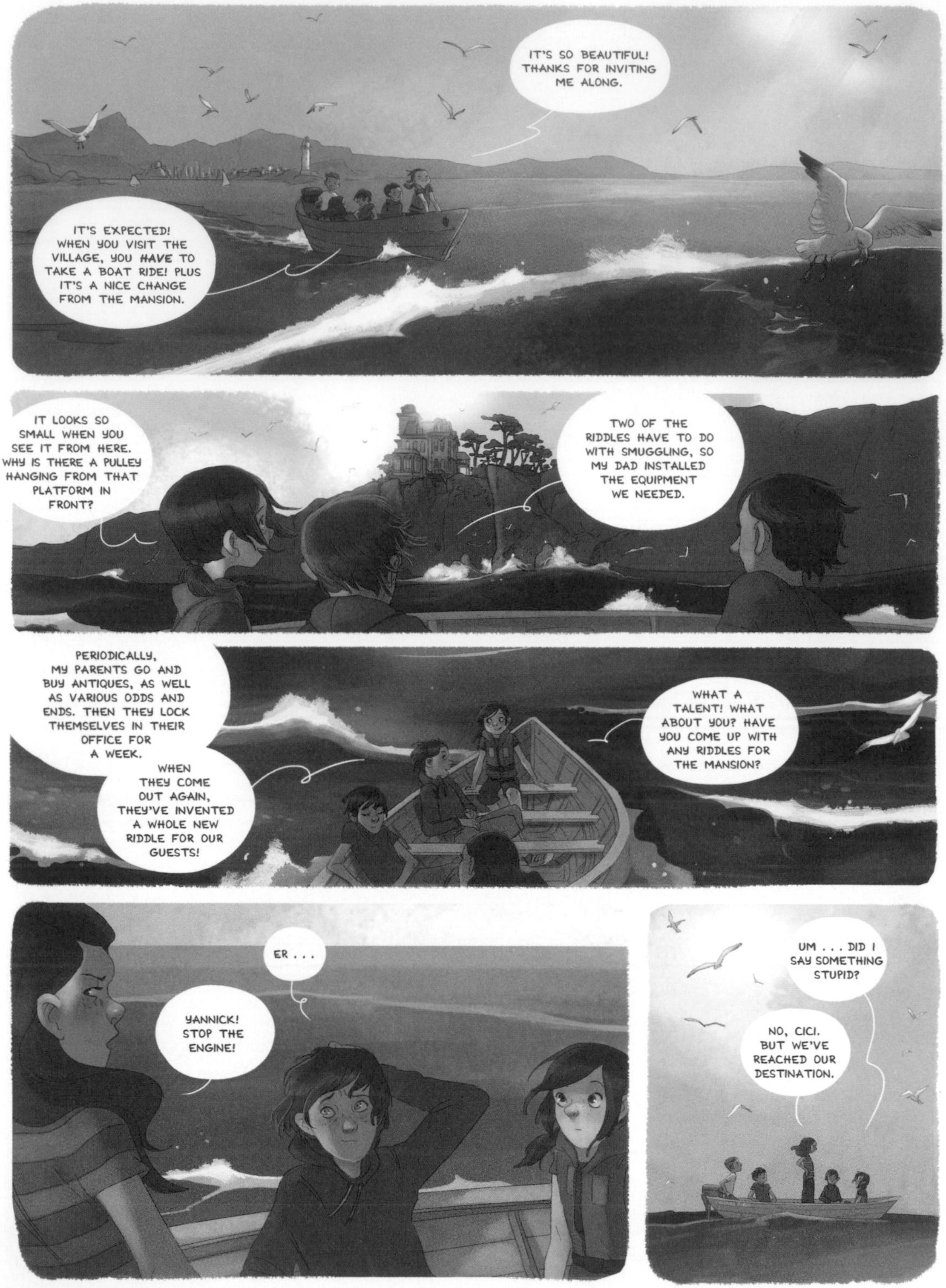
IT'S SO BEAUTIFUL! THANKS FOR INVITING ME ALONG.
IT'S EXPECTED! WHEN YOU VISIT THE VILLAGE, YOU HAVE TO TAKE A BOAT RIDE! PLUS IT'S A NICE CHANGE FROM THE MANSION.
IT LOOKS SO SMALL WHEN YOU SEE IT FROM HERE. WHY IS THERE A PULLEY HANGING FROM THAT PLATFORM IN FRONT?
TWO OF THE RIDDLES HAVE TO DO WITH SMUGGLING, SO MY DAD INSTALLED THE EQUIPMENT WE NEEDED.
PERIODICALLY, MY PARENTS GO AND BUY ANTIQUES, AS WELL AS VARIOUS ODDS AND ENDS. THEN THEY LOCK THEMSELVES IN THEIR OFFICE FOR A WEEK.
WHEN THEY COME OUT AGAIN, THEY'VE INVENTED A WHOLE NEW RIDDLE FOR OUR GUESTS!
WHAT A TALENT! WHAT ABOUT YOU? HAVE YOU COME UP WITH ANY RIDDLES FOR THE MANSION?
ER . . .
YANNICK! STOP THE ENGINE!
UM . . . DID I SAY SOMETHING STUPID?
NO, CICI. BUT WE'VE REACHED OUR DESTINATION.

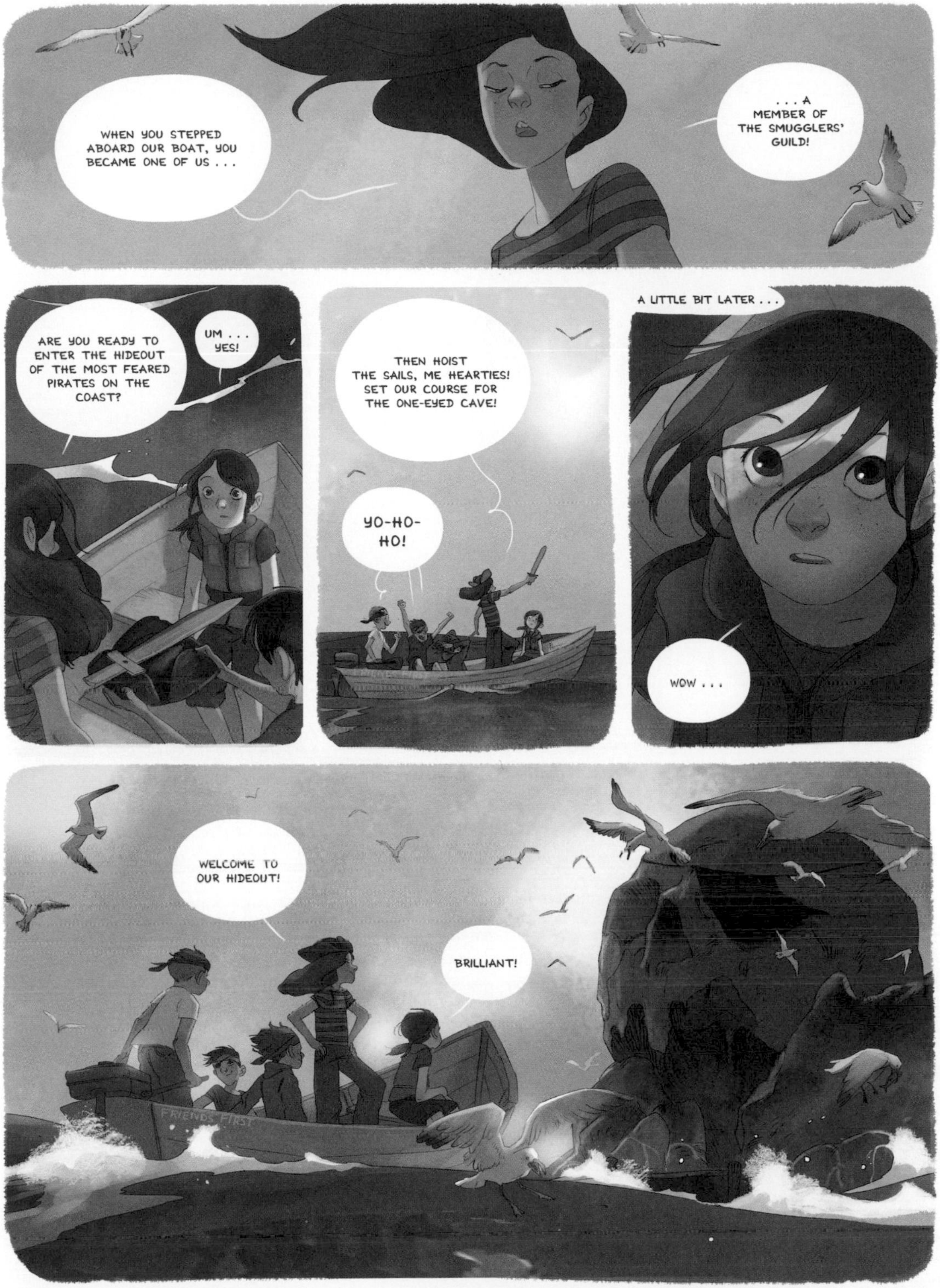
WHEN YOU STEPPED ABOARD OUR BOAT, YOU BECAME ONE OF US . . .
. . . A MEMBER OF THE SMUGGLERS' GUILD!
ARE YOU READY TO ENTER THE HIDEOUT OF THE MOST FEARED PIRATES ON THE COAST?
UM . . . YES!
THEN HOIST THE SAILS, ME HEARTIES! SET OUR COURSE FOR THE ONE-EYED CAVE!
YO-HO-HO!
A LITTLE BIT LATER . . .
WOW . . .
WELCOME TO OUR HIDEOUT!
BRILLIANT!
FRIENDS FIRST

Marvin and his friends have set up a real pirates' hideaway! It's part of a new riddle they're inventing for young people who visit the mansion!

BEWARE PIRATES!
ENTER AT YOUR OWN RISK!
ABANDON HOPE

While we were there, Anthony told me about his great-uncle, the bookstore owner. According to his parents, it was a failed romance that made Mr. Georges so bitter. At one time, he was one of the artists who lived at the mansion. He fell in love with Marvin's grandmother, but things didn't work out.

I also discovered why he's always looking out the window of his shop—he wants to see how his paintings are selling. ***He*** painted our central clue—"La Belle Vénus"! I have a hard time imagining him as a painter . . .

GRR
GRR
GRR
GRR
GRR

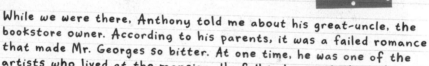

According to Anthony, Mr. Georges keeps the missing piece of our painting in his office. I asked if Mr. Georges would let me see it, but Anthony shook his head. What a shame! He's going to ask anyway, though. One last surprise: Marvin didn't even know our painting was in the mansion!

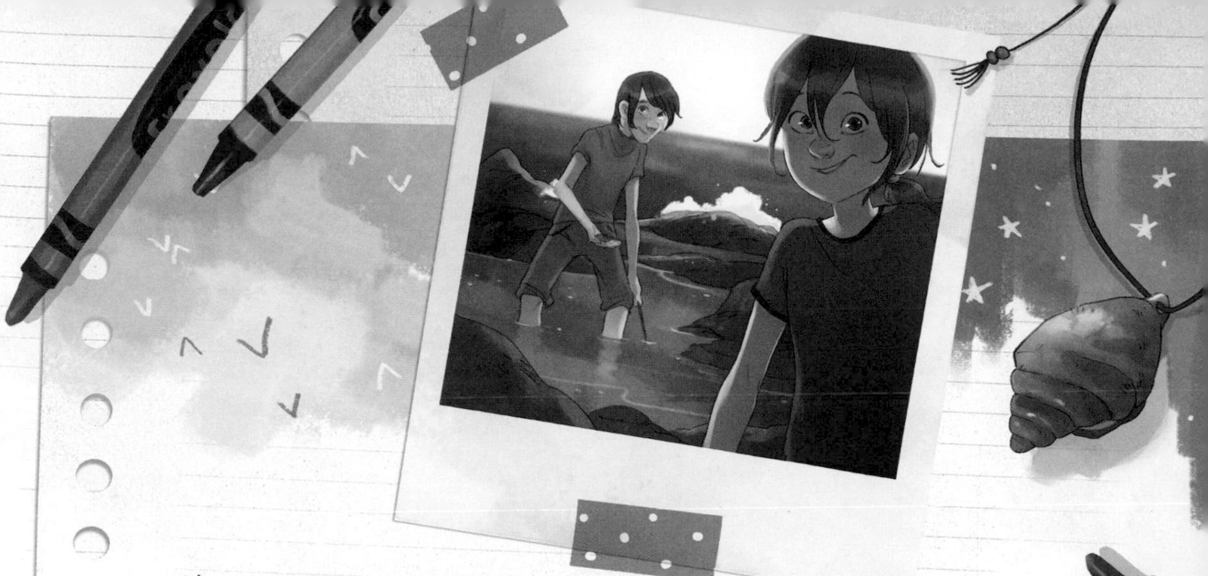

We spent a super afternoon on the Smugglers' Guild's island. I visited their secret cave and we climbed on the oceanside rocks. Anthony found a pretty shell and made it into a necklace; then he gave it to me as a souvenir! Finally, we had to leave so we could get back before it got dark.

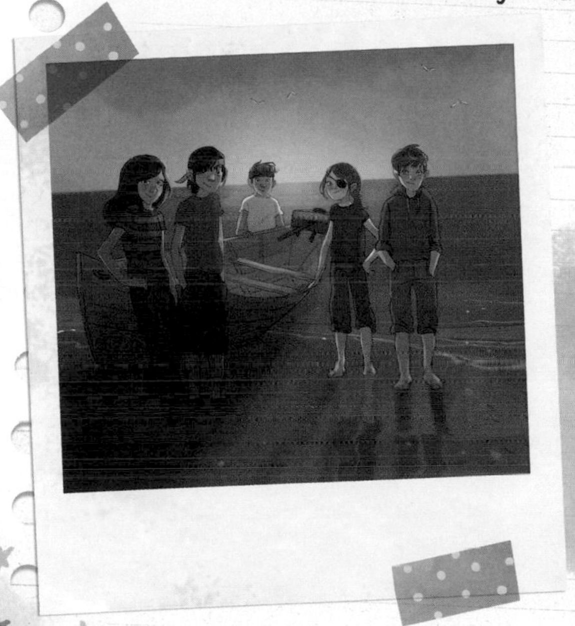

Marvin promised to show me some of the secret places in the mansion tomorrow.

I can't wait!

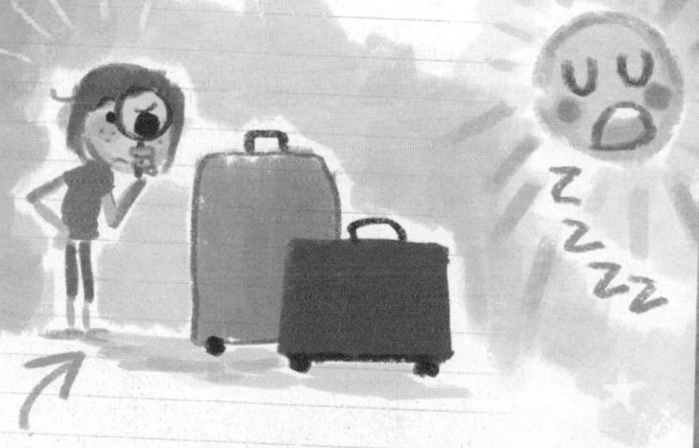

When I reached the cottage, a new mystery was waiting for me: two unknown suitcases were standing in the middle of the entryway. There's no way Mom had done that much shopping! Then, another mystery: there was no trace of Mom. Where was she hiding? I approached my room and heard whispers. At last I figured out what she meant about a storm. A veritable hurricane had entered my room!

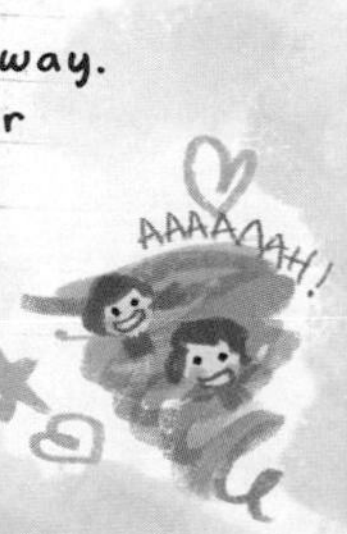
AAAAAAH!

THE SEATS ON THE TRAIN WERE SO UNCOMFORTABLE! MY BACK IS SORE!

HI, CICI!

LENA! ERICA! YOU'RE HERE! I'M SO HAPPY!!!

YOU DIDN'T THINK YOU WERE GOING TO SOLVE THOSE MYSTERIES WITHOUT US, DID YOU?

I WANTED IT TO BE A SURPRISE, SO I PICKED THEM UP AT THE RAILWAY STATION THIS AFTERNOON.

I HAVE TO THANK MARVIN FOR GIVING ME SUCH A GOOD EXCUSE TO GO OFF BY MYSELF!

THANKS, MOM! THIS IS AMAZING!

WE CAN ONLY STAY FOR TWO DAYS. I HAVE A DANCE RECITAL, AND ERICA HAS A GAME ON SATURDAY AFTERNOON.

I BROUGHT YOUR HAT, THOUGH—YOU ACCIDENTALLY LEFT IT AT MY HOUSE!

YOU GIRLS CHAT FOR A WHILE. I'LL GO MAKE DINNER!

SO, TELL US ABOUT THE MANSION!

AND WHO IS MARVIN?!

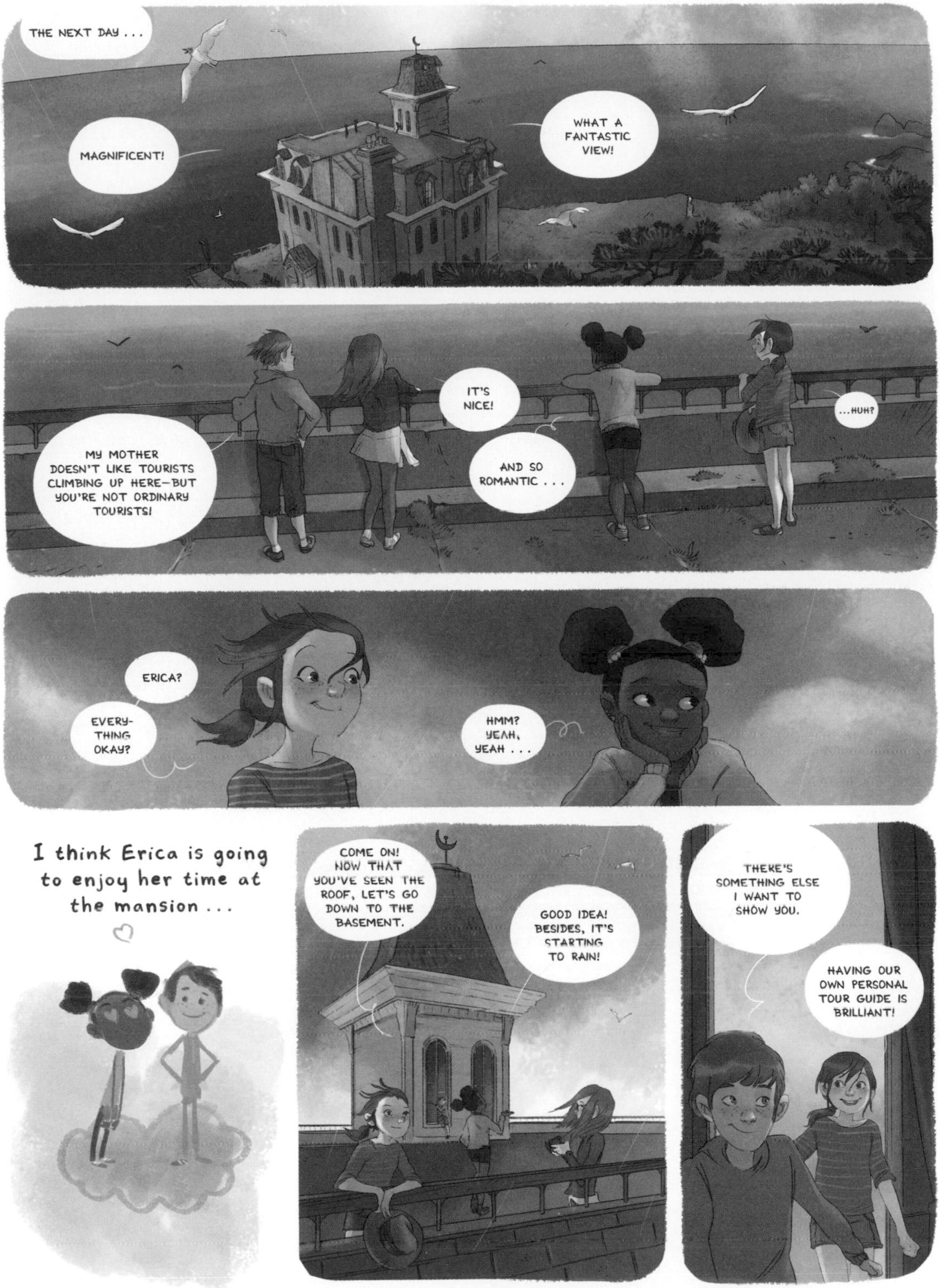
THE NEXT DAY . . .
MAGNIFICENT!
WHAT A FANTASTIC VIEW!
MY MOTHER DOESN'T LIKE TOURISTS CLIMBING UP HERE—BUT YOU'RE NOT ORDINARY TOURISTS!
IT'S NICE!
AND SO ROMANTIC . . .
. . . HUH?
ERICA?
EVERY-THING OKAY?
HMM? YEAH, YEAH . . .
I think Erica is going to enjoy her time at the mansion . . .
COME ON! NOW THAT YOU'VE SEEN THE ROOF, LET'S GO DOWN TO THE BASEMENT.
GOOD IDEA! BESIDES, IT'S STARTING TO RAIN!
THERE'S SOMETHING ELSE I WANT TO SHOW YOU.
HAVING OUR OWN PERSONAL TOUR GUIDE IS BRILLIANT!

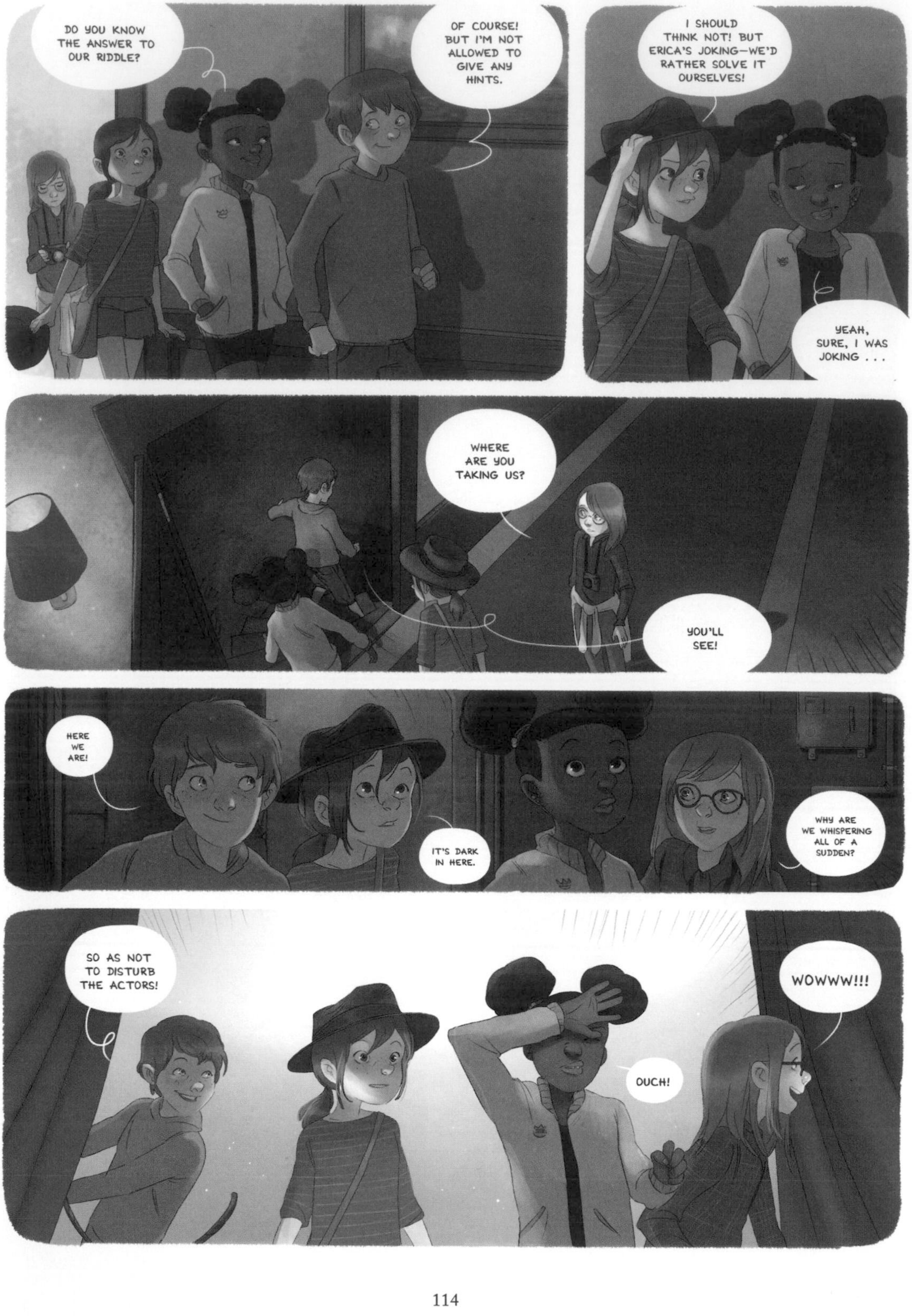
DO YOU KNOW THE ANSWER TO OUR RIDDLE?
OF COURSE! BUT I'M NOT ALLOWED TO GIVE ANY HINTS.
I SHOULD THINK NOT! BUT ERICA'S JOKING—WE'D RATHER SOLVE IT OURSELVES!
YEAH, SURE, I WAS JOKING . . .
WHERE ARE YOU TAKING US?
YOU'LL SEE!
HERE WE ARE!
IT'S DARK IN HERE.
WHY ARE WE WHISPERING ALL OF A SUDDEN?
SO AS NOT TO DISTURB THE ACTORS!
OUCH!
WOWWW!!!

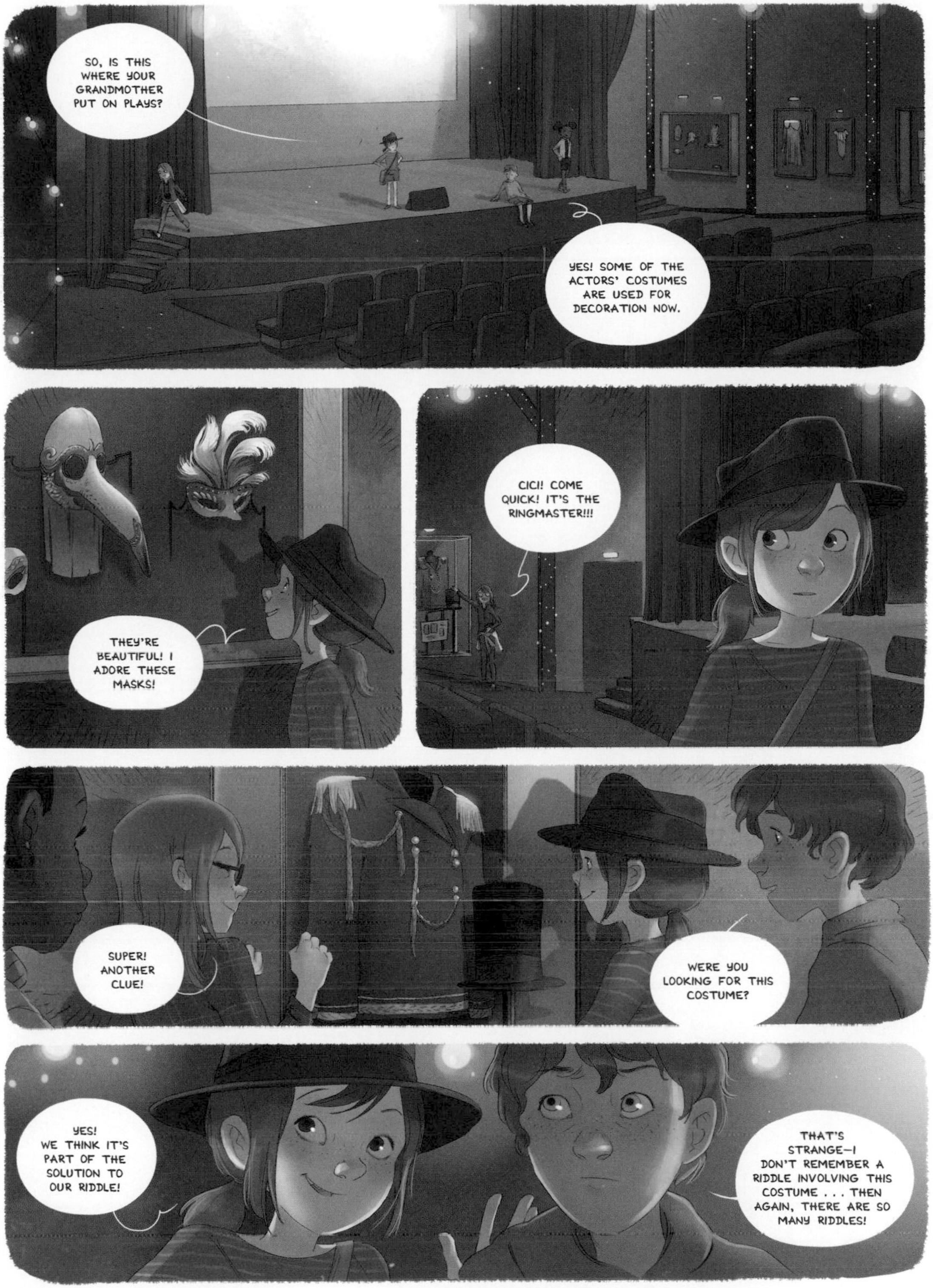
SO, IS THIS WHERE YOUR GRANDMOTHER PUT ON PLAYS?
YES! SOME OF THE ACTORS' COSTUMES ARE USED FOR DECORATION NOW.
THEY'RE BEAUTIFUL! I ADORE THESE MASKS!
CICI! COME QUICK! IT'S THE RINGMASTER!!!
SUPER! ANOTHER CLUE!
WERE YOU LOOKING FOR THIS COSTUME?
YES! WE THINK IT'S PART OF THE SOLUTION TO OUR RIDDLE!
THAT'S STRANGE—I DON'T REMEMBER A RIDDLE INVOLVING THIS COSTUME . . . THEN AGAIN, THERE ARE SO MANY RIDDLES!

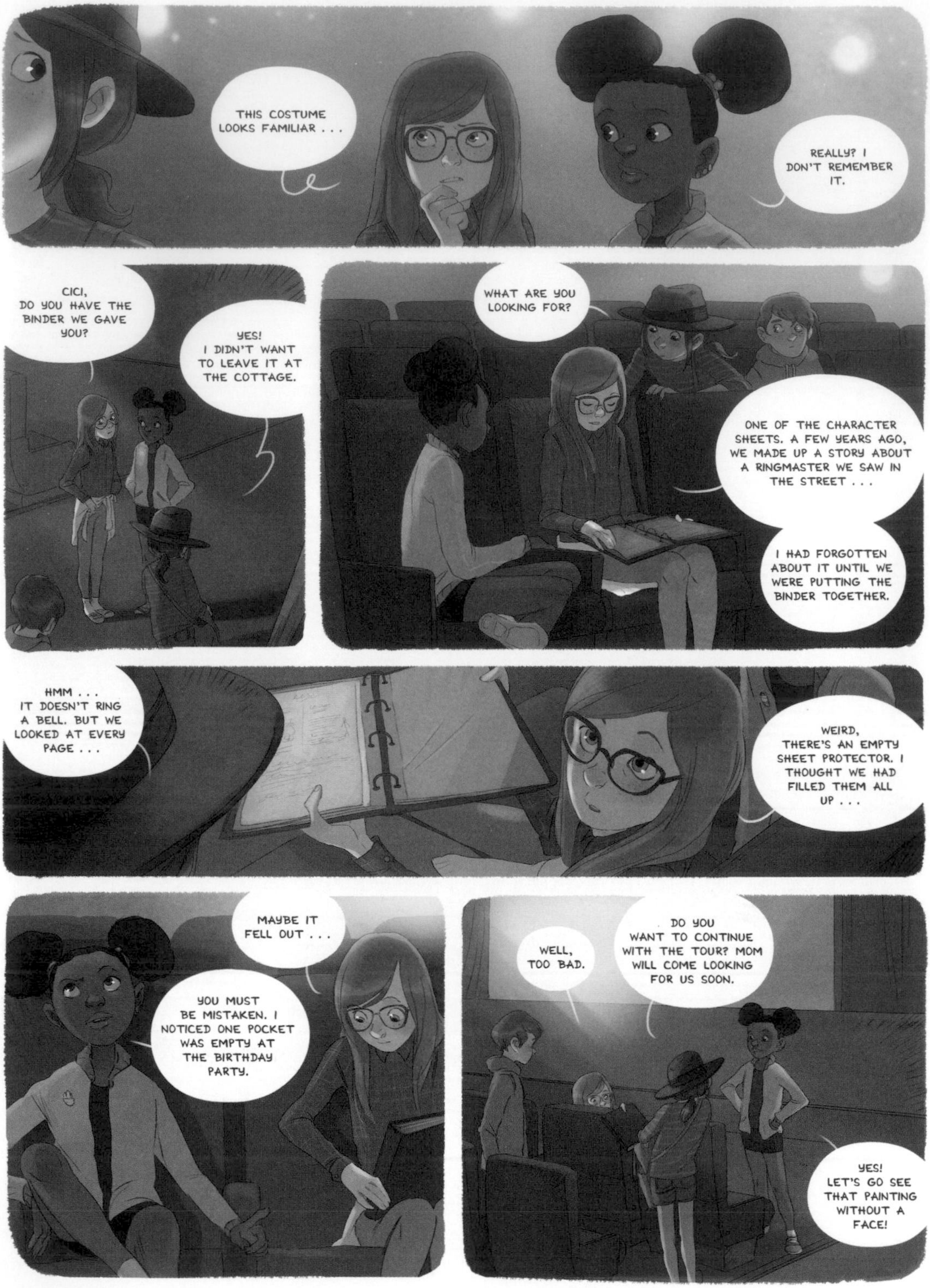
THIS COSTUME LOOKS FAMILIAR . . .
REALLY? I DON'T REMEMBER IT.
CICI, DO YOU HAVE THE BINDER WE GAVE YOU?
YES! I DIDN'T WANT TO LEAVE IT AT THE COTTAGE.
WHAT ARE YOU LOOKING FOR?
ONE OF THE CHARACTER SHEETS. A FEW YEARS AGO, WE MADE UP A STORY ABOUT A RINGMASTER WE SAW IN THE STREET . . .
I HAD FORGOTTEN ABOUT IT UNTIL WE WERE PUTTING THE BINDER TOGETHER.
HMM . . . IT DOESN'T RING A BELL. BUT WE LOOKED AT EVERY PAGE . . .
WEIRD, THERE'S AN EMPTY SHEET PROTECTOR. I THOUGHT WE HAD FILLED THEM ALL UP . . .
MAYBE IT FELL OUT . . .
YOU MUST BE MISTAKEN. I NOTICED ONE POCKET WAS EMPTY AT THE BIRTHDAY PARTY.
WELL, TOO BAD.
DO YOU WANT TO CONTINUE WITH THE TOUR? MOM WILL COME LOOKING FOR US SOON.
YES! LET'S GO SEE THAT PAINTING WITHOUT A FACE!

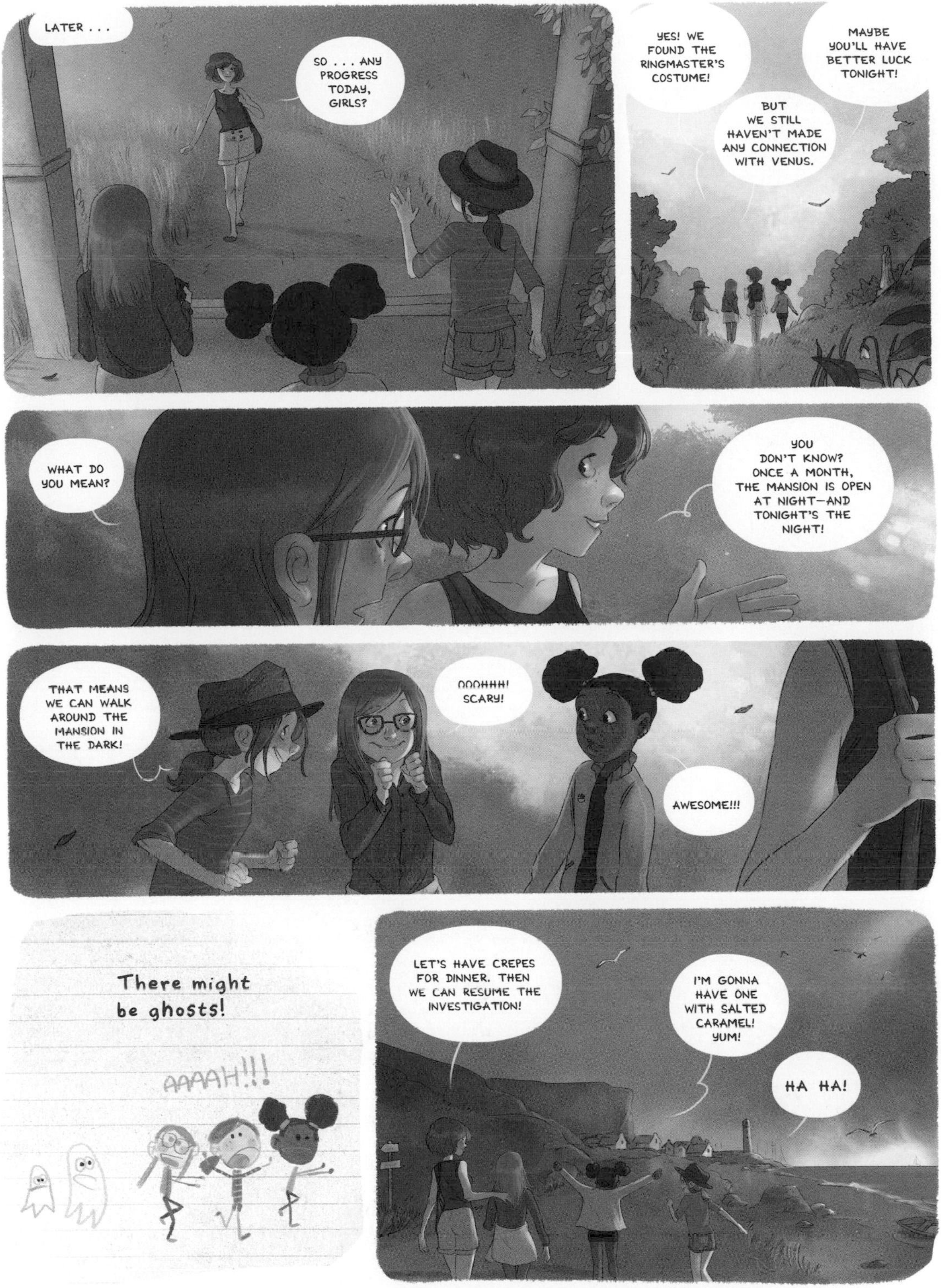
LATER . . .
SO . . . ANY PROGRESS TODAY, GIRLS?
YES! WE FOUND THE RINGMASTER'S COSTUME!
BUT WE STILL HAVEN'T MADE ANY CONNECTION WITH VENUS.
MAYBE YOU'LL HAVE BETTER LUCK TONIGHT!
WHAT DO YOU MEAN?
YOU DON'T KNOW? ONCE A MONTH, THE MANSION IS OPEN AT NIGHT—AND TONIGHT'S THE NIGHT!
THAT MEANS WE CAN WALK AROUND THE MANSION IN THE DARK!
OOOHHH! SCARY!
AWESOME!!!
There might be ghosts!
AAAAH!!!
LET'S HAVE CREPES FOR DINNER. THEN WE CAN RESUME THE INVESTIGATION!
I'M GONNA HAVE ONE WITH SALTED CARAMEL! YUM!
HA HA!

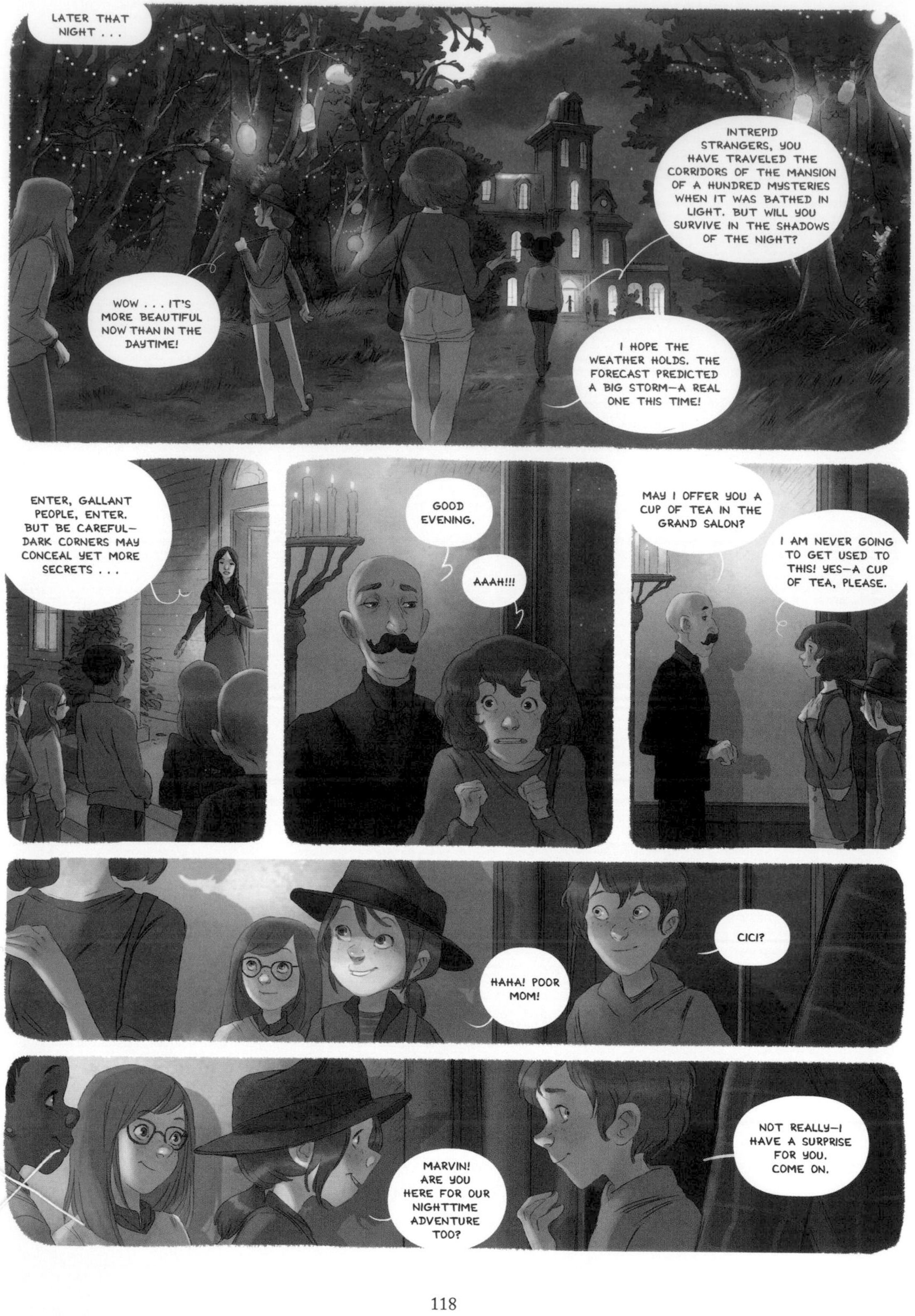
LATER THAT NIGHT . . .
INTREPID STRANGERS, YOU HAVE TRAVELED THE CORRIDORS OF THE MANSION OF A HUNDRED MYSTERIES WHEN IT WAS BATHED IN LIGHT. BUT WILL YOU SURVIVE IN THE SHADOWS OF THE NIGHT?
WOW . . . IT'S MORE BEAUTIFUL NOW THAN IN THE DAYTIME!
I HOPE THE WEATHER HOLDS. THE FORECAST PREDICTED A BIG STORM—A REAL ONE THIS TIME!
ENTER, GALLANT PEOPLE, ENTER. BUT BE CAREFUL—DARK CORNERS MAY CONCEAL YET MORE SECRETS . . .
GOOD EVENING.
AAAH!!!
MAY I OFFER YOU A CUP OF TEA IN THE GRAND SALON?
I AM NEVER GOING TO GET USED TO THIS! YES—A CUP OF TEA, PLEASE.
CICI?
HAHA! POOR MOM!
MARVIN! ARE YOU HERE FOR OUR NIGHTTIME ADVENTURE TOO?
NOT REALLY—I HAVE A SURPRISE FOR YOU. COME ON.

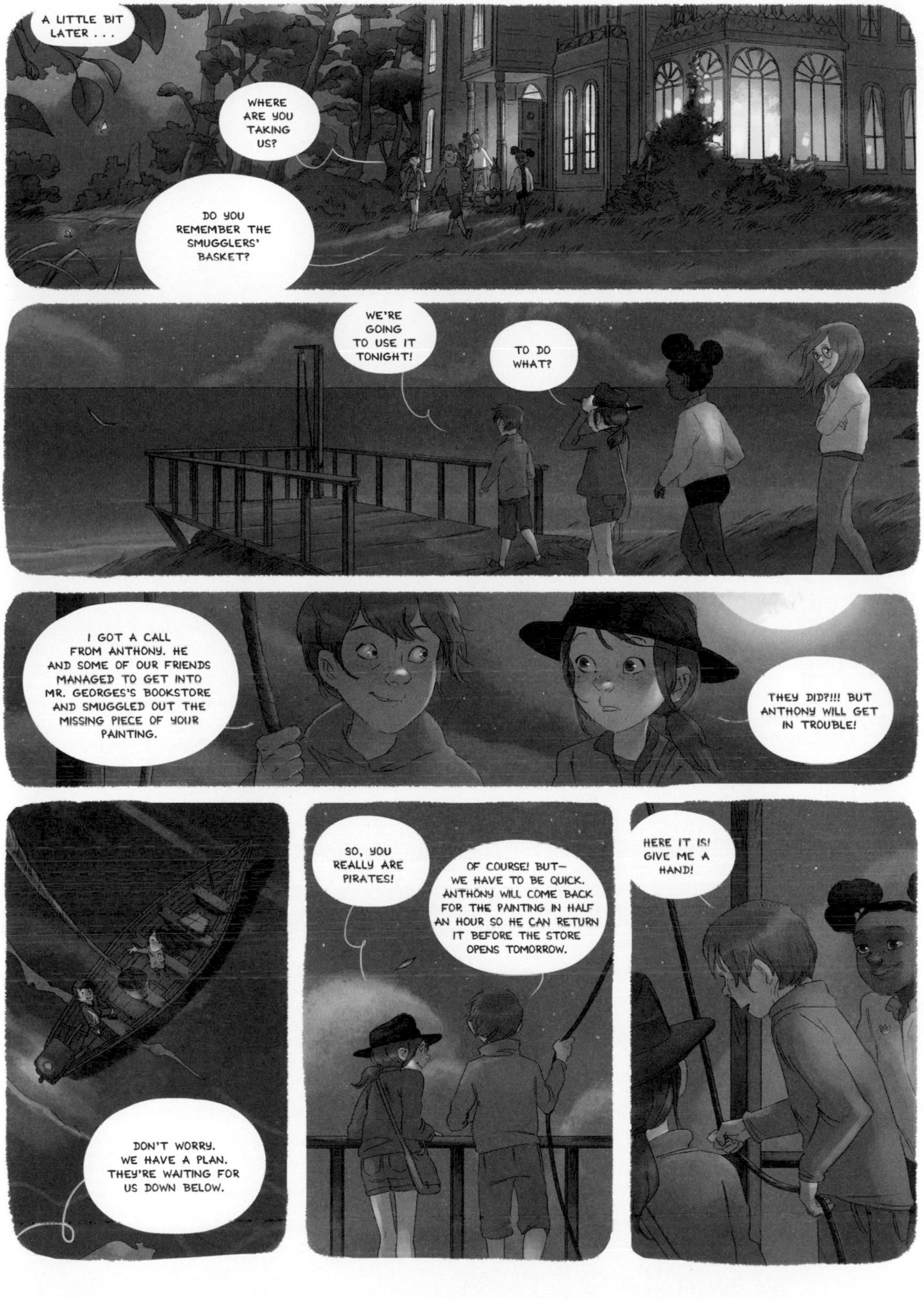
A LITTLE BIT LATER . . .
WHERE ARE YOU TAKING US?
DO YOU REMEMBER THE SMUGGLERS' BASKET?
WE'RE GOING TO USE IT TONIGHT!
TO DO WHAT?
I GOT A CALL FROM ANTHONY. HE AND SOME OF OUR FRIENDS MANAGED TO GET INTO MR. GEORGES'S BOOKSTORE AND SMUGGLED OUT THE MISSING PIECE OF YOUR PAINTING.
THEY DID?!!! BUT ANTHONY WILL GET IN TROUBLE!
DON'T WORRY. WE HAVE A PLAN. THEY'RE WAITING FOR US DOWN BELOW.
SO, YOU REALLY ARE PIRATES!
OF COURSE! BUT— WE HAVE TO BE QUICK. ANTHONY WILL COME BACK FOR THE PAINTING IN HALF AN HOUR SO HE CAN RETURN IT BEFORE THE STORE OPENS TOMORROW.
HERE IT IS! GIVE ME A HAND!

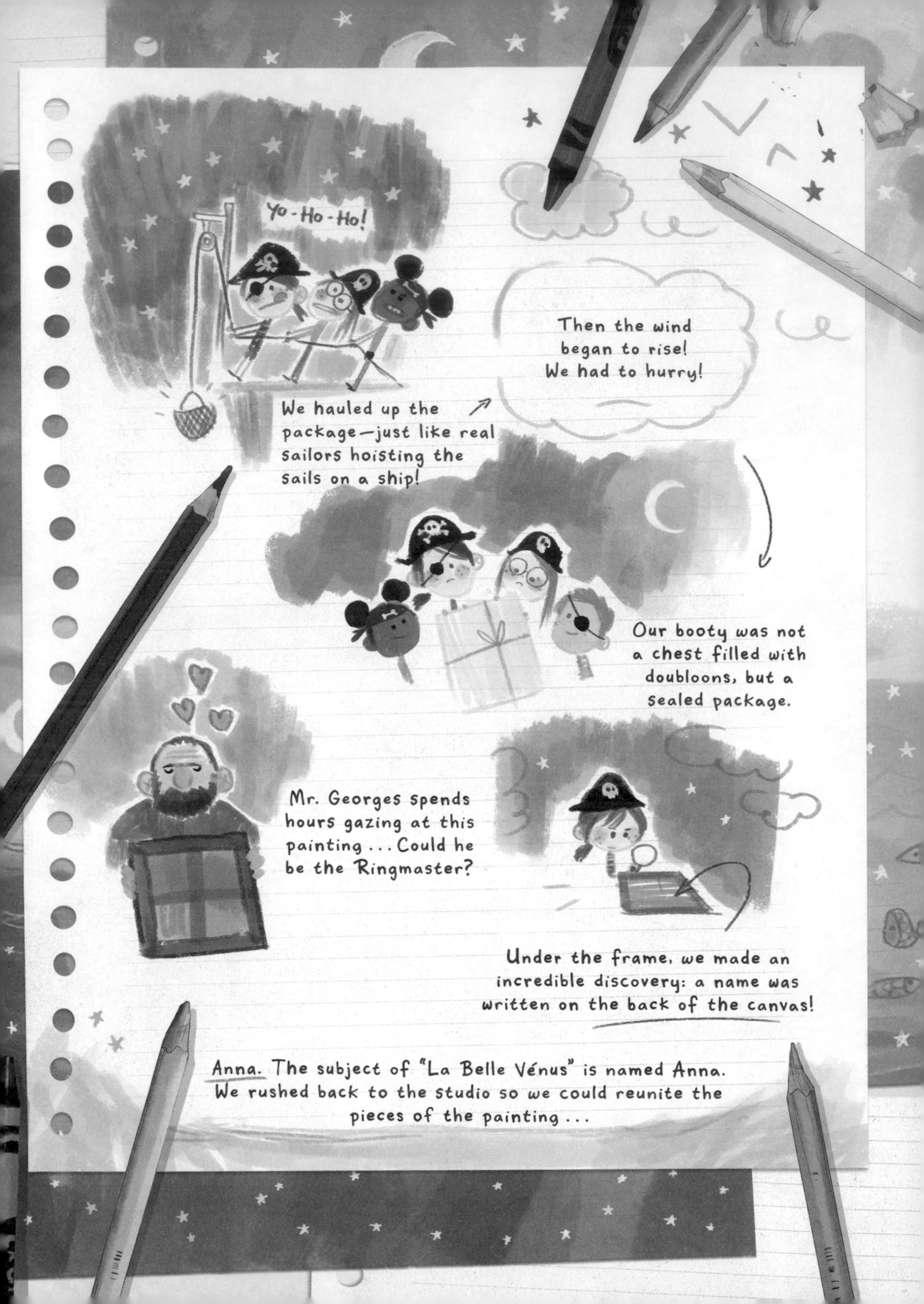
Yo-Ho-Ho!
We hauled up the package—just like real sailors hoisting the sails on a ship!
Then the wind began to rise! We had to hurry!
Our booty was not a chest filled with doubloons, but a sealed package.
Mr. Georges spends hours gazing at this painting . . . Could he be the Ringmaster?
Under the frame, we made an incredible discovery: a name was written on the back of the canvas!
Anna. The subject of "La Belle Vénus" is named Anna. We rushed back to the studio so we could reunite the pieces of the painting . . .

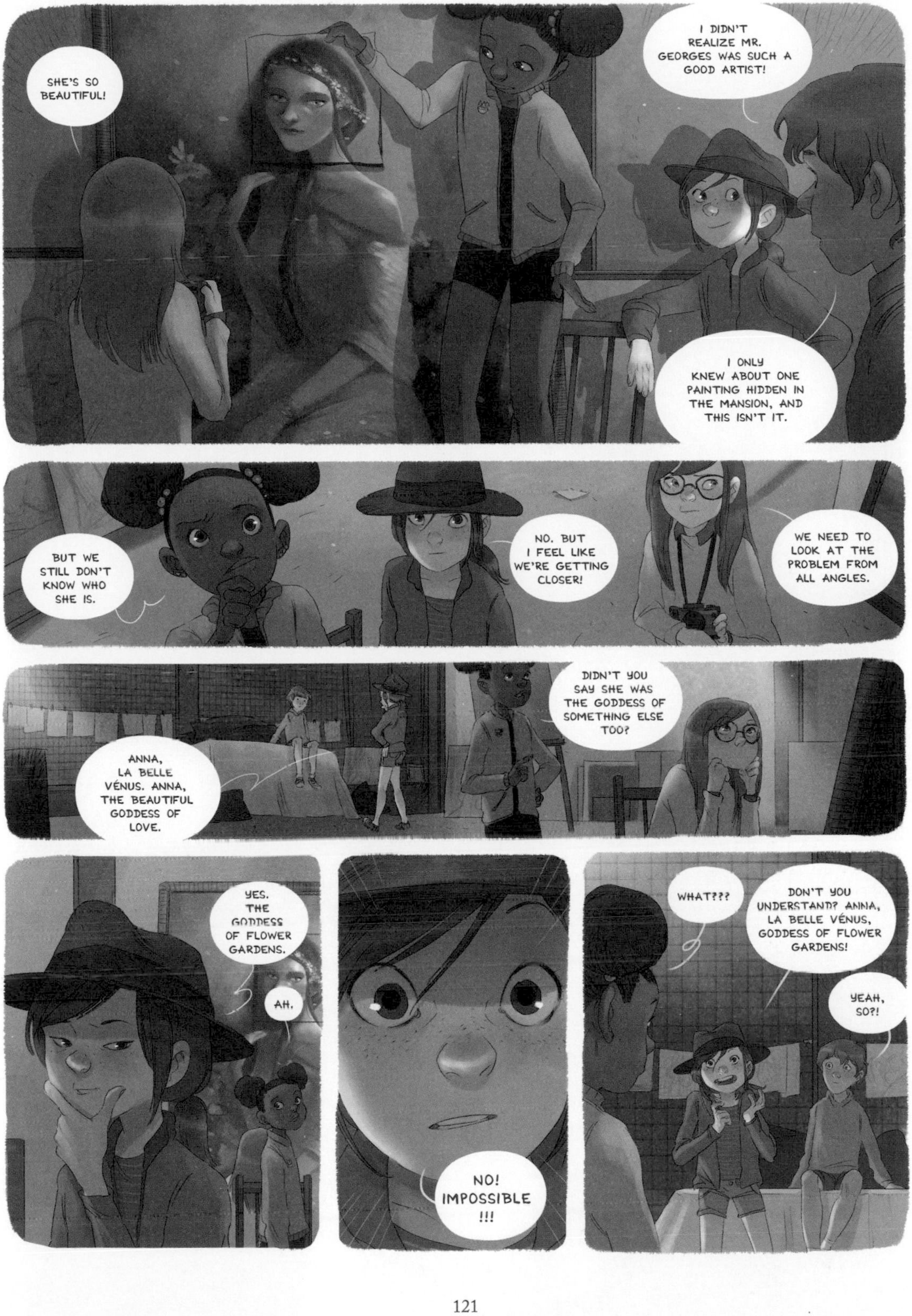
SHE'S SO BEAUTIFUL!
I DIDN'T REALIZE MR. GEORGES WAS SUCH A GOOD ARTIST!
I ONLY KNEW ABOUT ONE PAINTING HIDDEN IN THE MANSION, AND THIS ISN'T IT.
BUT WE STILL DON'T KNOW WHO SHE IS.
NO. BUT I FEEL LIKE WE'RE GETTING CLOSER!
WE NEED TO LOOK AT THE PROBLEM FROM ALL ANGLES.
DIDN'T YOU SAY SHE WAS THE GODDESS OF SOMETHING ELSE TOO?
ANNA, LA BELLE VÉNUS. ANNA, THE BEAUTIFUL GODDESS OF LOVE.
YES. THE GODDESS OF FLOWER GARDENS.
AH.
NO! IMPOSSIBLE !!!
WHAT???
DON'T YOU UNDERSTAND? ANNA, LA BELLE VÉNUS, GODDESS OF FLOWER GARDENS!
YEAH, SO?!

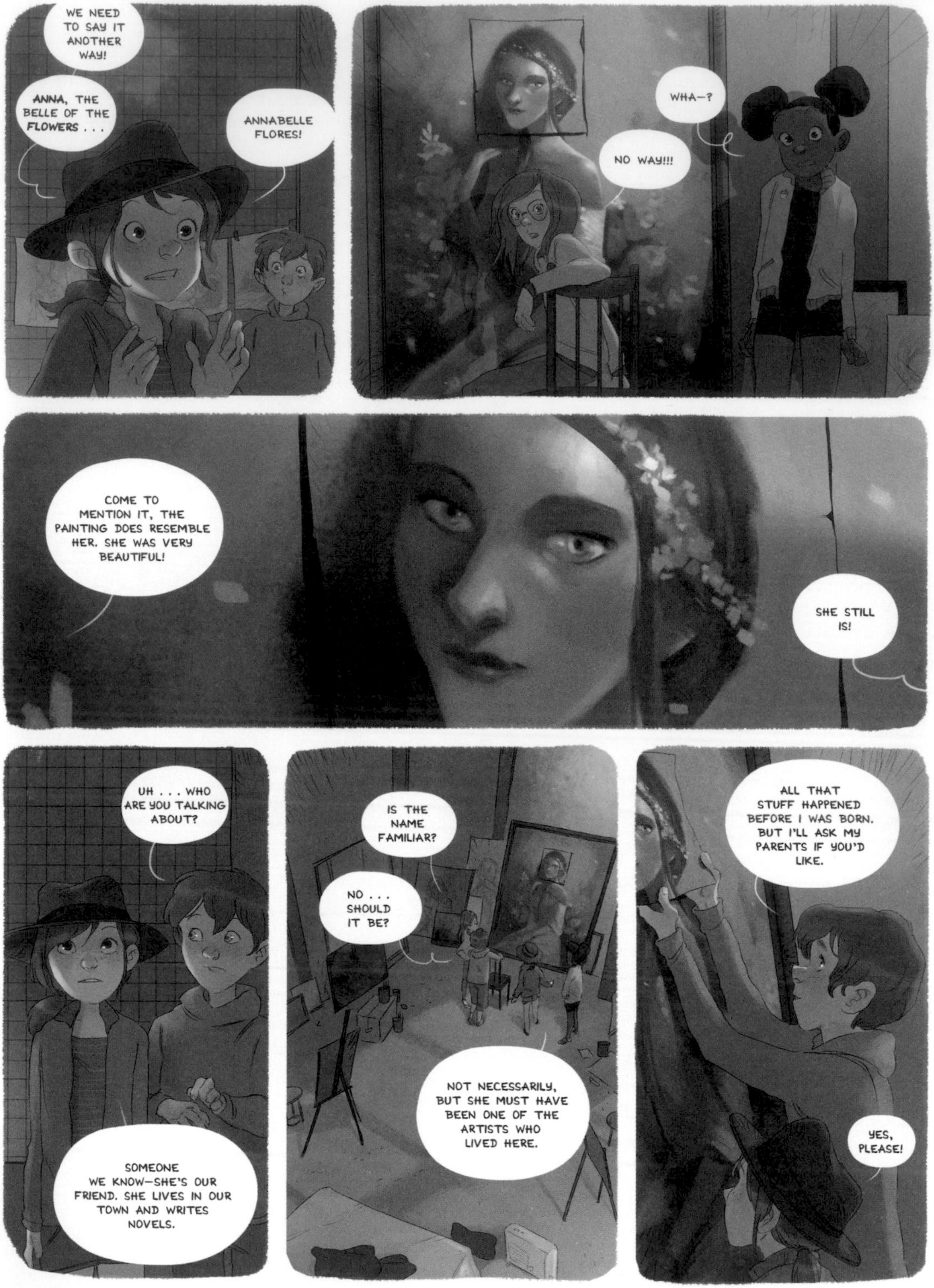
WE NEED TO SAY IT ANOTHER WAY!
ANNA, THE BELLE OF THE FLOWERS . . .
ANNABELLE FLORES!
WHA–?
NO WAY!!!
COME TO MENTION IT, THE PAINTING DOES RESEMBLE HER. SHE WAS VERY BEAUTIFUL!
SHE STILL IS!
UH . . . WHO ARE YOU TALKING ABOUT?
SOMEONE WE KNOW—SHE'S OUR FRIEND. SHE LIVES IN OUR TOWN AND WRITES NOVELS.
IS THE NAME FAMILIAR?
NO . . . SHOULD IT BE?
NOT NECESSARILY, BUT SHE MUST HAVE BEEN ONE OF THE ARTISTS WHO LIVED HERE.
ALL THAT STUFF HAPPENED BEFORE I WAS BORN. BUT I'LL ASK MY PARENTS IF YOU'D LIKE.
YES, PLEASE!

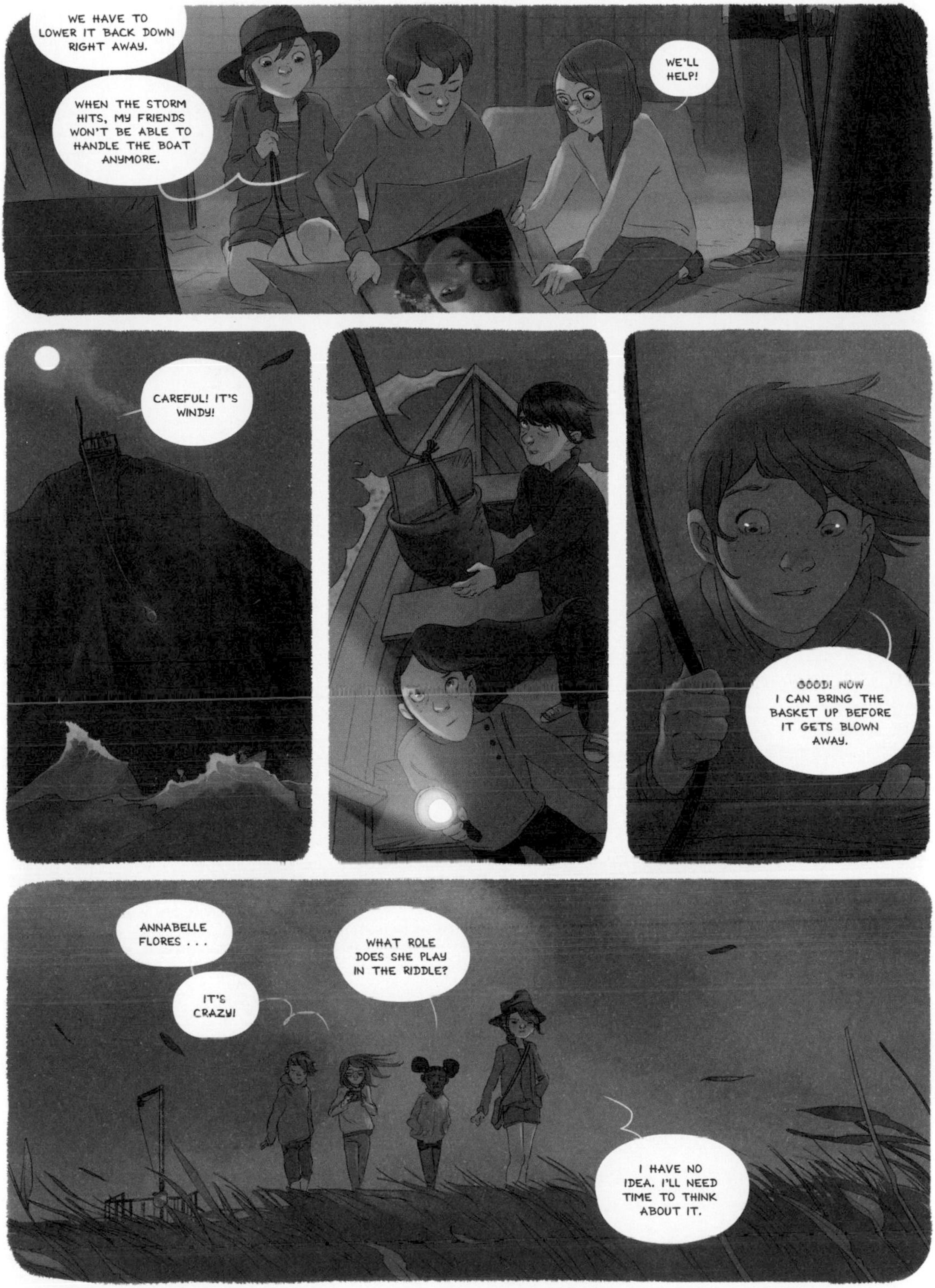
WE HAVE TO LOWER IT BACK DOWN RIGHT AWAY.
WHEN THE STORM HITS, MY FRIENDS WON'T BE ABLE TO HANDLE THE BOAT ANYMORE.
WE'LL HELP!
CAREFUL! IT'S WINDY!
GOOD! NOW I CAN BRING THE BASKET UP BEFORE IT GETS BLOWN AWAY.
ANNABELLE FLORES . . .
IT'S CRAZY!
WHAT ROLE DOES SHE PLAY IN THE RIDDLE?
I HAVE NO IDEA. I'LL NEED TIME TO THINK ABOUT IT.

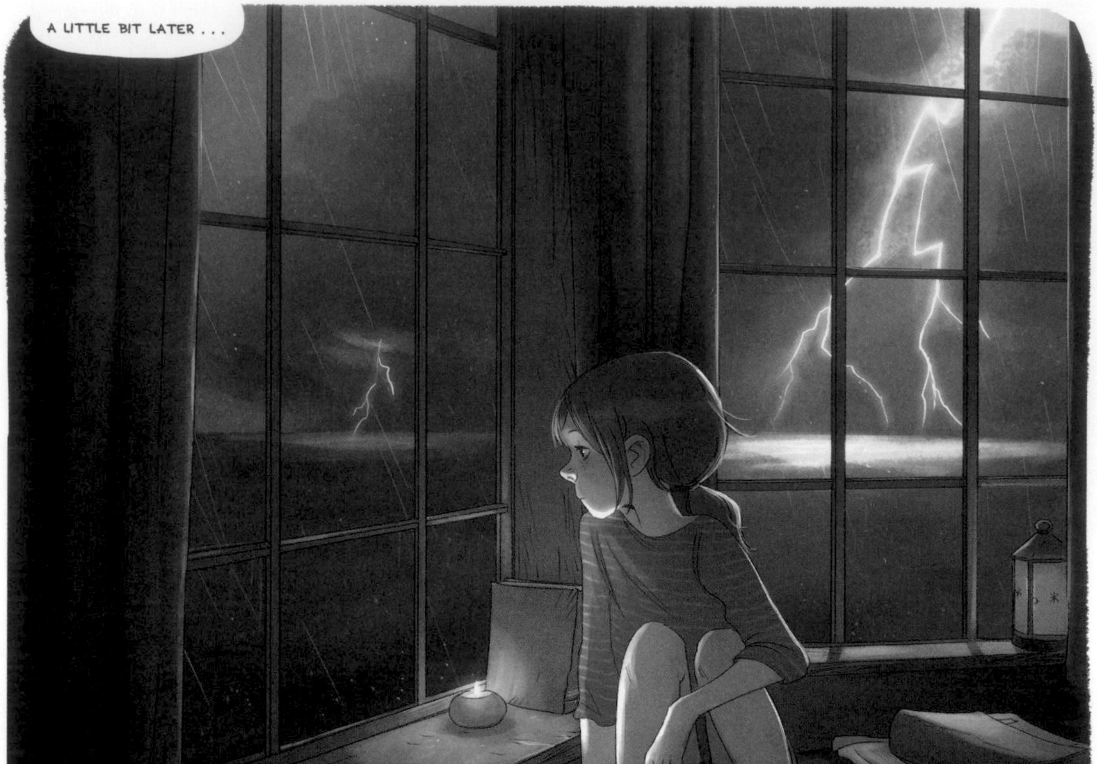
A LITTLE BIT LATER . . .

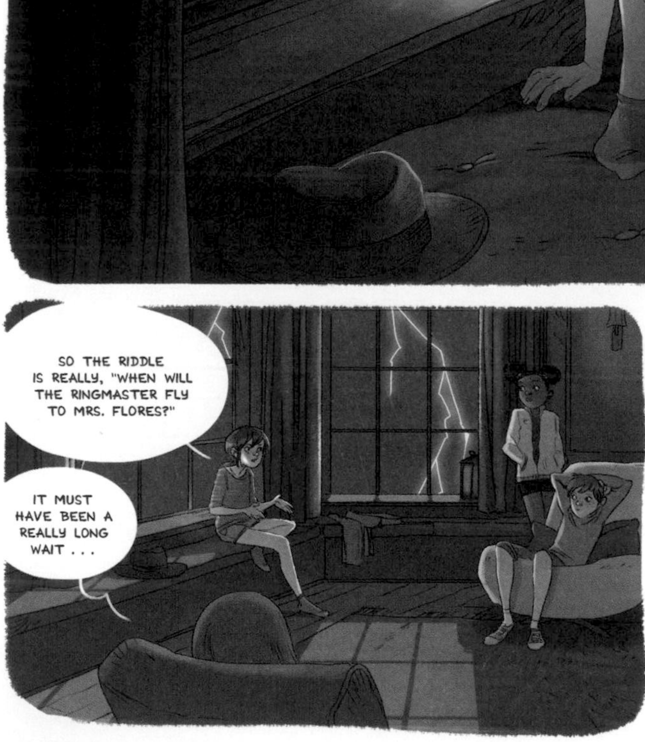
SO THE RIDDLE IS REALLY, "WHEN WILL THE RINGMASTER FLY TO MRS. FLORES?"
IT MUST HAVE BEEN A REALLY LONG WAIT . . .

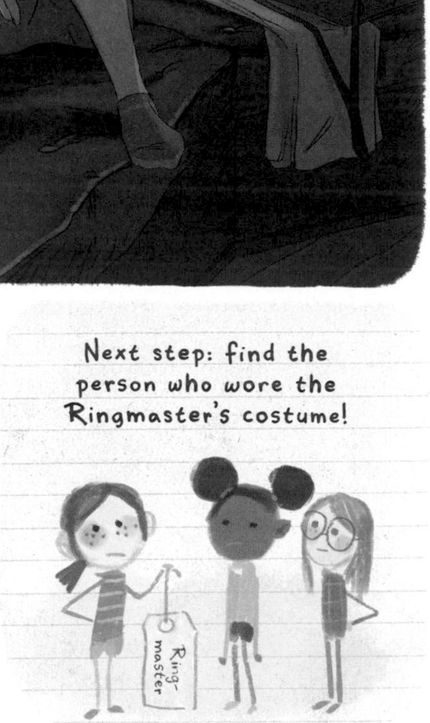
Next step: find the person who wore the Ringmaster's costume!
Ring-master

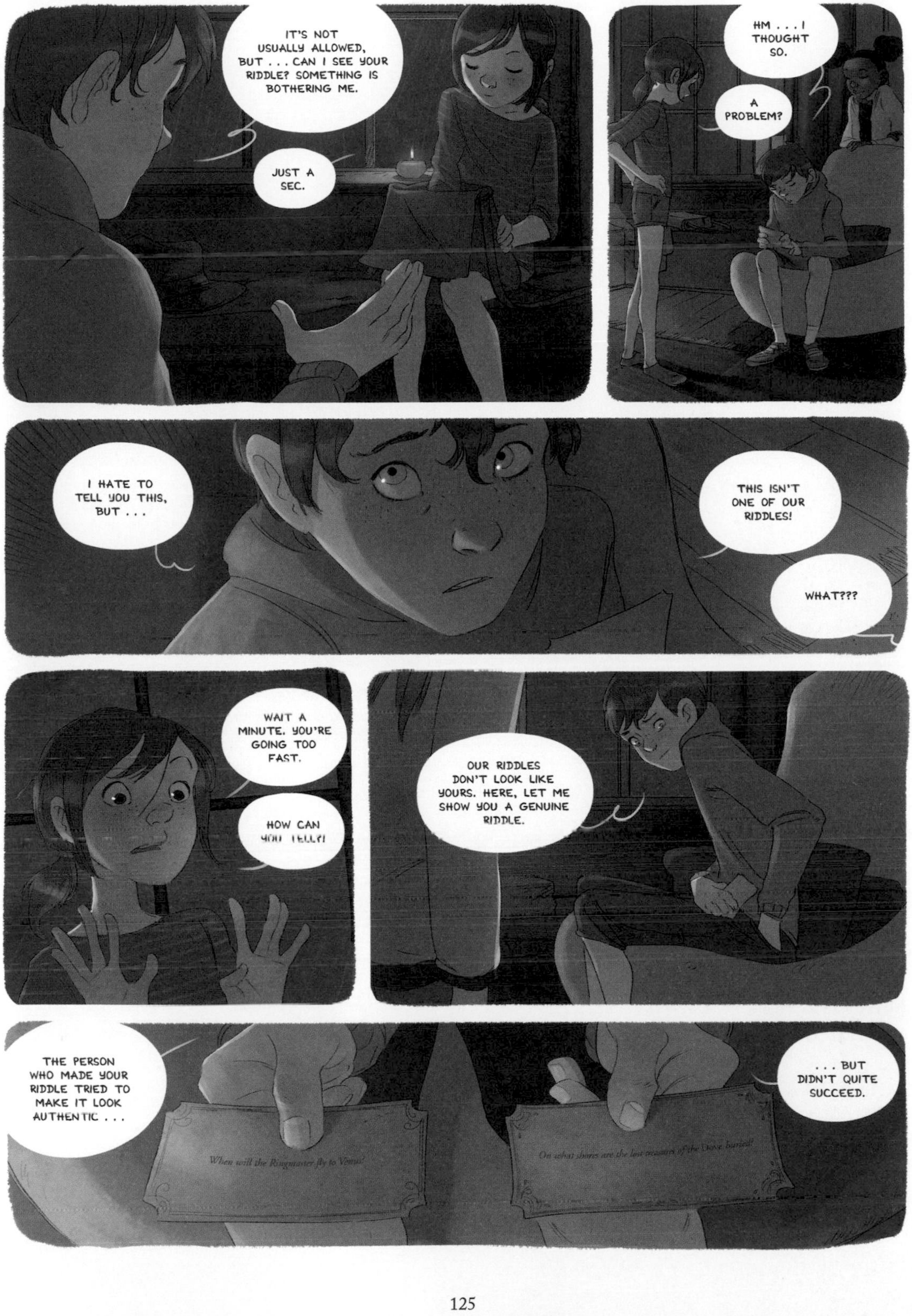
IT'S NOT USUALLY ALLOWED, BUT . . . CAN I SEE YOUR RIDDLE? SOMETHING IS BOTHERING ME.
JUST A SEC.
HM . . . I THOUGHT SO.
A PROBLEM?
I HATE TO TELL YOU THIS, BUT . . .
THIS ISN'T ONE OF OUR RIDDLES!
WHAT???
WAIT A MINUTE. YOU'RE GOING TOO FAST.
HOW CAN YOU TELL?!
OUR RIDDLES DON'T LOOK LIKE YOURS. HERE, LET ME SHOW YOU A GENUINE RIDDLE.
THE PERSON WHO MADE YOUR RIDDLE TRIED TO MAKE IT LOOK AUTHENTIC . . .
When will the Ringmaster fly to Venus?
On what shores are the lost treasures of the Dove buried?
. . . BUT DIDN'T QUITE SUCCEED.

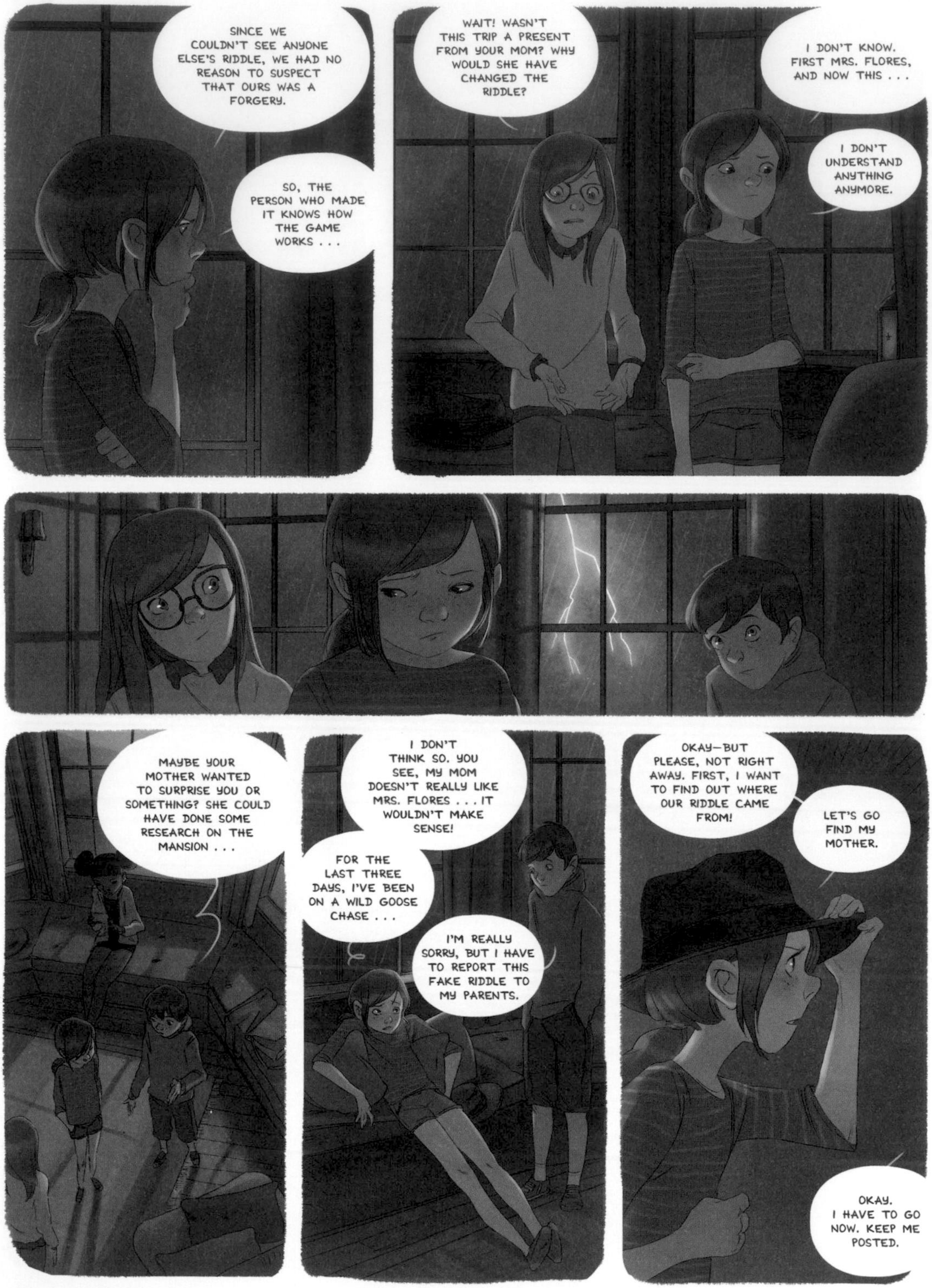
SINCE WE COULDN'T SEE ANYONE ELSE'S RIDDLE, WE HAD NO REASON TO SUSPECT THAT OURS WAS A FORGERY.
SO, THE PERSON WHO MADE IT KNOWS HOW THE GAME WORKS . . .
WAIT! WASN'T THIS TRIP A PRESENT FROM YOUR MOM? WHY WOULD SHE HAVE CHANGED THE RIDDLE?
I DON'T KNOW. FIRST MRS. FLORES, AND NOW THIS . . .
I DON'T UNDERSTAND ANYTHING ANYMORE.
MAYBE YOUR MOTHER WANTED TO SURPRISE YOU OR SOMETHING? SHE COULD HAVE DONE SOME RESEARCH ON THE MANSION . . .
I DON'T THINK SO. YOU SEE, MY MOM DOESN'T REALLY LIKE MRS. FLORES . . . IT WOULDN'T MAKE SENSE!
FOR THE LAST THREE DAYS, I'VE BEEN ON A WILD GOOSE CHASE . . .
I'M REALLY SORRY, BUT I HAVE TO REPORT THIS FAKE RIDDLE TO MY PARENTS.
OKAY—BUT PLEASE, NOT RIGHT AWAY. FIRST, I WANT TO FIND OUT WHERE OUR RIDDLE CAME FROM!
LET'S GO FIND MY MOTHER.
OKAY. I HAVE TO GO NOW. KEEP ME POSTED.

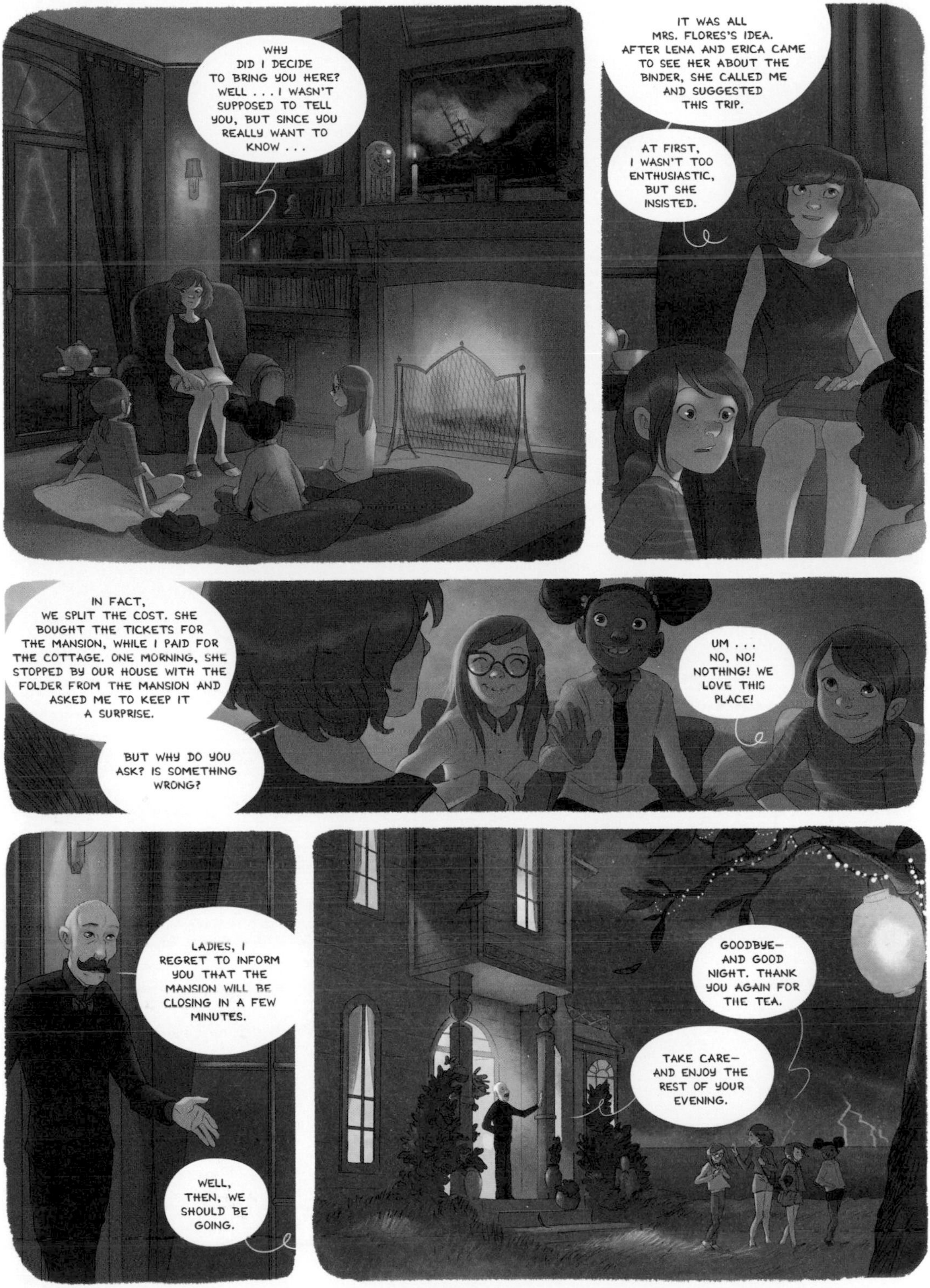
WHY DID I DECIDE TO BRING YOU HERE? WELL . . . I WASN'T SUPPOSED TO TELL YOU, BUT SINCE YOU REALLY WANT TO KNOW . . .
IT WAS ALL MRS. FLORES'S IDEA. AFTER LENA AND ERICA CAME TO SEE HER ABOUT THE BINDER, SHE CALLED ME AND SUGGESTED THIS TRIP.
AT FIRST, I WASN'T TOO ENTHUSIASTIC, BUT SHE INSISTED.
IN FACT, WE SPLIT THE COST. SHE BOUGHT THE TICKETS FOR THE MANSION, WHILE I PAID FOR THE COTTAGE. ONE MORNING, SHE STOPPED BY OUR HOUSE WITH THE FOLDER FROM THE MANSION AND ASKED ME TO KEEP IT A SURPRISE.
BUT WHY DO YOU ASK? IS SOMETHING WRONG?
UM . . . NO, NO! NOTHING! WE LOVE THIS PLACE!
LADIES, I REGRET TO INFORM YOU THAT THE MANSION WILL BE CLOSING IN A FEW MINUTES.
WELL, THEN, WE SHOULD BE GOING.
GOODBYE— AND GOOD NIGHT. THANK YOU AGAIN FOR THE TEA.
TAKE CARE— AND ENJOY THE REST OF YOUR EVENING.

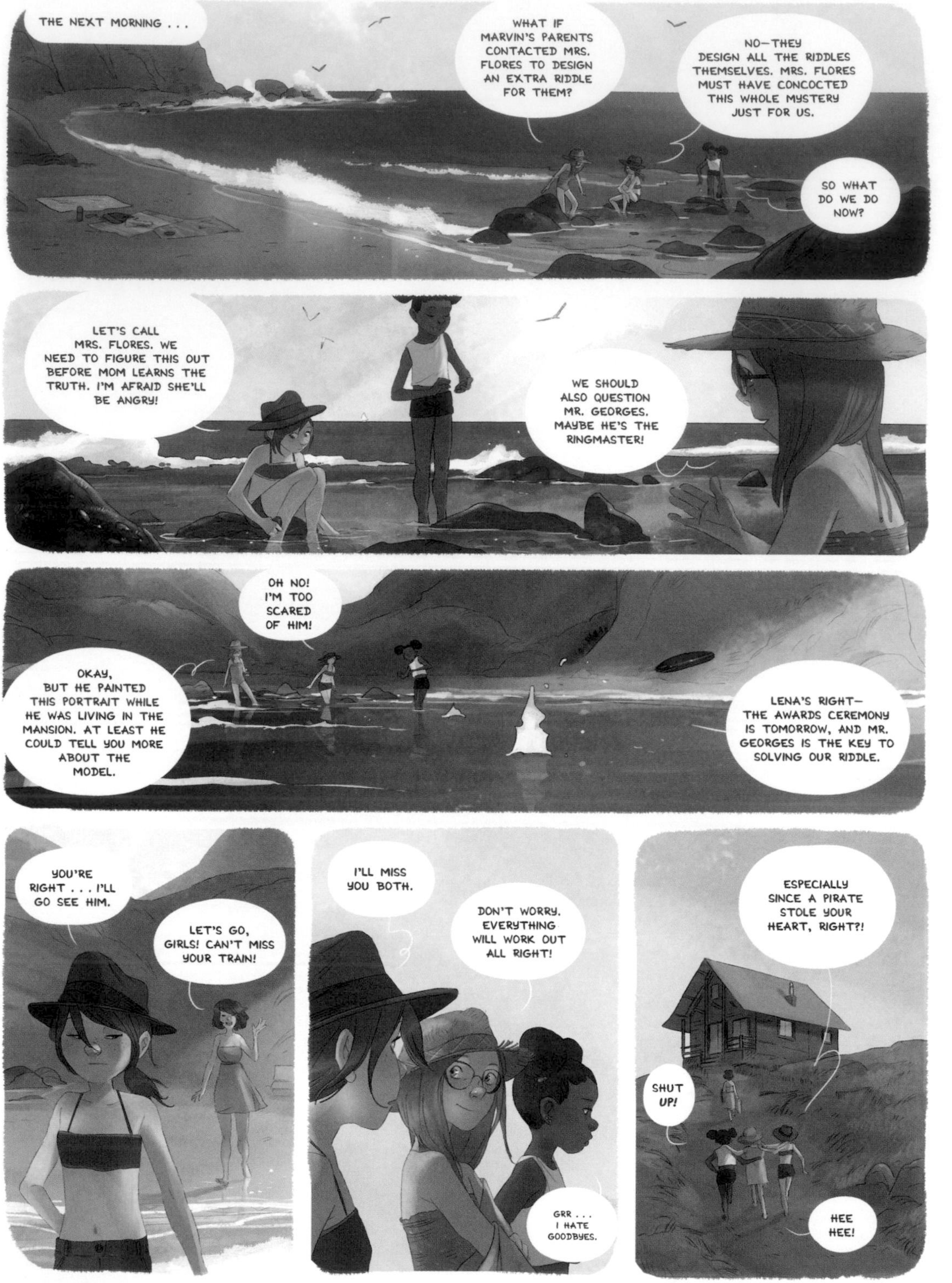
THE NEXT MORNING . . .
WHAT IF MARVIN'S PARENTS CONTACTED MRS. FLORES TO DESIGN AN EXTRA RIDDLE FOR THEM?
NO—THEY DESIGN ALL THE RIDDLES THEMSELVES. MRS. FLORES MUST HAVE CONCOCTED THIS WHOLE MYSTERY JUST FOR US.
SO WHAT DO WE DO NOW?
LET'S CALL MRS. FLORES. WE NEED TO FIGURE THIS OUT BEFORE MOM LEARNS THE TRUTH. I'M AFRAID SHE'LL BE ANGRY!
WE SHOULD ALSO QUESTION MR. GEORGES. MAYBE HE'S THE RINGMASTER!
OH NO! I'M TOO SCARED OF HIM!
OKAY, BUT HE PAINTED THIS PORTRAIT WHILE HE WAS LIVING IN THE MANSION. AT LEAST HE COULD TELL YOU MORE ABOUT THE MODEL.
LENA'S RIGHT—THE AWARDS CEREMONY IS TOMORROW, AND MR. GEORGES IS THE KEY TO SOLVING OUR RIDDLE.
YOU'RE RIGHT . . . I'LL GO SEE HIM.
LET'S GO, GIRLS! CAN'T MISS YOUR TRAIN!
I'LL MISS YOU BOTH.
DON'T WORRY. EVERYTHING WILL WORK OUT ALL RIGHT!
GRR . . . I HATE GOODBYES.
ESPECIALLY SINCE A PIRATE STOLE YOUR HEART, RIGHT?!
SHUT UP!
HEE HEE!

Let's start from the top . . .
Square One
I turned 12!
My friends' gift gave Mrs. Flores a strange idea . . .
She devised a plan to send me in her place . . .
. . . to the Mansion of a Hundred Mysteries . . .
. . . to find the answer to this riddle:
When will the Ringmaster fly to Venus?
Mom and I began our investigation!
Next— Lena and Erica arrived!
We tried to call Mrs. Flores discreetly, but we couldn't get through.
Miss one turn.
The game ends tomorrow and Mom will find out everything!
Lena and Erica have to go to the railway station.
They want to know how the story ends, so they're going to try to get in touch with Mrs. Flores tomorrow morning. I hope they succeed— I'm counting on them.
I feel like I'm not going to be able to sleep tonight. Tomorrow, we pack our bags and tidy up. I have just enough time to see Mr. Georges before the awards ceremony.

What will Mom do when she finds out that Mrs. Flores forged the riddle we've been investigating? I'm not sad anymore like I was when the trip began— now I'm anxious!

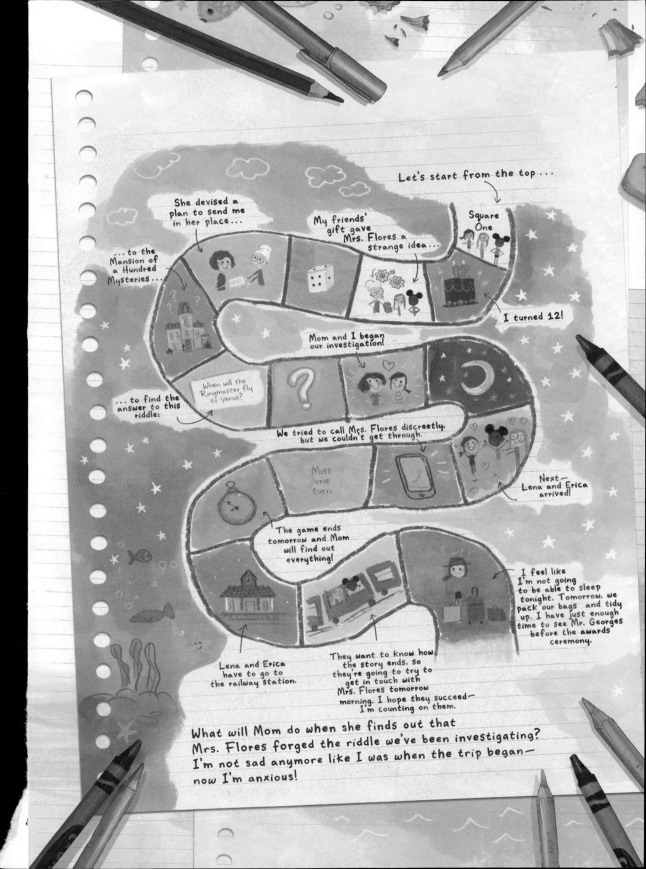

NO personal checks
YEAH, WHAT DO YOU WANT?
I'VE BEEN RESEARCHING THE MANSION. I KNOW THAT YOU'RE A PAINTER, SIR, AND THAT YOU PAINTED "LA BELLE VÉNUS." I ALSO LEARNED THAT YOU KEEP A TREASURED PIECE OF THAT PAINTING IN YOUR OFFICE.
I JUST WANT TO LEARN MORE ABOUT YOUR MODEL, ANNA.
HM . . .
Sorry CLOSED
SO YOU'RE THE ONE MY GRAND-NEPHEW SHOWED THE PORTRAIT TO LAST NIGHT . . . WELL, FINE.
I'M VERY SORRY. I DIDN'T MEAN . . .
NO MATTER. WHAT'S DONE IS DONE. COME IN AND TELL ME WHAT YOU WANT TO KNOW.
I KNOW ANNABELLE FLORES—SHE'S MY NEIGHBOR BACK HOME. SHE'S ALSO MY FRIEND.
I CAN TELL YOU KNOW THAT NAME. WHO WAS SHE BACK THEN, WHEN YOU PAINTED HER?
WHAT CAN I SAY? SHE WAS . . .

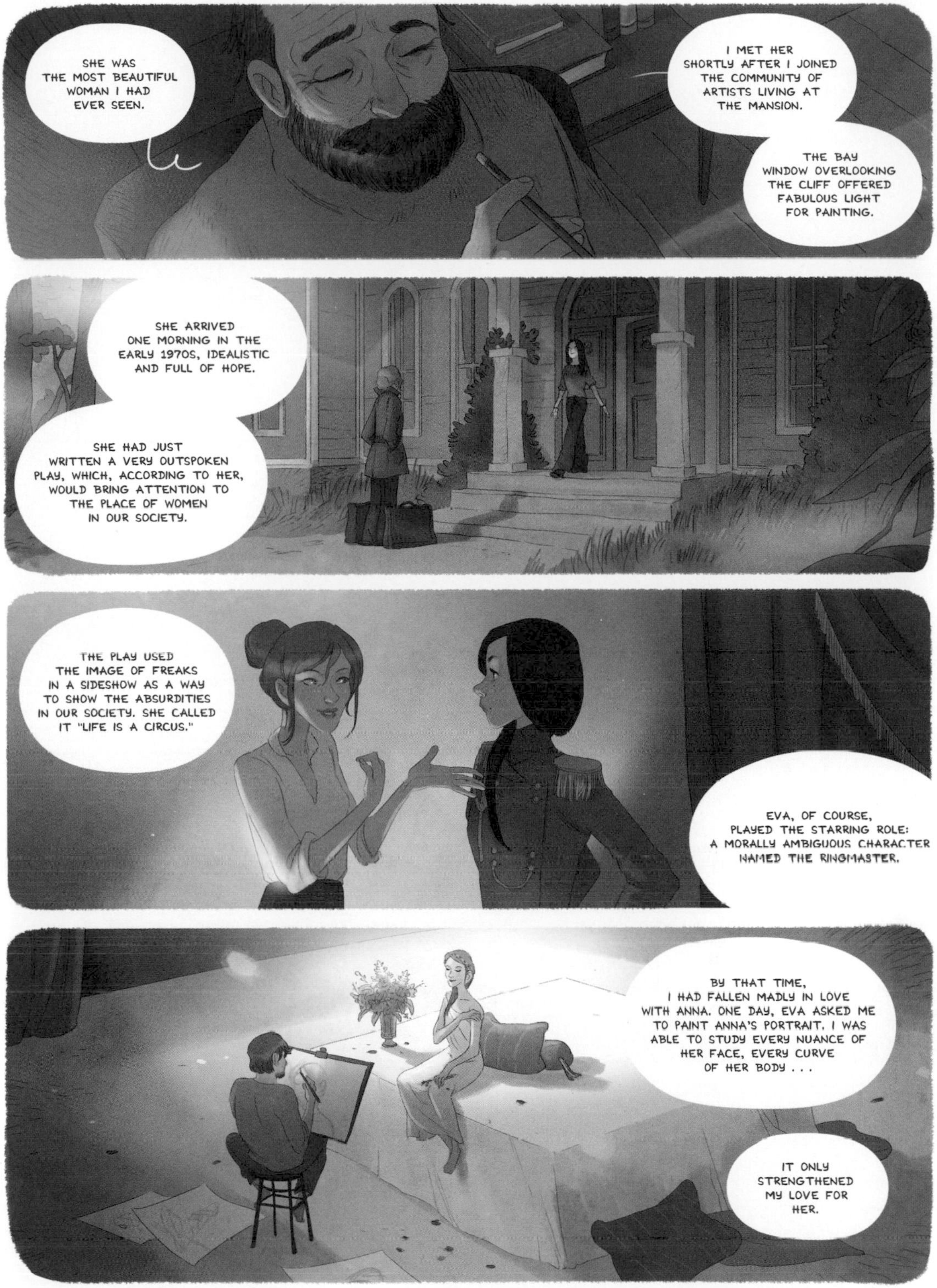
SHE WAS THE MOST BEAUTIFUL WOMAN I HAD EVER SEEN.
I MET HER SHORTLY AFTER I JOINED THE COMMUNITY OF ARTISTS LIVING AT THE MANSION.
THE BAY WINDOW OVERLOOKING THE CLIFF OFFERED FABULOUS LIGHT FOR PAINTING.
SHE ARRIVED ONE MORNING IN THE EARLY 1970S, IDEALISTIC AND FULL OF HOPE.
SHE HAD JUST WRITTEN A VERY OUTSPOKEN PLAY, WHICH, ACCORDING TO HER, WOULD BRING ATTENTION TO THE PLACE OF WOMEN IN OUR SOCIETY.
THE PLAY USED THE IMAGE OF FREAKS IN A SIDESHOW AS A WAY TO SHOW THE ABSURDITIES IN OUR SOCIETY. SHE CALLED IT "LIFE IS A CIRCUS."
EVA, OF COURSE, PLAYED THE STARRING ROLE: A MORALLY AMBIGUOUS CHARACTER NAMED THE RINGMASTER.
BY THAT TIME, I HAD FALLEN MADLY IN LOVE WITH ANNA. ONE DAY, EVA ASKED ME TO PAINT ANNA'S PORTRAIT. I WAS ABLE TO STUDY EVERY NUANCE OF HER FACE, EVERY CURVE OF HER BODY . . .
IT ONLY STRENGTHENED MY LOVE FOR HER.

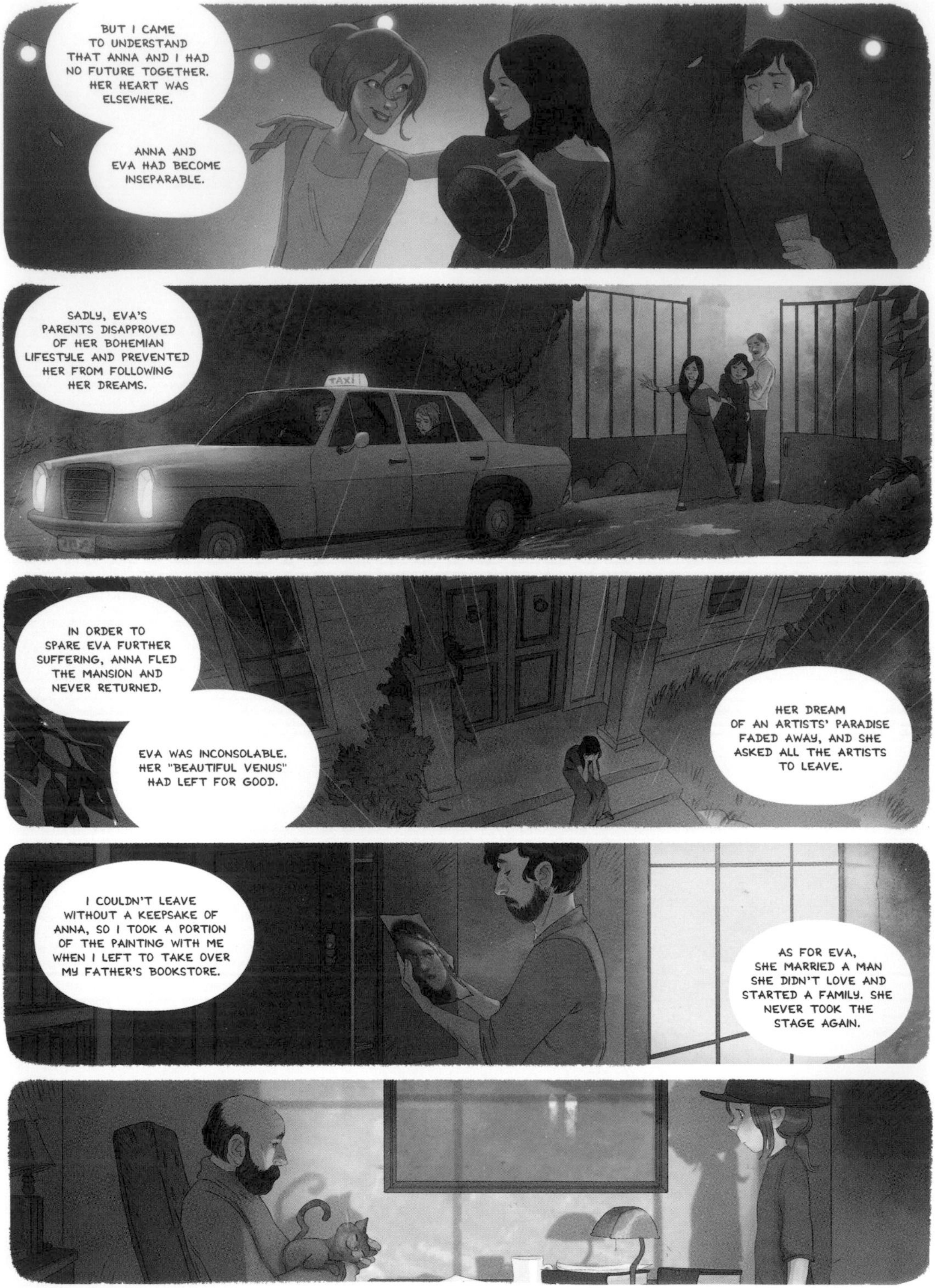
BUT I CAME TO UNDERSTAND THAT ANNA AND I HAD NO FUTURE TOGETHER. HER HEART WAS ELSEWHERE.
ANNA AND EVA HAD BECOME INSEPARABLE.
SADLY, EVA'S PARENTS DISAPPROVED OF HER BOHEMIAN LIFESTYLE AND PREVENTED HER FROM FOLLOWING HER DREAMS.
TAXI
IN ORDER TO SPARE EVA FURTHER SUFFERING, ANNA FLED THE MANSION AND NEVER RETURNED.
EVA WAS INCONSOLABLE. HER "BEAUTIFUL VENUS" HAD LEFT FOR GOOD.
HER DREAM OF AN ARTISTS' PARADISE FADED AWAY, AND SHE ASKED ALL THE ARTISTS TO LEAVE.
I COULDN'T LEAVE WITHOUT A KEEPSAKE OF ANNA, SO I TOOK A PORTION OF THE PAINTING WITH ME WHEN I LEFT TO TAKE OVER MY FATHER'S BOOKSTORE.
AS FOR EVA, SHE MARRIED A MAN SHE DIDN'T LOVE AND STARTED A FAMILY. SHE NEVER TOOK THE STAGE AGAIN.

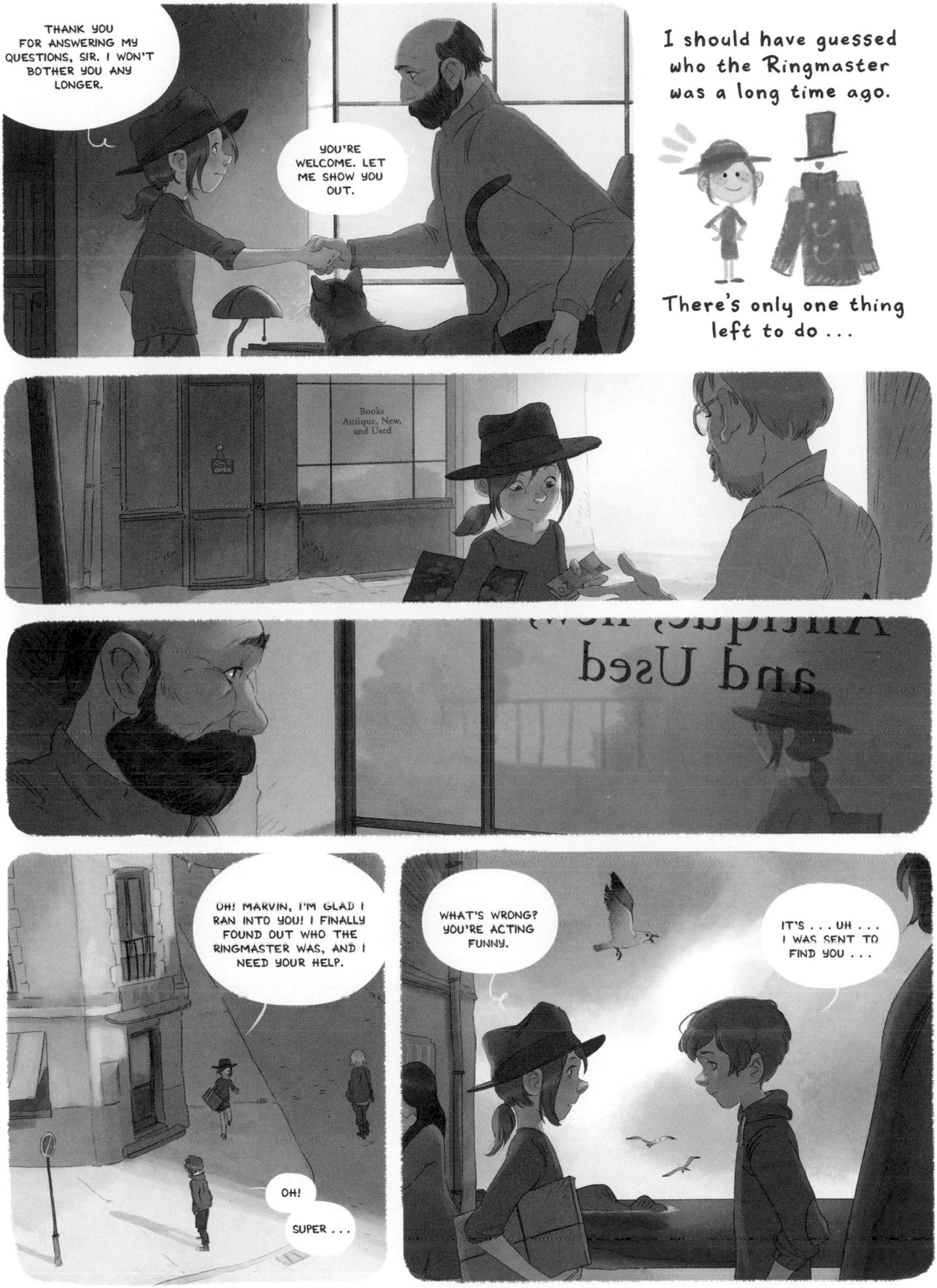
THANK YOU FOR ANSWERING MY QUESTIONS, SIR. I WON'T BOTHER YOU ANY LONGER.
YOU'RE WELCOME. LET ME SHOW YOU OUT.
I should have guessed who the Ringmaster was a long time ago.
There's only one thing left to do . . .
Books Antique, New, and Used
OPEN
OH! MARVIN, I'M GLAD I RAN INTO YOU! I FINALLY FOUND OUT WHO THE RINGMASTER WAS, AND I NEED YOUR HELP.
OH!
SUPER . . .
WHAT'S WRONG? YOU'RE ACTING FUNNY.
IT'S . . . UH . . . I WAS SENT TO FIND YOU . . .

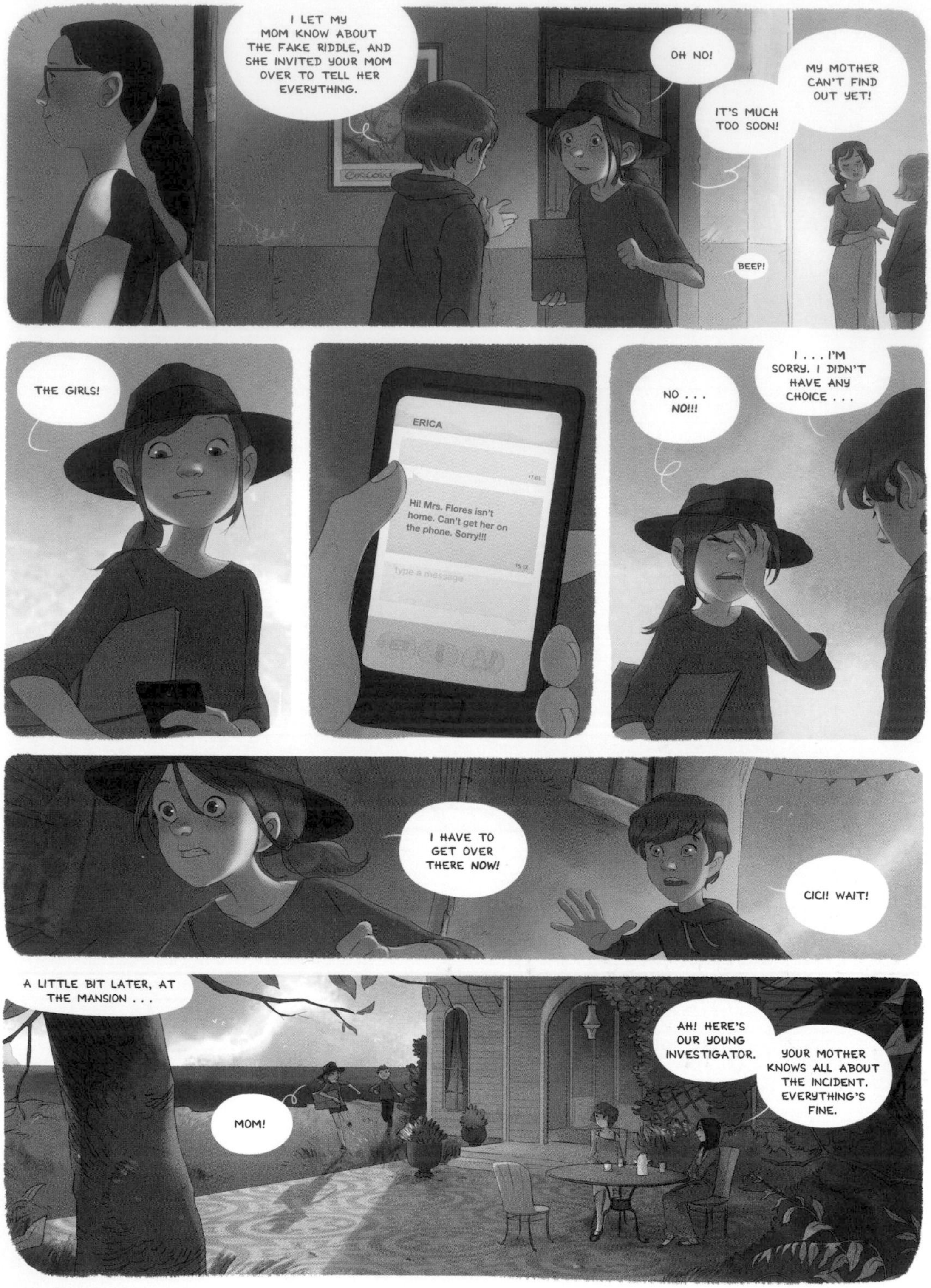
I LET MY MOM KNOW ABOUT THE FAKE RIDDLE, AND SHE INVITED YOUR MOM OVER TO TELL HER EVERYTHING.
OH NO!
IT'S MUCH TOO SOON!
MY MOTHER CAN'T FIND OUT YET!
BEEP!
THE GIRLS!
ERICA
Hi! Mrs. Flores isn't home. Can't get her on the phone. Sorry!!!
type a message
NO . . . NO!!!
I . . . I'M SORRY. I DIDN'T HAVE ANY CHOICE . . .
I HAVE TO GET OVER THERE NOW!
CICI! WAIT!
A LITTLE BIT LATER, AT THE MANSION . . .
MOM!
AH! HERE'S OUR YOUNG INVESTIGATOR.
YOUR MOTHER KNOWS ALL ABOUT THE INCIDENT. EVERYTHING'S FINE.

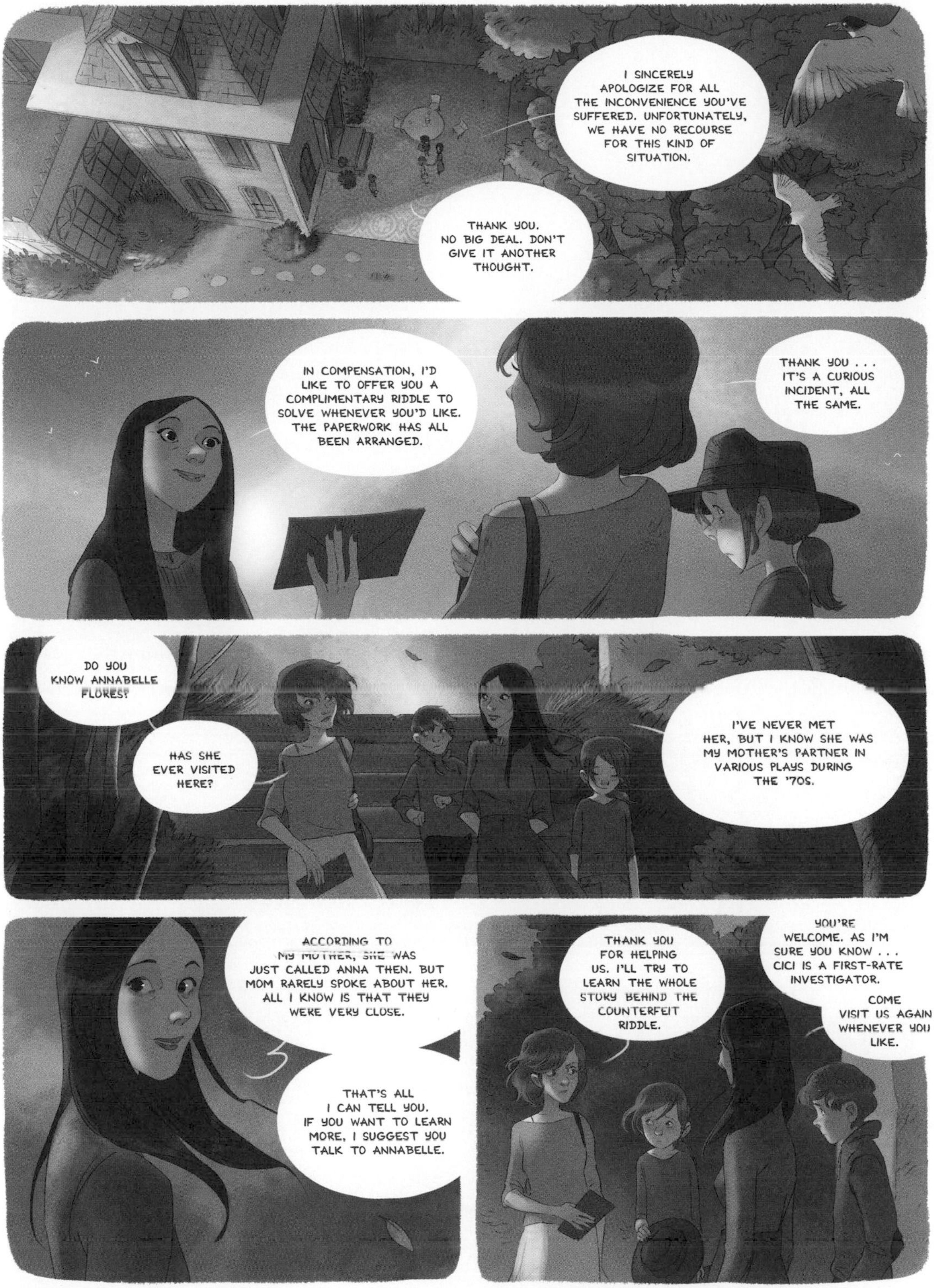
I SINCERELY APOLOGIZE FOR ALL THE INCONVENIENCE YOU'VE SUFFERED. UNFORTUNATELY, WE HAVE NO RECOURSE FOR THIS KIND OF SITUATION.
THANK YOU. NO BIG DEAL. DON'T GIVE IT ANOTHER THOUGHT.
IN COMPENSATION, I'D LIKE TO OFFER YOU A COMPLIMENTARY RIDDLE TO SOLVE WHENEVER YOU'D LIKE. THE PAPERWORK HAS ALL BEEN ARRANGED.
THANK YOU . . . IT'S A CURIOUS INCIDENT, ALL THE SAME.
DO YOU KNOW ANNABELLE FLORES?
HAS SHE EVER VISITED HERE?
I'VE NEVER MET HER, BUT I KNOW SHE WAS MY MOTHER'S PARTNER IN VARIOUS PLAYS DURING THE '70S.
ACCORDING TO MY MOTHER, SHE WAS JUST CALLED ANNA THEN. BUT MOM RARELY SPOKE ABOUT HER. ALL I KNOW IS THAT THEY WERE VERY CLOSE.
THAT'S ALL I CAN TELL YOU. IF YOU WANT TO LEARN MORE, I SUGGEST YOU TALK TO ANNABELLE.
THANK YOU FOR HELPING US. I'LL TRY TO LEARN THE WHOLE STORY BEHIND THE COUNTERFEIT RIDDLE.
YOU'RE WELCOME. AS I'M SURE YOU KNOW . . . CICI IS A FIRST-RATE INVESTIGATOR.
COME VISIT US AGAIN WHENEVER YOU LIKE.

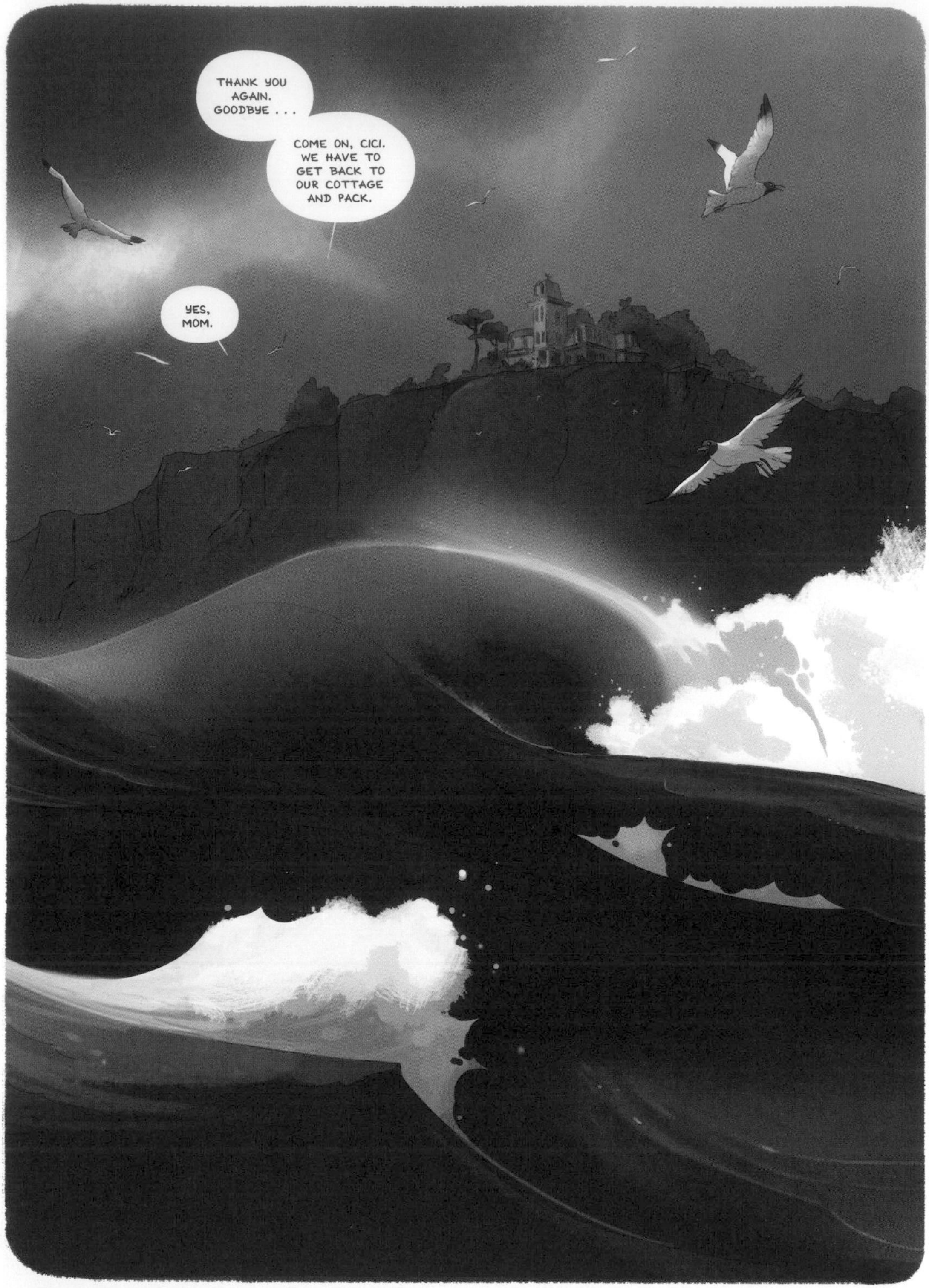
THANK YOU AGAIN. GOODBYE . . .
COME ON, CICI. WE HAVE TO GET BACK TO OUR COTTAGE AND PACK.
YES, MOM.

Marvin came to see me and say goodbye. He asked me for Erica's telephone number. I was right—they like each other! She's going to be happy. He made me promise to return once the Smugglers' Guild finally comes up with a mystery that can be solved in their lair. I hope they succeed.

He told me how sorry he was that he had reported the counterfeit riddle to his mother. But he had no choice. I didn't want him to feel guilty, so I told him it was no big deal and that he did the right thing.

But none of what I said is true! What's going to happen now will be terrible! And I can't do anything to fix it. It's horrible!

Everything is out of my control. And it all happened so fast! This has never happened to me before, and it makes me sick to my stomach . . .

Everything was going so well. My mom and I were having fun and laughing together! For the first time, we were investigating the same mystery. I felt ready to share all my feelings with her. I was going to do it . . .

But then Mrs. Flores had to set a trap for us . . .

Oh, Mrs. Flores, why did you do that?

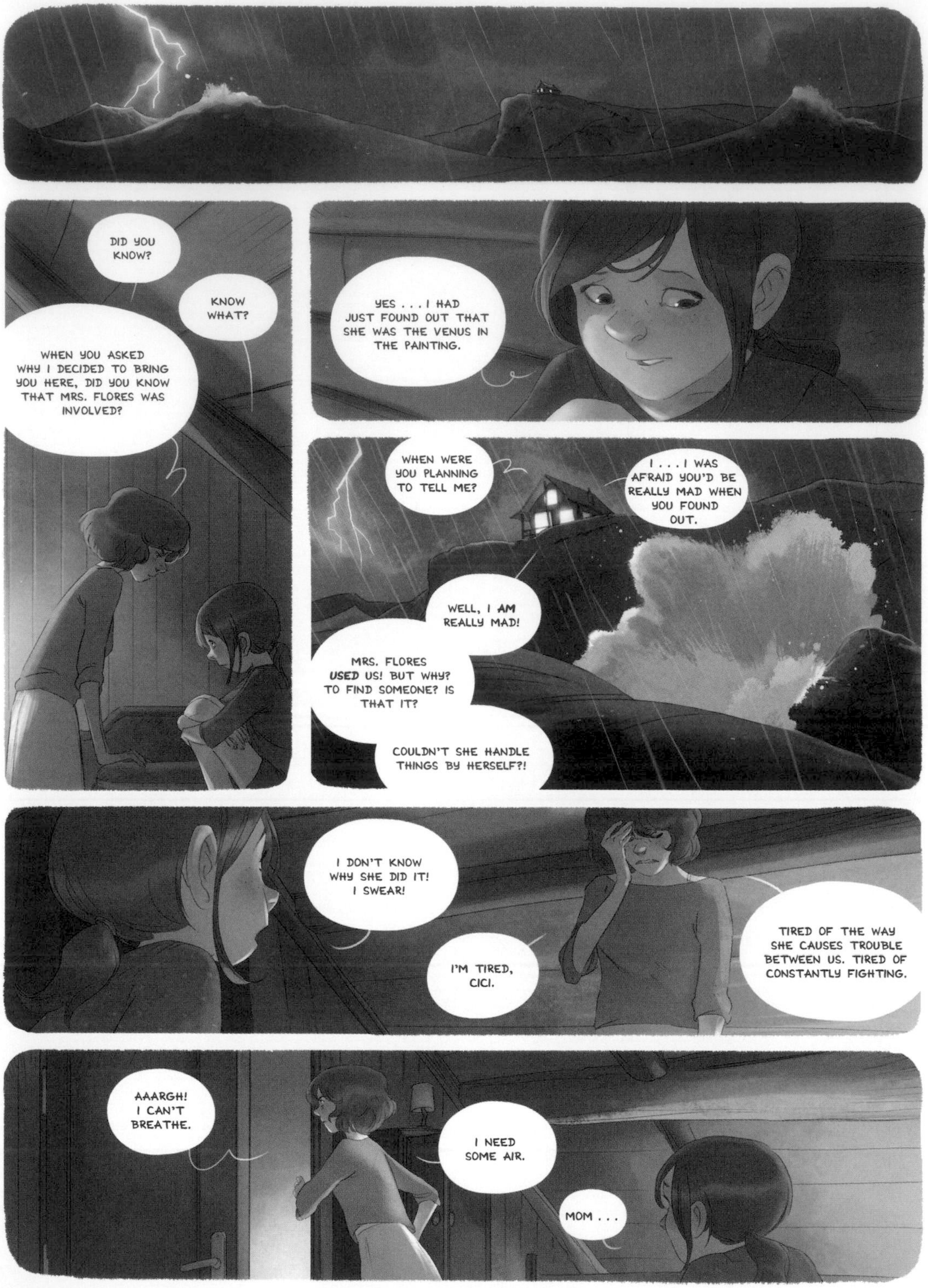
DID YOU KNOW?
KNOW WHAT?
WHEN YOU ASKED WHY I DECIDED TO BRING YOU HERE, DID YOU KNOW THAT MRS. FLORES WAS INVOLVED?
YES . . . I HAD JUST FOUND OUT THAT SHE WAS THE VENUS IN THE PAINTING.
WHEN WERE YOU PLANNING TO TELL ME?
I . . . I WAS AFRAID YOU'D BE REALLY MAD WHEN YOU FOUND OUT.
WELL, I **AM** REALLY MAD!
MRS. FLORES ***USED*** US! BUT WHY? TO FIND SOMEONE? IS THAT IT?
COULDN'T SHE HANDLE THINGS BY HERSELF?!
I DON'T KNOW WHY SHE DID IT! I SWEAR!
I'M TIRED, CICI.
TIRED OF THE WAY SHE CAUSES TROUBLE BETWEEN US. TIRED OF CONSTANTLY FIGHTING.
AAARGH! I CAN'T BREATHE.
I NEED SOME AIR.
MOM . . .

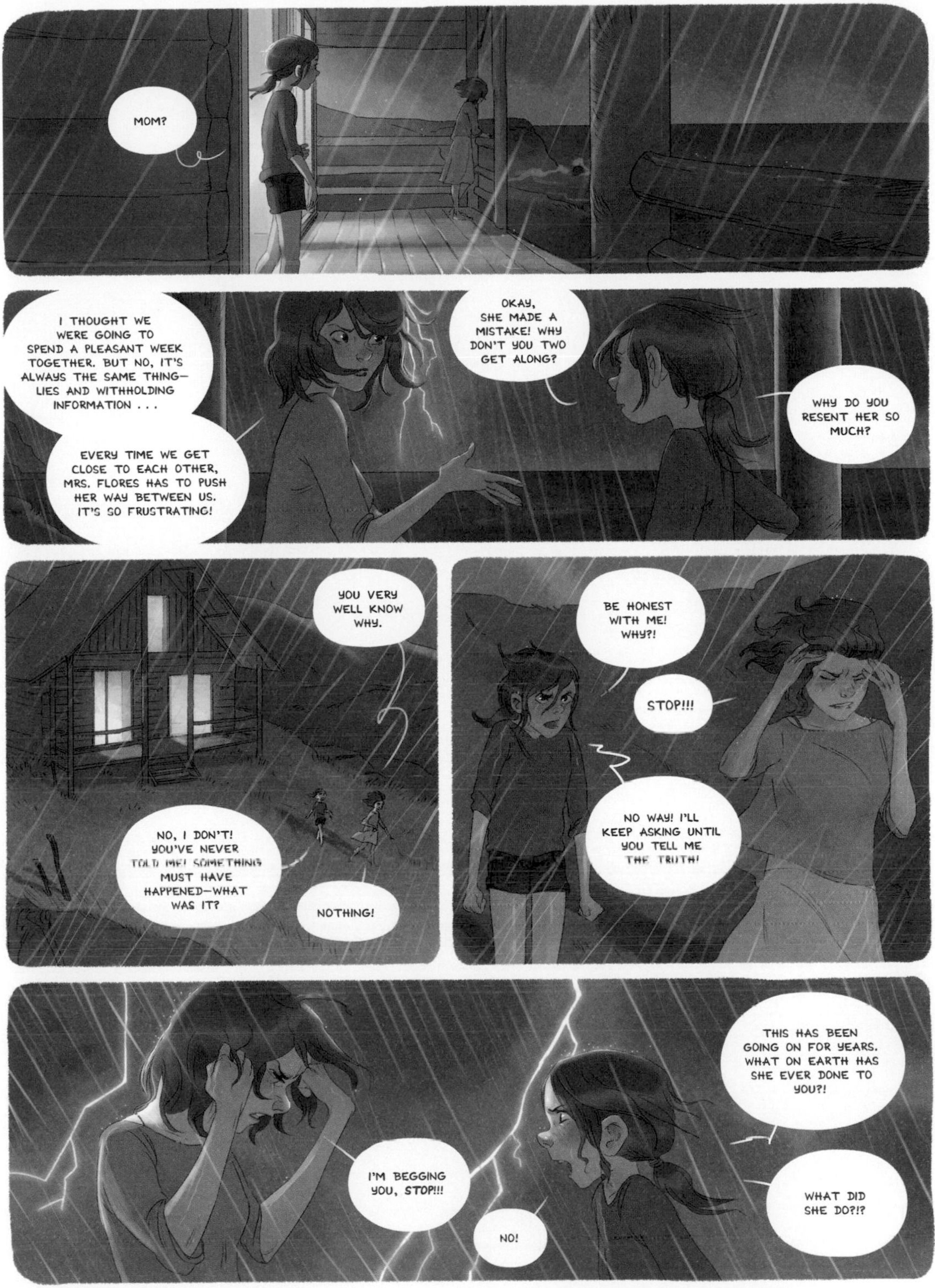
MOM?
I THOUGHT WE WERE GOING TO SPEND A PLEASANT WEEK TOGETHER. BUT NO, IT'S ALWAYS THE SAME THING—LIES AND WITHHOLDING INFORMATION . . .
EVERY TIME WE GET CLOSE TO EACH OTHER, MRS. FLORES HAS TO PUSH HER WAY BETWEEN US. IT'S SO FRUSTRATING!
OKAY, SHE MADE A MISTAKE! WHY DON'T YOU TWO GET ALONG?
WHY DO YOU RESENT HER SO MUCH?
YOU VERY WELL KNOW WHY.
NO, I DON'T! YOU'VE NEVER TOLD ME! SOMETHING MUST HAVE HAPPENED—WHAT WAS IT?
NOTHING!
BE HONEST WITH ME! WHY?!
STOP!!!
NO WAY! I'LL KEEP ASKING UNTIL YOU TELL ME THE TRUTH!
THIS HAS BEEN GOING ON FOR YEARS. WHAT ON EARTH HAS SHE EVER DONE TO YOU?!
I'M BEGGING YOU, STOP!!!
WHAT DID SHE DO?!?
NO!

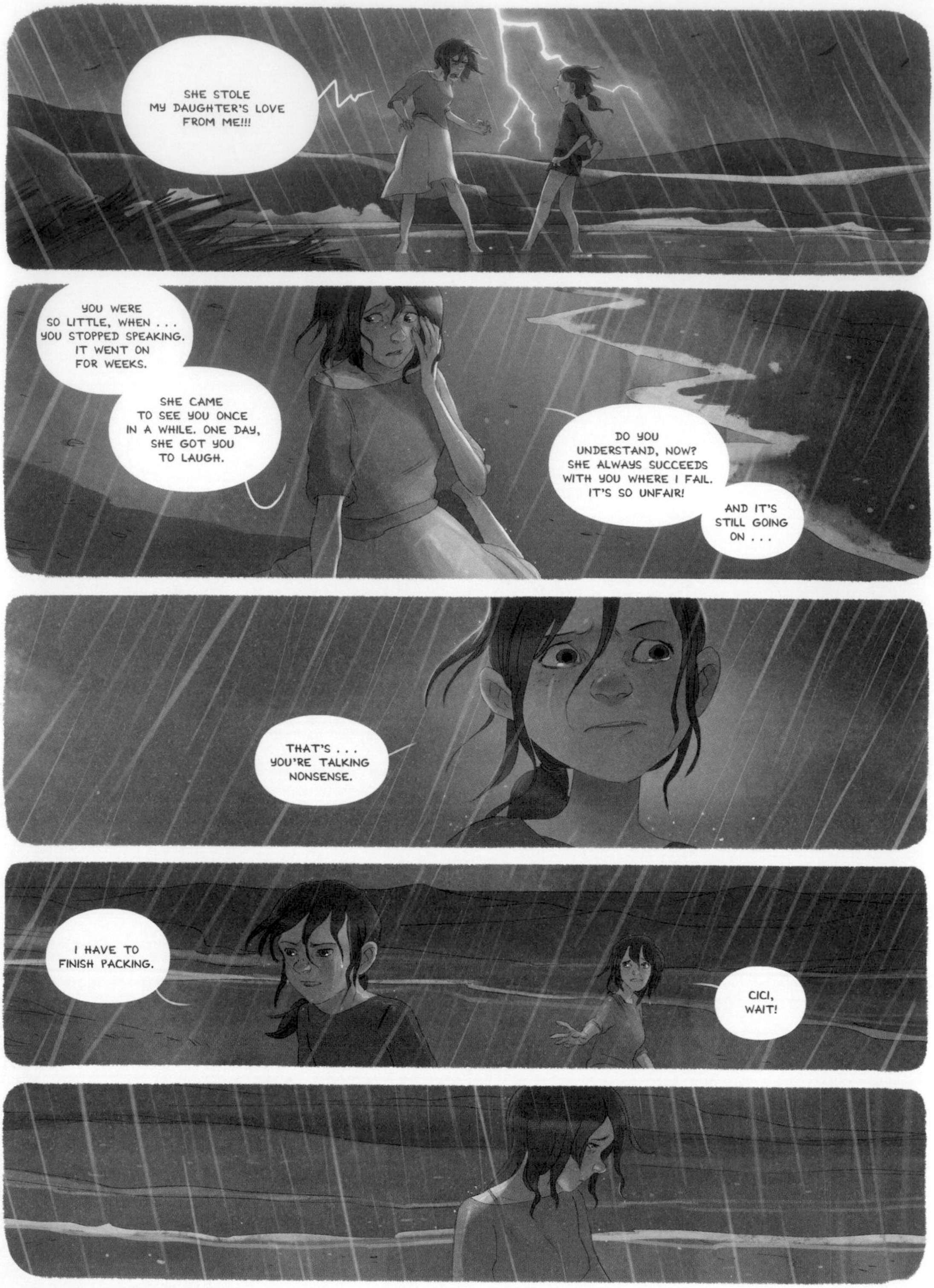
SHE STOLE MY DAUGHTER'S LOVE FROM ME!!!
YOU WERE SO LITTLE, WHEN . . . YOU STOPPED SPEAKING. IT WENT ON FOR WEEKS.
SHE CAME TO SEE YOU ONCE IN A WHILE. ONE DAY, SHE GOT YOU TO LAUGH.
DO YOU UNDERSTAND, NOW? SHE ALWAYS SUCCEEDS WITH YOU WHERE I FAIL. IT'S SO UNFAIR!
AND IT'S STILL GOING ON . . .
THAT'S . . . YOU'RE TALKING NONSENSE.
I HAVE TO FINISH PACKING.
CICI, WAIT!

On the way home, I managed to survive the worst car trip of my life. Mom and I didn't say a word to each other the whole time. She seemed both mad and sad at the same time. As for me, I didn't know what to say. I had hoped that this vacation would help chase away my sadness. Well, my hopes came true. Now, instead of feeling a little sad, I feel completely lost.

When we got home, Mom immediately called Mrs. Flores, but got no answer. Mom left a ferocious message on her answering machine. She forbade Mrs. Flores from coming near me ever again. Mom said that since Mrs. Flores came into our lives, there has been nothing but lies and heartache, and she wanted it to stop. Now.

I don't know what to do! I care for both Mom and Mrs. Flores, and I'm being forced to choose between them. No matter which choice I make, I'll lose. I feel like I am being torn in half.

In any case, I can't bring myself to abandon Mrs. Flores without first solving her riddle.

Before I lose her, I want to make sure she's okay. Mom will hate me for it, but it's something I must do.

I will finish the game. But I won't have to do it all by myself.

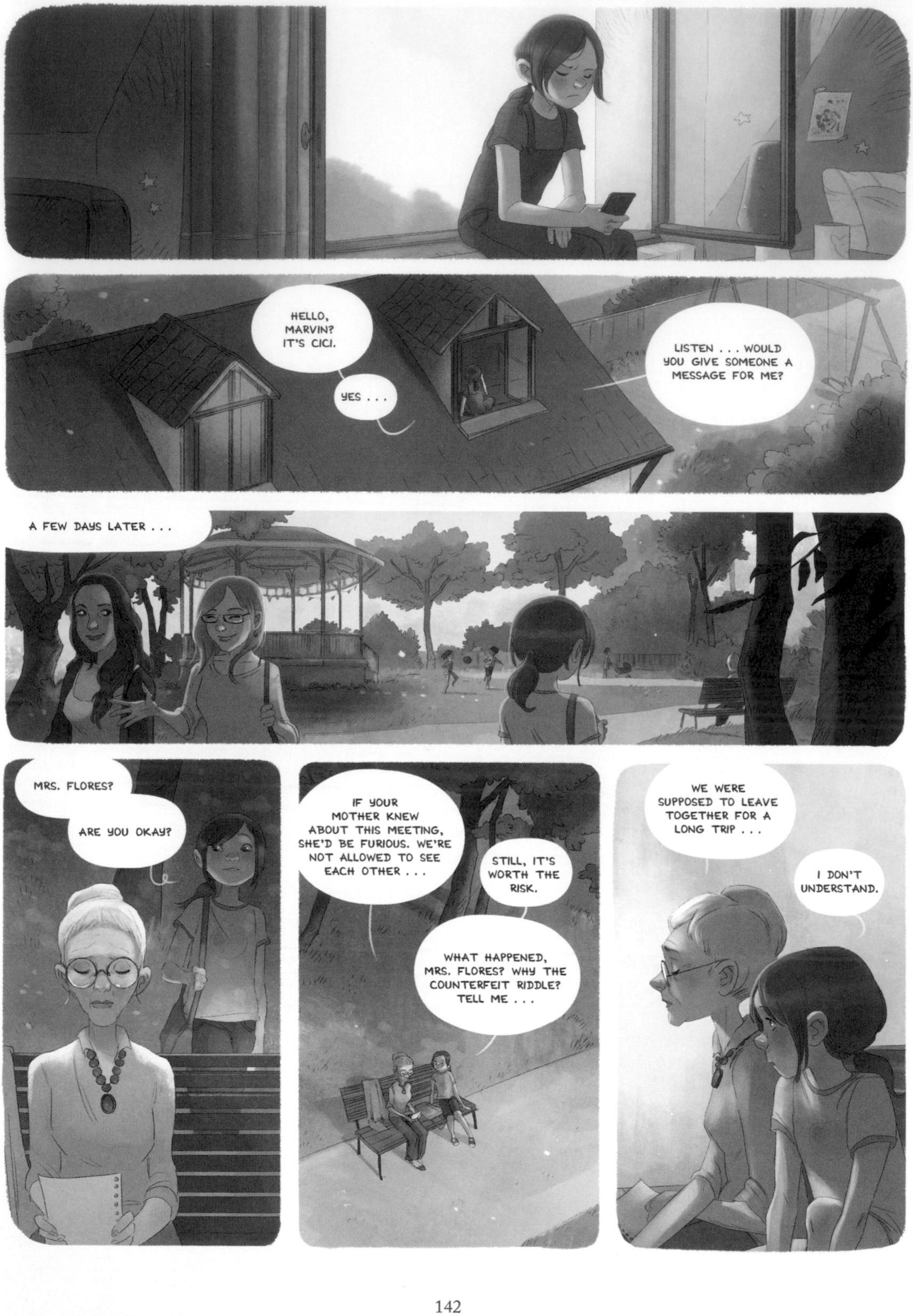
HELLO, MARVIN? IT'S CICI.
YES . . .
LISTEN . . . WOULD YOU GIVE SOMEONE A MESSAGE FOR ME?
A FEW DAYS LATER . . .
MRS. FLORES?
ARE YOU OKAY?
IF YOUR MOTHER KNEW ABOUT THIS MEETING, SHE'D BE FURIOUS. WE'RE NOT ALLOWED TO SEE EACH OTHER . . .
STILL, IT'S WORTH THE RISK.
WHAT HAPPENED, MRS. FLORES? WHY THE COUNTERFEIT RIDDLE? TELL ME . . .
WE WERE SUPPOSED TO LEAVE TOGETHER FOR A LONG TRIP . . .
I DON'T UNDERSTAND.

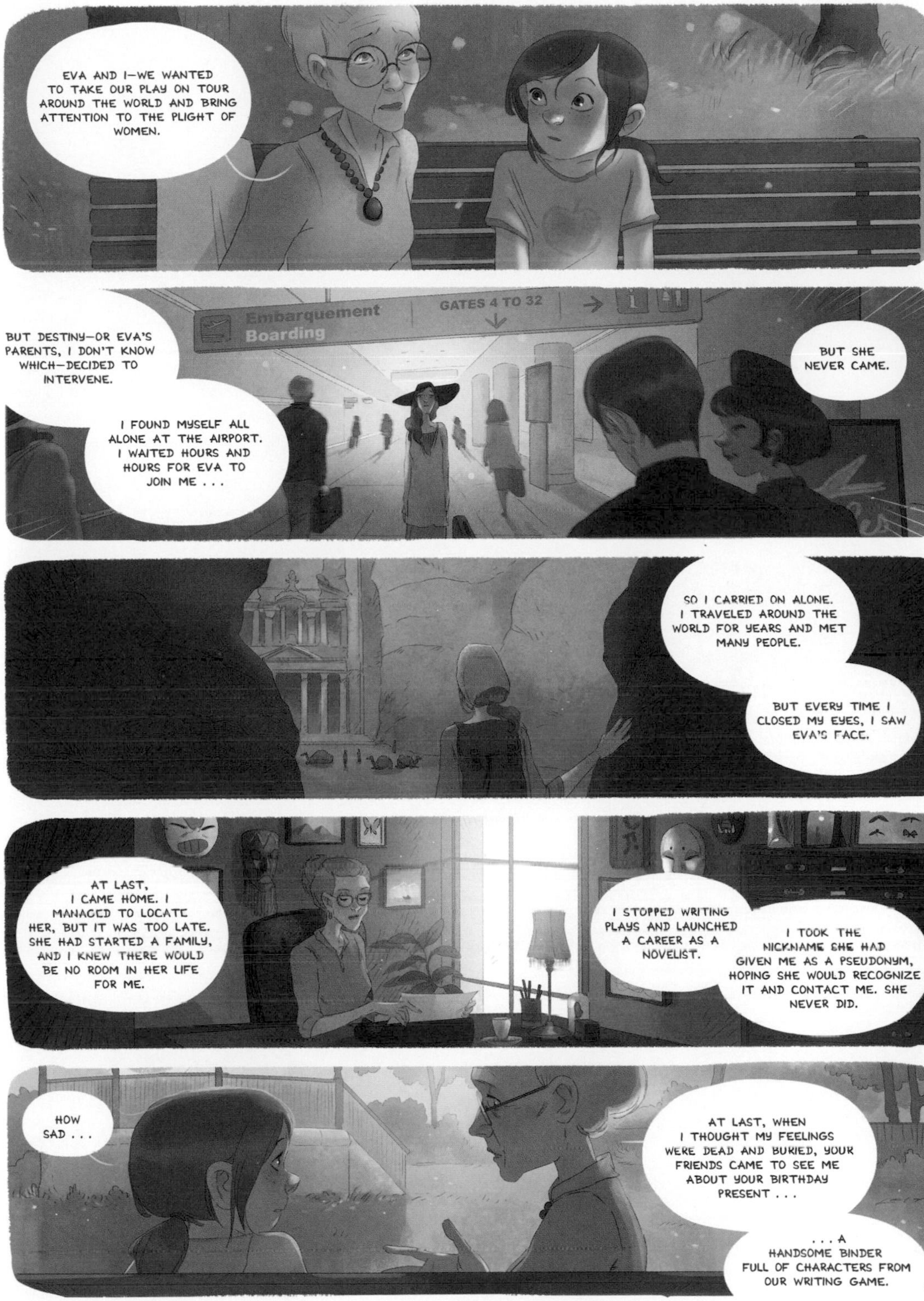
EVA AND I—WE WANTED TO TAKE OUR PLAY ON TOUR AROUND THE WORLD AND BRING ATTENTION TO THE PLIGHT OF WOMEN.
Embarquement
Boarding
GATES 4 TO 32
BUT DESTINY—OR EVA'S PARENTS, I DON'T KNOW WHICH—DECIDED TO INTERVENE.
I FOUND MYSELF ALL ALONE AT THE AIRPORT. I WAITED HOURS AND HOURS FOR EVA TO JOIN ME . . .
BUT SHE NEVER CAME.
SO I CARRIED ON ALONE. I TRAVELED AROUND THE WORLD FOR YEARS AND MET MANY PEOPLE.
BUT EVERY TIME I CLOSED MY EYES, I SAW EVA'S FACE.
AT LAST, I CAME HOME. I MANAGED TO LOCATE HER, BUT IT WAS TOO LATE. SHE HAD STARTED A FAMILY, AND I KNEW THERE WOULD BE NO ROOM IN HER LIFE FOR ME.
I STOPPED WRITING PLAYS AND LAUNCHED A CAREER AS A NOVELIST.
I TOOK THE NICKNAME SHE HAD GIVEN ME AS A PSEUDONYM, HOPING SHE WOULD RECOGNIZE IT AND CONTACT ME. SHE NEVER DID.
HOW SAD . . .
AT LAST, WHEN I THOUGHT MY FEELINGS WERE DEAD AND BURIED, YOUR FRIENDS CAME TO SEE ME ABOUT YOUR BIRTHDAY PRESENT . . .
. . . A HANDSOME BINDER FULL OF CHARACTERS FROM OUR WRITING GAME.

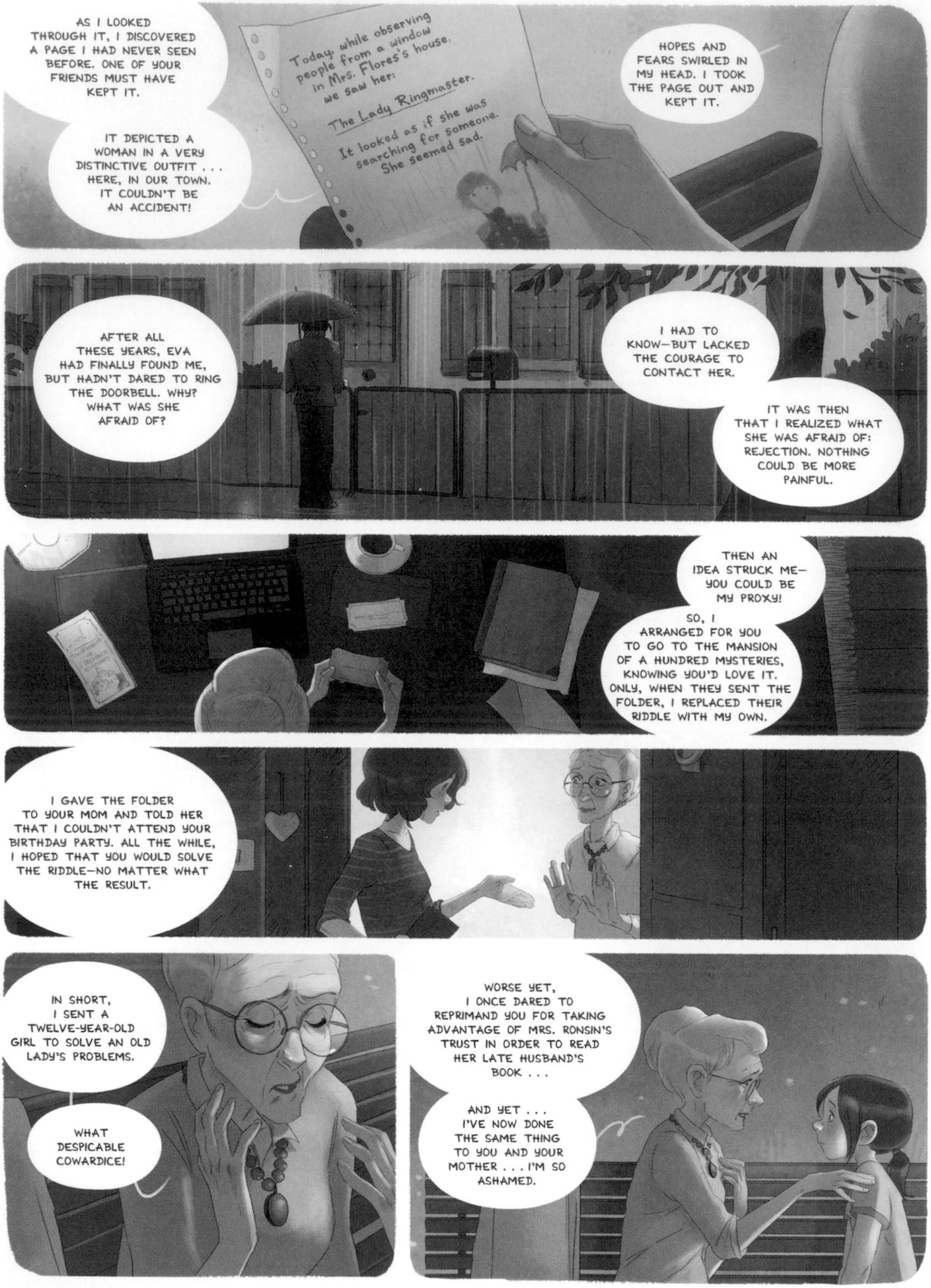
AS I LOOKED THROUGH IT, I DISCOVERED A PAGE I HAD NEVER SEEN BEFORE. ONE OF YOUR FRIENDS MUST HAVE KEPT IT.
IT DEPICTED A WOMAN IN A VERY DISTINCTIVE OUTFIT . . . HERE, IN OUR TOWN. IT COULDN'T BE AN ACCIDENT!
Today, while observing people from a window in Mrs. Flores's house, we saw her:
The Lady Ringmaster.
It looked as if she was searching for someone. She seemed sad.
HOPES AND FEARS SWIRLED IN MY HEAD. I TOOK THE PAGE OUT AND KEPT IT.
AFTER ALL THESE YEARS, EVA HAD FINALLY FOUND ME, BUT HADN'T DARED TO RING THE DOORBELL. WHY? WHAT WAS SHE AFRAID OF?
I HAD TO KNOW—BUT LACKED THE COURAGE TO CONTACT HER.
IT WAS THEN THAT I REALIZED WHAT SHE WAS AFRAID OF: REJECTION. NOTHING COULD BE MORE PAINFUL.
THEN AN IDEA STRUCK ME—YOU COULD BE MY PROXY!
SO, I ARRANGED FOR YOU TO GO TO THE MANSION OF A HUNDRED MYSTERIES, KNOWING YOU'D LOVE IT. ONLY, WHEN THEY SENT THE FOLDER, I REPLACED THEIR RIDDLE WITH MY OWN.
I GAVE THE FOLDER TO YOUR MOM AND TOLD HER THAT I COULDN'T ATTEND YOUR BIRTHDAY PARTY. ALL THE WHILE, I HOPED THAT YOU WOULD SOLVE THE RIDDLE—NO MATTER WHAT THE RESULT.
IN SHORT, I SENT A TWELVE-YEAR-OLD GIRL TO SOLVE AN OLD LADY'S PROBLEMS.
WHAT DESPICABLE COWARDICE!
WORSE YET, I ONCE DARED TO REPRIMAND YOU FOR TAKING ADVANTAGE OF MRS. RONSIN'S TRUST IN ORDER TO READ HER LATE HUSBAND'S BOOK . . .
AND YET . . . I'VE NOW DONE THE SAME THING TO YOU AND YOUR MOTHER . . . I'M SO ASHAMED.

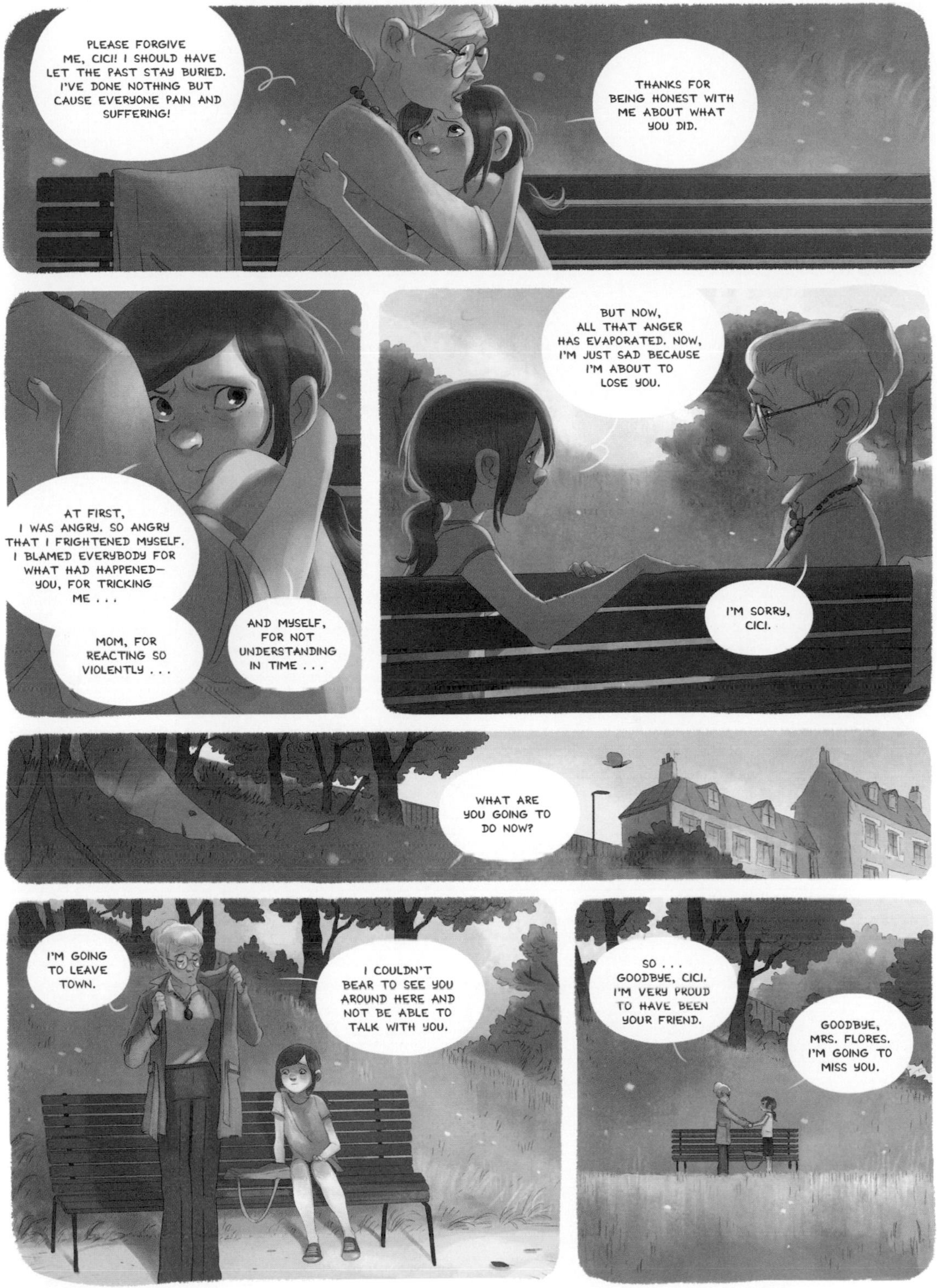
PLEASE FORGIVE ME, CICI! I SHOULD HAVE LET THE PAST STAY BURIED. I'VE DONE NOTHING BUT CAUSE EVERYONE PAIN AND SUFFERING!
THANKS FOR BEING HONEST WITH ME ABOUT WHAT YOU DID.
AT FIRST, I WAS ANGRY. SO ANGRY THAT I FRIGHTENED MYSELF. I BLAMED EVERYBODY FOR WHAT HAD HAPPENED— YOU, FOR TRICKING ME . . .
MOM, FOR REACTING SO VIOLENTLY . . .
AND MYSELF, FOR NOT UNDERSTANDING IN TIME . . .
BUT NOW, ALL THAT ANGER HAS EVAPORATED. NOW, I'M JUST SAD BECAUSE I'M ABOUT TO LOSE YOU.
I'M SORRY, CICI.
WHAT ARE YOU GOING TO DO NOW?
I'M GOING TO LEAVE TOWN.
I COULDN'T BEAR TO SEE YOU AROUND HERE AND NOT BE ABLE TO TALK WITH YOU.
SO . . . GOODBYE, CICI. I'M VERY PROUD TO HAVE BEEN YOUR FRIEND.
GOODBYE, MRS. FLORES. I'M GOING TO MISS YOU.

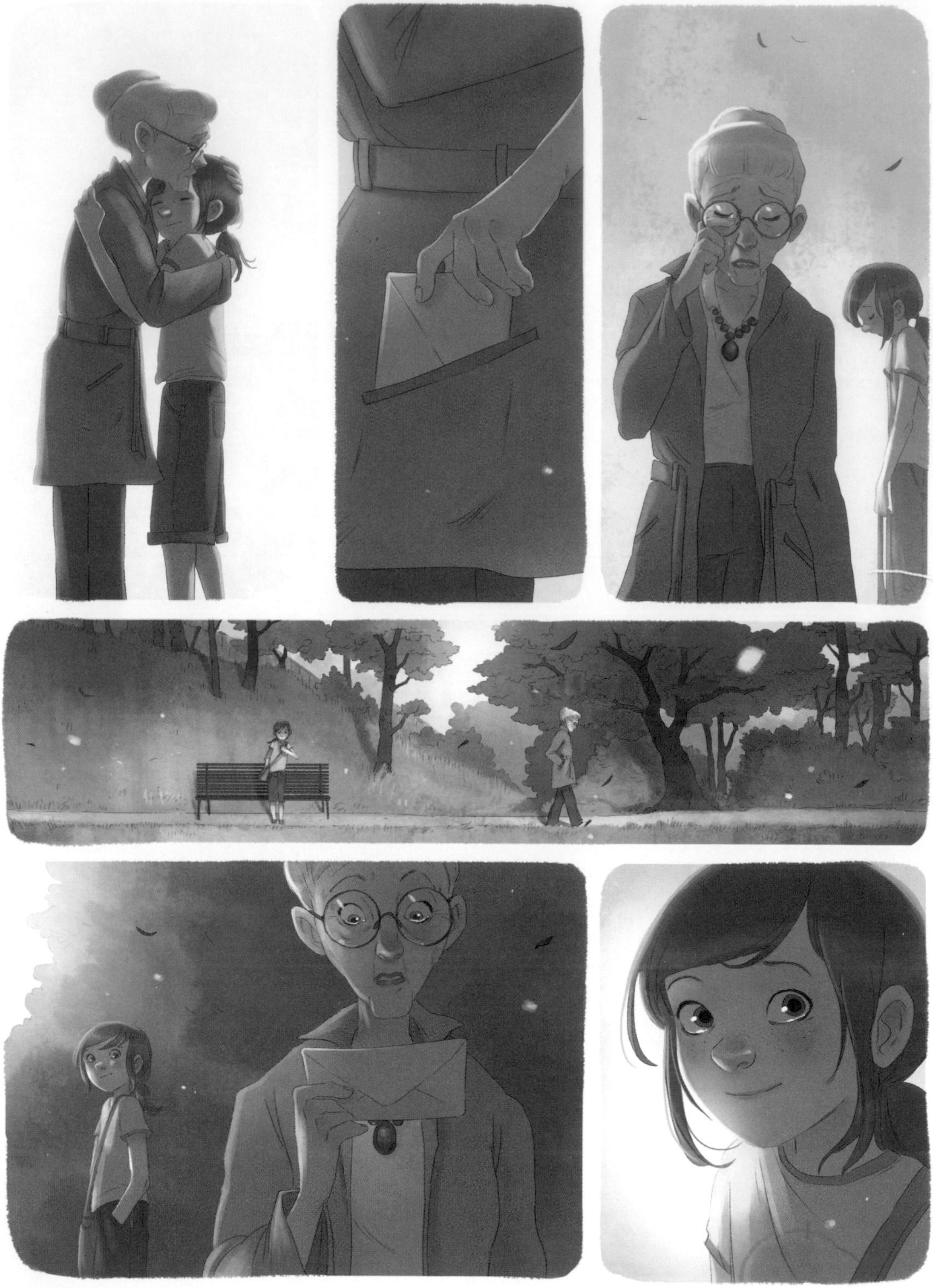

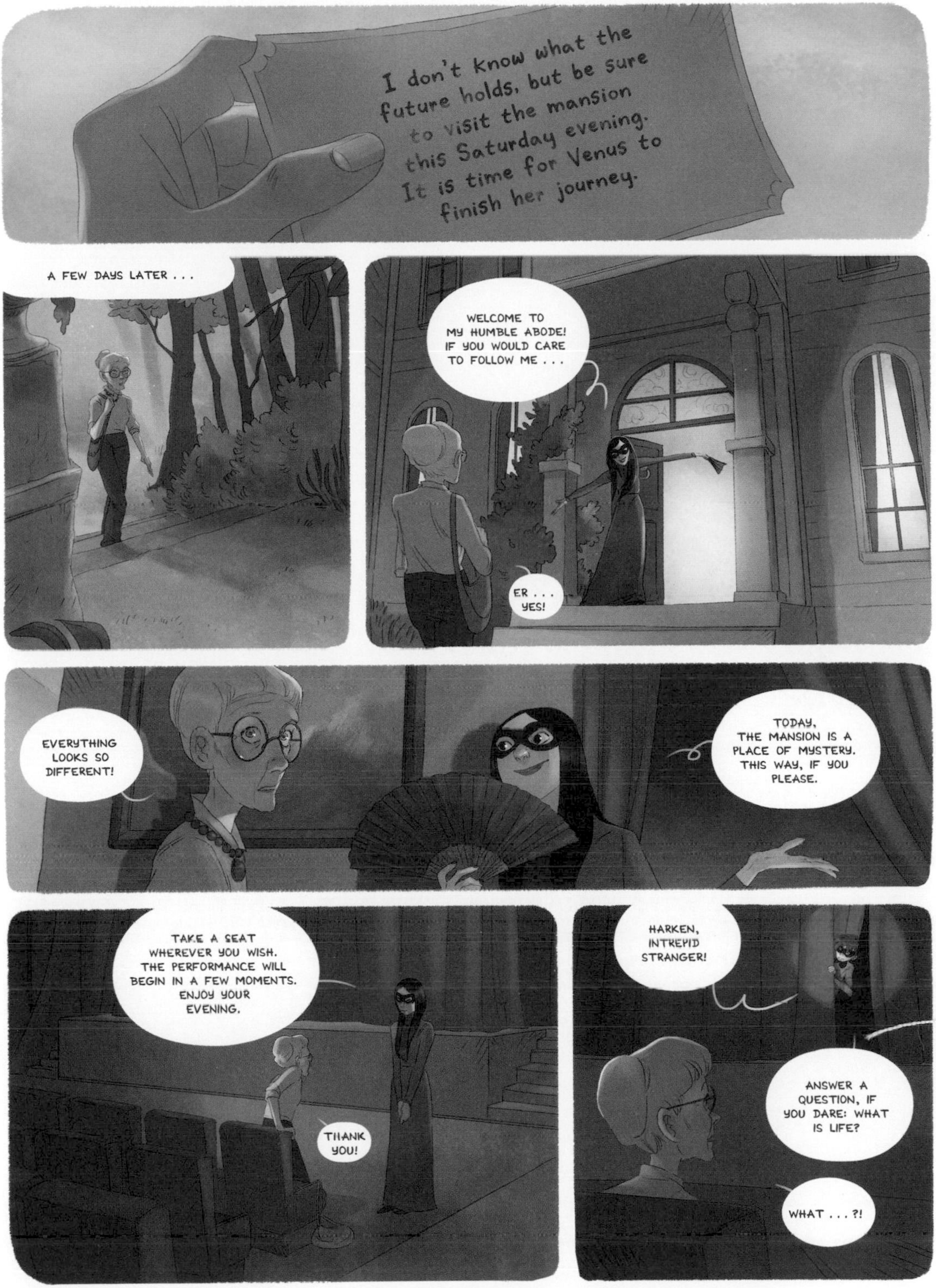
I don't know what the future holds, but be sure to visit the mansion this Saturday evening. It is time for Venus to finish her journey.
A FEW DAYS LATER . . .
WELCOME TO MY HUMBLE ABODE! IF YOU WOULD CARE TO FOLLOW ME . . .
ER . . . YES!
EVERYTHING LOOKS SO DIFFERENT!
TODAY, THE MANSION IS A PLACE OF MYSTERY. THIS WAY, IF YOU PLEASE.
TAKE A SEAT WHEREVER YOU WISH. THE PERFORMANCE WILL BEGIN IN A FEW MOMENTS. ENJOY YOUR EVENING.
THANK YOU!
HARKEN, INTREPID STRANGER!
ANSWER A QUESTION, IF YOU DARE: WHAT IS LIFE?
WHAT . . . ?!

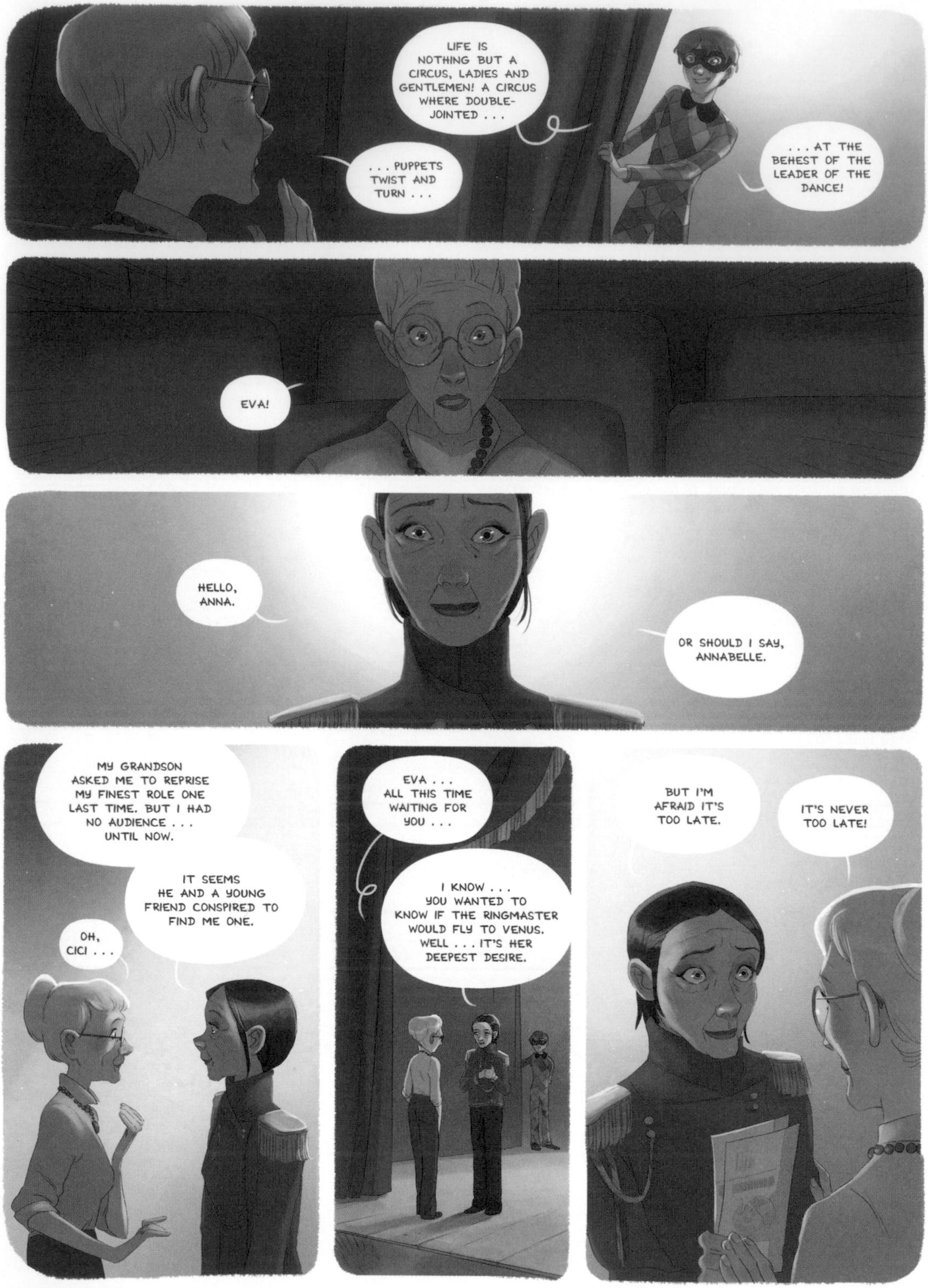
LIFE IS NOTHING BUT A CIRCUS, LADIES AND GENTLEMEN! A CIRCUS WHERE DOUBLE-JOINTED . . .
. . . PUPPETS TWIST AND TURN . . .
. . . AT THE BEHEST OF THE LEADER OF THE DANCE!
EVA!
HELLO, ANNA.
OR SHOULD I SAY, ANNABELLE.
MY GRANDSON ASKED ME TO REPRISE MY FINEST ROLE ONE LAST TIME. BUT I HAD NO AUDIENCE . . . UNTIL NOW.
IT SEEMS HE AND A YOUNG FRIEND CONSPIRED TO FIND ME ONE.
OH, CICI . . .
EVA . . . ALL THIS TIME WAITING FOR YOU . . .
I KNOW . . . YOU WANTED TO KNOW IF THE RINGMASTER WOULD FLY TO VENUS. WELL . . . IT'S HER DEEPEST DESIRE.
BUT I'M AFRAID IT'S TOO LATE.
IT'S NEVER TOO LATE!

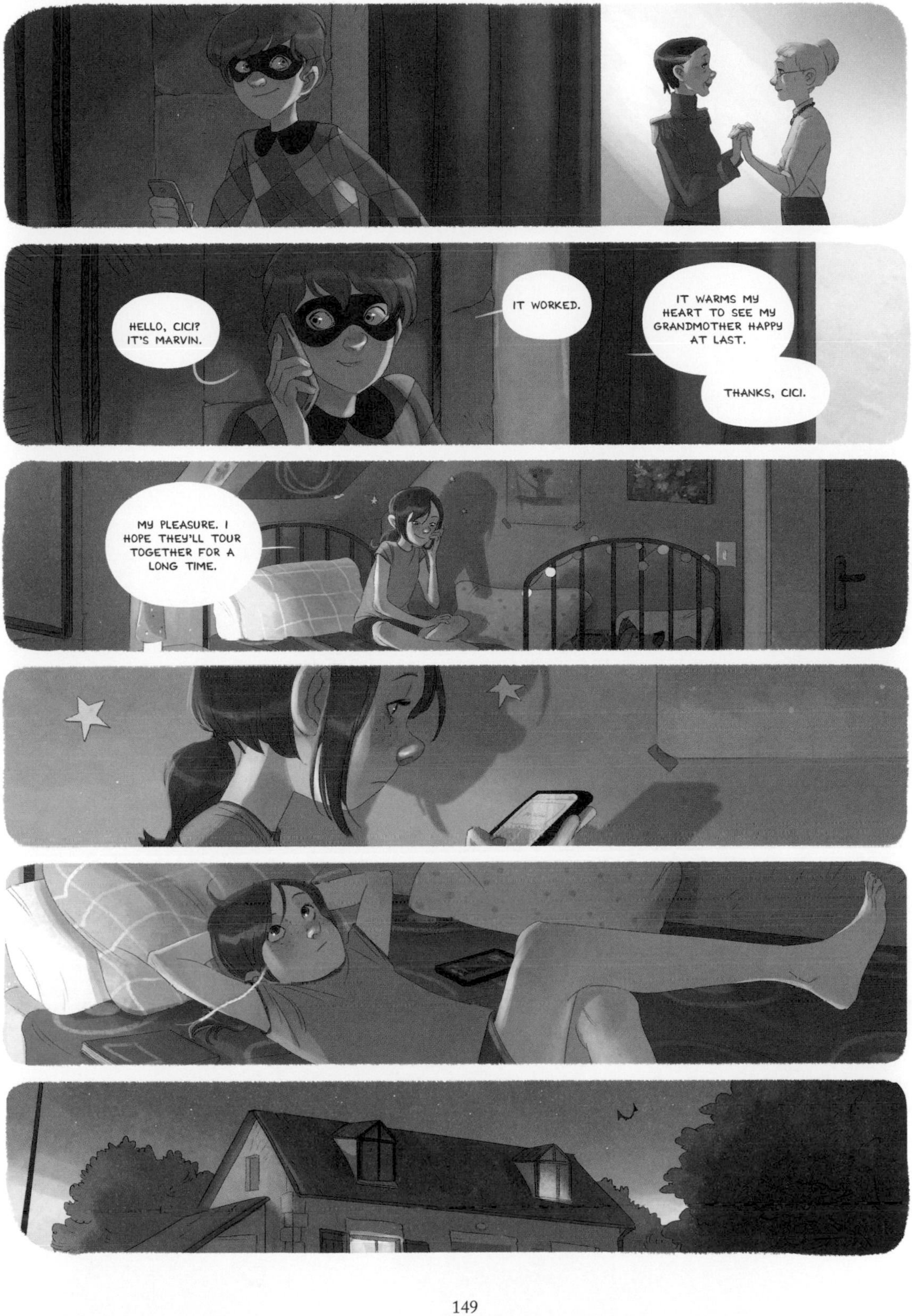
HELLO, CICI? IT'S MARVIN.
IT WORKED.
IT WARMS MY HEART TO SEE MY GRANDMOTHER HAPPY AT LAST.
THANKS, CICI.
MY PLEASURE. I HOPE THEY'LL TOUR TOGETHER FOR A LONG TIME.

My dearest Cici,

If you are reading this letter, it means that Lena carried out my instructions to deliver it to you discreetly. I wish I could contact you directly, but if your mother were to find out, I fear she would react badly, and quite rightly so. Above all else, I wish to spare you such distress.

Eva and I are catching up on the forty years we spent apart. It's been marvelous! Despite that, however, my heart bleeds for having lost you. When I conceived my desperate plan, I knew it would require a sacrifice. No matter how fervently I hoped otherwise, I was afraid that to regain one friend, I would have to lose another.

I will never forgive myself for using our friendship for my own selfish purposes. Never again will I betray anyone's trust—especially the trust of a child. Know that I will never have peace until I can repair the harm I've caused.

Your mother fears that I have stolen your love. I know it is not true. Still, she has been deeply wounded, and I wish I could have spared you the pain of hearing her make that claim. Please do not dwell on the sorrow I have caused. One day, I will return and ask for her forgiveness. I sincerely hope she will decide to hear me out, but if not, I will respect her wishes.

I don't know if I shall ever see you again. Whatever the future holds, know that I have always loved you as a daughter, or to be slightly more precise, as a granddaughter.

Goodbye, Cici. May your life be filled with joy.

Your friend, Venus

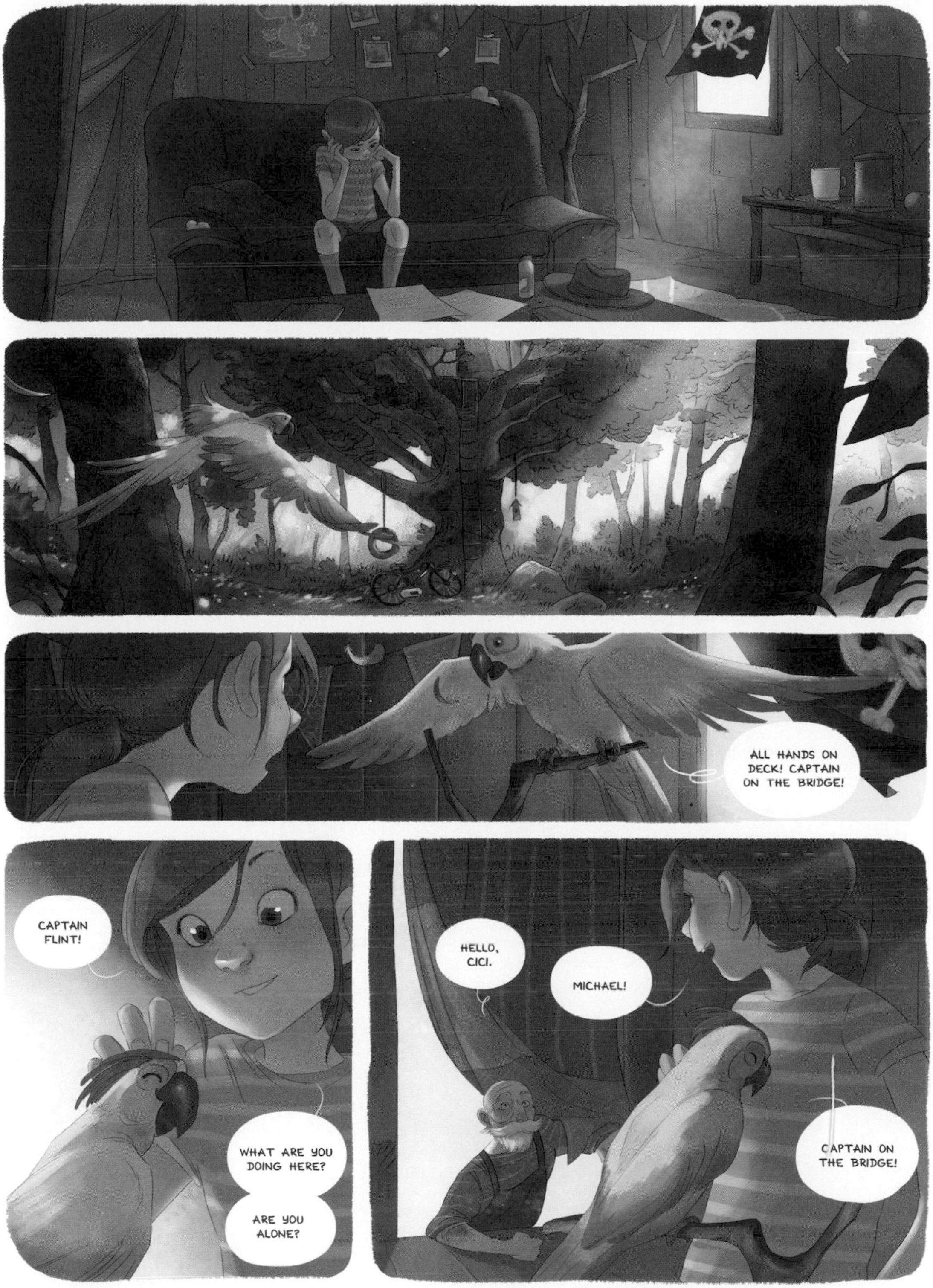
ALL HANDS ON DECK! CAPTAIN ON THE BRIDGE!
CAPTAIN FLINT!
WHAT ARE YOU DOING HERE?
ARE YOU ALONE?
HELLO, CICI.
MICHAEL!
CAPTAIN ON THE BRIDGE!

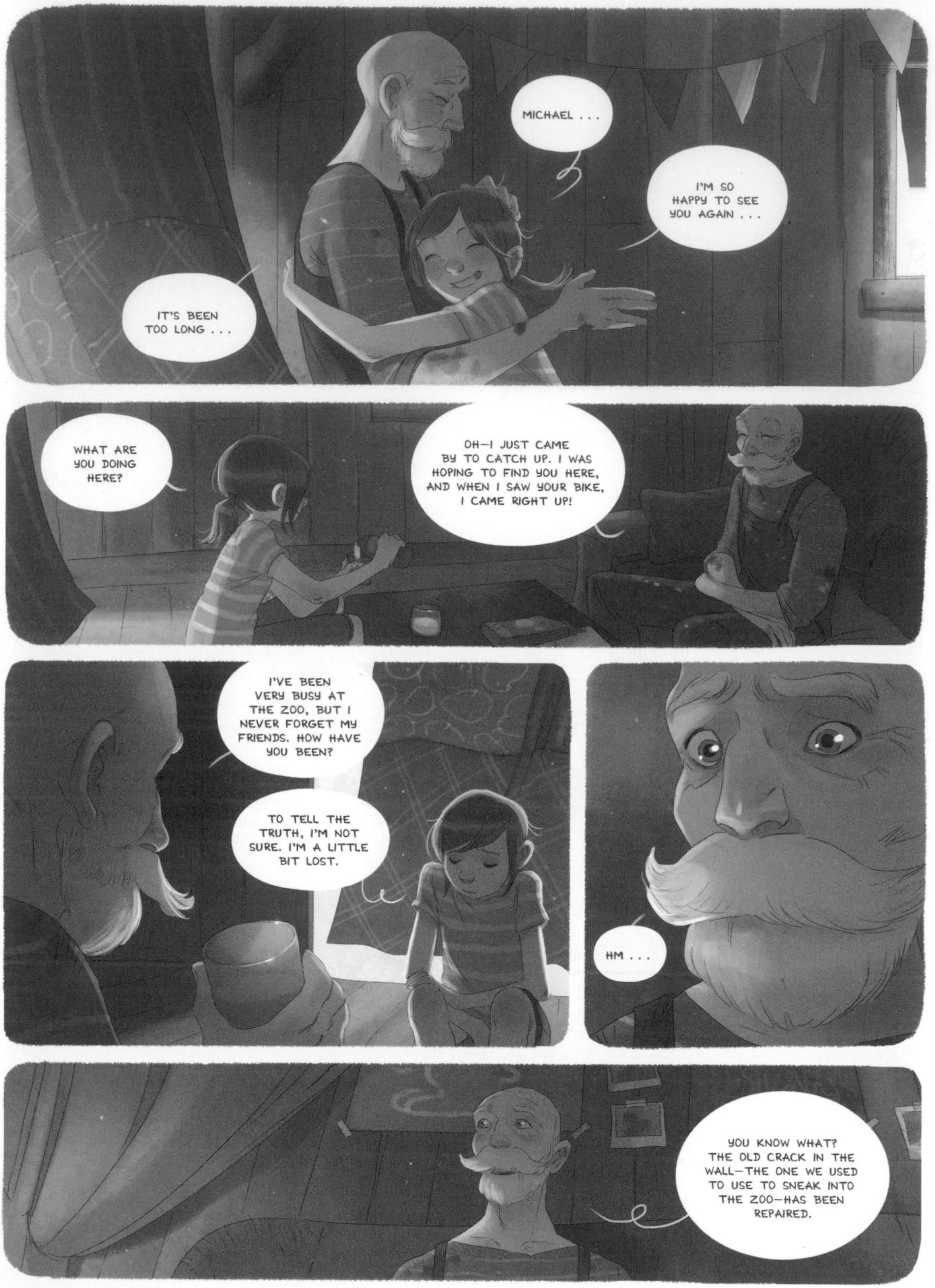
MICHAEL . . .
I'M SO HAPPY TO SEE YOU AGAIN . . .
IT'S BEEN TOO LONG . . .
WHAT ARE YOU DOING HERE?
OH—I JUST CAME BY TO CATCH UP. I WAS HOPING TO FIND YOU HERE, AND WHEN I SAW YOUR BIKE, I CAME RIGHT UP!
I'VE BEEN VERY BUSY AT THE ZOO, BUT I NEVER FORGET MY FRIENDS. HOW HAVE YOU BEEN?
TO TELL THE TRUTH, I'M NOT SURE. I'M A LITTLE BIT LOST.
HM . . .
YOU KNOW WHAT? THE OLD CRACK IN THE WALL—THE ONE WE USED TO USE TO SNEAK INTO THE ZOO—HAS BEEN REPAIRED.

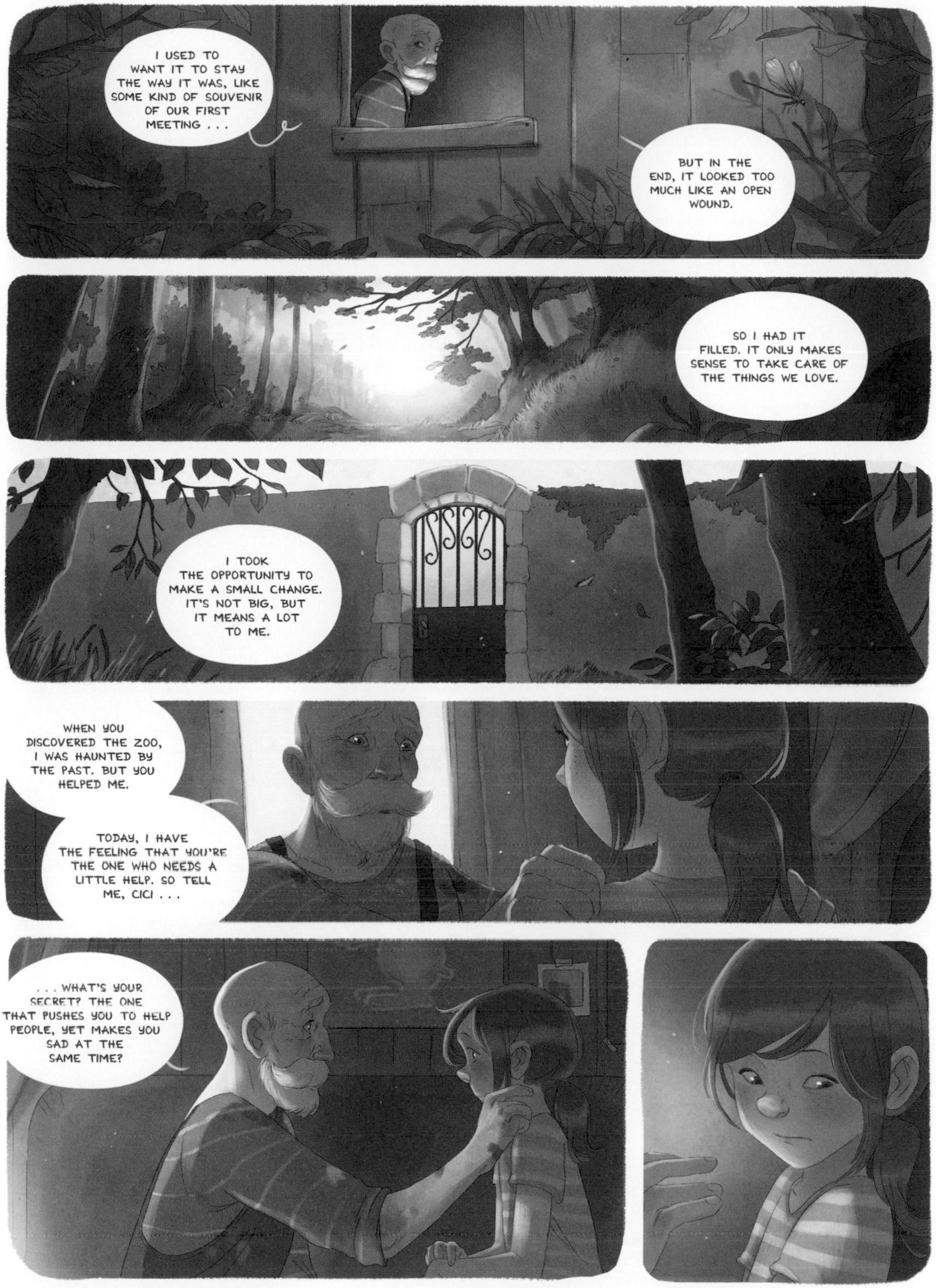
I USED TO WANT IT TO STAY THE WAY IT WAS, LIKE SOME KIND OF SOUVENIR OF OUR FIRST MEETING . . .
BUT IN THE END, IT LOOKED TOO MUCH LIKE AN OPEN WOUND.
SO I HAD IT FILLED. IT ONLY MAKES SENSE TO TAKE CARE OF THE THINGS WE LOVE.
I TOOK THE OPPORTUNITY TO MAKE A SMALL CHANGE. IT'S NOT BIG, BUT IT MEANS A LOT TO ME.
WHEN YOU DISCOVERED THE ZOO, I WAS HAUNTED BY THE PAST. BUT YOU HELPED ME.
TODAY, I HAVE THE FEELING THAT YOU'RE THE ONE WHO NEEDS A LITTLE HELP. SO TELL ME, CICI . . .
. . . WHAT'S YOUR SECRET? THE ONE THAT PUSHES YOU TO HELP PEOPLE, YET MAKES YOU SAD AT THE SAME TIME?

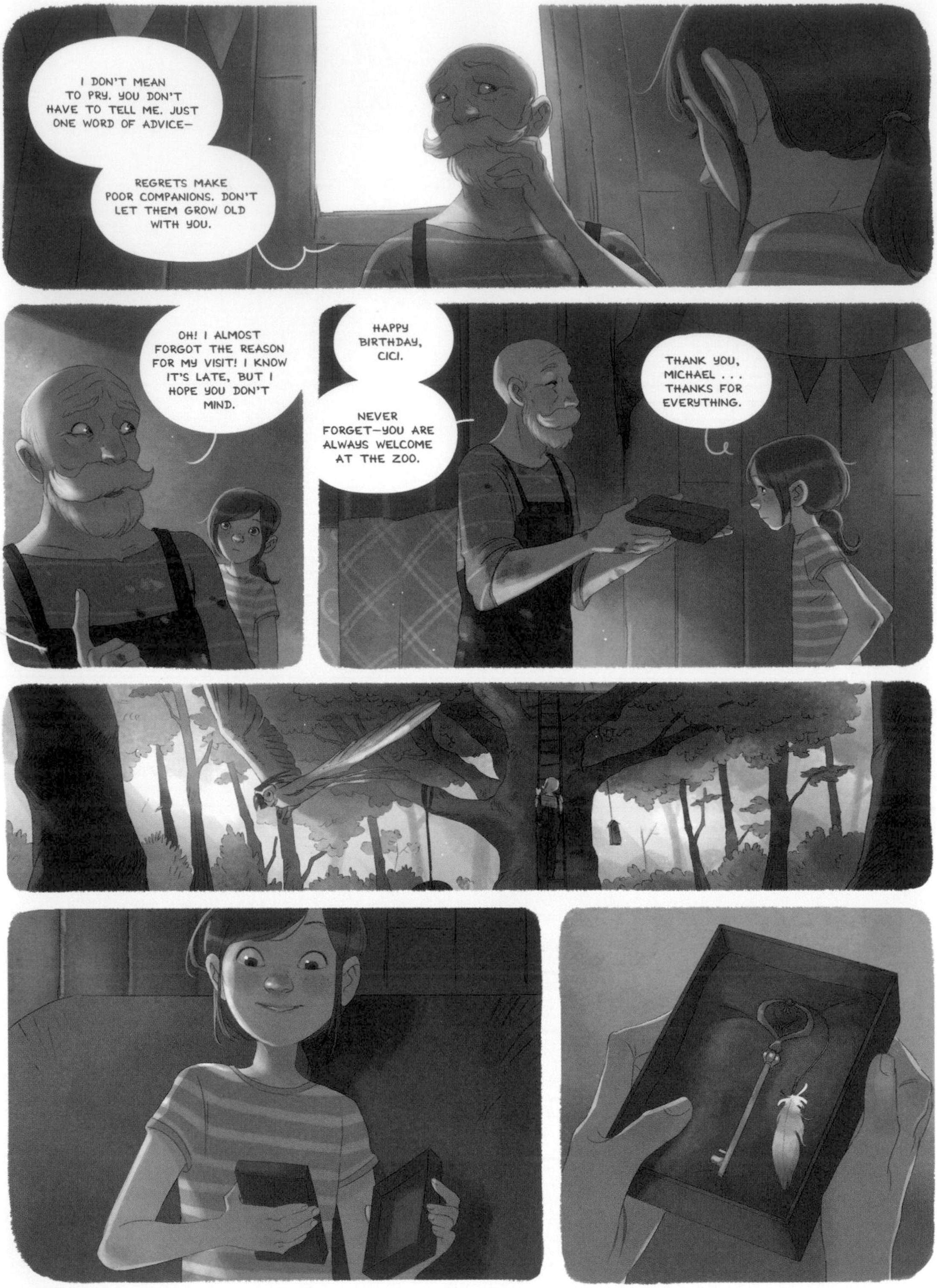
I DON'T MEAN TO PRY. YOU DON'T HAVE TO TELL ME. JUST ONE WORD OF ADVICE—
REGRETS MAKE POOR COMPANIONS. DON'T LET THEM GROW OLD WITH YOU.
OH! I ALMOST FORGOT THE REASON FOR MY VISIT! I KNOW IT'S LATE, BUT I HOPE YOU DON'T MIND.
HAPPY BIRTHDAY, CICI.
NEVER FORGET—YOU ARE ALWAYS WELCOME AT THE ZOO.
THANK YOU, MICHAEL . . . THANKS FOR EVERYTHING.

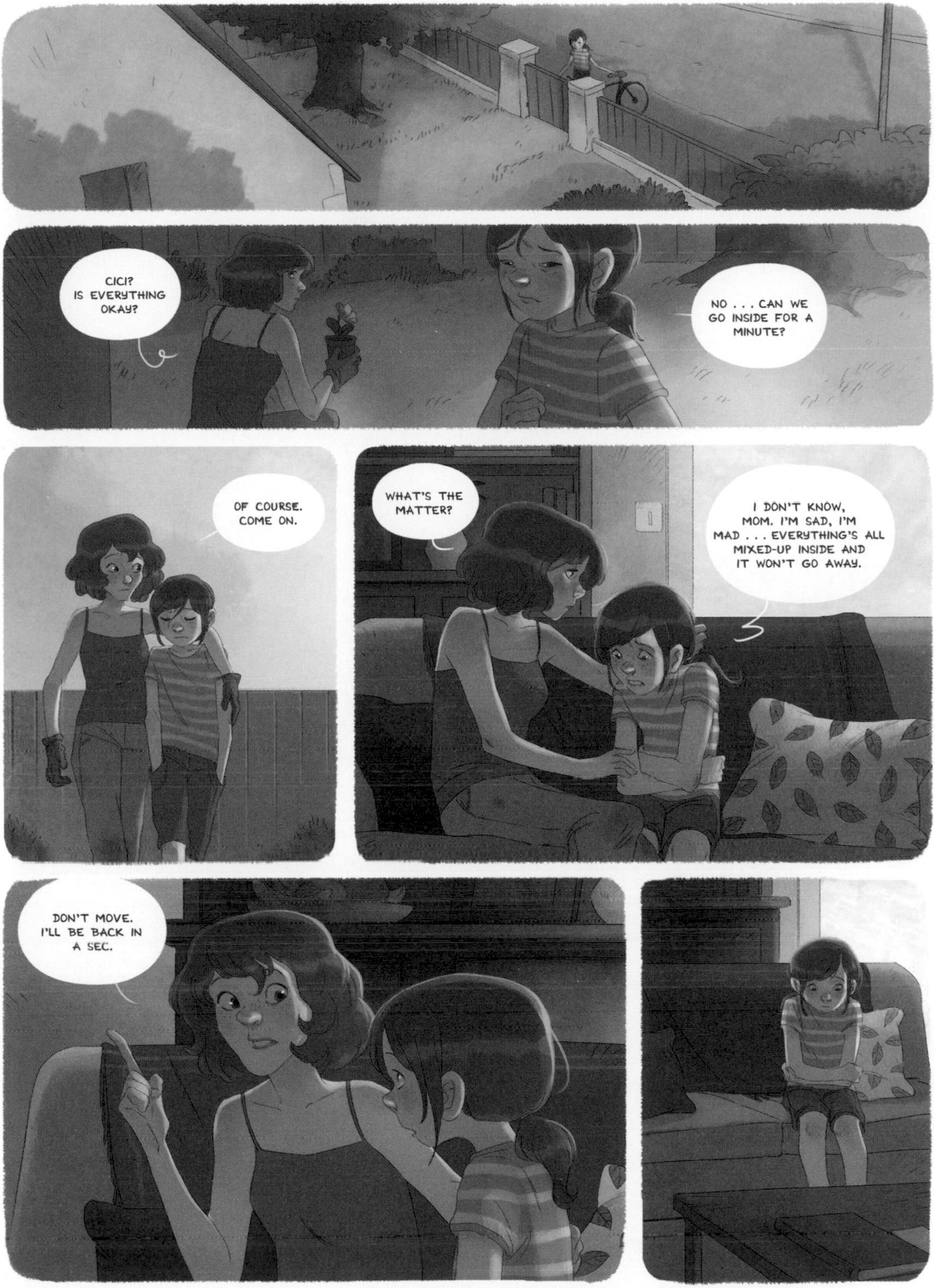
CICI? IS EVERYTHING OKAY?
NO . . . CAN WE GO INSIDE FOR A MINUTE?
OF COURSE. COME ON.
WHAT'S THE MATTER?
I DON'T KNOW, MOM. I'M SAD, I'M MAD . . . EVERYTHING'S ALL MIXED-UP INSIDE AND IT WON'T GO AWAY.
DON'T MOVE. I'LL BE BACK IN A SEC.

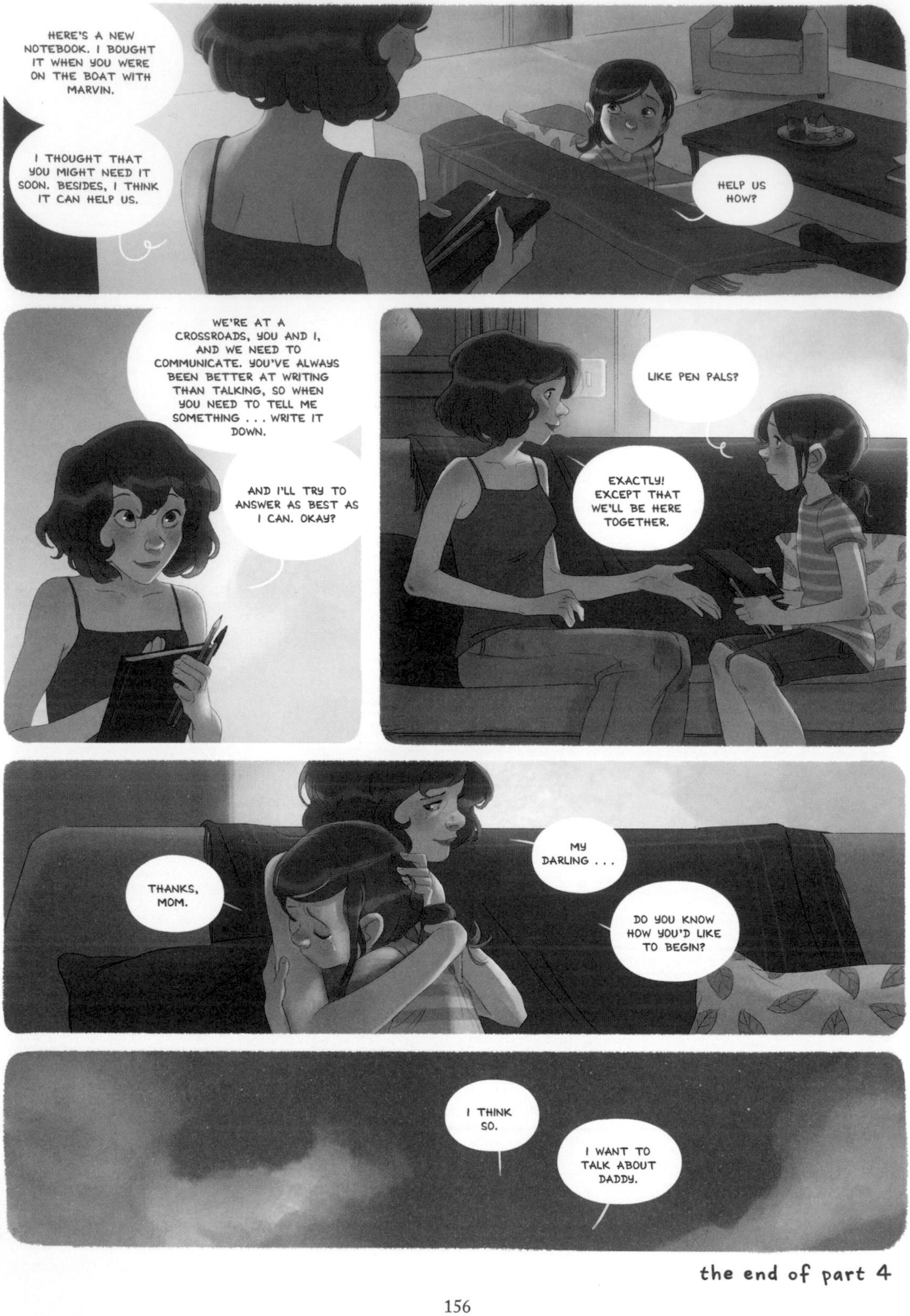
HERE'S A NEW NOTEBOOK. I BOUGHT IT WHEN YOU WERE ON THE BOAT WITH MARVIN.
I THOUGHT THAT YOU MIGHT NEED IT SOON. BESIDES, I THINK IT CAN HELP US.
HELP US HOW?
WE'RE AT A CROSSROADS, YOU AND I, AND WE NEED TO COMMUNICATE. YOU'VE ALWAYS BEEN BETTER AT WRITING THAN TALKING, SO WHEN YOU NEED TO TELL ME SOMETHING . . . WRITE IT DOWN.
AND I'LL TRY TO ANSWER AS BEST AS I CAN. OKAY?
LIKE PEN PALS?
EXACTLY! EXCEPT THAT WE'LL BE HERE TOGETHER.
THANKS, MOM.
MY DARLING . . .
DO YOU KNOW HOW YOU'D LIKE TO BEGIN?
I THINK SO.
I WANT TO TALK ABOUT DADDY.

the end of part 4

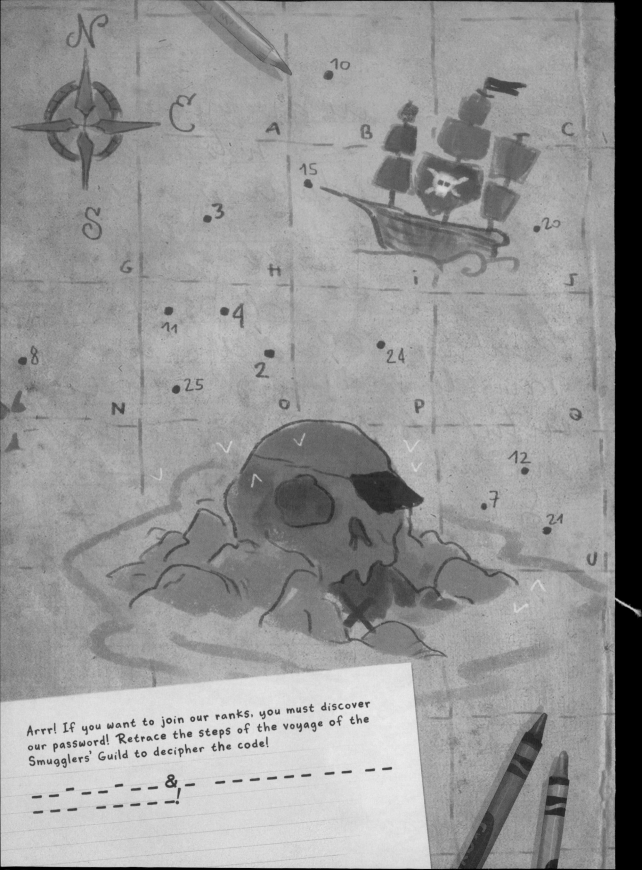

Arrr! If you want to join our ranks, you must discover our password! Retrace the steps of the voyage of the Smugglers' Guild to decipher the code!

_ _ _ _ _ _ _ & _ _ _ _ _ _ _ _ _ _ _
_ _ _ _ _ _ _ _ _ !

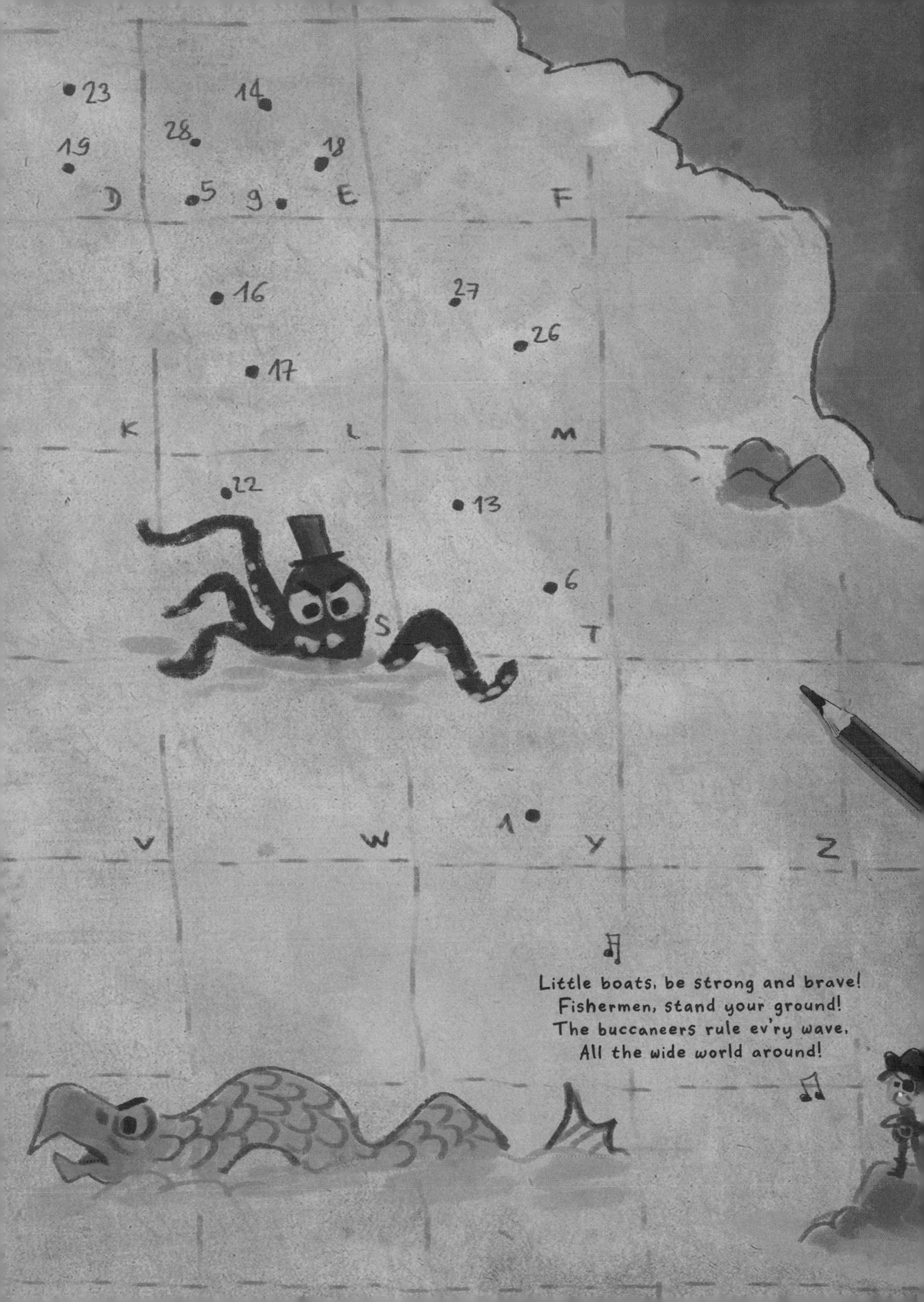
D
E
F
K
L
M
S
T
V
W
Y
Z
Little boats, be strong and brave!
Fishermen, stand your ground!
The buccaneers rule ev'ry wave,
All the wide world around!

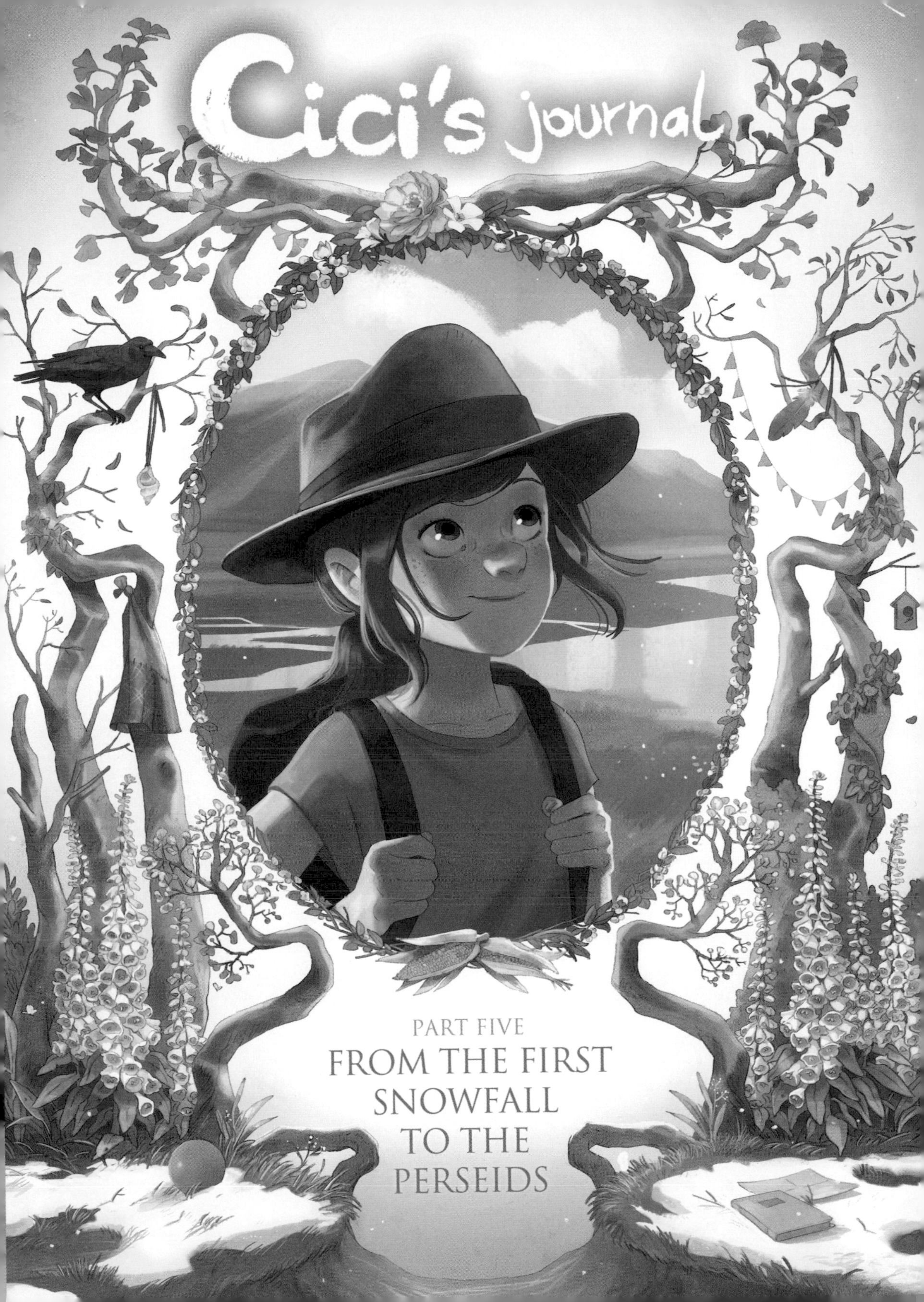
Cici's journal

PART FIVE

FROM THE FIRST SNOWFALL TO THE PERSEIDS

Vacation time!!!

Once upon a time . . .

Dear Santa Claus . . .

I'm twelve years old!

I had no trouble starting my earlier journals, but this time, I don't know how to begin. So many things are jostling around in my head that it feels like it's going to explode. But when I try to talk, the words get all jumbled up in my throat.

To make this easier, let me just go through everything in order. Over Christmas vacation, I helped Sandra recover part of her lost childhood by going on a treasure hunt that was organized by her late father . . . It was so touching!

Like her, I feel like my life is a puzzle that is missing several pieces. Until I find them,
I won't feel whole.

But I don't know how to go about it. I really want to find those missing pieces, but whenever I think about looking for them, I get scared and angry and I don't know why.

I was four years old when Daddy passed away. I can barely remember how he laughed or what he smelled like.

Mom, I feel guilty for not being able to remember more.

Can you help me remember?

Darling Cici,

After reading your first entry in this notebook, my stomach is all knotted up. It hurts to know that you carry so much grief. It's not wrong to be unable to remember more about your dad, so you shouldn't feel guilty. You were so little. Don't blame yourself. Sometimes, even I find myself forgetting the color of his eyes.

I promise to do my best to help you discover the missing pieces of your past so you feel whole again. I promise to do all I can to drive away your sadness, as you have so cleverly done for so many others.

This time, the "mysterious character" in your notebook is you.

You'll have to launch an investigation into your own past. It's the only way to discover what is hurting you so much and how you can feel better.

The journey will be long and sometimes painful, but I will never let go of your hand. I will be with you every step of the way. I promise.

Where shall we begin our journey together? I know—tell me, what is your earliest memory?

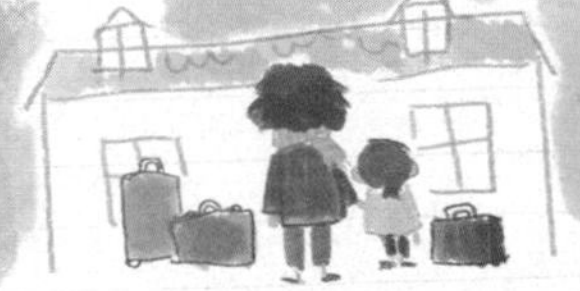

I remember arriving in this big house for the first time. I think it was a gift from your uncle. Before that, everything's foggy. I especially remember my first day of school. It was snowing—the first snowfall of the season.

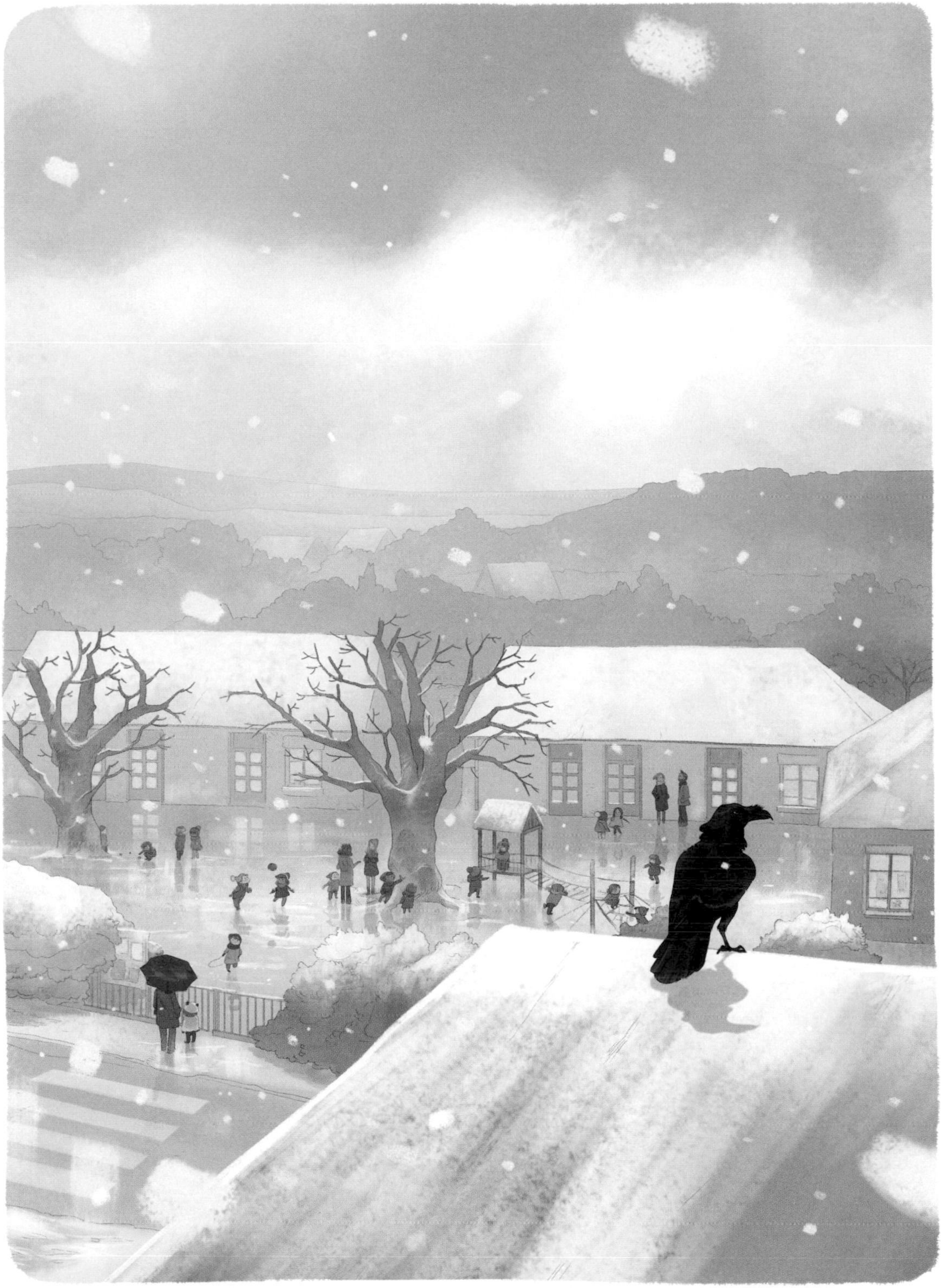

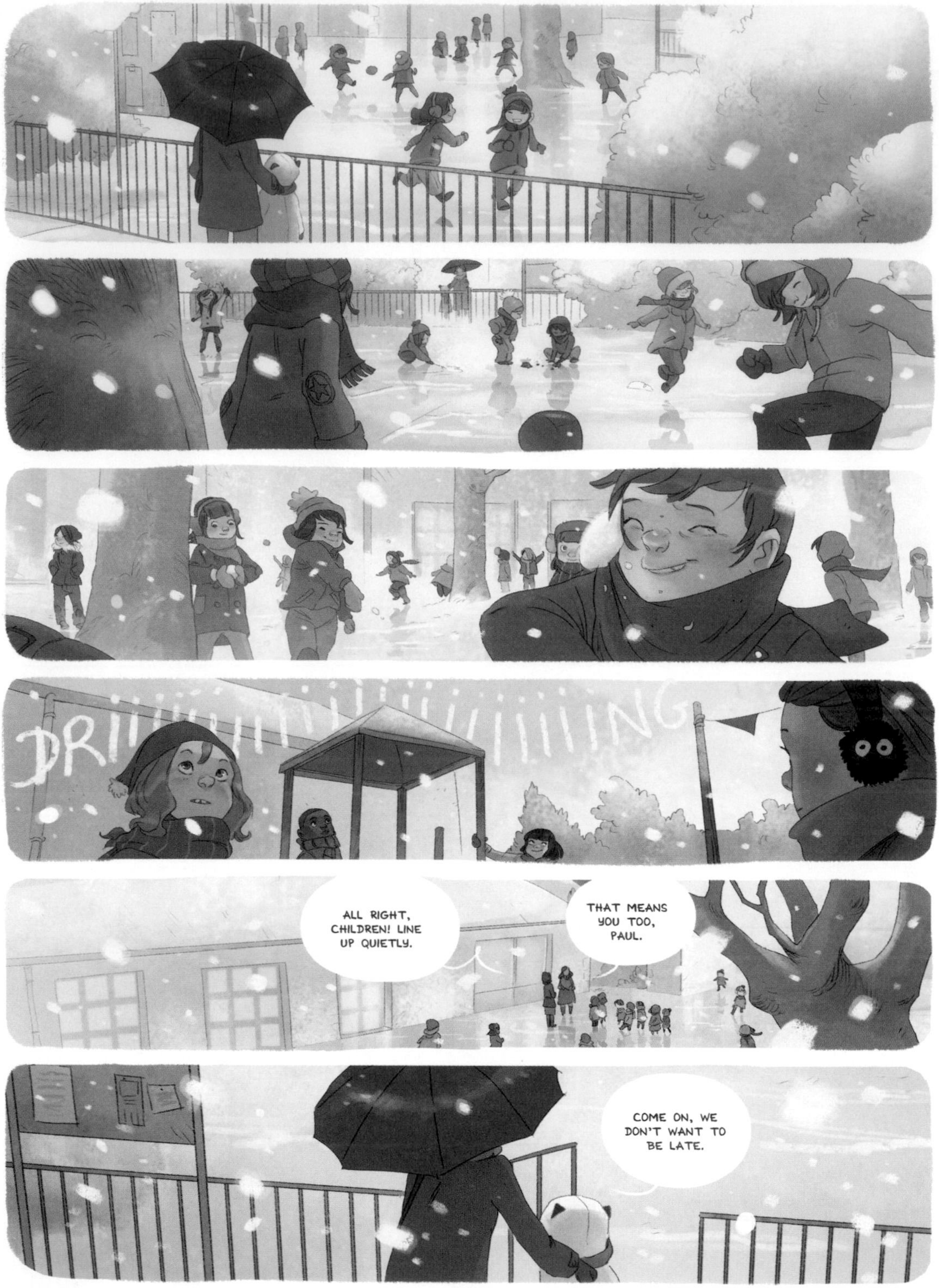
DRIIIIIIIIIIIIIIIIIING
ALL RIGHT, CHILDREN! LINE UP QUIETLY.
THAT MEANS YOU TOO, PAUL.
COME ON, WE DON'T WANT TO BE LATE.

HELLO, MA'AM. I'M MR. MOREAU, THE SCHOOL PRINCIPAL.

WE SPOKE ON THE PHONE LAST WEEK.

PLEASED TO MEET YOU.

HELLO, YOUNG LADY! WOULD YOU LIKE TO COME WITH ME AND SEE YOUR NEW CLASS?

THIS WAY, PLEASE.

WE HAVE A BIG ACTIVITY ROOM, A COMPUTER LAB FOR BEGINNERS, A LIBRARY . . .

AND EVEN A CAFETERIA WHERE A COOK COMES EVERY DAY AT NOON TO PREPARE US LUNCH USING LOCALLY GROWN INGREDIENTS!

HOW NICE!

THIS IS MRS. NICOLE'S CLASSROOM.

MRS. NIC

MRS. NIC

WAIT JUST A MOMENT. I'LL LET THEM KNOW YOU'RE HERE.

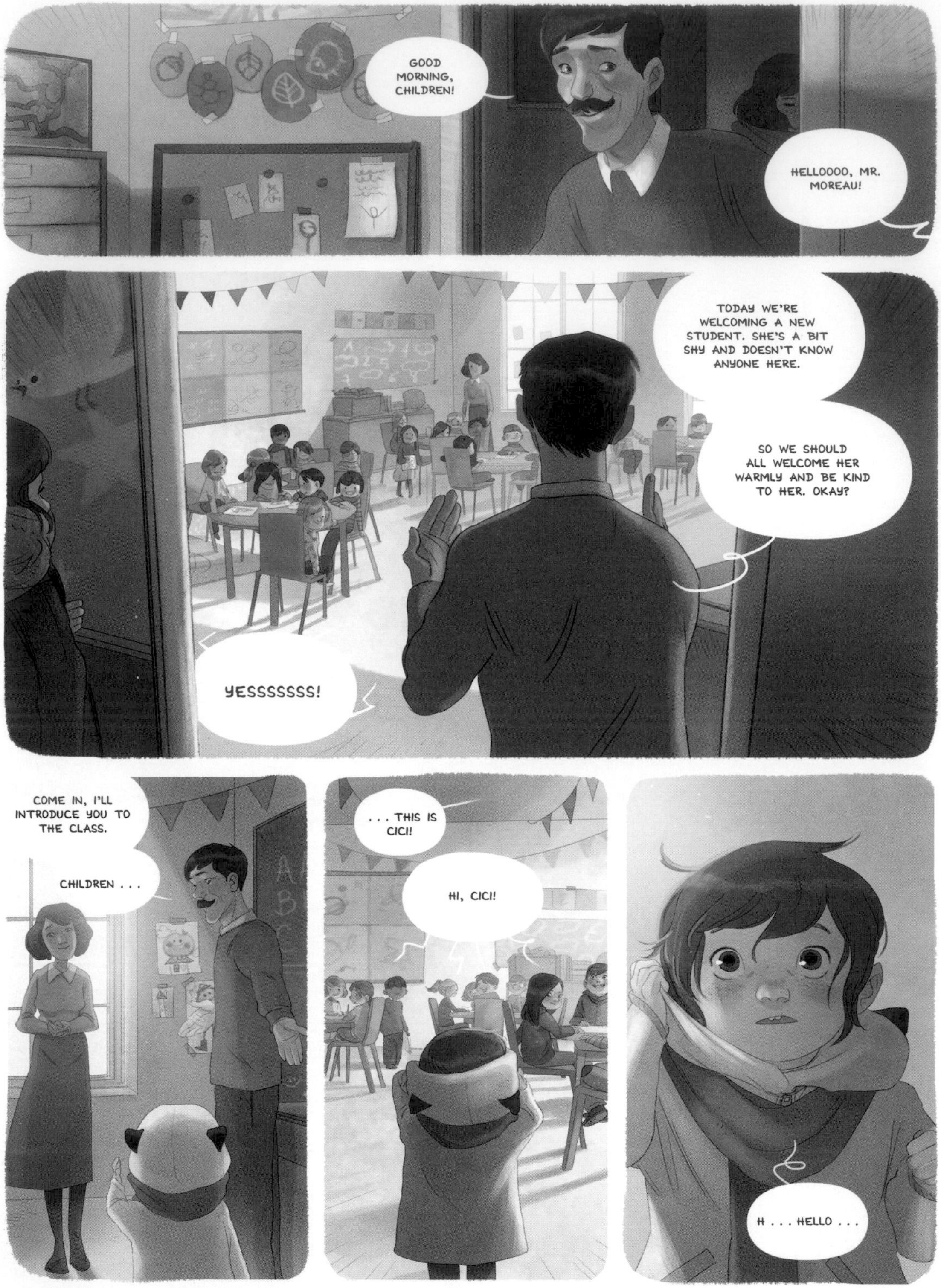
GOOD MORNING, CHILDREN!
HELLOOOO, MR. MOREAU!
TODAY WE'RE WELCOMING A NEW STUDENT. SHE'S A BIT SHY AND DOESN'T KNOW ANYONE HERE.
SO WE SHOULD ALL WELCOME HER WARMLY AND BE KIND TO HER. OKAY?
YESSSSSSS!
COME IN, I'LL INTRODUCE YOU TO THE CLASS.
CHILDREN . . .
. . . THIS IS CICI!
HI, CICI!
H . . . HELLO . . .

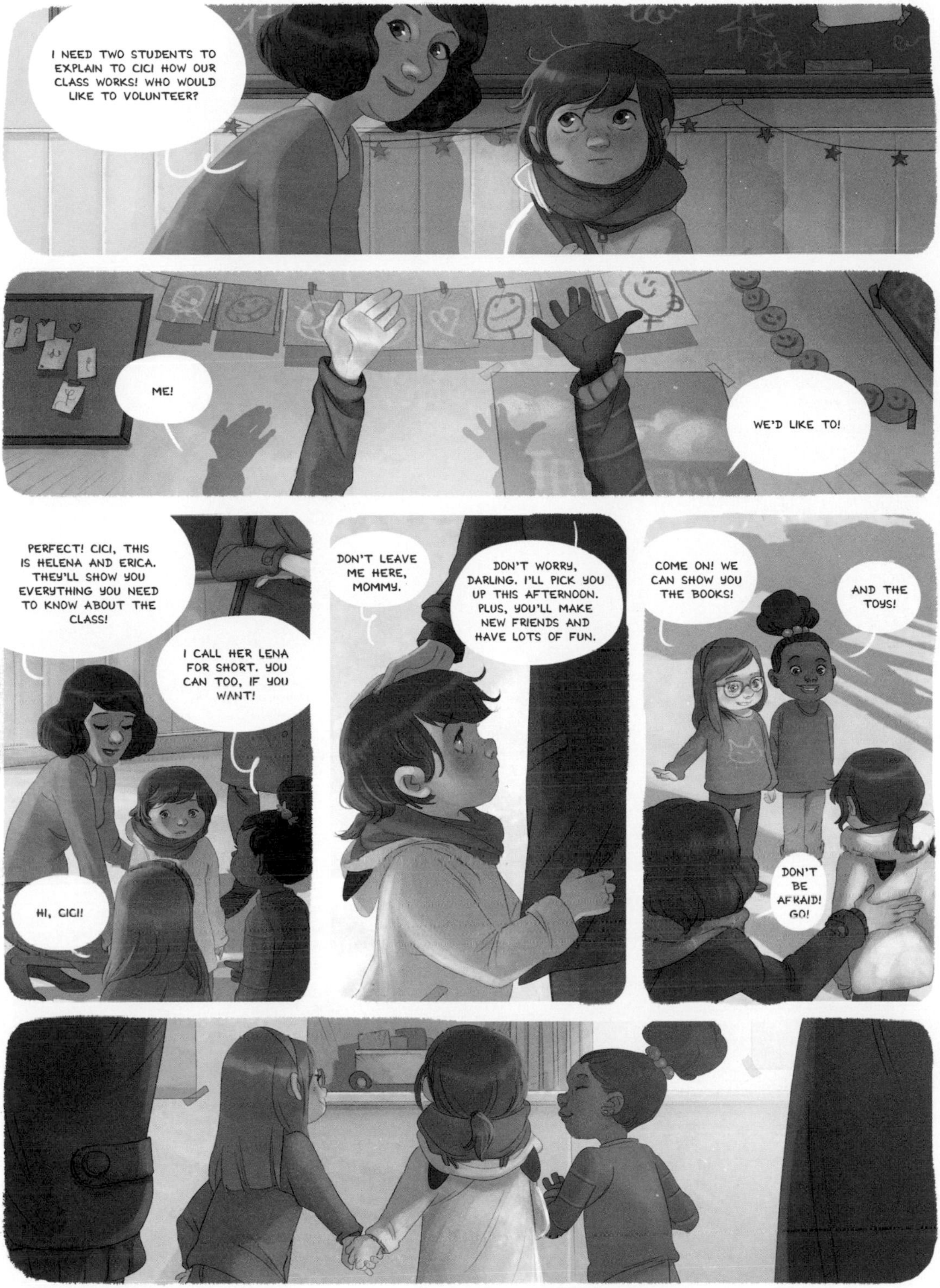
I NEED TWO STUDENTS TO EXPLAIN TO CICI HOW OUR CLASS WORKS! WHO WOULD LIKE TO VOLUNTEER?
ME!
WE'D LIKE TO!
PERFECT! CICI, THIS IS HELENA AND ERICA. THEY'LL SHOW YOU EVERYTHING YOU NEED TO KNOW ABOUT THE CLASS!
I CALL HER LENA FOR SHORT. YOU CAN TOO, IF YOU WANT!
HI, CICI!
DON'T LEAVE ME HERE, MOMMY.
DON'T WORRY, DARLING. I'LL PICK YOU UP THIS AFTERNOON. PLUS, YOU'LL MAKE NEW FRIENDS AND HAVE LOTS OF FUN.
COME ON! WE CAN SHOW YOU THE BOOKS!
AND THE TOYS!
DON'T BE AFRAID! GO!

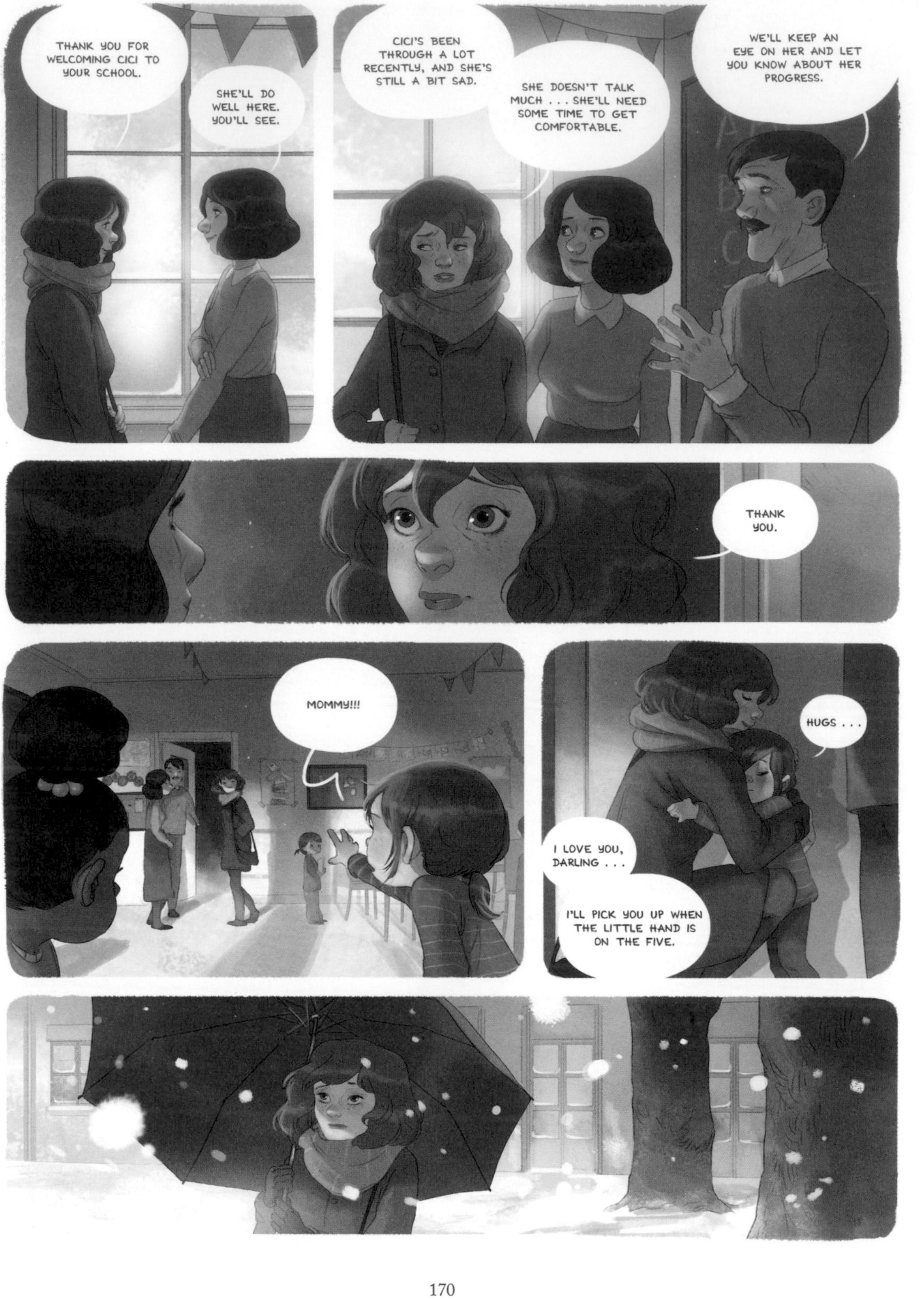
THANK YOU FOR WELCOMING CICI TO YOUR SCHOOL.
SHE'LL DO WELL HERE. YOU'LL SEE.
CICI'S BEEN THROUGH A LOT RECENTLY, AND SHE'S STILL A BIT SAD.
SHE DOESN'T TALK MUCH . . . SHE'LL NEED SOME TIME TO GET COMFORTABLE.
WE'LL KEEP AN EYE ON HER AND LET YOU KNOW ABOUT HER PROGRESS.
THANK YOU.
MOMMY!!!
HUGS . . .
I LOVE YOU, DARLING . . .
I'LL PICK YOU UP WHEN THE LITTLE HAND IS ON THE FIVE.

Lena and Erica were super kind to me. Until now, I never realized how much I owe them. Despite seeing that I wanted to keep to myself, they did everything they could to get me to laugh. We became friends almost right away and they often invited me over to their houses.

Elliot hadn't even been born yet!

I love this photo!

Lena and Erica told me they first met at day care, where their parents hit it off. They grew up together. Since Erica's parents worked a lot, she often went to play at Lena's house. I would love to have been there too!

Even though they were already best friends (really, they were more like sisters than friends), they accepted me without hesitation, as if we all belonged together.

I can never thank them enough for that.

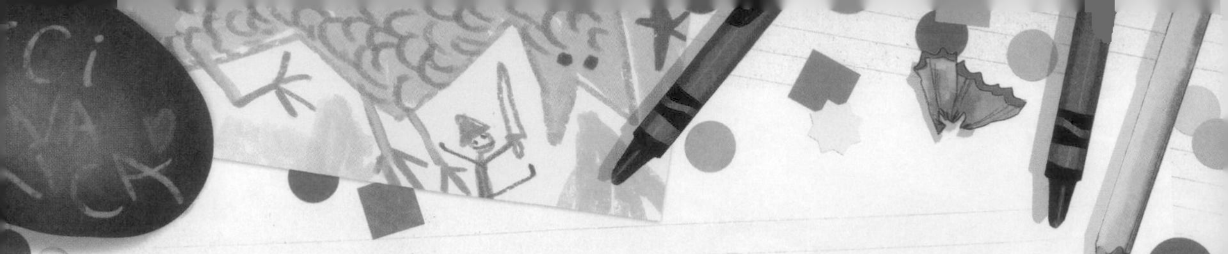

The three of us had so much fun! We quickly became inseparable. Whether on field trips or in the cafeteria, we could always be found side by side.

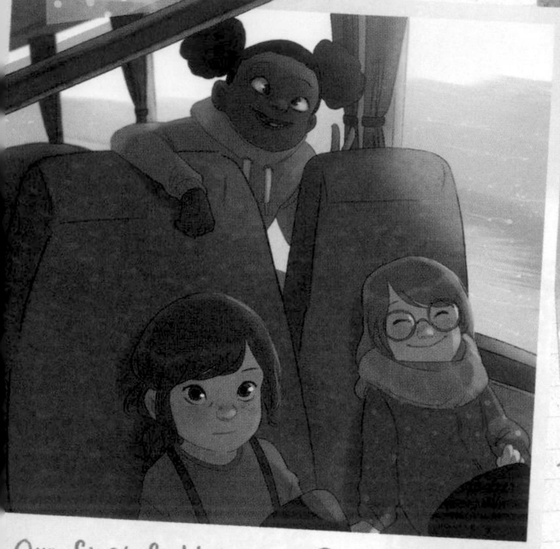

Our first field trip to Paris!

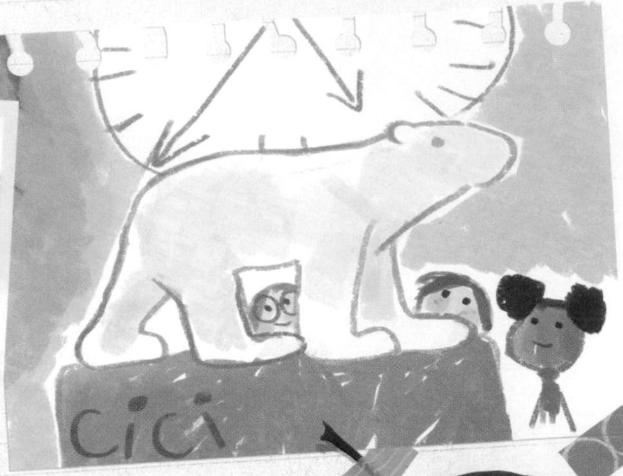
cici

My drawing of Pompon's polar bear at the Musée d'Orsay!

Since I had an unusual name, a pale complexion, and a sad expression most of the time, the other kids would make fun of me. I didn't know how to respond, but Lena and Erica came to my rescue. They stuck up for me and made the teasing stop.

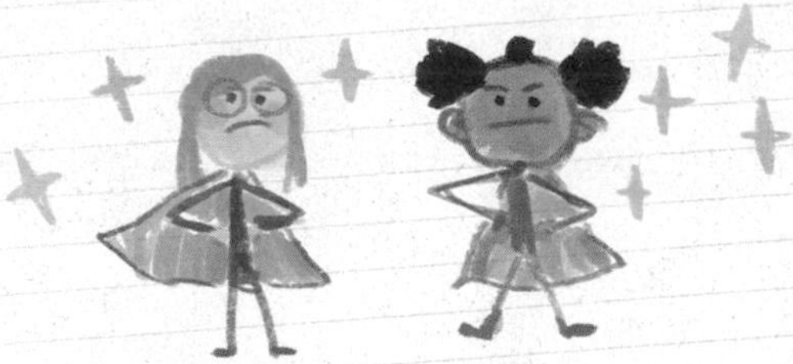

Then, one day, the other kids in my class found out I could already do something they were having trouble with.

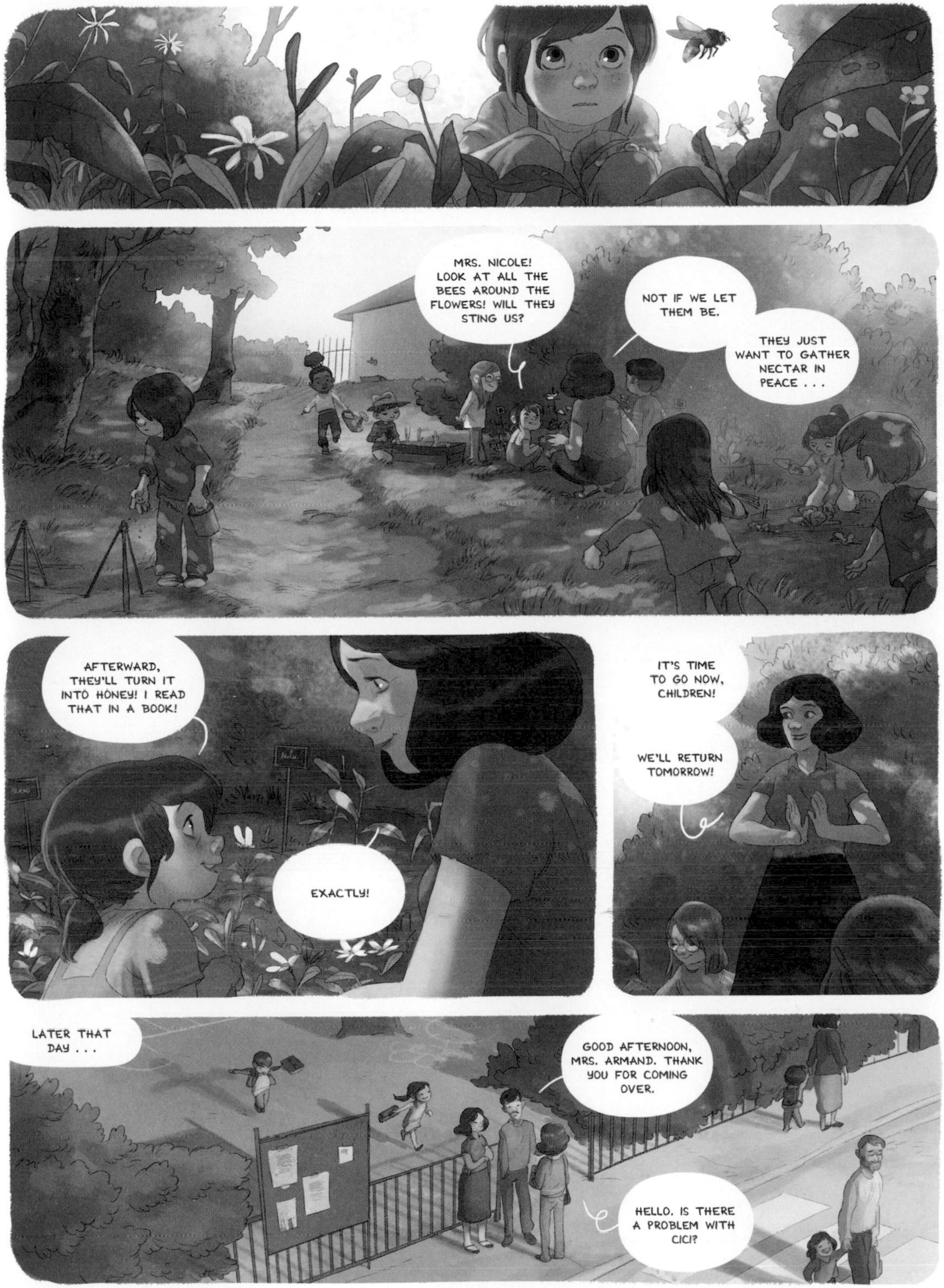
MRS. NICOLE! LOOK AT ALL THE BEES AROUND THE FLOWERS! WILL THEY STING US?
NOT IF WE LET THEM BE.
THEY JUST WANT TO GATHER NECTAR IN PEACE . . .
AFTERWARD, THEY'LL TURN IT INTO HONEY! I READ THAT IN A BOOK!
EXACTLY!
IT'S TIME TO GO NOW, CHILDREN!
WE'LL RETURN TOMORROW!
LATER THAT DAY . . .
GOOD AFTERNOON, MRS. ARMAND. THANK YOU FOR COMING OVER.
HELLO. IS THERE A PROBLEM WITH CICI?

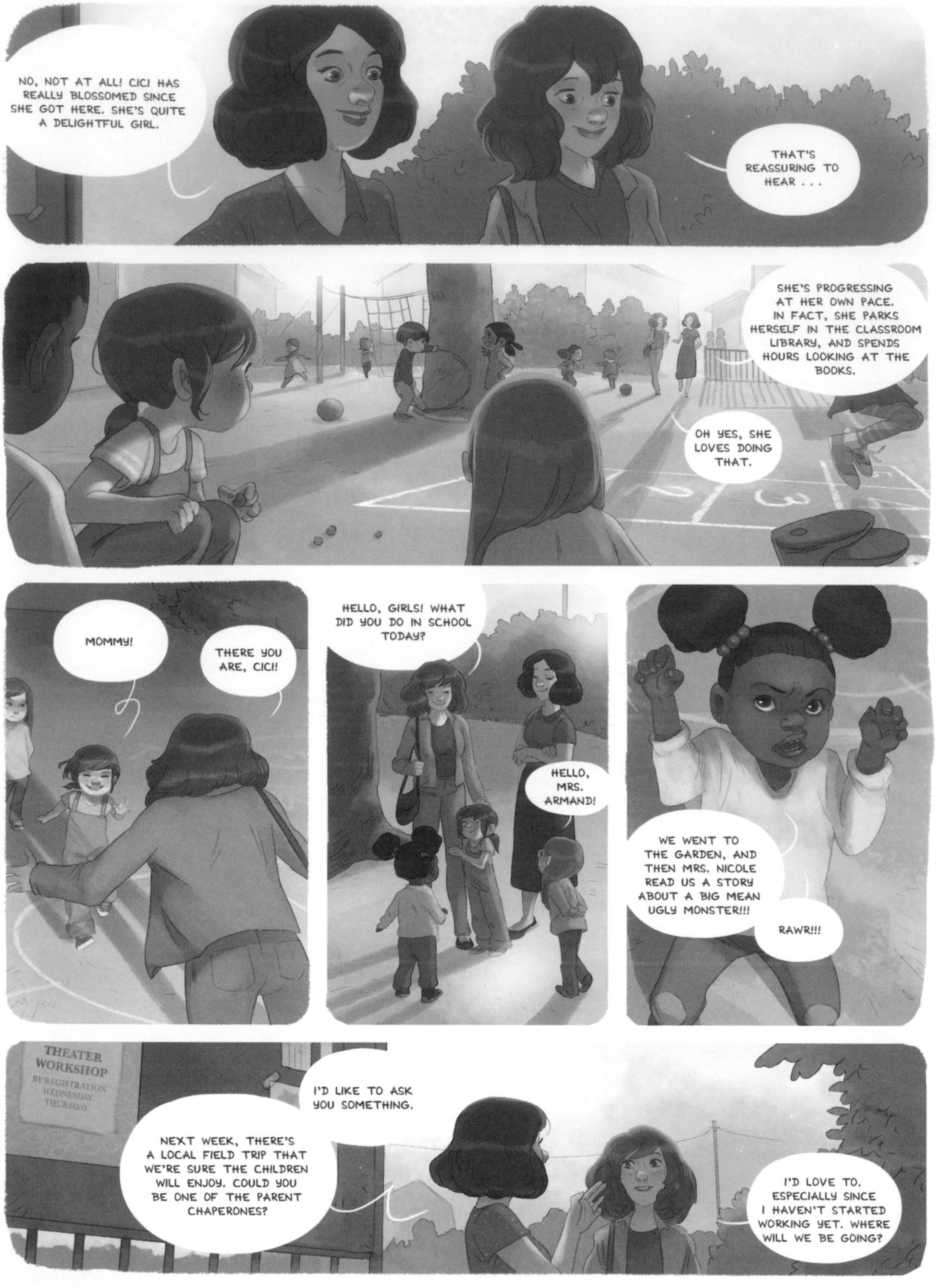
NO, NOT AT ALL! CICI HAS REALLY BLOSSOMED SINCE SHE GOT HERE. SHE'S QUITE A DELIGHTFUL GIRL.
THAT'S REASSURING TO HEAR . . .
SHE'S PROGRESSING AT HER OWN PACE. IN FACT, SHE PARKS HERSELF IN THE CLASSROOM LIBRARY, AND SPENDS HOURS LOOKING AT THE BOOKS.
OH YES, SHE LOVES DOING THAT.
MOMMY!
THERE YOU ARE, CICI!
HELLO, GIRLS! WHAT DID YOU DO IN SCHOOL TODAY?
HELLO, MRS. ARMAND!
WE WENT TO THE GARDEN, AND THEN MRS. NICOLE READ US A STORY ABOUT A BIG MEAN UGLY MONSTER!!!
RAWR!!!
THEATER WORKSHOP
BY REGISTRATION
WEDNESDAY
THURSDAY
I'D LIKE TO ASK YOU SOMETHING.
NEXT WEEK, THERE'S A LOCAL FIELD TRIP THAT WE'RE SURE THE CHILDREN WILL ENJOY. COULD YOU BE ONE OF THE PARENT CHAPERONES?
I'D LOVE TO. ESPECIALLY SINCE I HAVEN'T STARTED WORKING YET. WHERE WILL WE BE GOING?

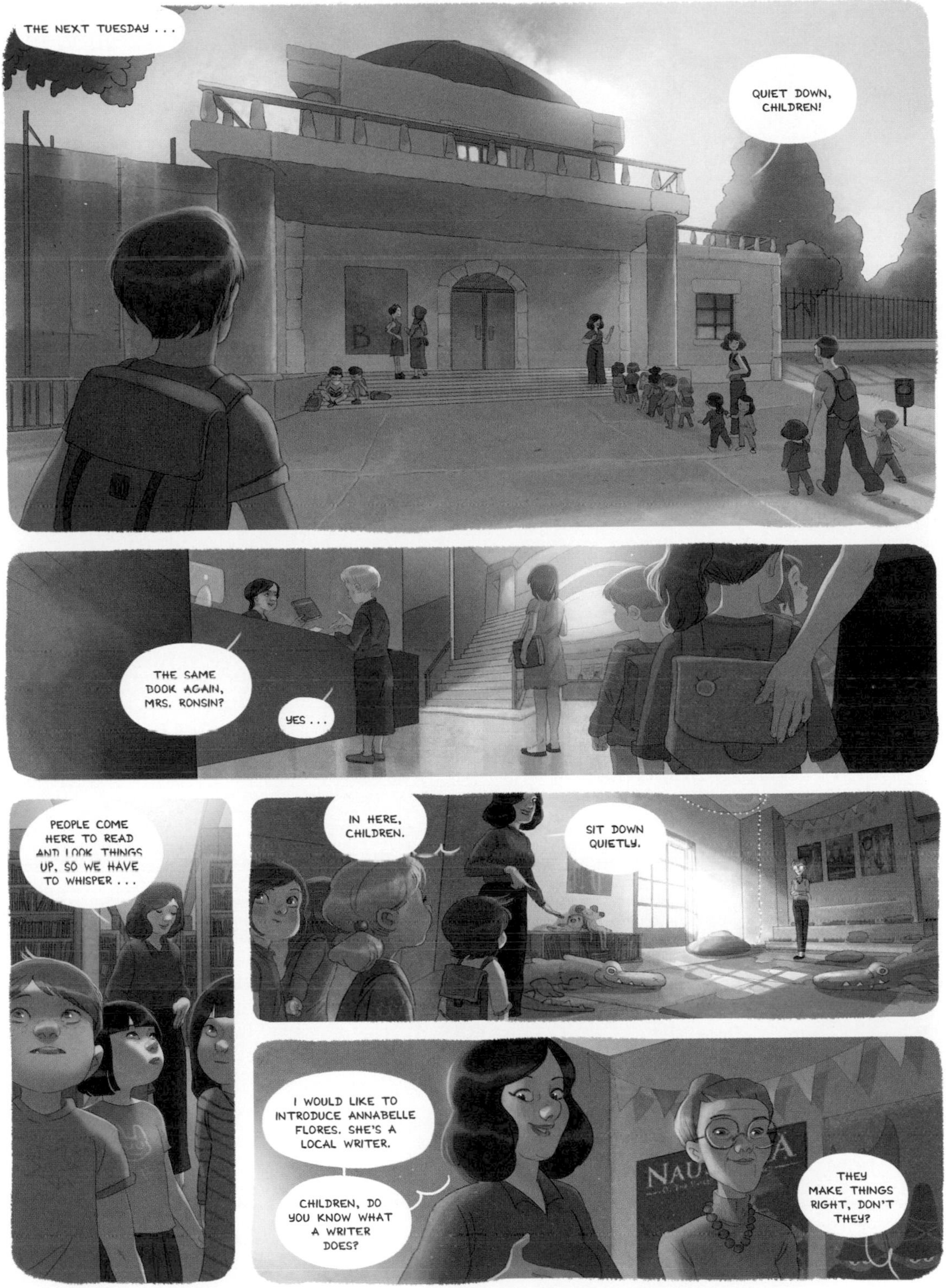
THE NEXT TUESDAY . . .
QUIET DOWN, CHILDREN!
THE SAME BOOK AGAIN, MRS. RONSIN?
YES . . .
PEOPLE COME HERE TO READ AND LOOK THINGS UP, SO WE HAVE TO WHISPER . . .
IN HERE, CHILDREN.
SIT DOWN QUIETLY.
I WOULD LIKE TO INTRODUCE ANNABELLE FLORES. SHE'S A LOCAL WRITER.
CHILDREN, DO YOU KNOW WHAT A WRITER DOES?
THEY MAKE THINGS RIGHT, DON'T THEY?

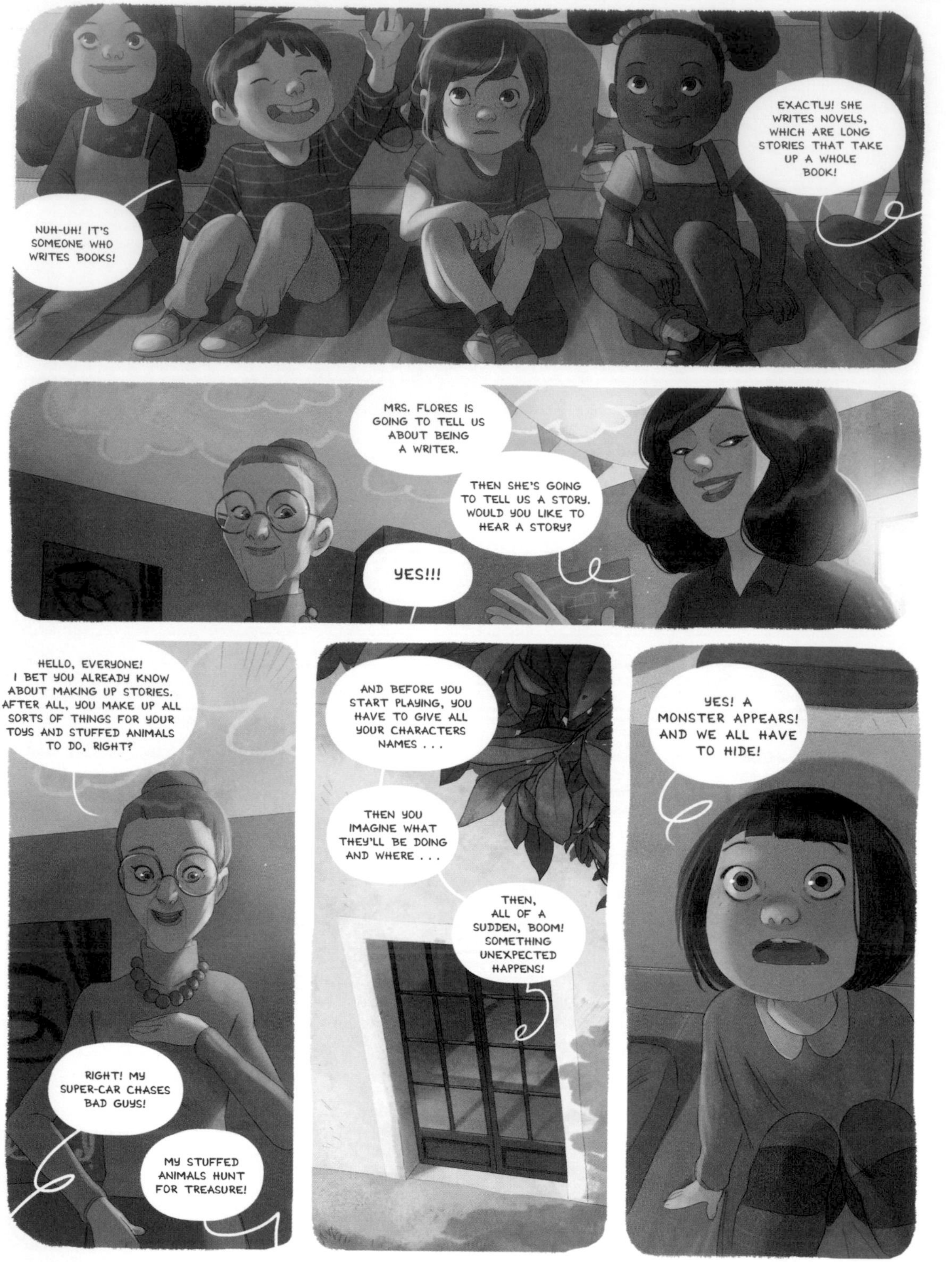
NUH-UH! IT'S SOMEONE WHO WRITES BOOKS!
EXACTLY! SHE WRITES NOVELS, WHICH ARE LONG STORIES THAT TAKE UP A WHOLE BOOK!
MRS. FLORES IS GOING TO TELL US ABOUT BEING A WRITER.
THEN SHE'S GOING TO TELL US A STORY. WOULD YOU LIKE TO HEAR A STORY?
YES!!!
HELLO, EVERYONE! I BET YOU ALREADY KNOW ABOUT MAKING UP STORIES. AFTER ALL, YOU MAKE UP ALL SORTS OF THINGS FOR YOUR TOYS AND STUFFED ANIMALS TO DO, RIGHT?
RIGHT! MY SUPER-CAR CHASES BAD GUYS!
MY STUFFED ANIMALS HUNT FOR TREASURE!
AND BEFORE YOU START PLAYING, YOU HAVE TO GIVE ALL YOUR CHARACTERS NAMES . . .
THEN YOU IMAGINE WHAT THEY'LL BE DOING AND WHERE . . .
THEN, ALL OF A SUDDEN, BOOM! SOMETHING UNEXPECTED HAPPENS!
YES! A MONSTER APPEARS! AND WE ALL HAVE TO HIDE!

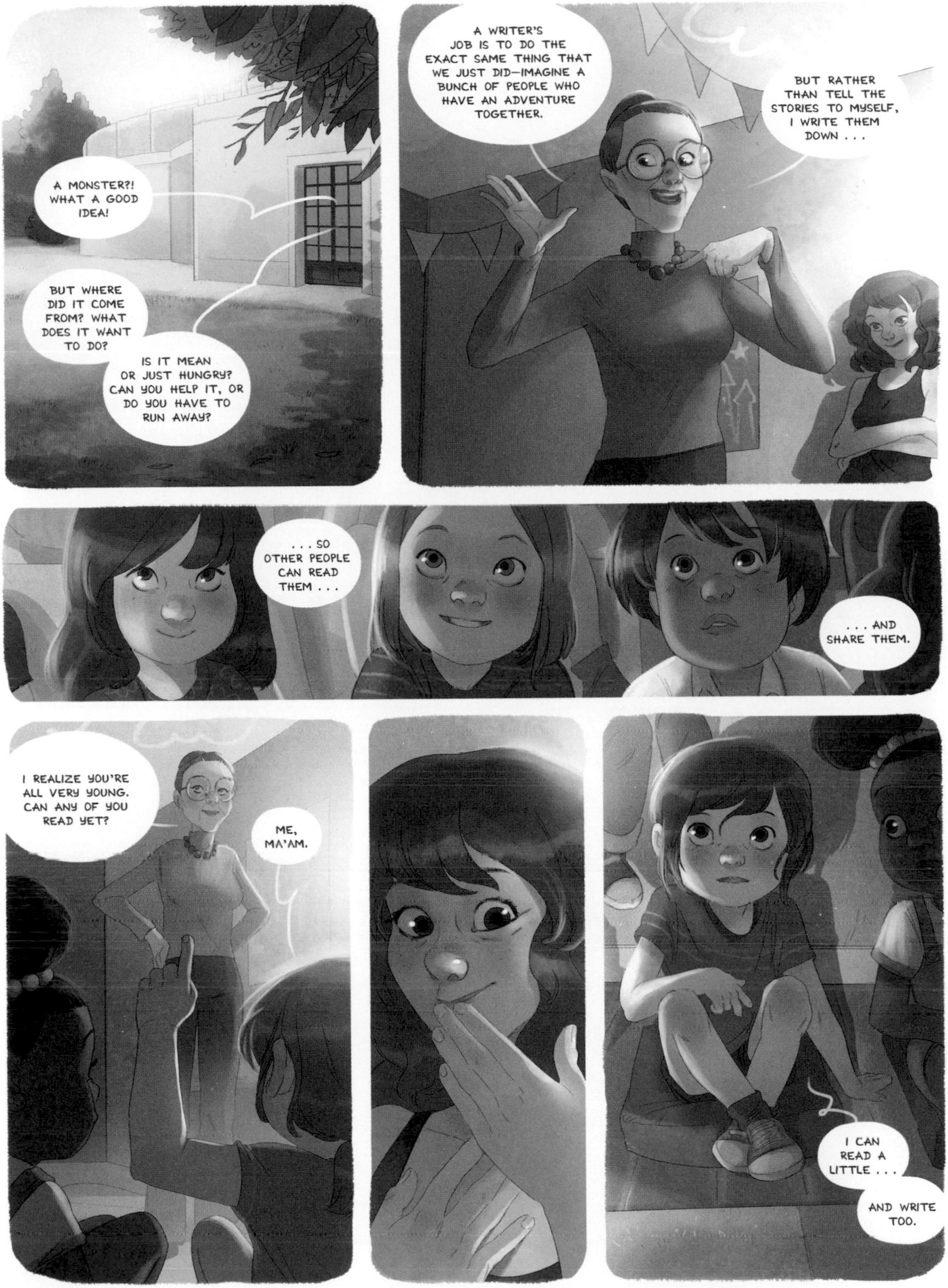
A MONSTER?! WHAT A GOOD IDEA!
BUT WHERE DID IT COME FROM? WHAT DOES IT WANT TO DO?
IS IT MEAN OR JUST HUNGRY? CAN YOU HELP IT, OR DO YOU HAVE TO RUN AWAY?
A WRITER'S JOB IS TO DO THE EXACT SAME THING THAT WE JUST DID—IMAGINE A BUNCH OF PEOPLE WHO HAVE AN ADVENTURE TOGETHER.
BUT RATHER THAN TELL THE STORIES TO MYSELF, I WRITE THEM DOWN . . .
. . . SO OTHER PEOPLE CAN READ THEM . . .
. . . AND SHARE THEM.
I REALIZE YOU'RE ALL VERY YOUNG. CAN ANY OF YOU READ YET?
ME, MA'AM.
I CAN READ A LITTLE . . .
AND WRITE TOO.

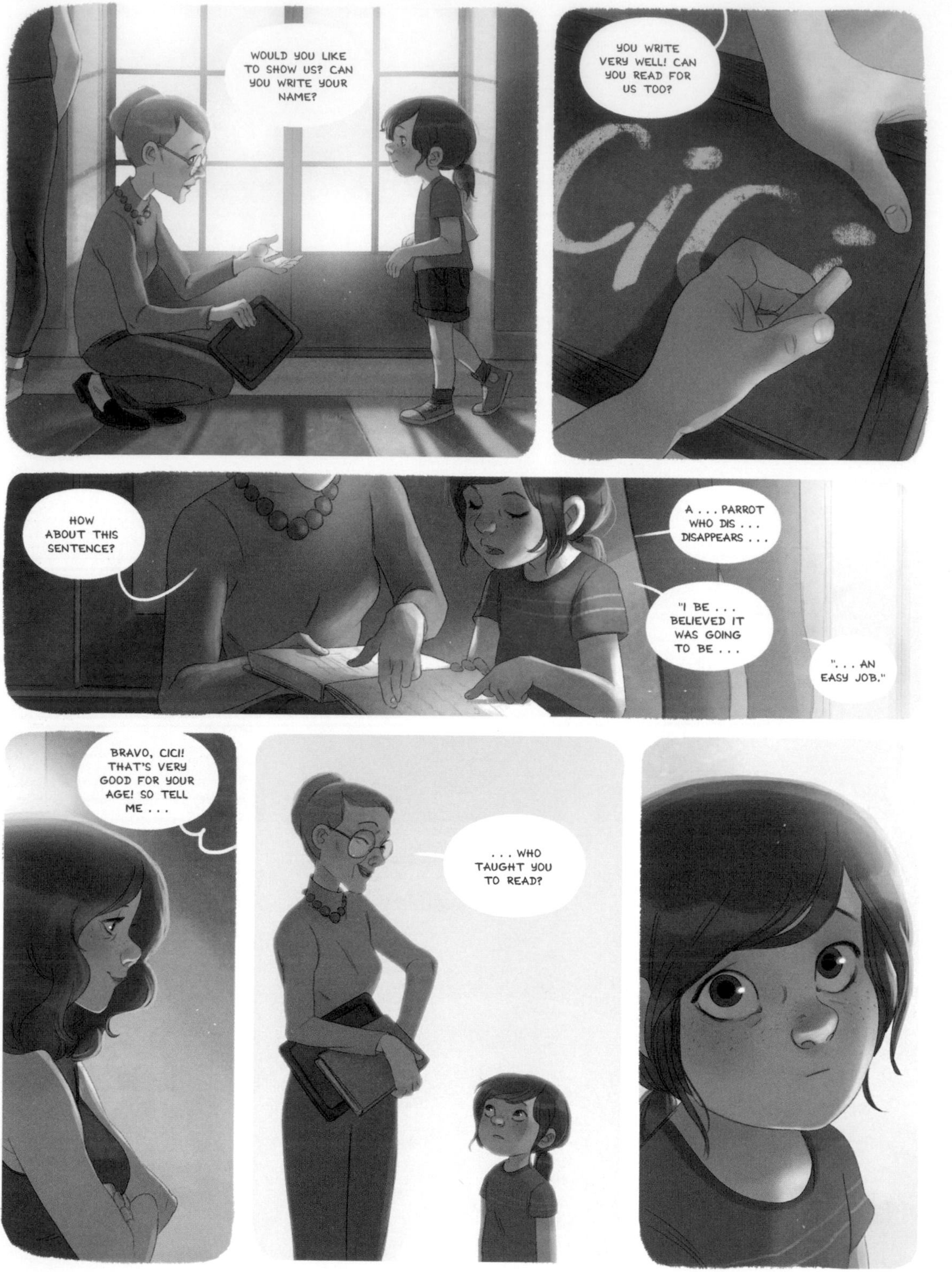
WOULD YOU LIKE TO SHOW US? CAN YOU WRITE YOUR NAME?
YOU WRITE VERY WELL! CAN YOU READ FOR US TOO?
HOW ABOUT THIS SENTENCE?
A . . . PARROT WHO DIS . . . DISAPPEARS . . .
"I BE . . . BELIEVED IT WAS GOING TO BE . . .
". . . AN EASY JOB."
BRAVO, CICI! THAT'S VERY GOOD FOR YOUR AGE! SO TELL ME . . .
. . . WHO TAUGHT YOU TO READ?

Hello? Hello? Memories?

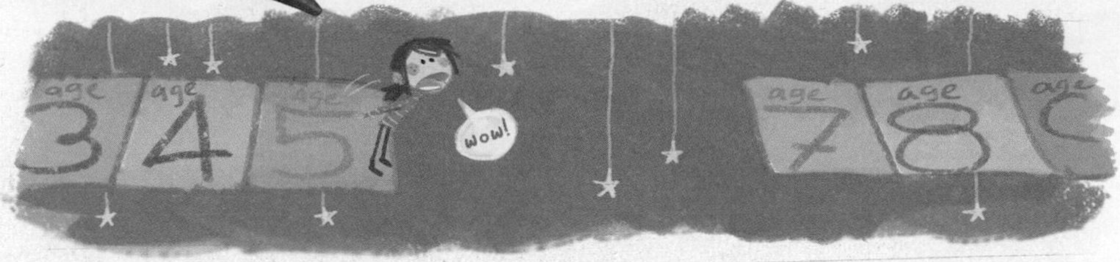
age 3
age 4
age 5
wow!
age 7
age 8

I don't remember too much more after that. What do you remember?

I'll never forget—it was so sad. Mrs. Flores had brought up the topic that must never be mentioned. You told her that your daddy had taught you to read and write.

Then the tears began to flow. All the tears you had kept bottled up inside since your dad passed away. You were inconsolable. I think that Mrs. Flores still blames herself for that.

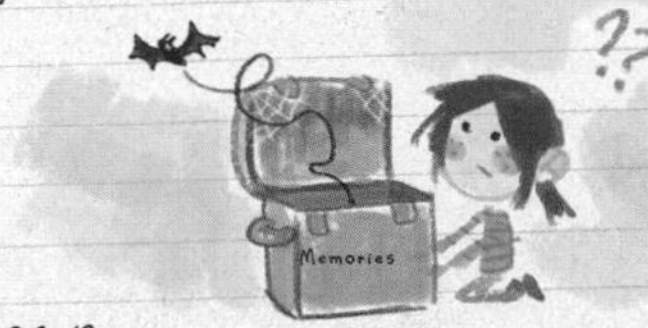
??
Memories

I don't remember that at all.

For weeks, you didn't say a word or leave your room. There was nothing I could do. The doctors we called diagnosed you with childhood depression. I didn't even know such a thing existed. No parent should ever have to hear such a diagnosis.

So that's why I was sick for so long . . . I always thought I had the flu or something.

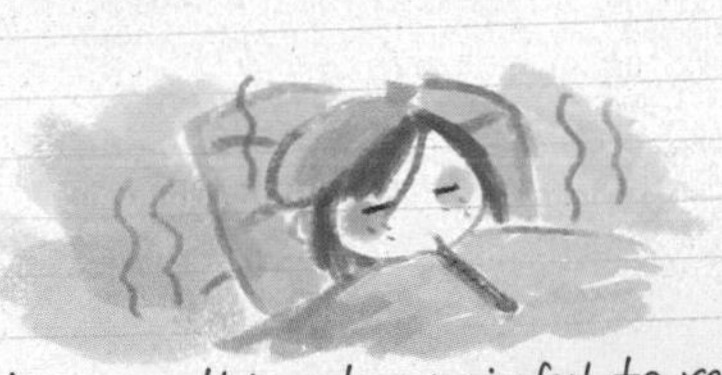

When we encounter something too painful to remember, our minds often protect us by substituting a harmless fiction.

So, I had memory problems just like Sandra did...
How long was I sick?

Way too long, in my opinion. According to a psychologist I consulted, depression is a normal stage of the grieving process, following shock and denial. I was told that your depression might last weeks—even years!

It broke my heart. You were so little! Despite my own grief, I did everything I could to support you. Every day was a challenge, but I had faith you would heal.

And I wasn't the only one who did...

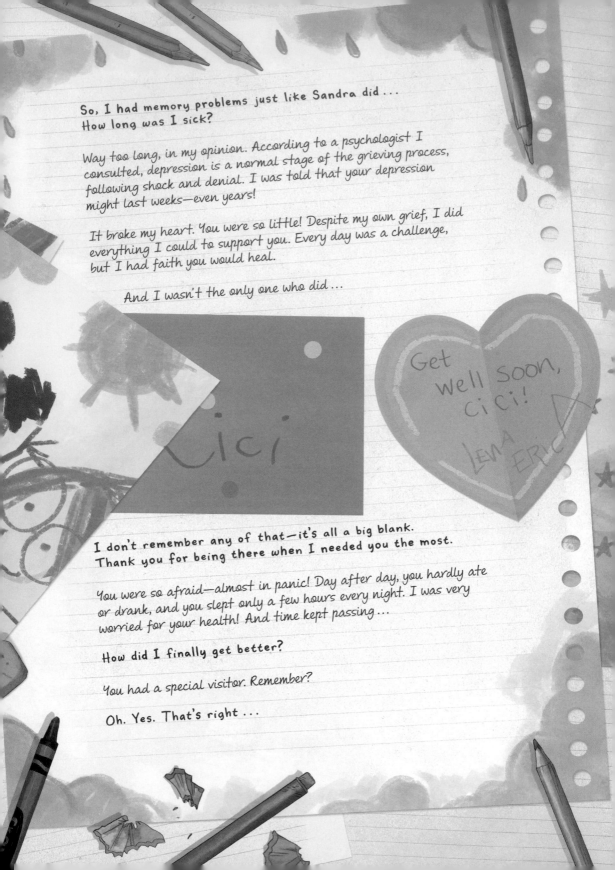

Get well soon, Cici!
Lena
Eric

Cici

I don't remember any of that—it's all a big blank.
Thank you for being there when I needed you the most.

You were so afraid—almost in panic! Day after day, you hardly ate or drank, and you slept only a few hours every night. I was very worried for your health! And time kept passing...

How did I finally get better?

You had a special visitor. Remember?

Oh. Yes. That's right...

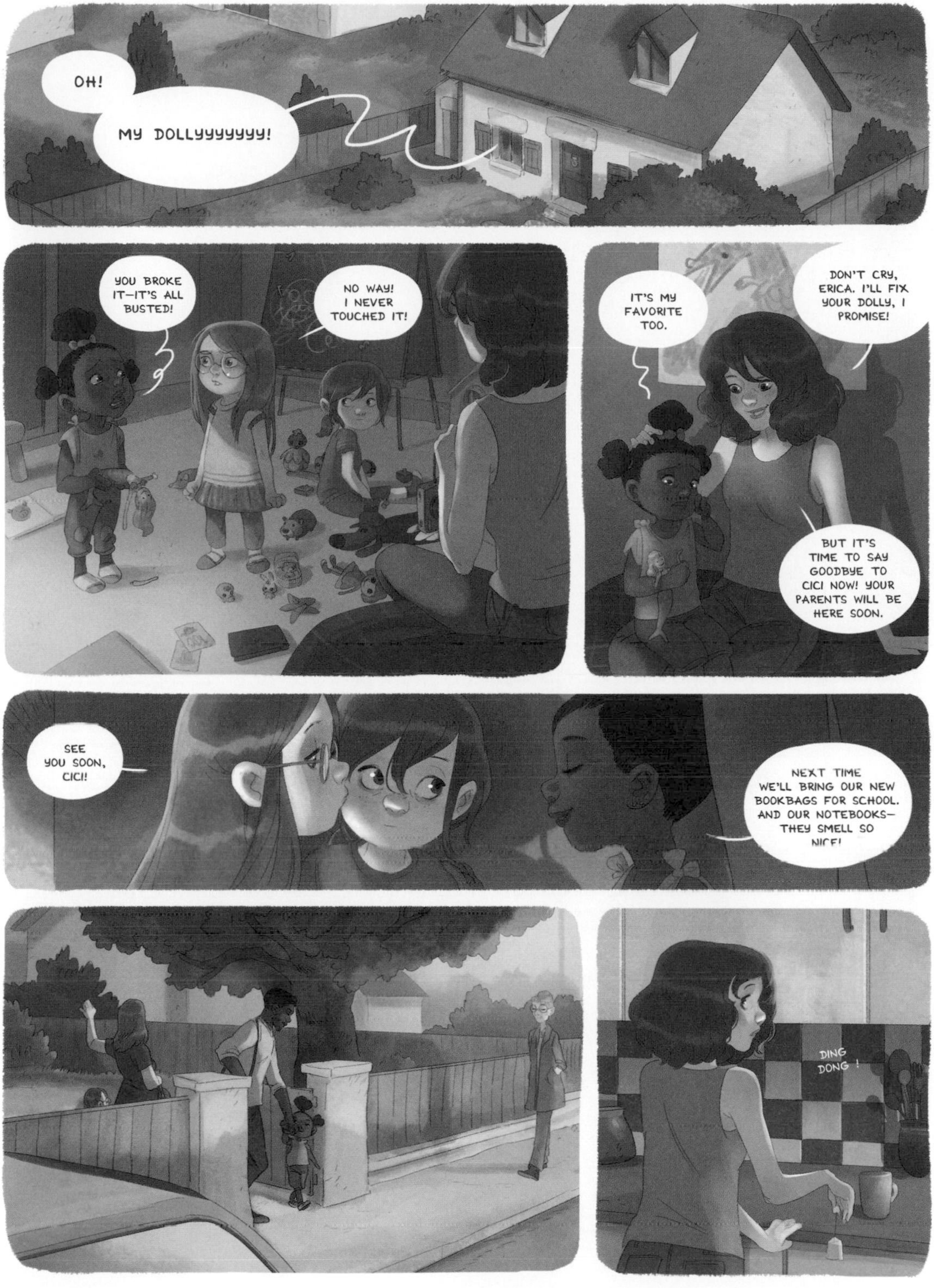
OH!
MY DOLLYYYYYYY!
YOU BROKE IT—IT'S ALL BUSTED!
NO WAY! I NEVER TOUCHED IT!
IT'S MY FAVORITE TOO.
DON'T CRY, ERICA. I'LL FIX YOUR DOLLY, I PROMISE!
BUT IT'S TIME TO SAY GOODBYE TO CICI NOW! YOUR PARENTS WILL BE HERE SOON.
SEE YOU SOON, CICI!
NEXT TIME WE'LL BRING OUR NEW BOOKBAGS FOR SCHOOL. AND OUR NOTEBOOKS—THEY SMELL SO NICE!
DING DONG !

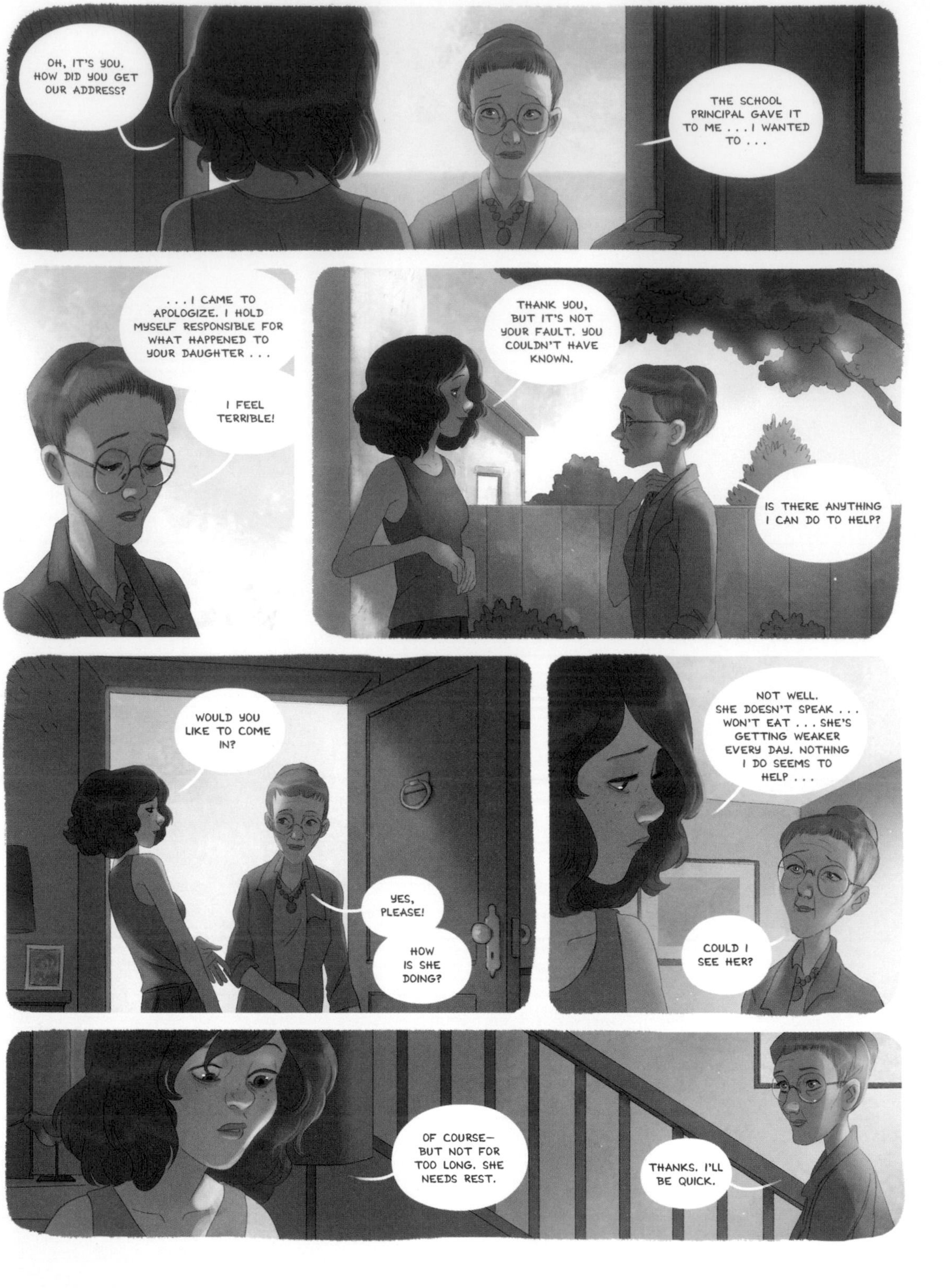
OH, IT'S YOU. HOW DID YOU GET OUR ADDRESS?
THE SCHOOL PRINCIPAL GAVE IT TO ME . . . I WANTED TO . . .
. . . I CAME TO APOLOGIZE. I HOLD MYSELF RESPONSIBLE FOR WHAT HAPPENED TO YOUR DAUGHTER . . .
I FEEL TERRIBLE!
THANK YOU, BUT IT'S NOT YOUR FAULT. YOU COULDN'T HAVE KNOWN.
IS THERE ANYTHING I CAN DO TO HELP?
WOULD YOU LIKE TO COME IN?
YES, PLEASE!
HOW IS SHE DOING?
NOT WELL. SHE DOESN'T SPEAK . . . WON'T EAT . . . SHE'S GETTING WEAKER EVERY DAY. NOTHING I DO SEEMS TO HELP . . .
COULD I SEE HER?
OF COURSE— BUT NOT FOR TOO LONG. SHE NEEDS REST.
THANKS. I'LL BE QUICK.

KNOCK
KNOCK?

HELLO!

CICI? IT'S
ANNABELLE FLORES.
DO YOU REMEMBER
ME?

THERE'S
SOMETHING I
HAVE TO TELL
YOU . . .

I'M SO SORRY—
I NEVER SHOULD HAVE
ASKED YOU THAT
QUESTION.

BUT YOU WERE
SUCH A BRIGHT LITTLE
GIRL, IT MADE ME CURIOUS.
PLEASE FORGIVE ME.

IF EVER YOU
NEED SOMEONE TO TALK
TO, PLEASE LET ME
KNOW. I'D LIKE TO
BE YOUR FRIEND.

WELL . . . I'LL
GO NOW.

YOU NEED
TO REST.

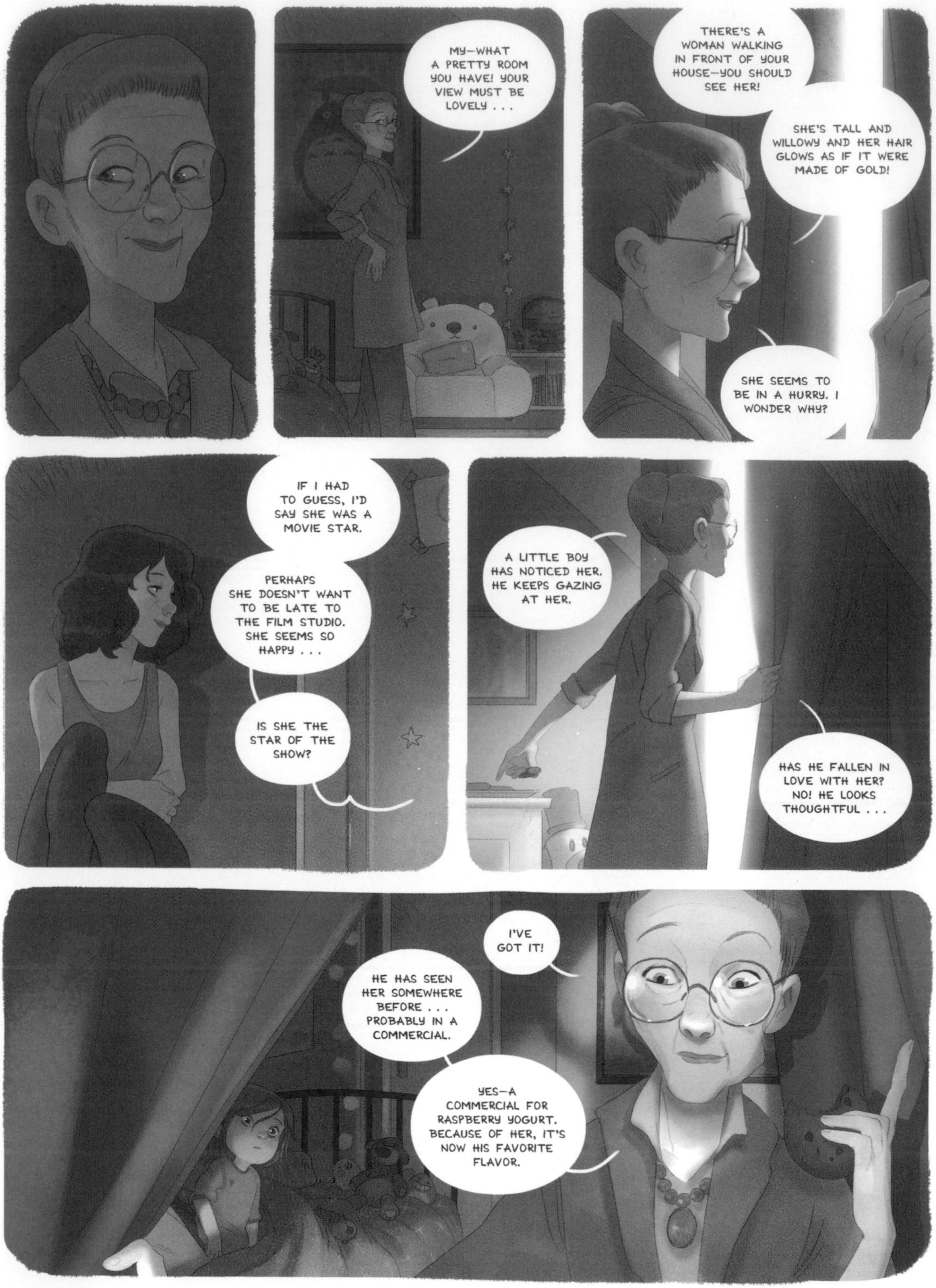
MY—WHAT A PRETTY ROOM YOU HAVE! YOUR VIEW MUST BE LOVELY . . .
THERE'S A WOMAN WALKING IN FRONT OF YOUR HOUSE—YOU SHOULD SEE HER!
SHE'S TALL AND WILLOWY AND HER HAIR GLOWS AS IF IT WERE MADE OF GOLD!
SHE SEEMS TO BE IN A HURRY. I WONDER WHY?
IF I HAD TO GUESS, I'D SAY SHE WAS A MOVIE STAR.
PERHAPS SHE DOESN'T WANT TO BE LATE TO THE FILM STUDIO. SHE SEEMS SO HAPPY . . .
IS SHE THE STAR OF THE SHOW?
A LITTLE BOY HAS NOTICED HER. HE KEEPS GAZING AT HER.
HAS HE FALLEN IN LOVE WITH HER? NO! HE LOOKS THOUGHTFUL . . .
I'VE GOT IT!
HE HAS SEEN HER SOMEWHERE BEFORE . . . PROBABLY IN A COMMERCIAL.
YES—A COMMERCIAL FOR RASPBERRY YOGURT. BECAUSE OF HER, IT'S NOW HIS FAVORITE FLAVOR.

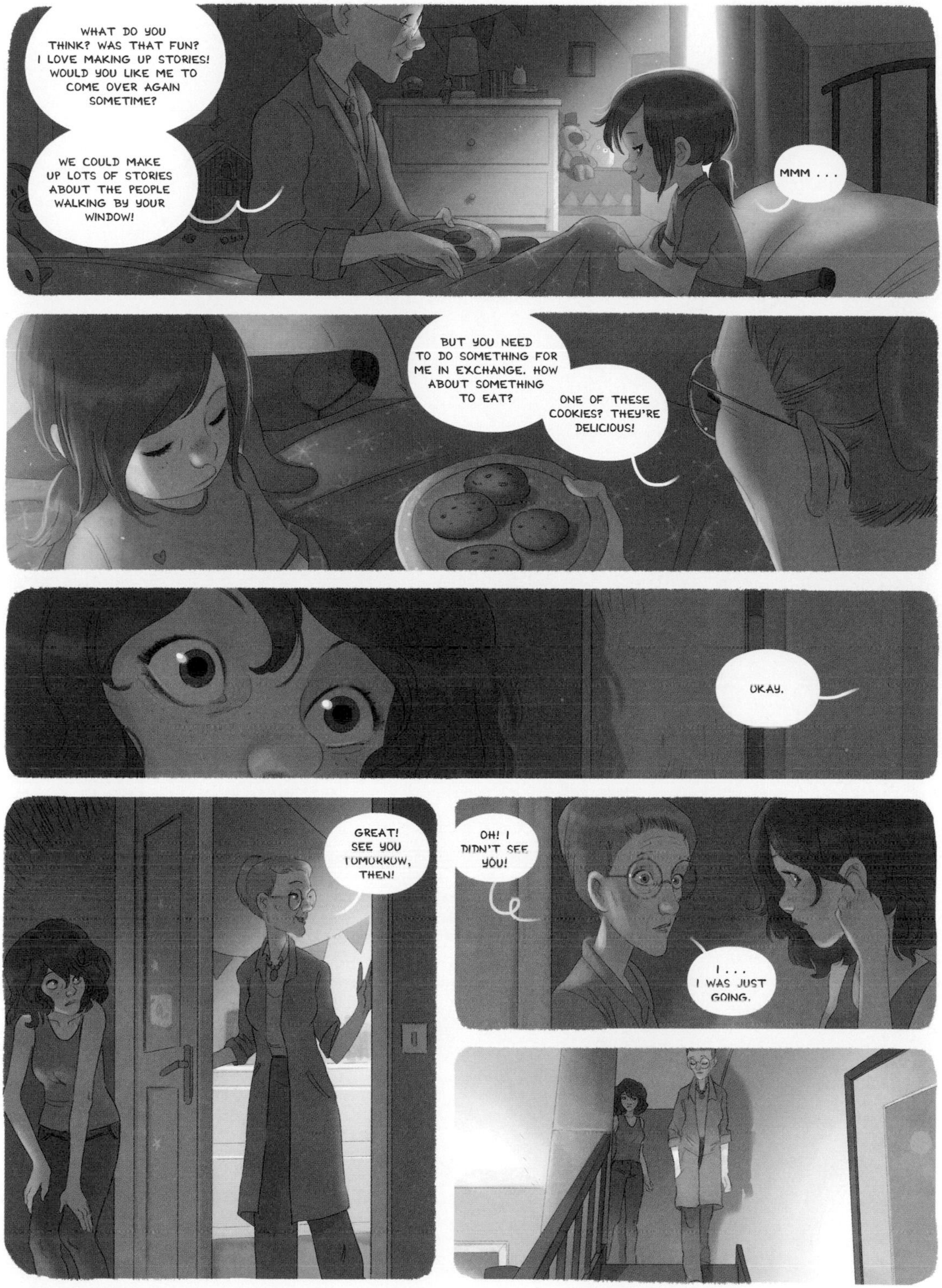
WHAT DO YOU THINK? WAS THAT FUN? I LOVE MAKING UP STORIES! WOULD YOU LIKE ME TO COME OVER AGAIN SOMETIME?
WE COULD MAKE UP LOTS OF STORIES ABOUT THE PEOPLE WALKING BY YOUR WINDOW!
MMM . . .
BUT YOU NEED TO DO SOMETHING FOR ME IN EXCHANGE. HOW ABOUT SOMETHING TO EAT?
ONE OF THESE COOKIES? THEY'RE DELICIOUS!
OKAY.
GREAT! SEE YOU TOMORROW, THEN!
OH! I DIDN'T SEE YOU!
I . . . I WAS JUST GOING.

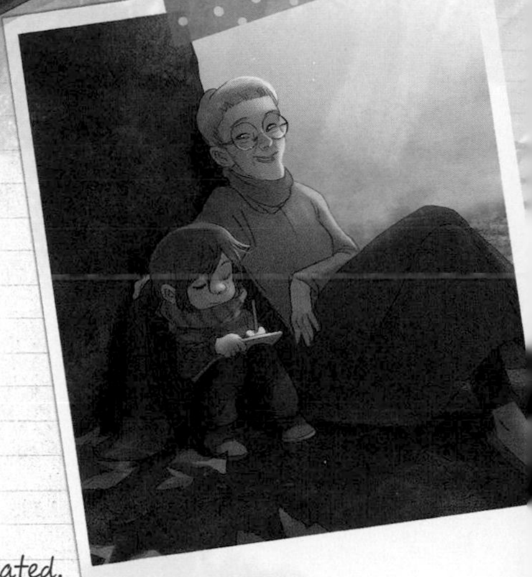

Mrs. Flores came over regularly for the next few weeks. With her help, I was able to go back to work. That's when the writing game, with all your character pages, began.

At first, she would write and you would draw. You two gradually developed quite a close bond.

You never said a word, but you were clearly fascinated. You hung on her every word. And when she offered you food, you ate without hesitation.

Thanks to her, you gradually got your strength back. But I had mixed feelings—I was happy to see you becoming more lively, but I was frustrated because you responded to Mrs. Flores, but not to me.

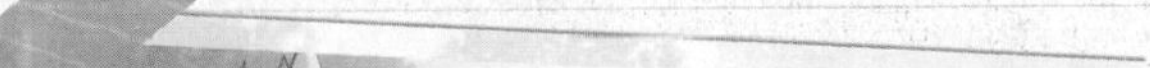

Lena and Erica also did their best to make you happy.

They even got you to wear a Halloween costume and go trick-or-treating.

One evening, I came home from work and found you both sitting at the top of the stairs. Mrs. Flores was telling a story while you drew pictures.

I took a photo of you, and as I went to put the camera away, something wonderful happened...

You began to laugh. A happy laugh, full of life! It had been months since I had heard that sound. I ran back so I wouldn't miss a moment...

But as soon as you saw me, you stopped laughing. Immediately.

I was heartbroken, and anger welled up inside me.

Mrs. Flores probably sensed my frustration. She left and never returned to our home. As for you, you went back to your room without saying a word.

You see, it was now clear to me that our relationship had changed. You were fine with Mrs. Flores—but not with me.

It hurt. Deep down inside, it hurt. But what mattered most was that you were feeling better.

TIME PASSED. YOU WENT BACK TO SCHOOL. FIRST GRADE WAS A NEW START FOR YOU.

THANKS TO THE WRITING GAME, YOU WOULD GO OUT WITH YOUR FRIENDS. THE YEAR PASSED PEACEFULLY, AND YOUR SMILE GRADUALLY RETURNED.

THEN, ALL OF A SUDDEN, YOU BOXED UP ALL YOUR TOYS—YOUR STUFFED TOY HAMSTER, YOUR FAVORITE DOLL . . .

YOU TOOK THE BOX UP TO THE ATTIC AND RETURNED CARRYING YOUR GREAT-UNCLE'S THINGS. IT WAS AS IF ONE CHAPTER IN YOUR LIFE HAD ENDED AND ANOTHER HAD BEGUN.

YOU WERE A BIG GIRL NOW.

THAT'S WHEN THE LIES BEGAN.

YOU COAXED YOUR FRIENDS TO GIVE YOU ALIBIS, YOU VISITED MRS. FLORES IN SECRET, AND YOU WOULD NEVER LOOK ME STRAIGHT IN THE EYE . . .

I DIDN'T KNOW HOW TO HELP YOU. SO I GAVE YOU THE FREEDOM TO FIND YOUR OWN PATH.

ALTHOUGH YOUR FATHER'S PARENTS DESPERATELY WANTED TO SEE YOU, I NEVER FORCED YOU TO VISIT THEM.

THEY TOO RECOGNIZED THAT YOU NEEDED TIME. SO THEY WERE CONTENT WITH THE PHOTOS THAT I SENT THEM AS OFTEN AS POSSIBLE.

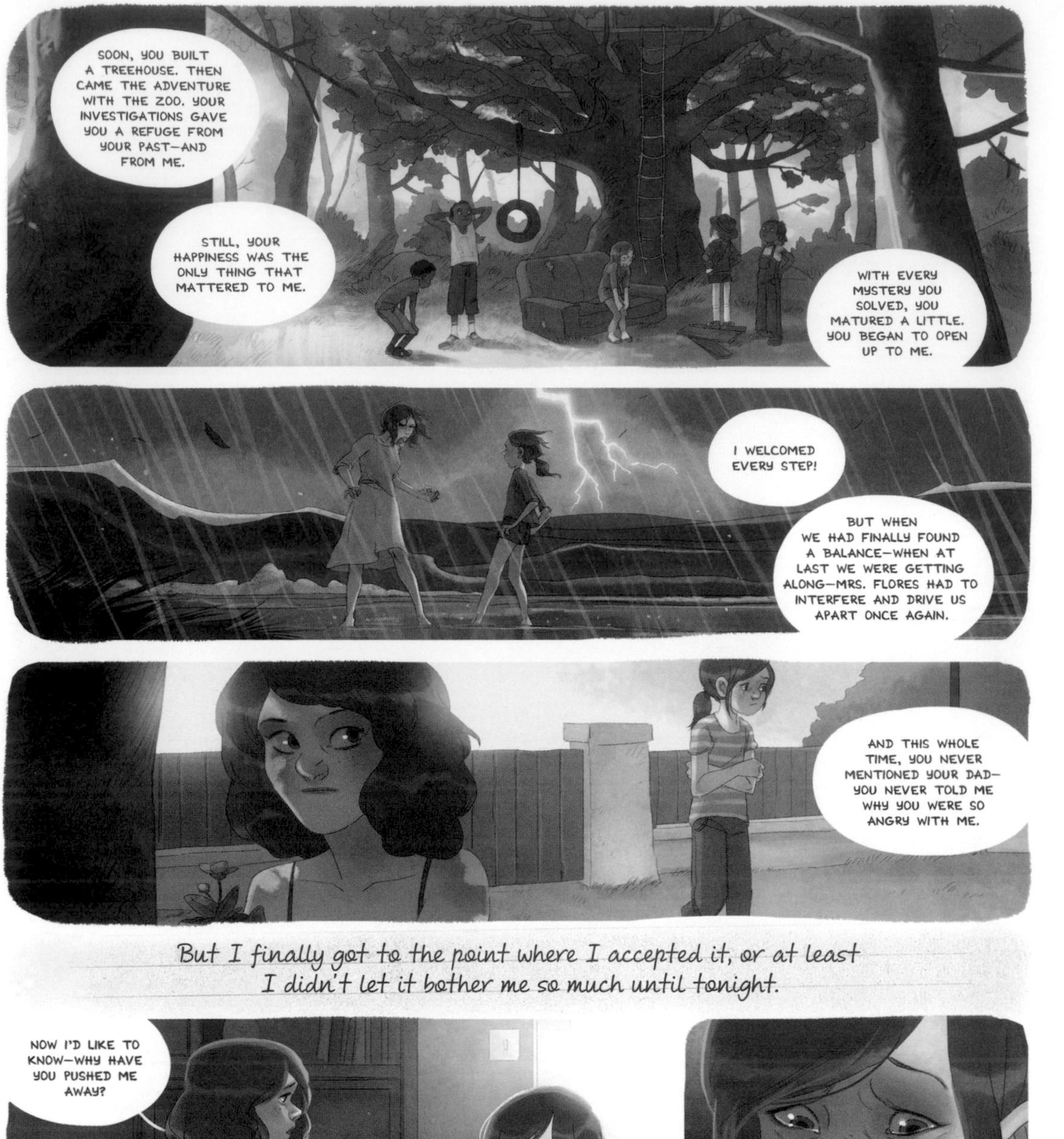
SOON, YOU BUILT A TREEHOUSE. THEN CAME THE ADVENTURE WITH THE ZOO. YOUR INVESTIGATIONS GAVE YOU A REFUGE FROM YOUR PAST—AND FROM ME.
STILL, YOUR HAPPINESS WAS THE ONLY THING THAT MATTERED TO ME.
WITH EVERY MYSTERY YOU SOLVED, YOU MATURED A LITTLE. YOU BEGAN TO OPEN UP TO ME.
I WELCOMED EVERY STEP!
BUT WHEN WE HAD FINALLY FOUND A BALANCE—WHEN AT LAST WE WERE GETTING ALONG—MRS. FLORES HAD TO INTERFERE AND DRIVE US APART ONCE AGAIN.
AND THIS WHOLE TIME, YOU NEVER MENTIONED YOUR DAD—YOU NEVER TOLD ME WHY YOU WERE SO ANGRY WITH ME.

But I finally got to the point where I accepted it, or at least I didn't let it bother me so much until tonight.

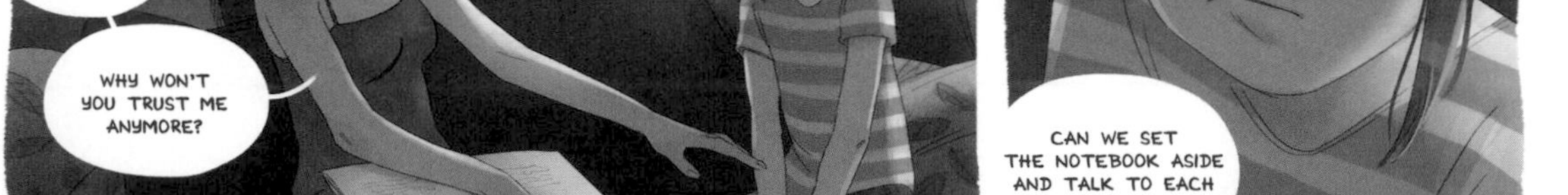
NOW I'D LIKE TO KNOW—WHY HAVE YOU PUSHED ME AWAY?
WHY ALL THE SILENCE?
WHY WON'T YOU TRUST ME ANYMORE?
CAN WE SET THE NOTEBOOK ASIDE AND TALK TO EACH OTHER AT LAST?

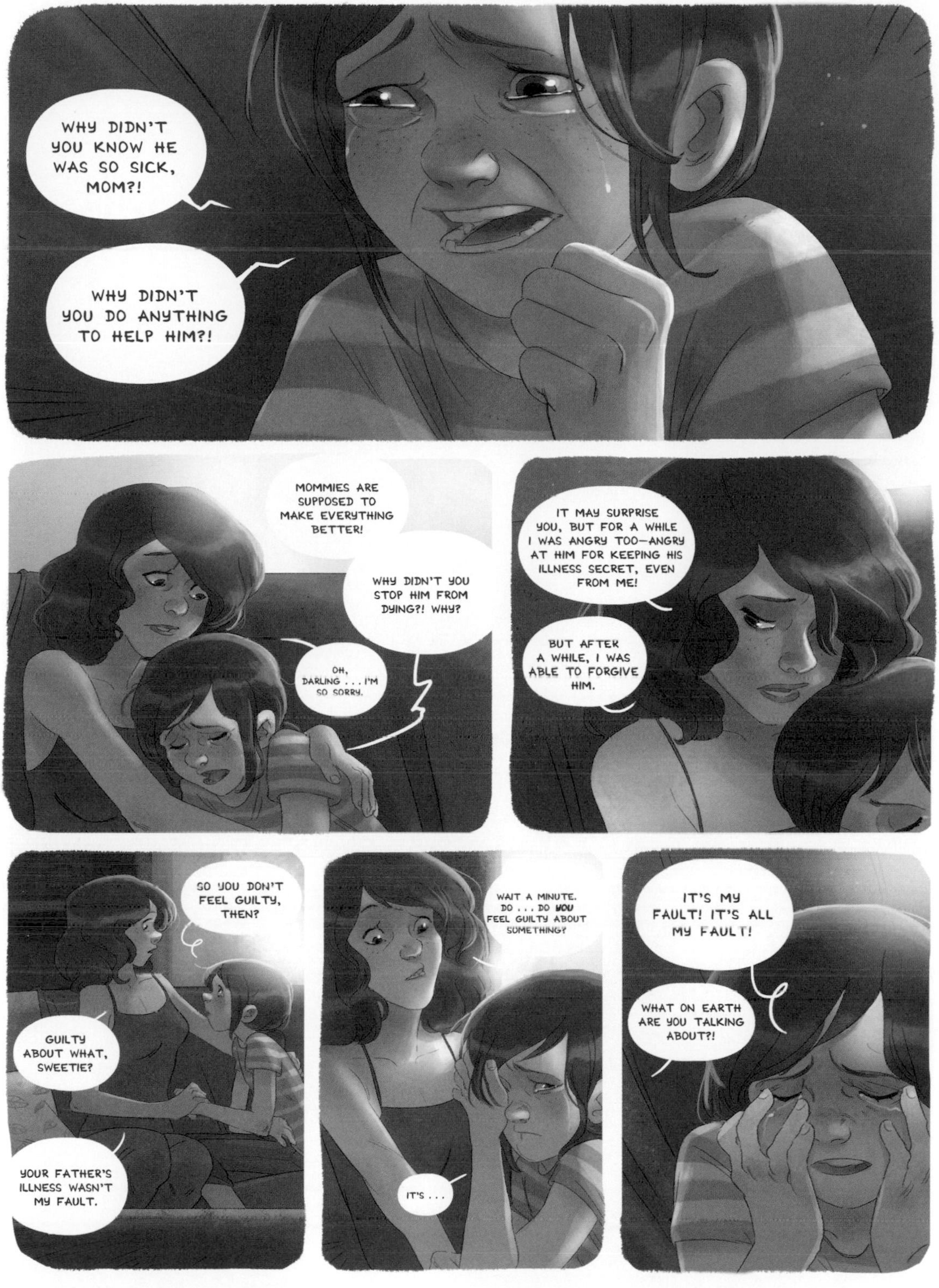
WHY DIDN'T YOU KNOW HE WAS SO SICK, MOM?!
WHY DIDN'T YOU DO ANYTHING TO HELP HIM?!
MOMMIES ARE SUPPOSED TO MAKE EVERYTHING BETTER!
WHY DIDN'T YOU STOP HIM FROM DYING?! WHY?
OH, DARLING . . . I'M SO SORRY.
IT MAY SURPRISE YOU, BUT FOR A WHILE I WAS ANGRY TOO—ANGRY AT HIM FOR KEEPING HIS ILLNESS SECRET, EVEN FROM ME!
BUT AFTER A WHILE, I WAS ABLE TO FORGIVE HIM.
SO YOU DON'T FEEL GUILTY, THEN?
GUILTY ABOUT WHAT, SWEETIE?
YOUR FATHER'S ILLNESS WASN'T MY FAULT.
WAIT A MINUTE. DO . . . DO YOU FEEL GUILTY ABOUT SOMETHING?
IT'S . . .
IT'S MY FAULT! IT'S ALL MY FAULT!
WHAT ON EARTH ARE YOU TALKING ABOUT?!

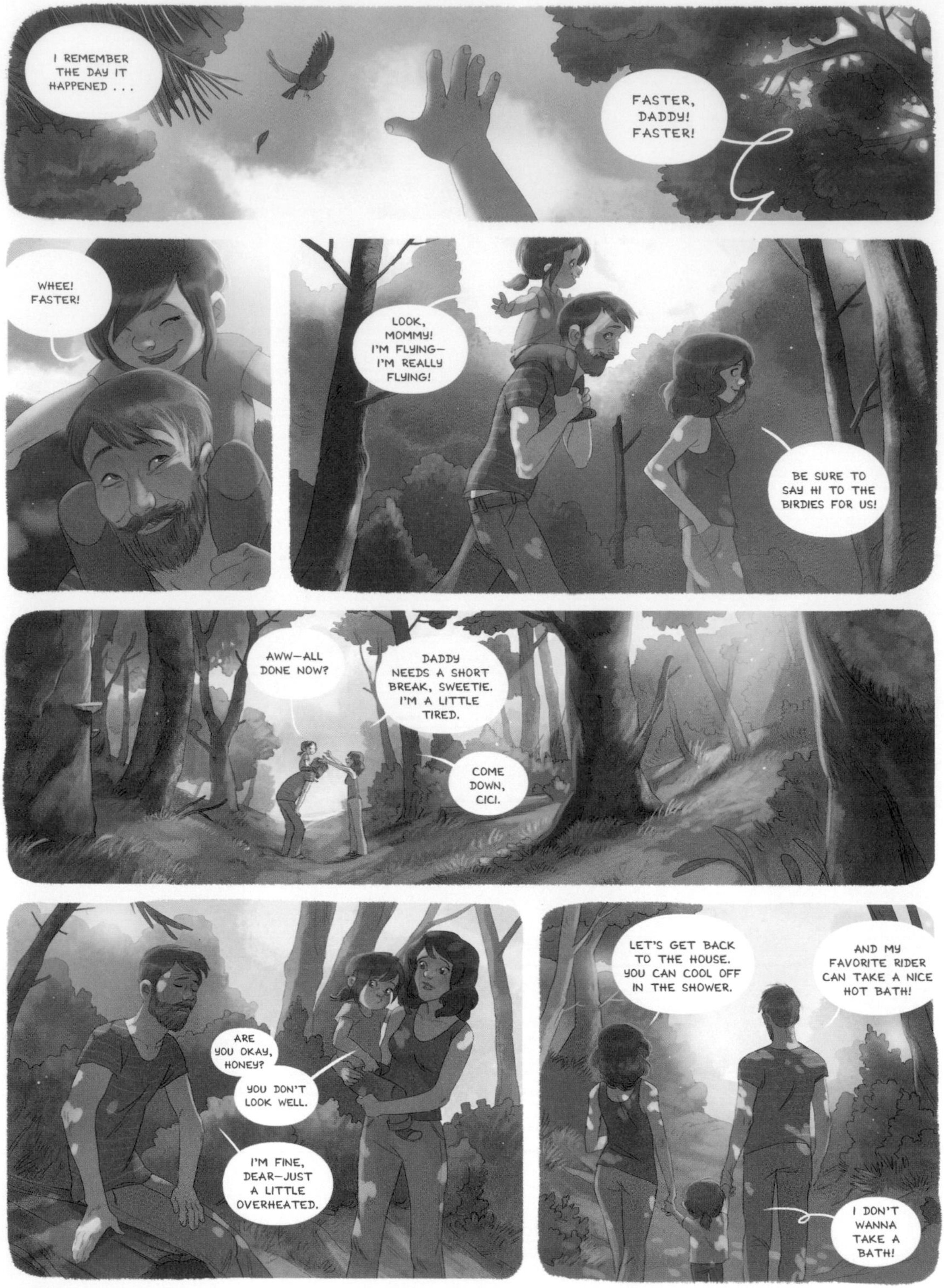
I REMEMBER THE DAY IT HAPPENED . . .
FASTER, DADDY! FASTER!
WHEE! FASTER!
LOOK, MOMMY! I'M FLYING— I'M REALLY FLYING!
BE SURE TO SAY HI TO THE BIRDIES FOR US!
AWW—ALL DONE NOW?
DADDY NEEDS A SHORT BREAK, SWEETIE. I'M A LITTLE TIRED.
COME DOWN, CICI.
ARE YOU OKAY, HONEY?
YOU DON'T LOOK WELL.
I'M FINE, DEAR—JUST A LITTLE OVERHEATED.
LET'S GET BACK TO THE HOUSE. YOU CAN COOL OFF IN THE SHOWER.
AND MY FAVORITE RIDER CAN TAKE A NICE HOT BATH!
I DON'T WANNA TAKE A BATH!

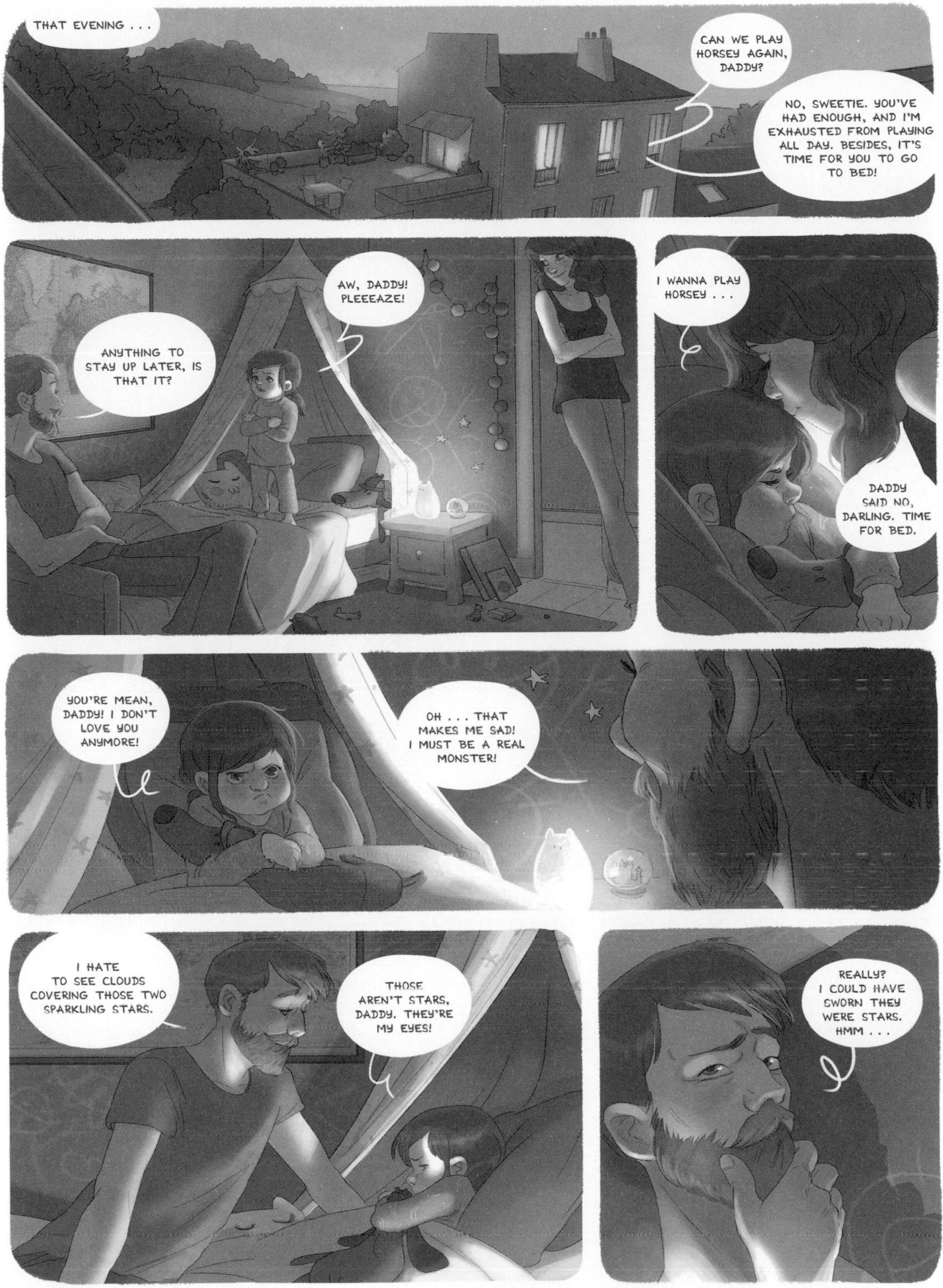
THAT EVENING . . .
CAN WE PLAY HORSEY AGAIN, DADDY?
NO, SWEETIE. YOU'VE HAD ENOUGH, AND I'M EXHAUSTED FROM PLAYING ALL DAY. BESIDES, IT'S TIME FOR YOU TO GO TO BED!
AW, DADDY! PLEEEAZE!
ANYTHING TO STAY UP LATER, IS THAT IT?
I WANNA PLAY HORSEY . . .
DADDY SAID NO, DARLING. TIME FOR BED.
YOU'RE MEAN, DADDY! I DON'T LOVE YOU ANYMORE!
OH . . . THAT MAKES ME SAD! I MUST BE A REAL MONSTER!
I HATE TO SEE CLOUDS COVERING THOSE TWO SPARKLING STARS.
THOSE AREN'T STARS, DADDY. THEY'RE MY EYES!
REALLY? I COULD HAVE SWORN THEY WERE STARS. HMM . . .

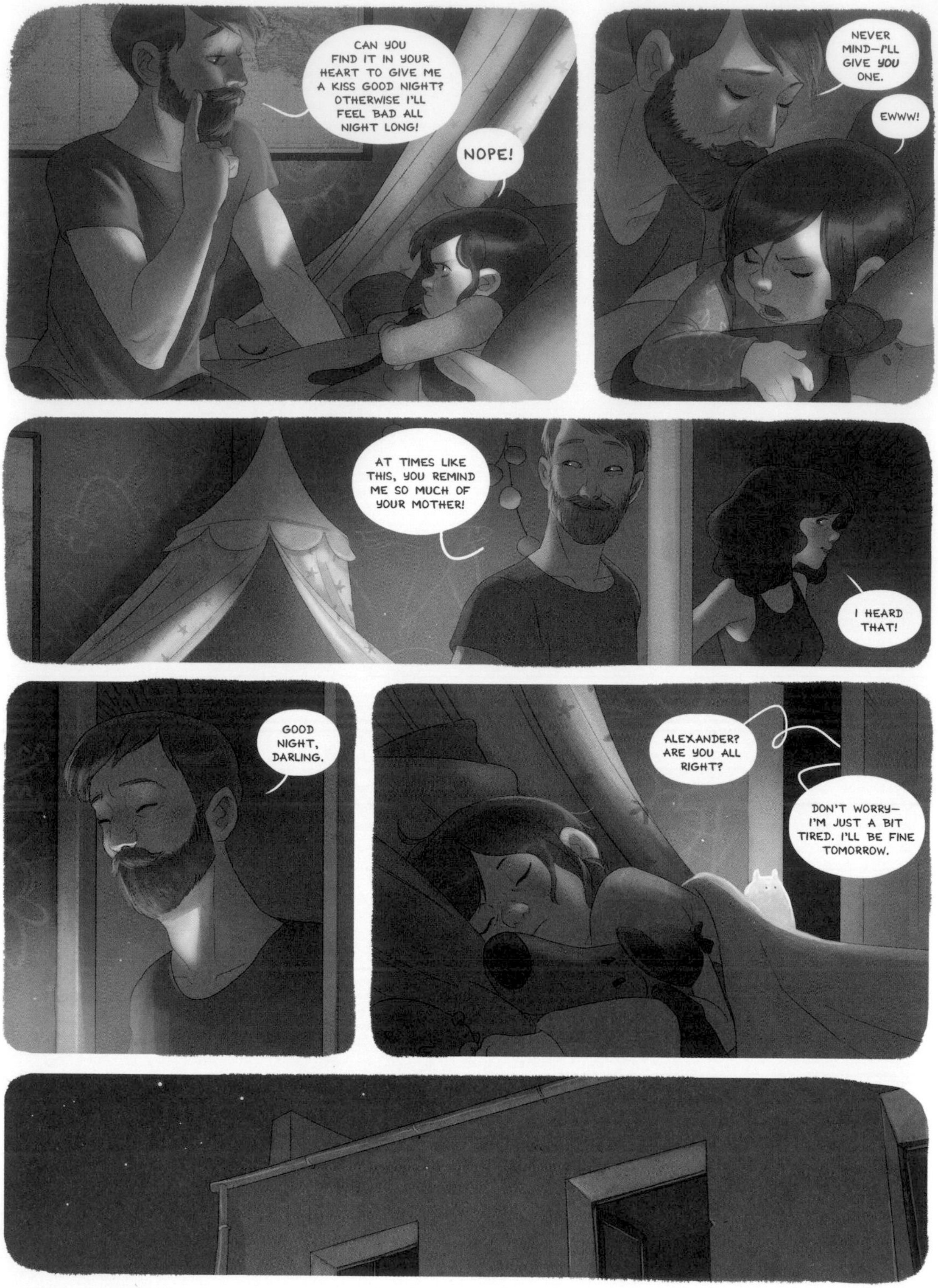
CAN YOU FIND IT IN YOUR HEART TO GIVE ME A KISS GOOD NIGHT? OTHERWISE I'LL FEEL BAD ALL NIGHT LONG!
NOPE!
NEVER MIND—I'LL GIVE YOU ONE.
EWWW!
AT TIMES LIKE THIS, YOU REMIND ME SO MUCH OF YOUR MOTHER!
I HEARD THAT!
GOOD NIGHT, DARLING.
ALEXANDER? ARE YOU ALL RIGHT?
DON'T WORRY—I'M JUST A BIT TIRED. I'LL BE FINE TOMORROW.

The next morning, I ran into your room to wake you both up. You laughed when I gave you your kiss, but when I went to kiss Daddy, his cheek was cold. I remember jumping on the bed to try and get him up, but he didn't move.

You reached over and tried to shake him awake. Then you began to cry and told me to get back to my room. I didn't want to—I had no idea what was going on. But you kept shouting at me, so I went.

I'll never forget that morning . . . I called an ambulance, then my sister—your Aunt Helen. First the ambulance came and the attendants wheeled your father away. When Helen arrived, she ushered us out of the house.

We spent a couple of days at Aunt Helen's house, didn't we? I remember I kept asking where Daddy was . . .

I couldn't bring myself to tell you. It was Helen who eventually explained to you that your father had died . . .

I still didn't understand. I only knew that I would never see Daddy again. And I kept remembering how tired he was, and how I kept asking him to play horsey, and how mean I was to him . . .

It was me—I made him get sick . . . I made him go away . . . If only . . .

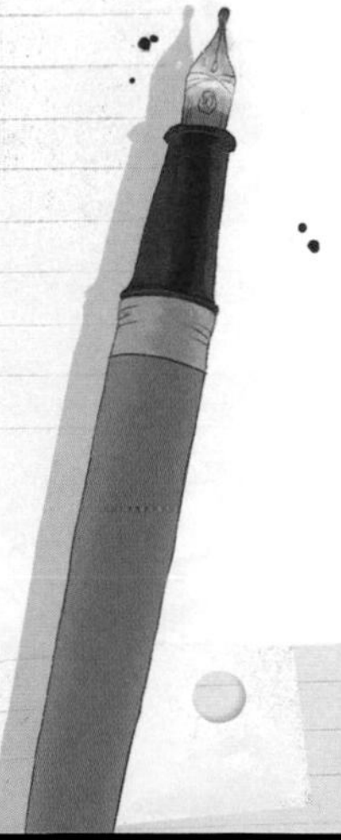

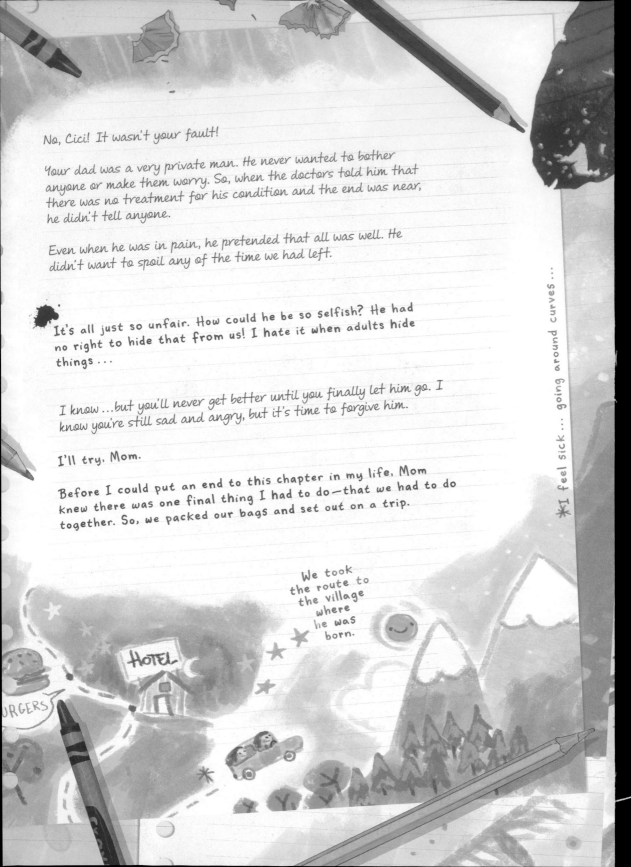

No, Cici! It wasn't your fault!

Your dad was a very private man. He never wanted to bother anyone or make them worry. So, when the doctors told him that there was no treatment for his condition and the end was near, he didn't tell anyone.

Even when he was in pain, he pretended that all was well. He didn't want to spoil any of the time we had left.

It's all just so unfair. How could he be so selfish? He had no right to hide that from us! I hate it when adults hide things . . .

I know . . . but you'll never get better until you finally let him go. I know you're still sad and angry, but it's time to forgive him.

I'll try, Mom.

Before I could put an end to this chapter in my life, Mom knew there was one final thing I had to do—that we had to do together. So, we packed our bags and set out on a trip.

We took the route to the village where he was born.

*I feel sick . . . going around curves . . .

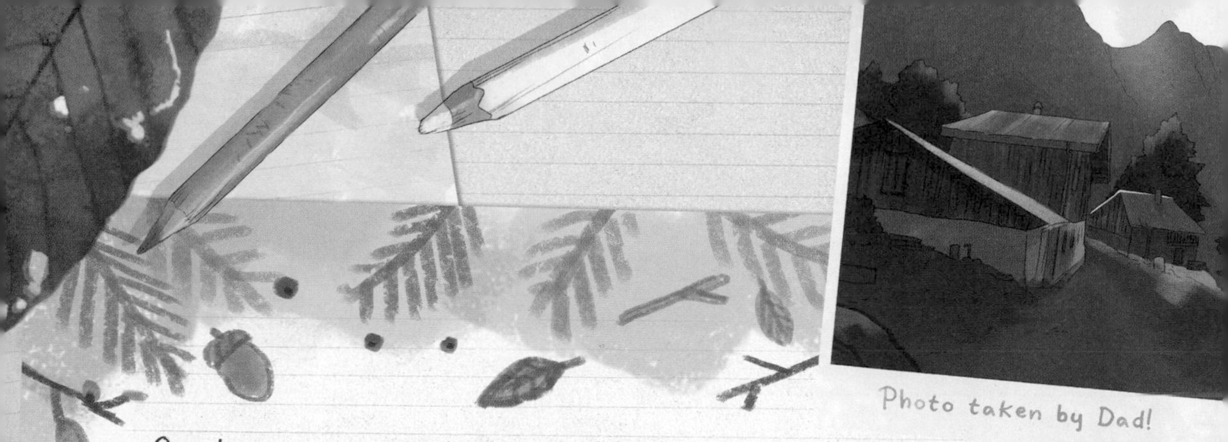

Photo taken by Dad!

Our destination—the village where Dad grew up. Mom and Dad often traveled there after they got married. Nanna and Poppa, my Dad's parents, still live there. It's a pretty town. Of course, I don't remember it—I was only three years old when we last visited. It turns out that their house, along with a few others, is located in a small clearing in the middle of a forest! We arrived just after noon. Lunch was a bit awkward, to say the least. I mean, we're family and we really wanted to see each other, but a lot had changed since I was little, and we had to get to know one another all over again.

It turns out that I have a strong connection with this forest. Not only did Daddy spend a lot of his childhood here, but so did I! Nanna told me that Daddy took me for walks here whenever we visited, and I built my first hideout among these very trees!

I remember the hideout—well, sort of.
I have a photo of it.

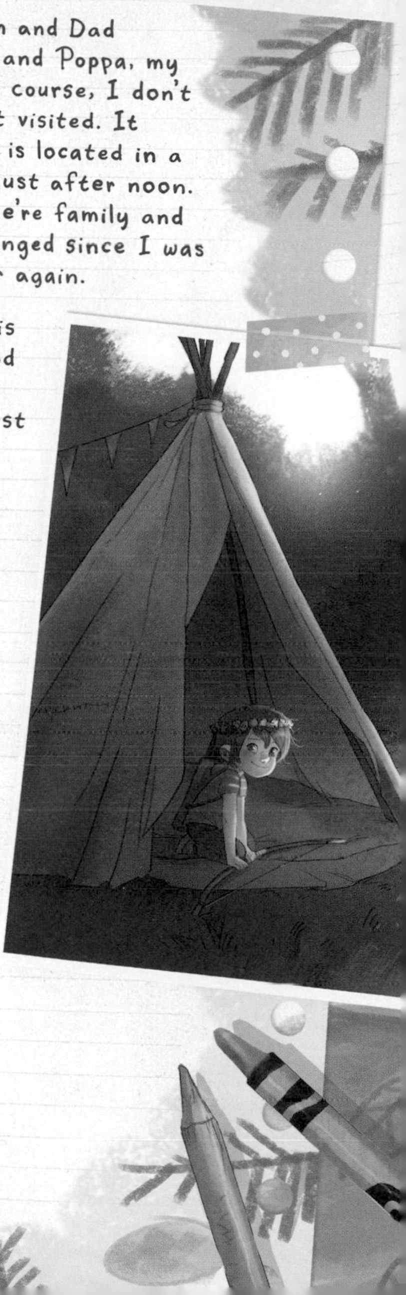

Here I am, practicing
to be a forest warrior!

In the afternoon, Nanna and Poppa went into town to do some shopping. At least, that's what they told us. I think they knew that Mom and I needed some time alone.

We took a long walk in the forest. It smells different than the forest back home. Older, somehow, full of the fragrance of moss, pine trees, and weathered stones. It's very calming. Mom began to tell me about her visits here with Daddy before I was born. Then came stories about my childhood and finally, quite naturally . . .

. . . she talked to me about Dad.

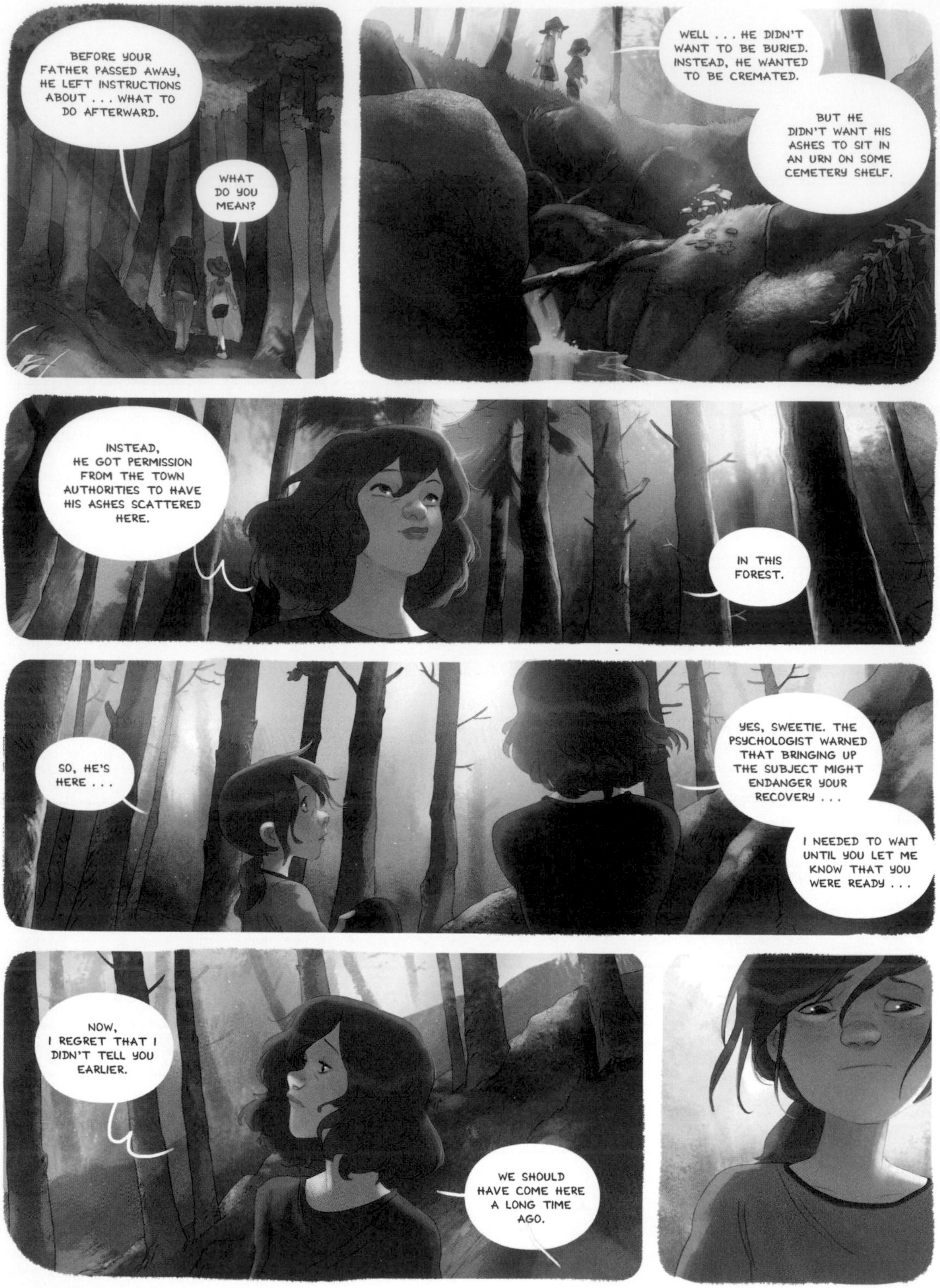
BEFORE YOUR FATHER PASSED AWAY, HE LEFT INSTRUCTIONS ABOUT . . . WHAT TO DO AFTERWARD.
WHAT DO YOU MEAN?
WELL . . . HE DIDN'T WANT TO BE BURIED. INSTEAD, HE WANTED TO BE CREMATED.
BUT HE DIDN'T WANT HIS ASHES TO SIT IN AN URN ON SOME CEMETERY SHELF.
INSTEAD, HE GOT PERMISSION FROM THE TOWN AUTHORITIES TO HAVE HIS ASHES SCATTERED HERE.
IN THIS FOREST.
SO, HE'S HERE . . .
YES, SWEETIE. THE PSYCHOLOGIST WARNED THAT BRINGING UP THE SUBJECT MIGHT ENDANGER YOUR RECOVERY . . .
I NEEDED TO WAIT UNTIL YOU LET ME KNOW THAT YOU WERE READY . . .
NOW, I REGRET THAT I DIDN'T TELL YOU EARLIER.
WE SHOULD HAVE COME HERE A LONG TIME AGO.

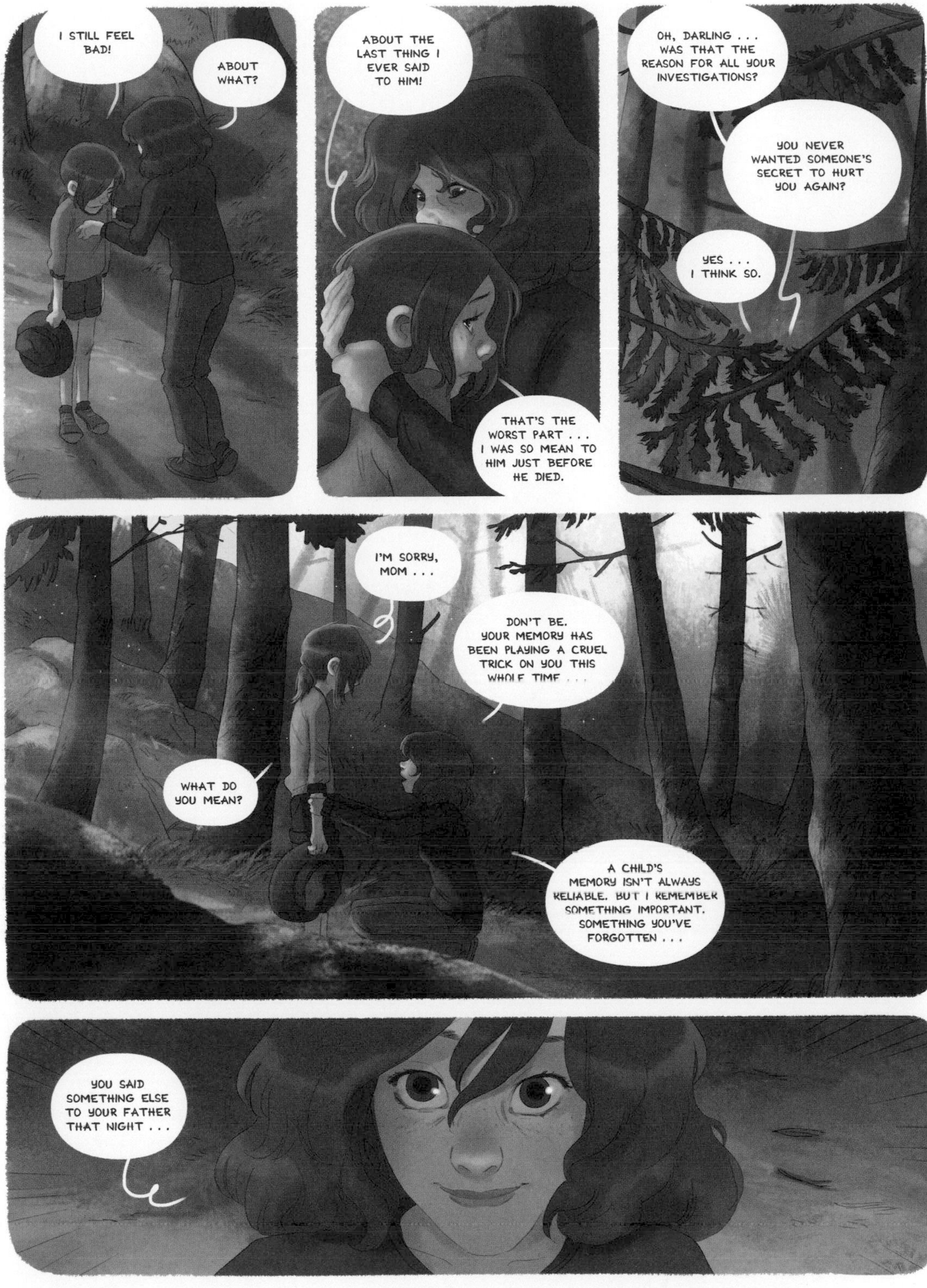
I STILL FEEL BAD!
ABOUT WHAT?
ABOUT THE LAST THING I EVER SAID TO HIM!
THAT'S THE WORST PART . . . I WAS SO MEAN TO HIM JUST BEFORE HE DIED.
OH, DARLING . . . WAS THAT THE REASON FOR ALL YOUR INVESTIGATIONS?
YOU NEVER WANTED SOMEONE'S SECRET TO HURT YOU AGAIN?
YES . . . I THINK SO.
I'M SORRY, MOM . . .
DON'T BE. YOUR MEMORY HAS BEEN PLAYING A CRUEL TRICK ON YOU THIS WHOLE TIME . . .
WHAT DO YOU MEAN?
A CHILD'S MEMORY ISN'T ALWAYS RELIABLE. BUT I REMEMBER SOMETHING IMPORTANT. SOMETHING YOU'VE FORGOTTEN . . .
YOU SAID SOMETHING ELSE TO YOUR FATHER THAT NIGHT . . .

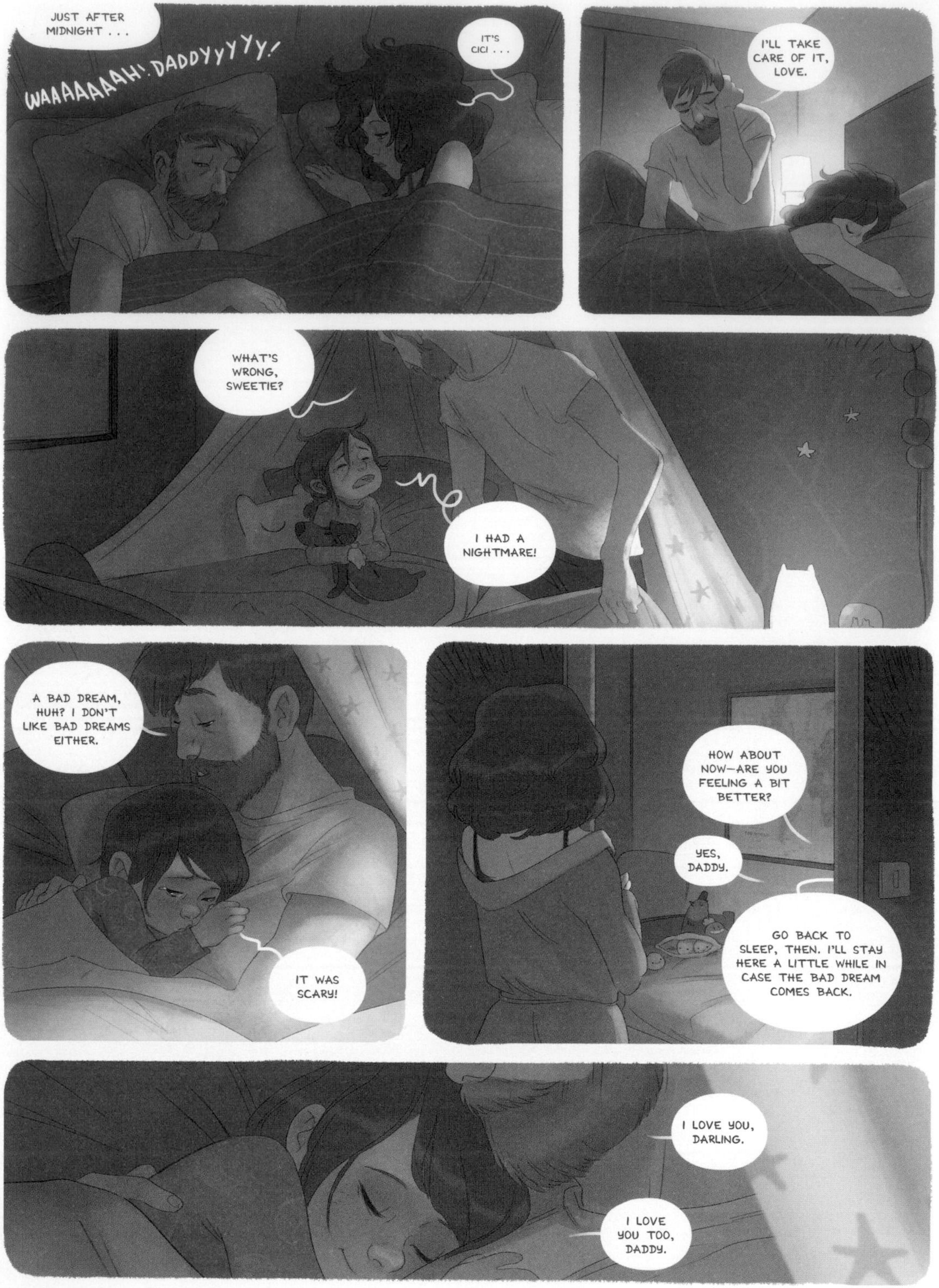
JUST AFTER MIDNIGHT . . .
WAAAAAAAH! DADDYYYYY!
IT'S CICI . . .
I'LL TAKE CARE OF IT, LOVE.
WHAT'S WRONG, SWEETIE?
I HAD A NIGHTMARE!
A BAD DREAM, HUH? I DON'T LIKE BAD DREAMS EITHER.
IT WAS SCARY!
HOW ABOUT NOW—ARE YOU FEELING A BIT BETTER?
YES, DADDY.
GO BACK TO SLEEP, THEN. I'LL STAY HERE A LITTLE WHILE IN CASE THE BAD DREAM COMES BACK.
I LOVE YOU, DARLING.
I LOVE YOU TOO, DADDY.

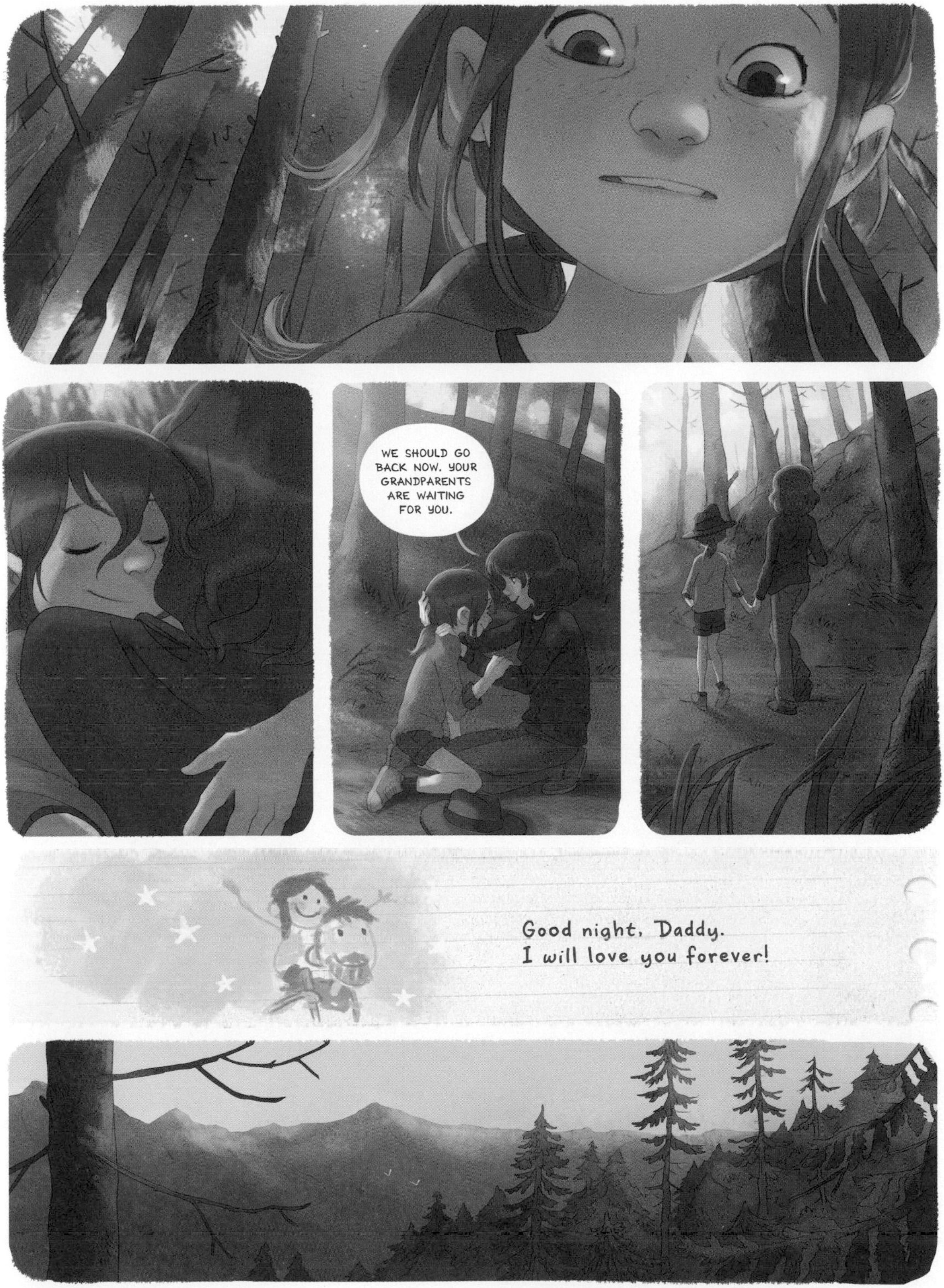
WE SHOULD GO BACK NOW. YOUR GRANDPARENTS ARE WAITING FOR YOU.
Good night, Daddy.
I will love you forever!

All my anger has drained away, Daddy. I've forgiven you, and more importantly, I've forgiven myself. Now it's time for me to make new memories about you with Mom's help—and Nanna and Poppa's help too!

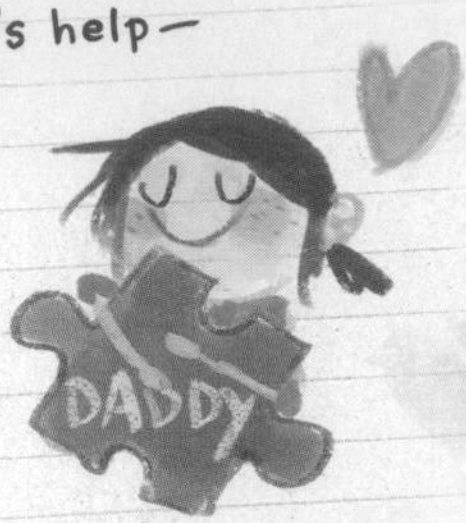
DADDY

When Mom and I got back to the house, Nanna and Poppa told me lots of stories about Daddy's childhood. It was super! They also gave me lots of photos of him when he was young. Some of them were even new to mom!

Daddy

Me so many years later . . .

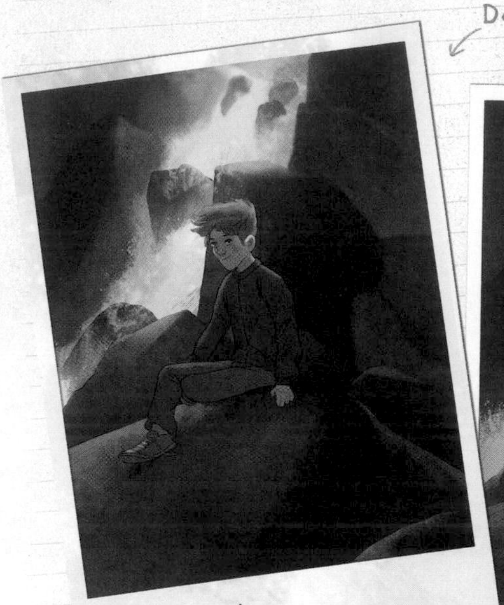

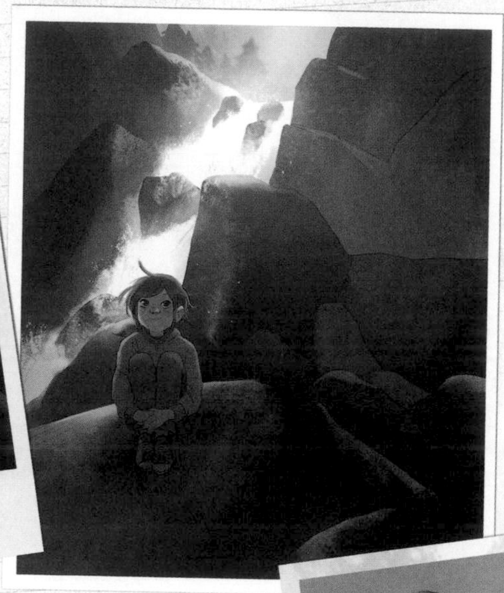

The next day, we all took a hike together! I enjoy walking in his footsteps!

My dad was an explorer!

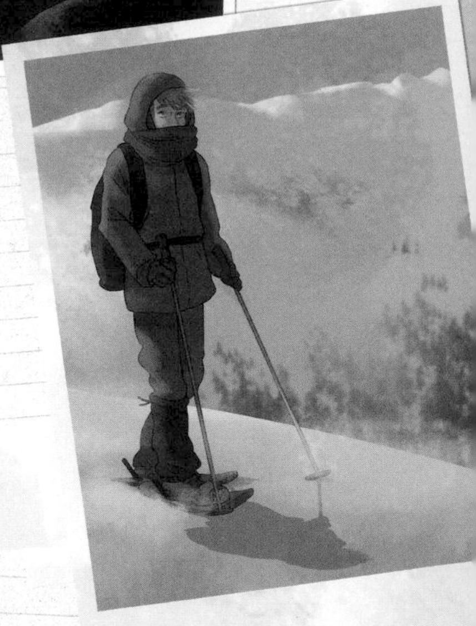

To be perfectly honest, Dad wasn't really an explorer; he delivered letters for the post office. Nanna told me the story of how he chose this career.

The winters in this mountainous area have always been very brutal. When my dad was little, the snow was sometimes so heavy that it blocked the roads and brought down the telephone lines. So for weeks on end, the villagers had to stay shut up in their houses, reading and playing games.

Once the snow melted enough for traffic to move again, everyone eagerly anticipated one thing: the delivery of the mail!

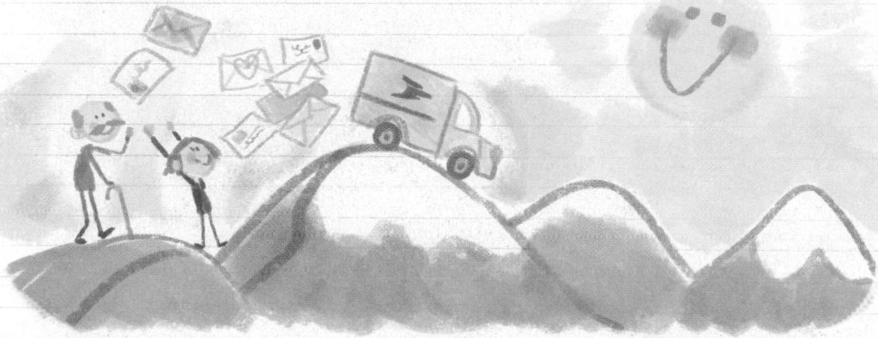

Dad loved to see the looks on people's faces when they finally received news about their family and friends. So, when the old postman finally retired, he applied for the position. Since Dad knew the mountain so well, he could deliver mail to even the most remote cabins. So, there was a bit of adventure in his job after all!

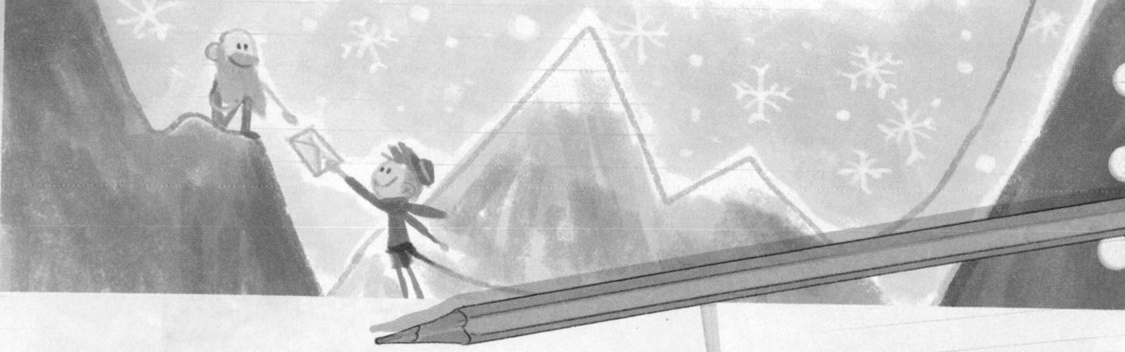

Poppa used to enjoy making videos when my mom, dad, and I visited them. One evening, we watched some of those videos, and memories of those trips came flooding back to me. I remembered especially afternoons when we camped along the banks of a mountain stream, and nights when we watched shooting stars fill the sky. Poppa told me their name: the Perseid meteor shower. They return every August. From now on, I will make a point of staying up late to see them. And whenever I do, I will remember this visit to my grandparents' home.

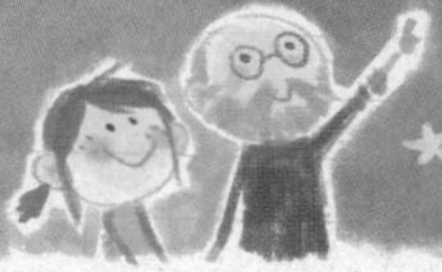

I wish we could've stayed up longer that evening, but Mom and I had to leave early the next morning. I promised to visit Nanna and Poppa more often. I never realized how important grandparents are. I'll be sure to take full advantage of these trips in the future!

Poppa promised me we could build secret hideouts together, and I'll get to visit my dad as often as I'd like.

All during the drive back, Mom told me stories about Dad—how they met, what she loved about him, and why he occasionally annoyed her.

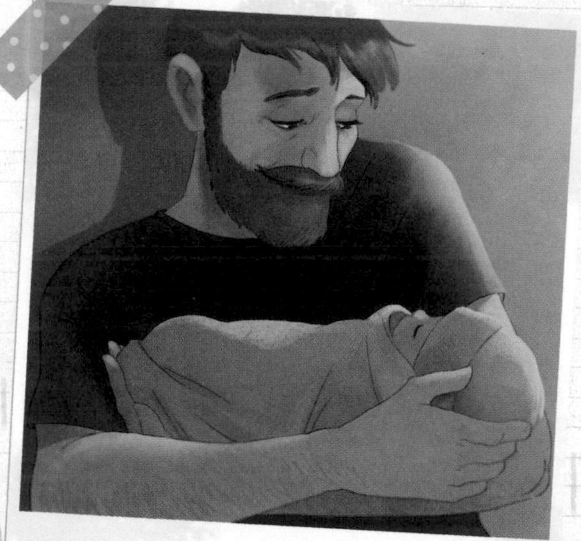

She confided in me that he was scared to become a father, but as soon as I was born, his fear evaporated.

It was still light when we arrived home, but we were drenched by a rainstorm. Warm summer rains—I love them!

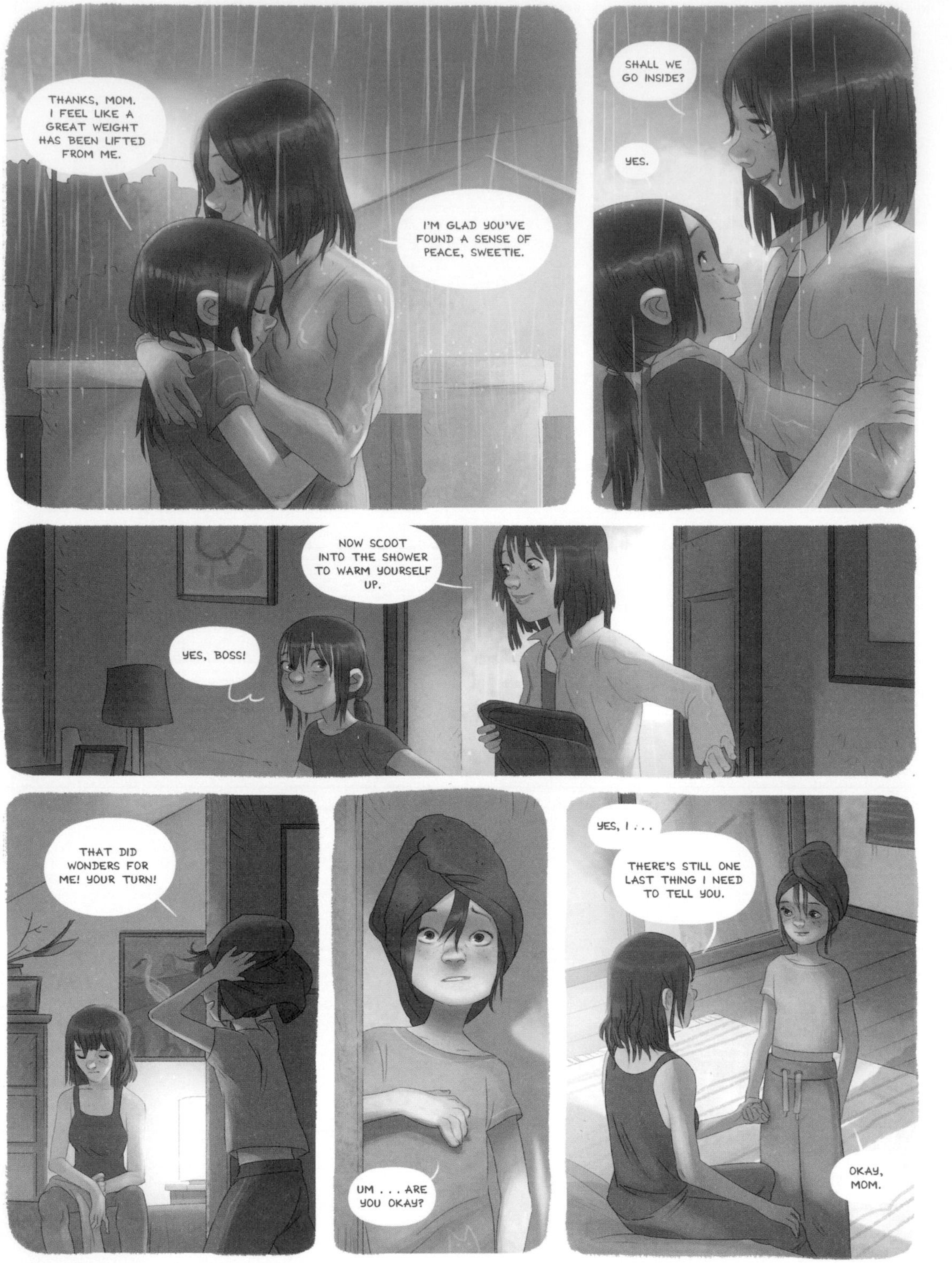
THANKS, MOM. I FEEL LIKE A GREAT WEIGHT HAS BEEN LIFTED FROM ME.
I'M GLAD YOU'VE FOUND A SENSE OF PEACE, SWEETIE.
SHALL WE GO INSIDE?
YES.
NOW SCOOT INTO THE SHOWER TO WARM YOURSELF UP.
YES, BOSS!
THAT DID WONDERS FOR ME! YOUR TURN!
UM . . . ARE YOU OKAY?
YES, I . . .
THERE'S STILL ONE LAST THING I NEED TO TELL YOU.
OKAY, MOM.

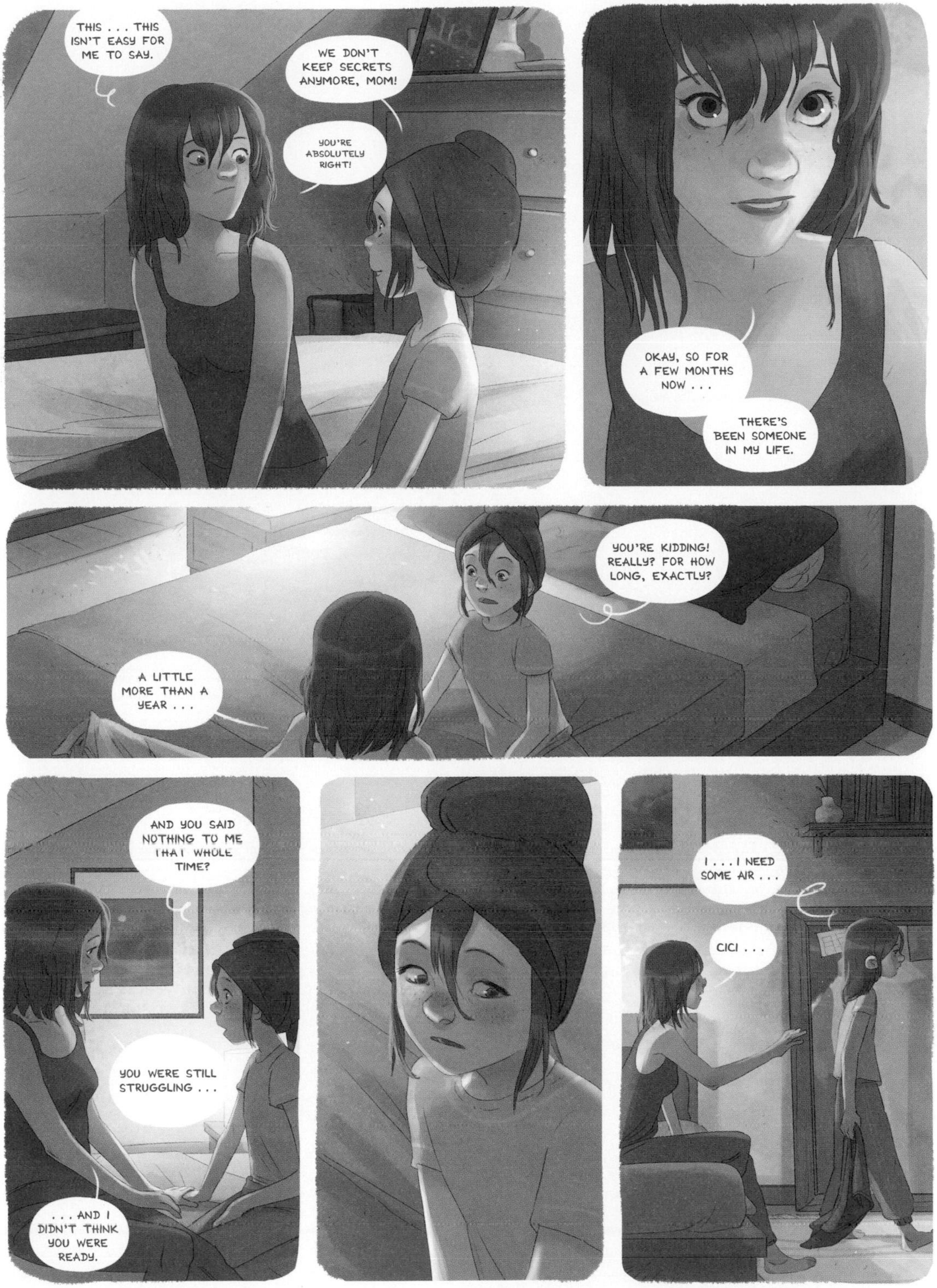
THIS . . . THIS ISN'T EASY FOR ME TO SAY.
WE DON'T KEEP SECRETS ANYMORE, MOM!
YOU'RE ABSOLUTELY RIGHT!
OKAY, SO FOR A FEW MONTHS NOW . . .
THERE'S BEEN SOMEONE IN MY LIFE.
YOU'RE KIDDING! REALLY? FOR HOW LONG, EXACTLY?
A LITTLE MORE THAN A YEAR . . .
AND YOU SAID NOTHING TO ME THAT WHOLE TIME?
YOU WERE STILL STRUGGLING . . .
. . . AND I DIDN'T THINK YOU WERE READY.
I . . . I NEED SOME AIR . . .
CICI . . .

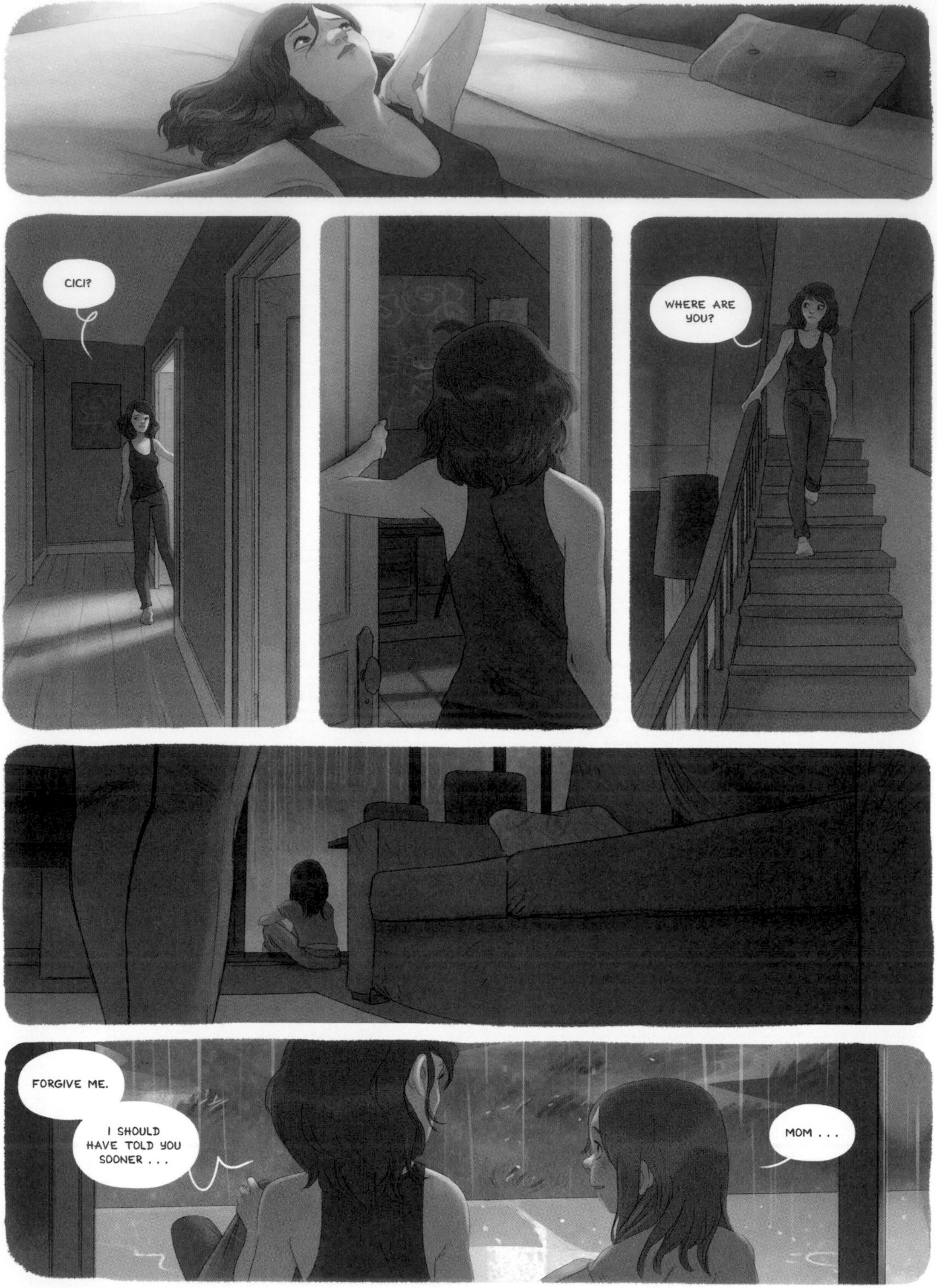
CICI?
WHERE ARE YOU?
FORGIVE ME.
I SHOULD HAVE TOLD YOU SOONER . . .
MOM . . .

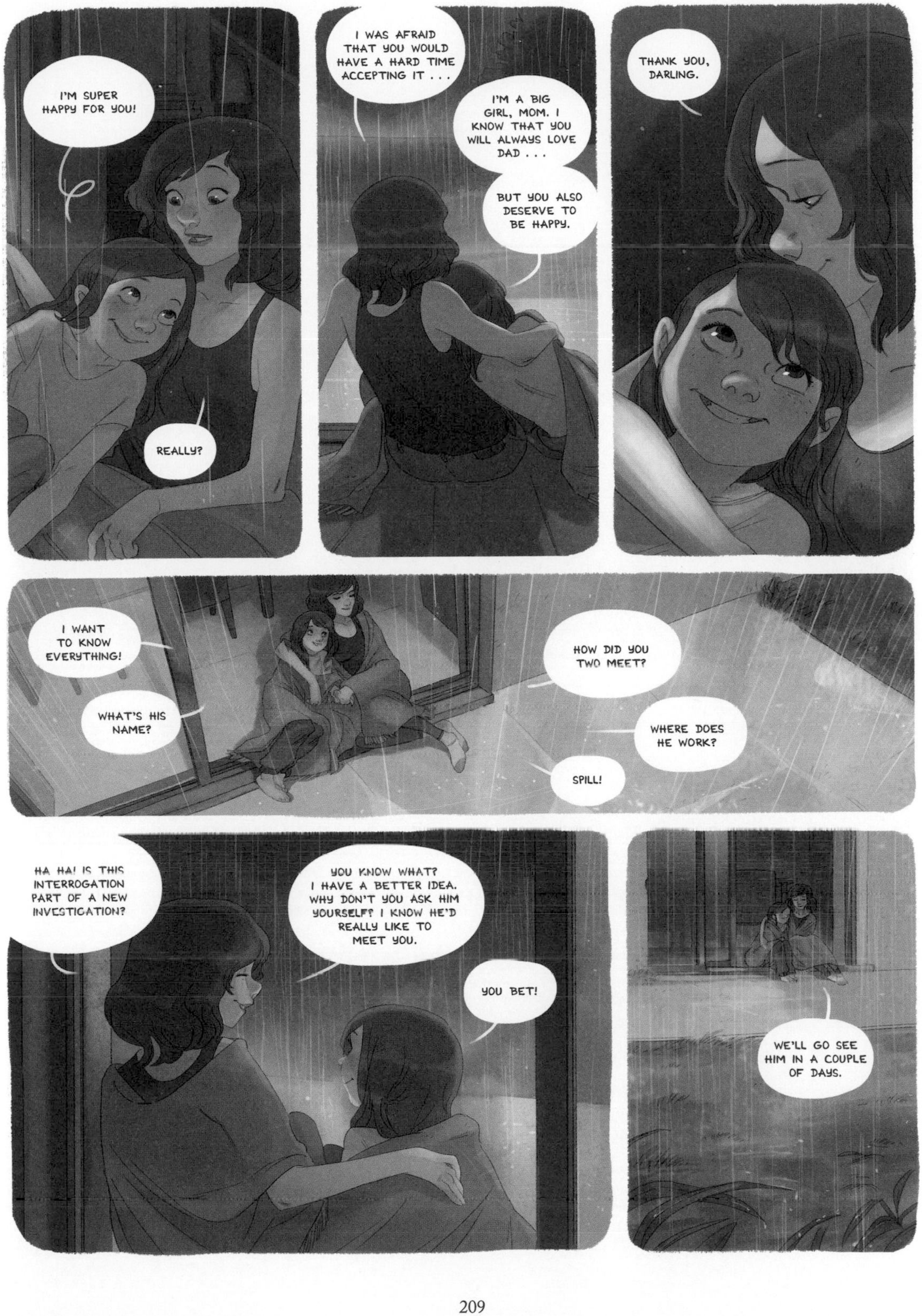
I'M SUPER HAPPY FOR YOU!
REALLY?
I WAS AFRAID THAT YOU WOULD HAVE A HARD TIME ACCEPTING IT . . .
I'M A BIG GIRL, MOM. I KNOW THAT YOU WILL ALWAYS LOVE DAD . . .
BUT YOU ALSO DESERVE TO BE HAPPY.
THANK YOU, DARLING.
I WANT TO KNOW EVERYTHING!
WHAT'S HIS NAME?
HOW DID YOU TWO MEET?
WHERE DOES HE WORK?
SPILL!
HA HA! IS THIS INTERROGATION PART OF A NEW INVESTIGATION?
YOU KNOW WHAT? I HAVE A BETTER IDEA. WHY DON'T YOU ASK HIM YOURSELF? I KNOW HE'D REALLY LIKE TO MEET YOU.
YOU BET!
WE'LL GO SEE HIM IN A COUPLE OF DAYS.

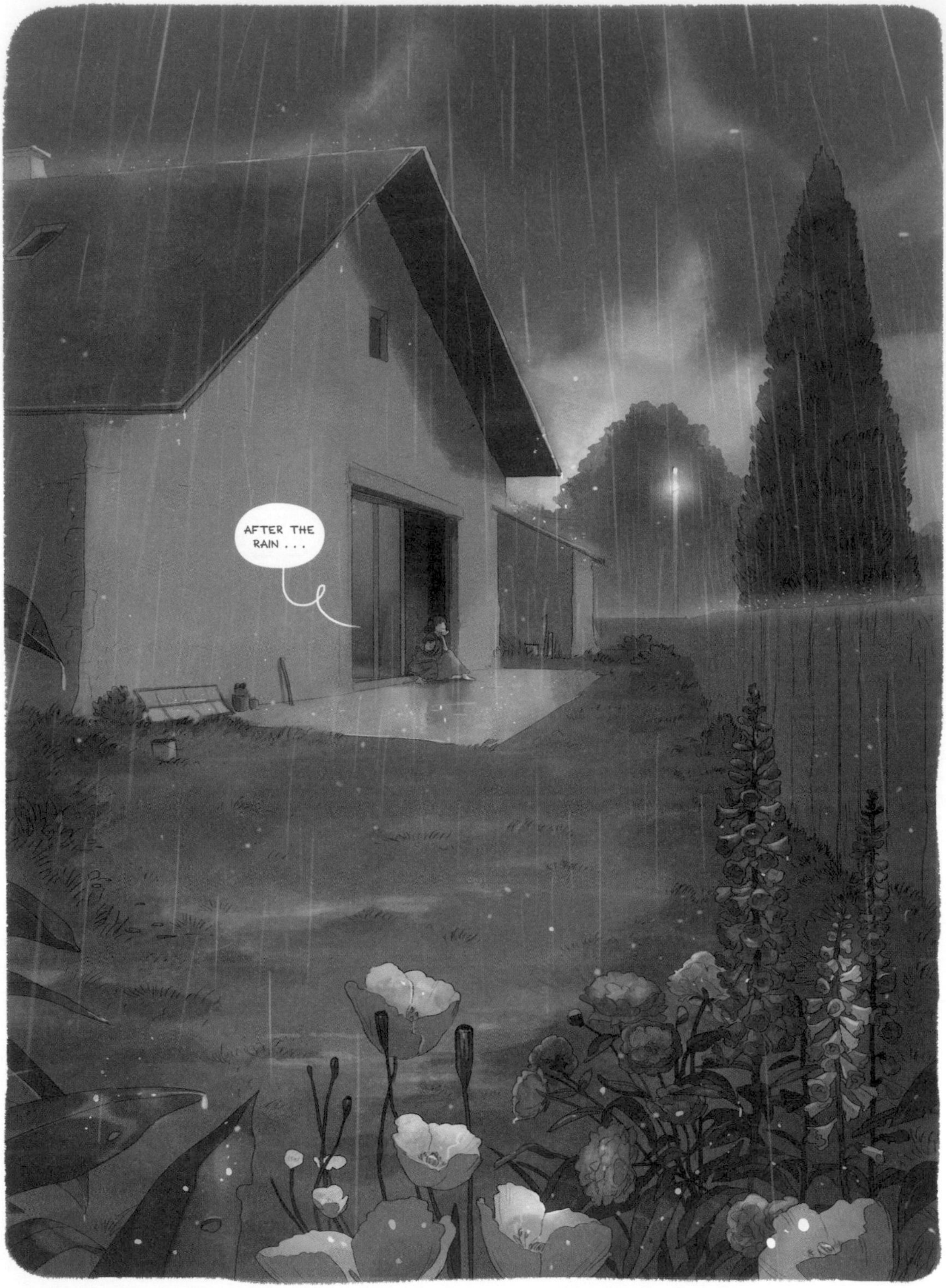
AFTER THE RAIN . . .

Mom has a new boyfriend!

Fantastic!

His name is Stephen and he lives in a small town not far away from us. She didn't tell me too much—she'd rather I find out about him myself.

Nevertheless, I managed to worm some details out of her to satisfy my curiosity.

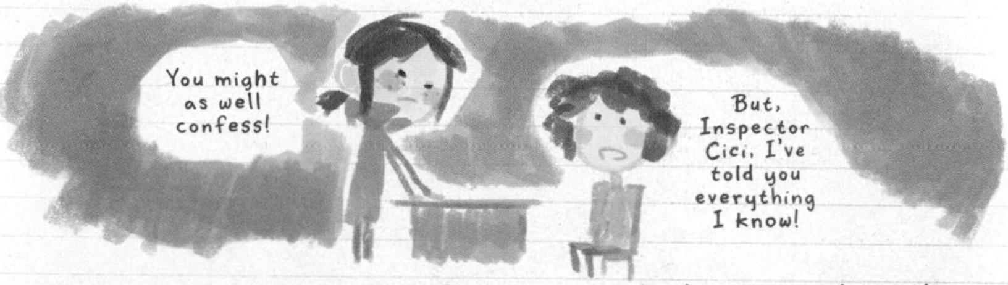
You might as well confess!
But, Inspector Cici, I've told you everything I know!

They have been together for a year, which means that their story began . . . at the same time as my encounter with Mrs. Ronsin at the library!

Now that I think about it, Mom has been coming home from work a little later than usual. And she's been a bit distracted. I wonder . . . When she drove me to the library, did she **really** go shopping?

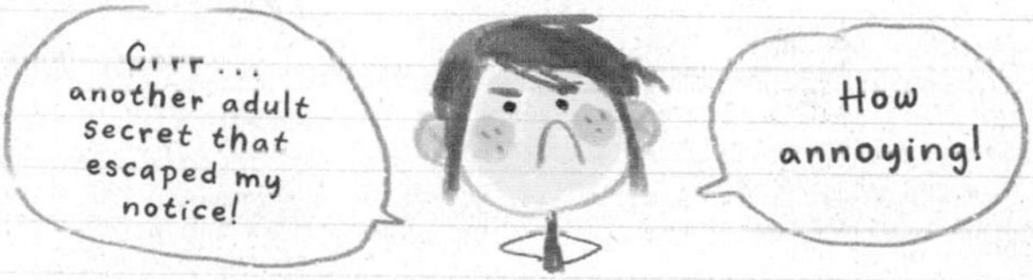
Grrr . . . another adult secret that escaped my notice!
How annoying!

According to Mom, they met at the beginning of last year while she was organizing a music festival. It seems that he's a musician and had to come to the civic center where Mom works to fill out some paperwork. There weren't any problems, but he kept inventing excuses to visit Mom's office. She's pretty savvy—she quickly figured out what he was up to. But they had a lot in common and took a liking to each other . . .

I honestly had no clue. Perhaps if I had paid a little more attention to her, I might have figured it out ... Mom seems very happy, though, and that's all that counts.

She told me how hard it was to be in a relationship again. She felt guilty at first, but then she realized that she was allowed to love someone again. Love is a wonderful thing—being in love with Stephen is not a betrayal of Dad, but an opportunity to find happiness again.

The hardest thing for Mom has been getting over the fear of losing someone she loves. It's hard for her to feel secure in a relationship—it was really traumatic for her when Dad passed away so suddenly! She still has nightmares about it sometimes. Stephen told her that he would be patient and give her all the time she needs to adjust.

He seems like a good guy. He makes her laugh, and when she talks about him, her eyes light up. It makes her even more beautiful!

I'll meet him for the first time tomorrow—I can't wait!

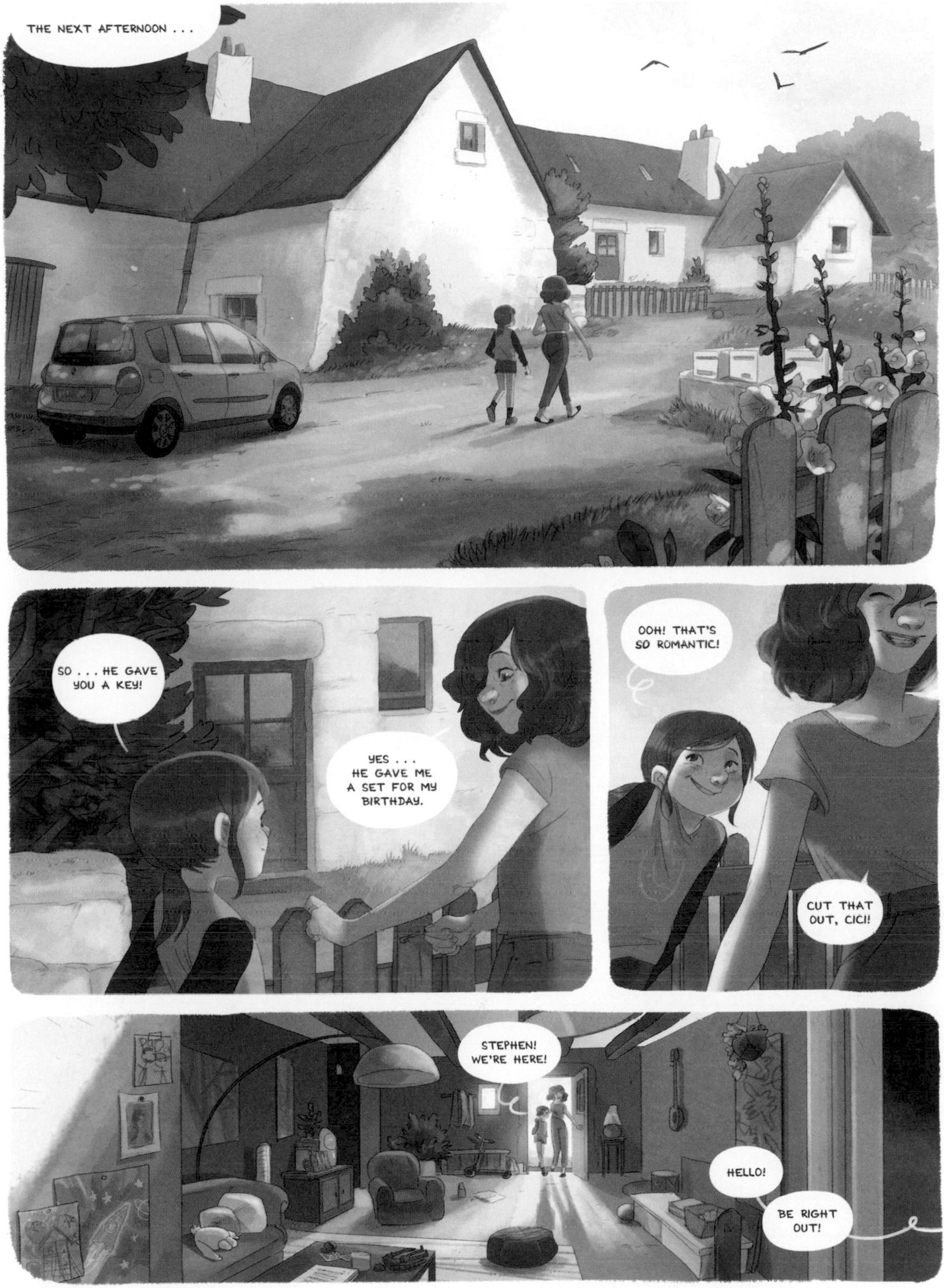
THE NEXT AFTERNOON . . .
SO . . . HE GAVE YOU A KEY!
YES . . . HE GAVE ME A SET FOR MY BIRTHDAY.
OOH! THAT'S SO ROMANTIC!
CUT THAT OUT, CICI!
STEPHEN! WE'RE HERE!
HELLO!
BE RIGHT OUT!

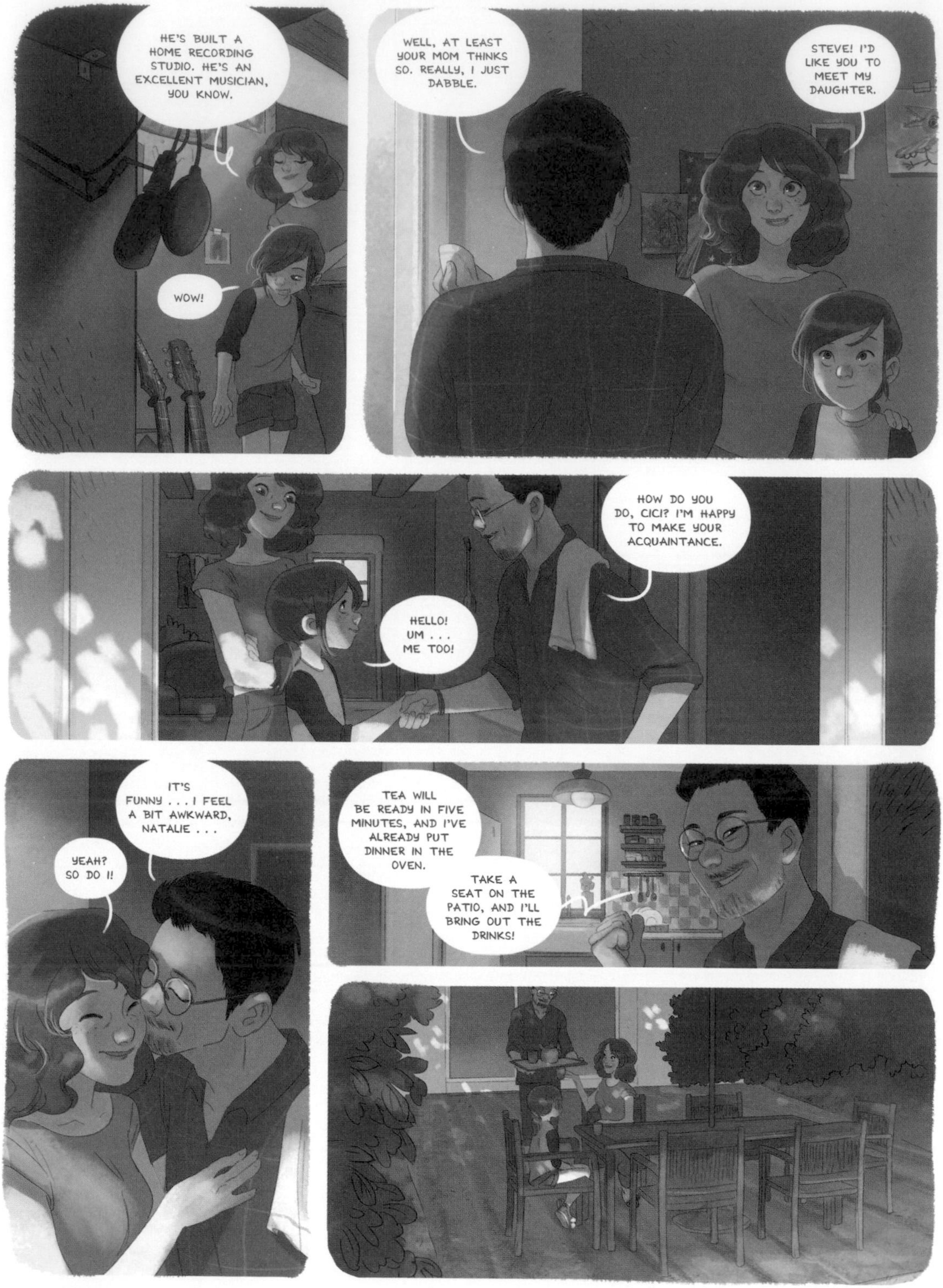
HE'S BUILT A HOME RECORDING STUDIO. HE'S AN EXCELLENT MUSICIAN, YOU KNOW.
WOW!
WELL, AT LEAST YOUR MOM THINKS SO. REALLY, I JUST DABBLE.
STEVE! I'D LIKE YOU TO MEET MY DAUGHTER.
HOW DO YOU DO, CICI? I'M HAPPY TO MAKE YOUR ACQUAINTANCE.
HELLO! UM . . . ME TOO!
IT'S FUNNY . . . I FEEL A BIT AWKWARD, NATALIE . . .
YEAH? SO DO I!
TEA WILL BE READY IN FIVE MINUTES, AND I'VE ALREADY PUT DINNER IN THE OVEN.
TAKE A SEAT ON THE PATIO, AND I'LL BRING OUT THE DRINKS!

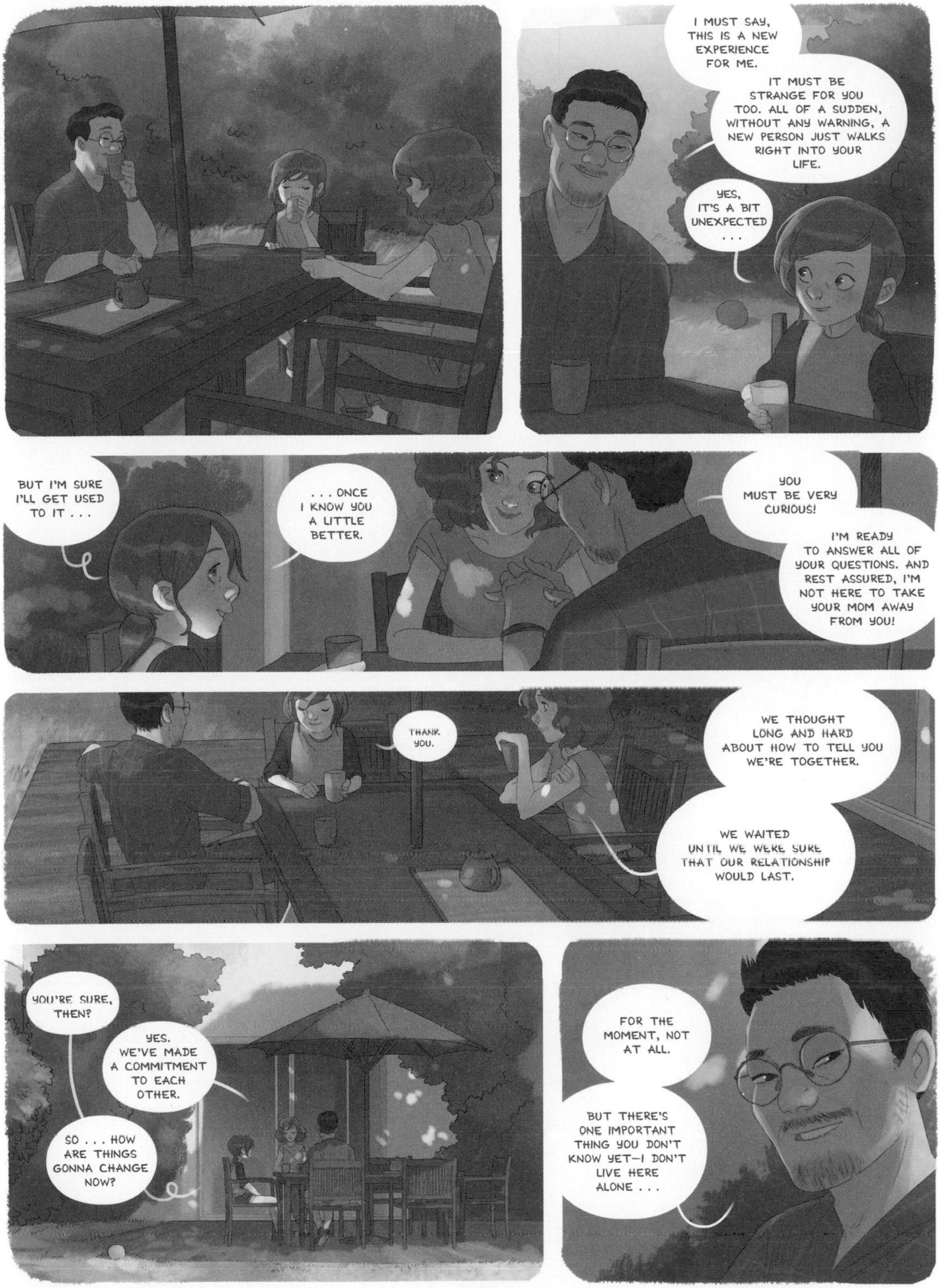

I MUST SAY, THIS IS A NEW EXPERIENCE FOR ME.
IT MUST BE STRANGE FOR YOU TOO. ALL OF A SUDDEN, WITHOUT ANY WARNING, A NEW PERSON JUST WALKS RIGHT INTO YOUR LIFE.
YES, IT'S A BIT UNEXPECTED . . .
BUT I'M SURE I'LL GET USED TO IT . . .
. . . ONCE I KNOW YOU A LITTLE BETTER.
YOU MUST BE VERY CURIOUS!
I'M READY TO ANSWER ALL OF YOUR QUESTIONS. AND REST ASSURED, I'M NOT HERE TO TAKE YOUR MOM AWAY FROM YOU!
THANK YOU.
WE THOUGHT LONG AND HARD ABOUT HOW TO TELL YOU WE'RE TOGETHER.
WE WAITED UNTIL WE WERE SURE THAT OUR RELATIONSHIP WOULD LAST.
YOU'RE SURE, THEN?
YES. WE'VE MADE A COMMITMENT TO EACH OTHER.
SO . . . HOW ARE THINGS GONNA CHANGE NOW?
FOR THE MOMENT, NOT AT ALL.
BUT THERE'S ONE IMPORTANT THING YOU DON'T KNOW YET—I DON'T LIVE HERE ALONE . . .

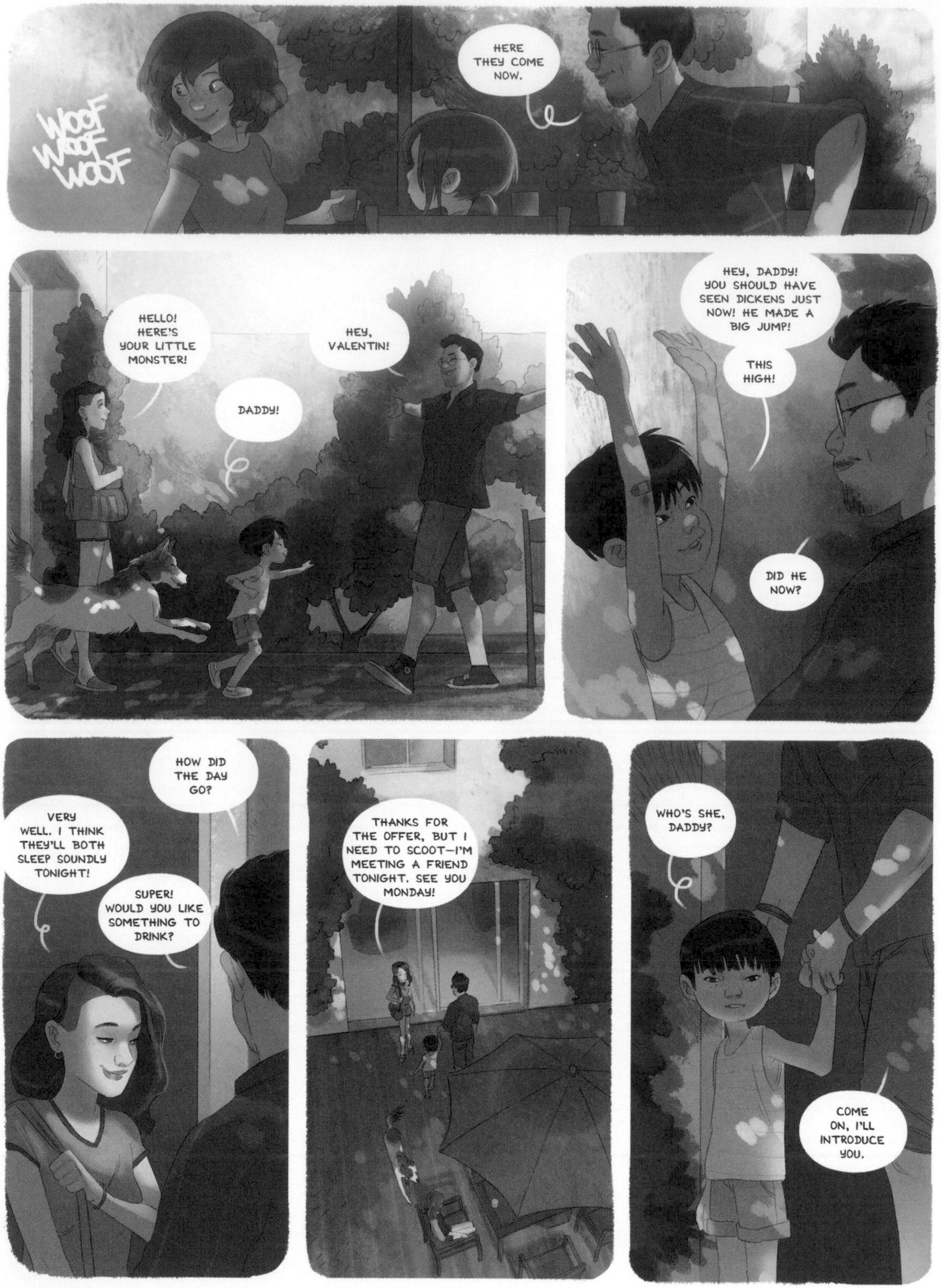
WOOF WOOF WOOF
HERE THEY COME NOW.
HELLO! HERE'S YOUR LITTLE MONSTER!
HEY, VALENTIN!
DADDY!
HEY, DADDY! YOU SHOULD HAVE SEEN DICKENS JUST NOW! HE MADE A BIG JUMP!
THIS HIGH!
DID HE NOW?
HOW DID THE DAY GO?
VERY WELL. I THINK THEY'LL BOTH SLEEP SOUNDLY TONIGHT!
SUPER! WOULD YOU LIKE SOMETHING TO DRINK?
THANKS FOR THE OFFER, BUT I NEED TO SCOOT—I'M MEETING A FRIEND TONIGHT. SEE YOU MONDAY!
WHO'S SHE, DADDY?
COME ON, I'LL INTRODUCE YOU.

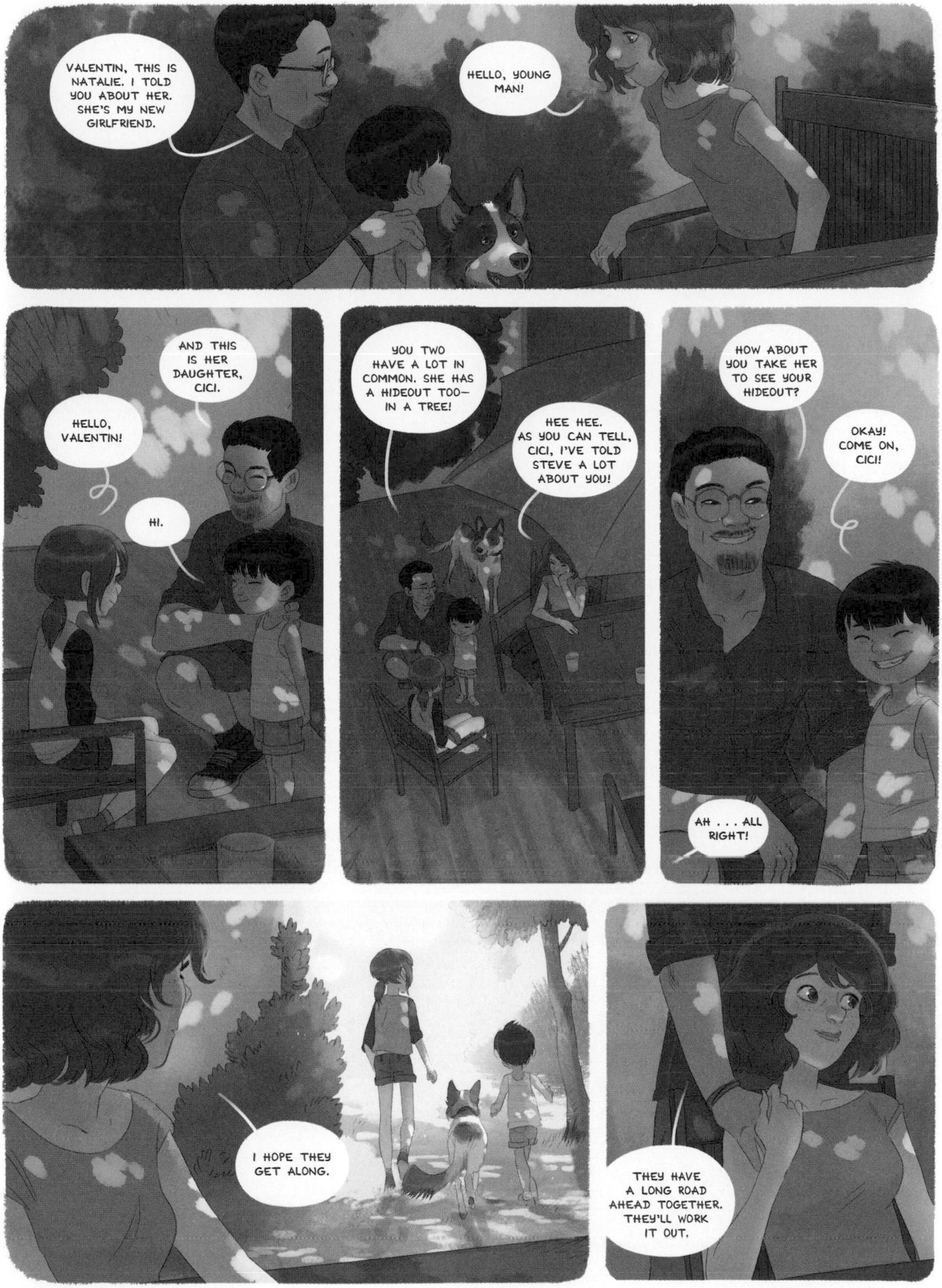
VALENTIN, THIS IS NATALIE. I TOLD YOU ABOUT HER. SHE'S MY NEW GIRLFRIEND.
HELLO, YOUNG MAN!
AND THIS IS HER DAUGHTER, CICI.
HELLO, VALENTIN!
HI.
YOU TWO HAVE A LOT IN COMMON. SHE HAS A HIDEOUT TOO— IN A TREE!
HEE HEE. AS YOU CAN TELL, CICI, I'VE TOLD STEVE A LOT ABOUT YOU!
HOW ABOUT YOU TAKE HER TO SEE YOUR HIDEOUT?
OKAY! COME ON, CICI!
AH . . . ALL RIGHT!
I HOPE THEY GET ALONG.
THEY HAVE A LONG ROAD AHEAD TOGETHER. THEY'LL WORK IT OUT.

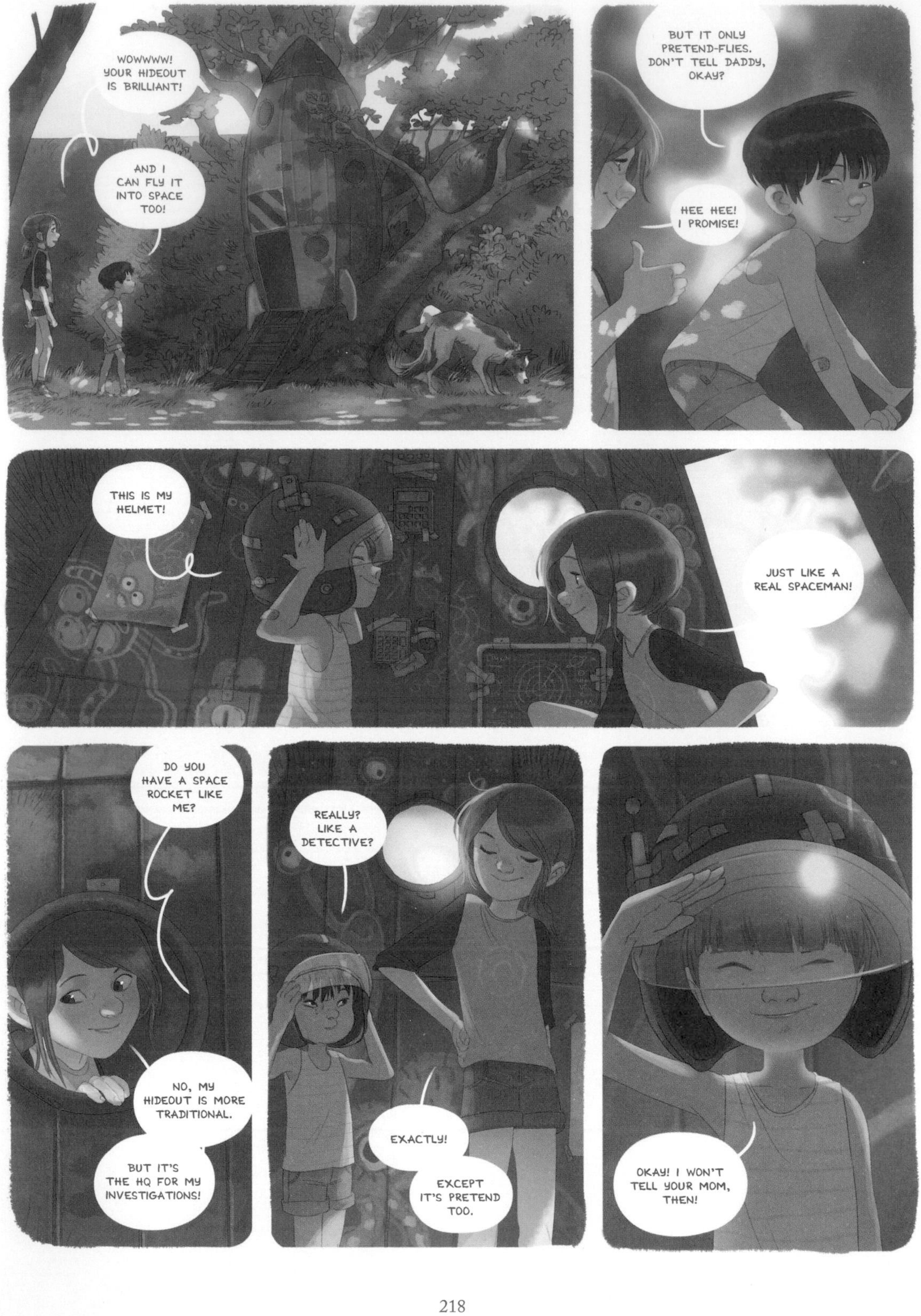
WOWWWW! YOUR HIDEOUT IS BRILLIANT!
AND I CAN FLY IT INTO SPACE TOO!
BUT IT ONLY PRETEND-FLIES. DON'T TELL DADDY, OKAY?
HEE HEE! I PROMISE!
THIS IS MY HELMET!
JUST LIKE A REAL SPACEMAN!
DO YOU HAVE A SPACE ROCKET LIKE ME?
NO, MY HIDEOUT IS MORE TRADITIONAL.
BUT IT'S THE HQ FOR MY INVESTIGATIONS!
REALLY? LIKE A DETECTIVE?
EXACTLY!
EXCEPT IT'S PRETEND TOO.
OKAY! I WON'T TELL YOUR MOM, THEN!

Valentin is so cute! His head is always in the stars.

His room is full of space stuff.

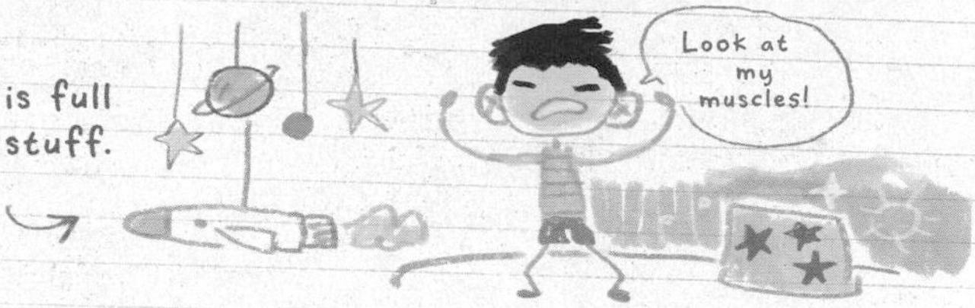
Look at my muscles!

His dream is to go to the moon! Nothing less will do!
He saw pictures of a moon landing on TV once and he loved it.
He's been passionate about space travel ever since.

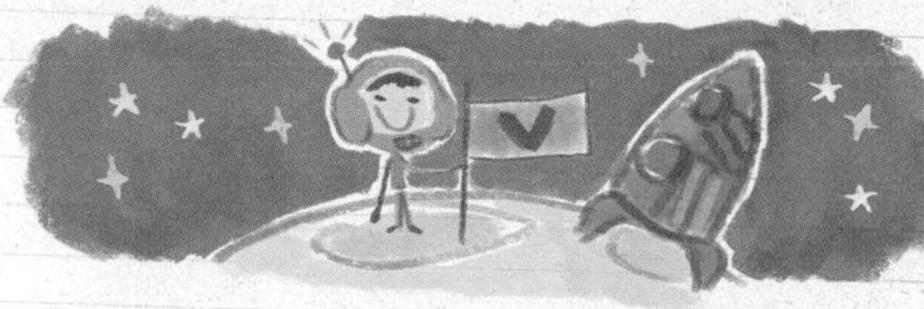

We spent the whole day together. We've already become partners:

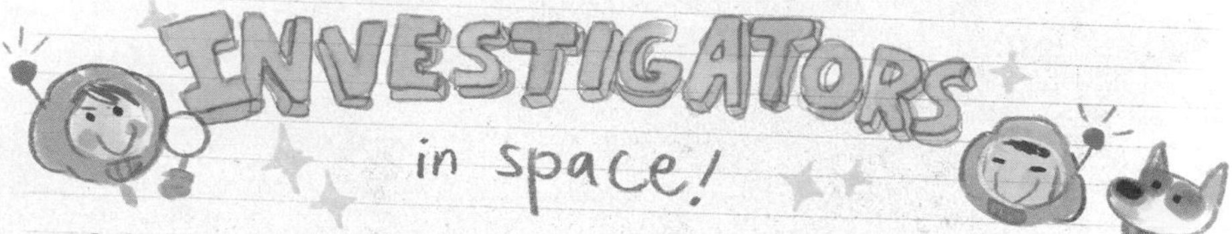
INVESTIGATORS
in space!

I found out that his mom left when he was just a baby. Apparently, she didn't like being a mom. But he isn't sad about it. He and his dad get along great! Anyway, we're really happy that our parents have fallen in love.

Mom really wanted to have the two of us in a picture. It's our first photo together—but I'm sure it won't be the last!

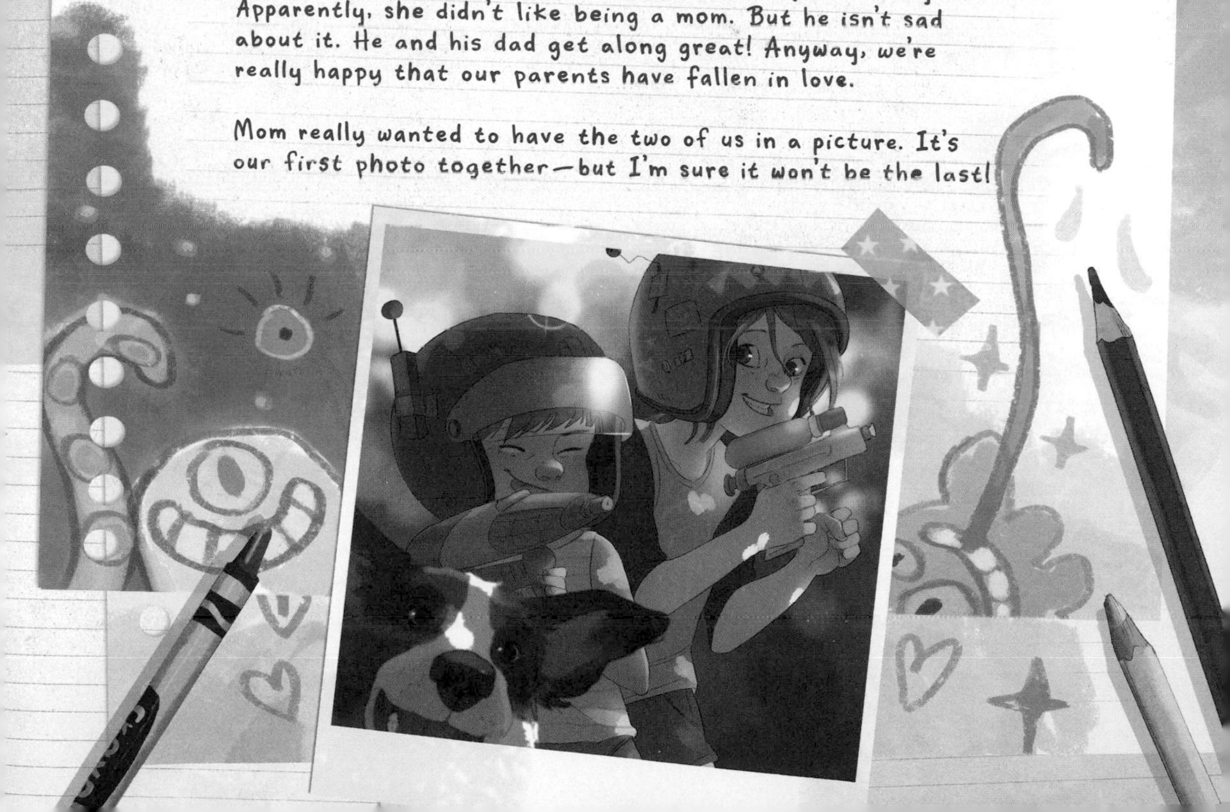

I always wanted to have a little brother or sister.

I've often wondered why Mom didn't get married again so she could have more kids. Now, all of a sudden, our family has doubled in size! I think I'm going to love being a big sister! Maybe Mom and Stephen will even have a baby together?

Valentin is crazy about his dog, Dickens. He told me Dickens has been asking a really important question: When our parents get married, which house will he sleep in? Valentin's? Mine? Or will they want to get a brand-new house together?

I don't actually think Dickens is the one who wants to know . . . ☺

Anyway, we went and asked our parents the question. They looked at each other without saying anything. Finally, Stephen spoke up. He said:

"Actually, there's another alternative we've been contemplating . . ."

You'll never believe what they suggested.
    Lena and Erica will be amazed—I can't wait to tell them!

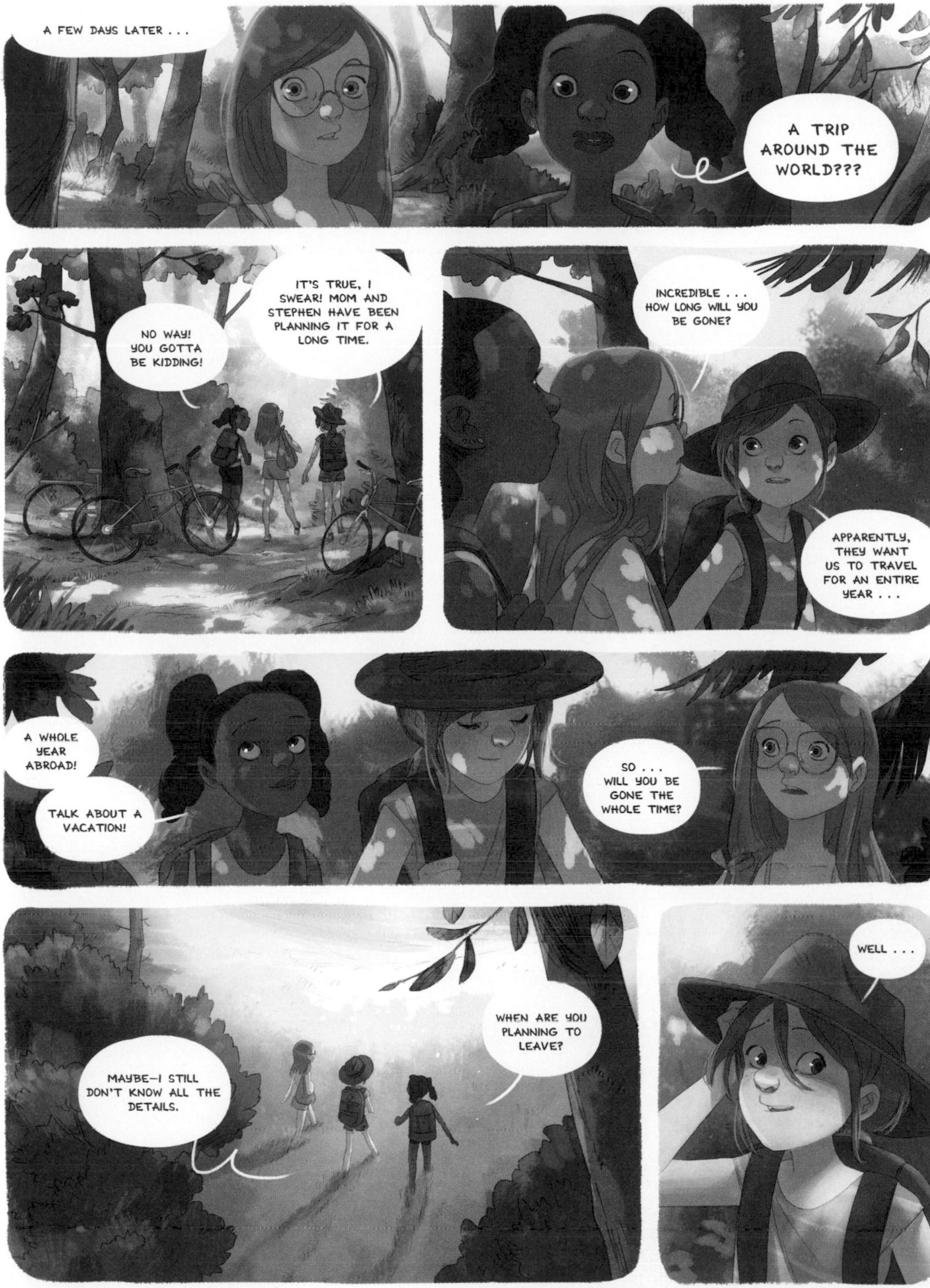
A FEW DAYS LATER . . .
A TRIP AROUND THE WORLD???
NO WAY! YOU GOTTA BE KIDDING!
IT'S TRUE, I SWEAR! MOM AND STEPHEN HAVE BEEN PLANNING IT FOR A LONG TIME.
INCREDIBLE . . . HOW LONG WILL YOU BE GONE?
APPARENTLY, THEY WANT US TO TRAVEL FOR AN ENTIRE YEAR . . .
A WHOLE YEAR ABROAD!
TALK ABOUT A VACATION!
SO . . . WILL YOU BE GONE THE WHOLE TIME?
WHEN ARE YOU PLANNING TO LEAVE?
MAYBE—I STILL DON'T KNOW ALL THE DETAILS.
WELL . . .

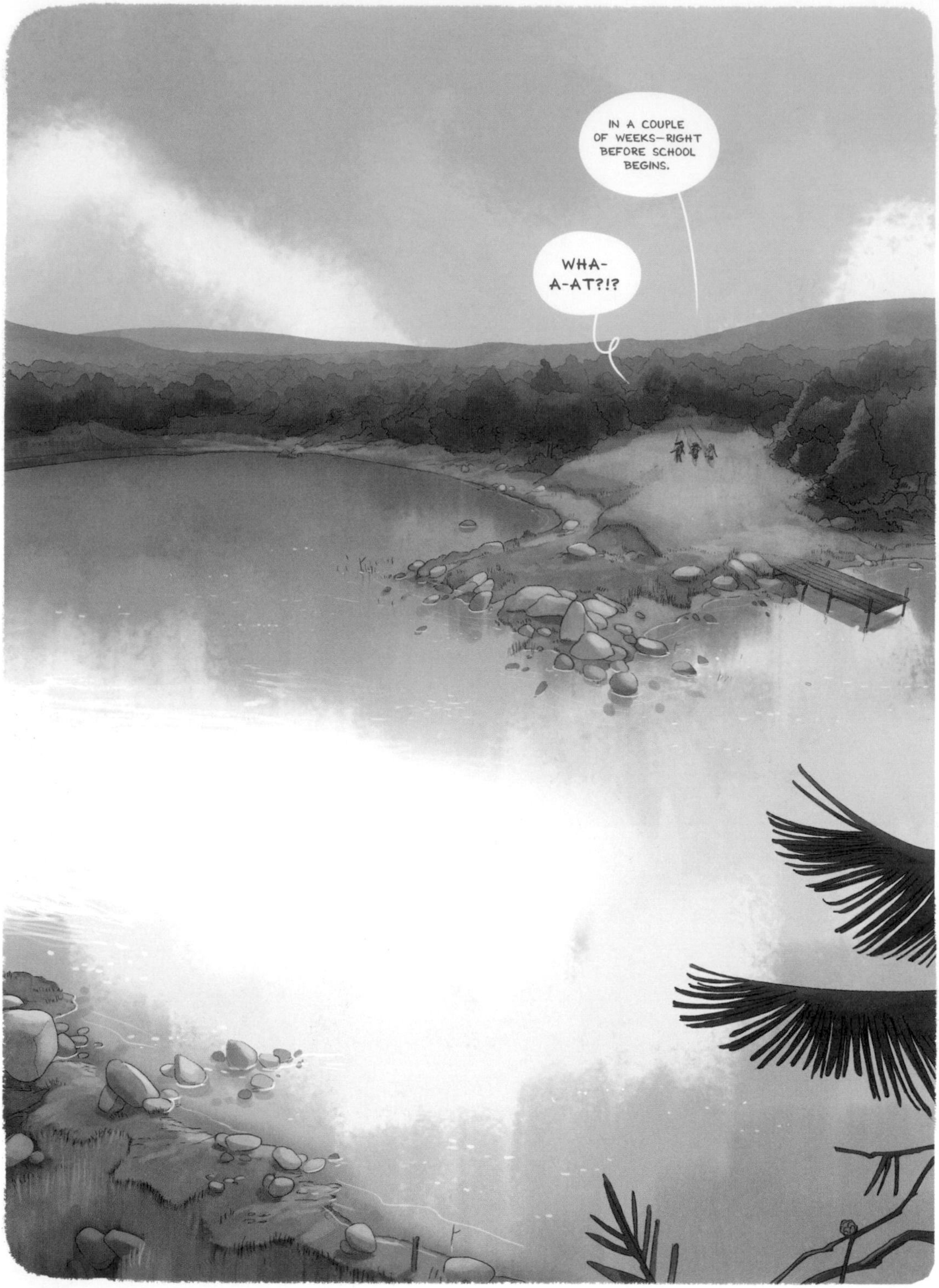
IN A COUPLE OF WEEKS—RIGHT BEFORE SCHOOL BEGINS.
WHA-A-AT?!?

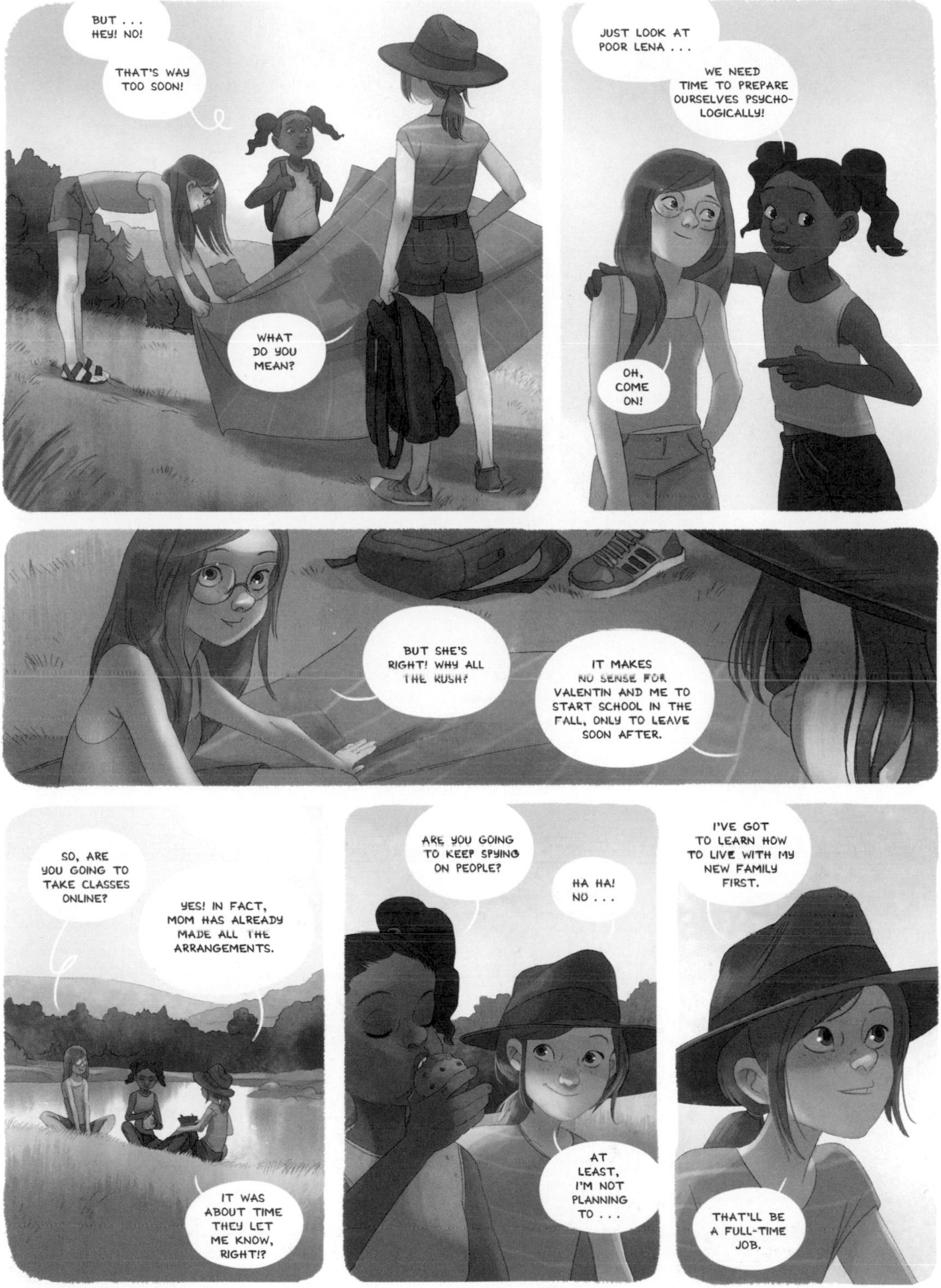

BUT . . . HEY! NO!
THAT'S WAY TOO SOON!
WHAT DO YOU MEAN?
JUST LOOK AT POOR LENA . . .
WE NEED TIME TO PREPARE OURSELVES PSYCHOLOGICALLY!
OH, COME ON!
BUT SHE'S RIGHT! WHY ALL THE RUSH?
IT MAKES NO SENSE FOR VALENTIN AND ME TO START SCHOOL IN THE FALL, ONLY TO LEAVE SOON AFTER.
SO, ARE YOU GOING TO TAKE CLASSES ONLINE?
YES! IN FACT, MOM HAS ALREADY MADE ALL THE ARRANGEMENTS.
IT WAS ABOUT TIME THEY LET ME KNOW, RIGHT!?
ARE YOU GOING TO KEEP SPYING ON PEOPLE?
HA HA! NO . . .
AT LEAST, I'M NOT PLANNING TO . . .
I'VE GOT TO LEARN HOW TO LIVE WITH MY NEW FAMILY FIRST.
THAT'LL BE A FULL-TIME JOB.

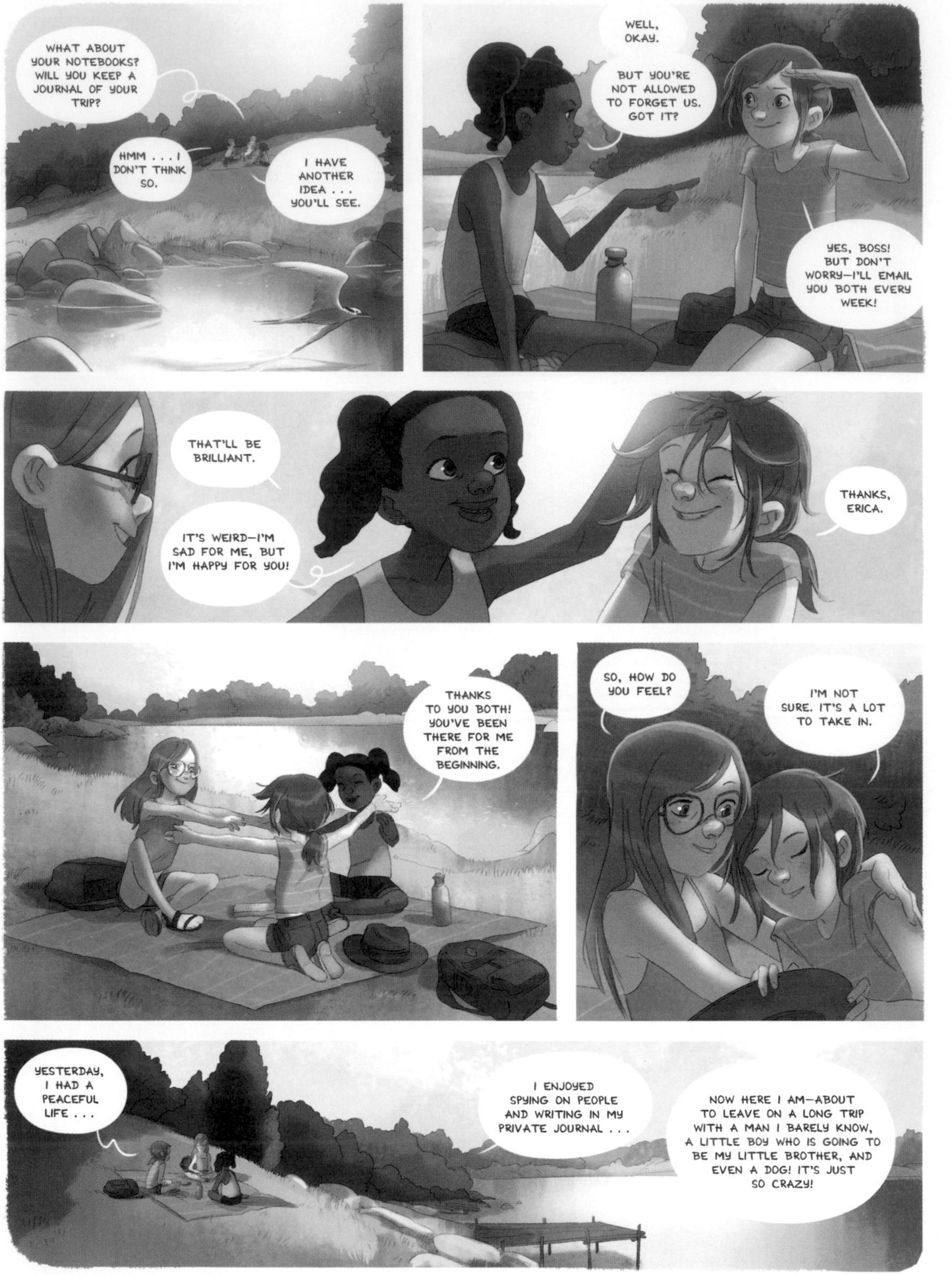
WHAT ABOUT YOUR NOTEBOOKS? WILL YOU KEEP A JOURNAL OF YOUR TRIP?
HMM . . . I DON'T THINK SO.
I HAVE ANOTHER IDEA . . . YOU'LL SEE.
WELL, OKAY.
BUT YOU'RE NOT ALLOWED TO FORGET US. GOT IT?
YES, BOSS! BUT DON'T WORRY—I'LL EMAIL YOU BOTH EVERY WEEK!
THAT'LL BE BRILLIANT.
IT'S WEIRD—I'M SAD FOR ME, BUT I'M HAPPY FOR YOU!
THANKS, ERICA.
THANKS TO YOU BOTH! YOU'VE BEEN THERE FOR ME FROM THE BEGINNING.
SO, HOW DO YOU FEEL?
I'M NOT SURE. IT'S A LOT TO TAKE IN.
YESTERDAY, I HAD A PEACEFUL LIFE . . .
I ENJOYED SPYING ON PEOPLE AND WRITING IN MY PRIVATE JOURNAL . . .
NOW HERE I AM—ABOUT TO LEAVE ON A LONG TRIP WITH A MAN I BARELY KNOW, A LITTLE BOY WHO IS GOING TO BE MY LITTLE BROTHER, AND EVEN A DOG! IT'S JUST SO CRAZY!

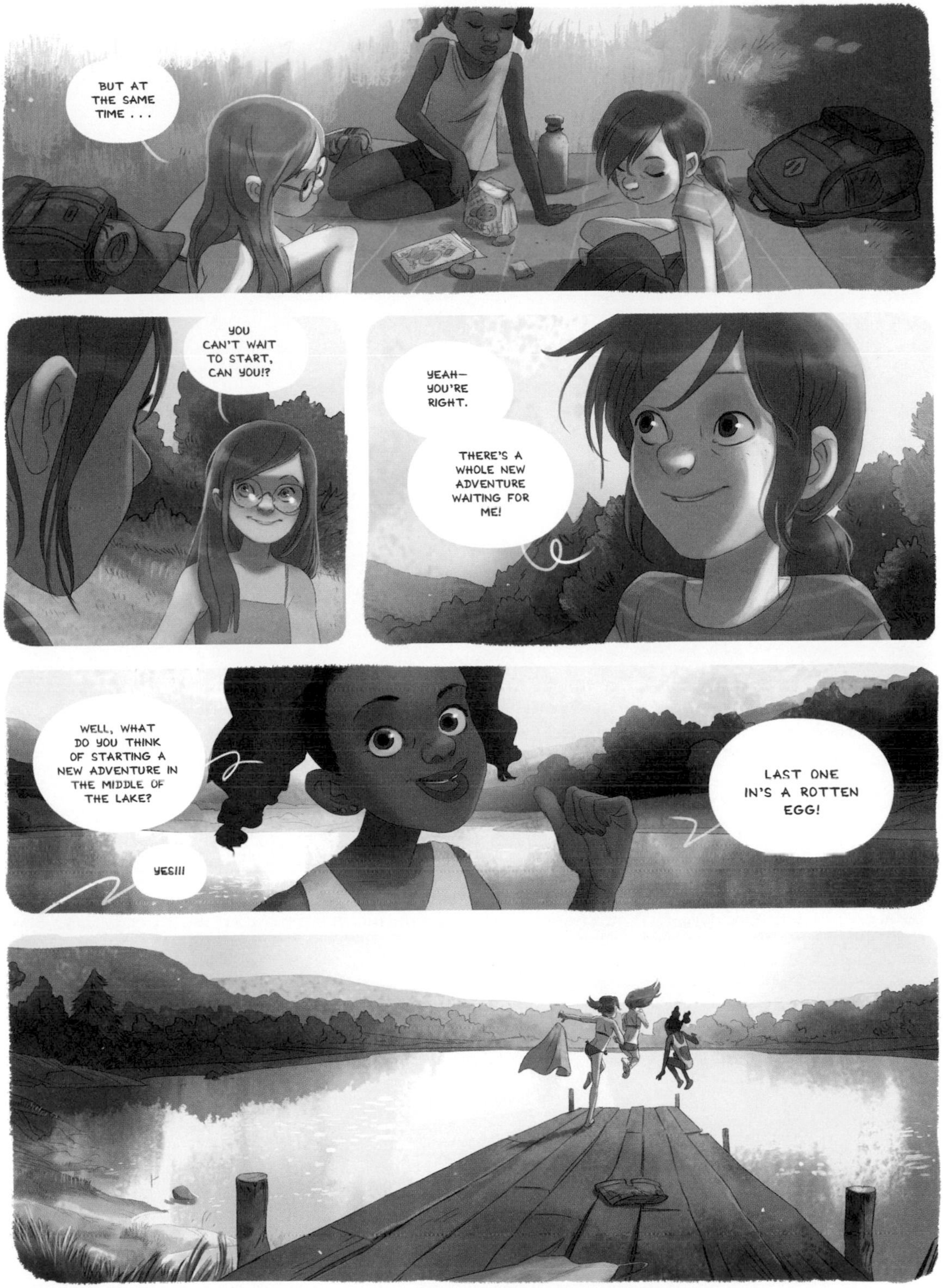
BUT AT THE SAME TIME . . .
YOU CAN'T WAIT TO START, CAN YOU!?
YEAH— YOU'RE RIGHT.
THERE'S A WHOLE NEW ADVENTURE WAITING FOR ME!
WELL, WHAT DO YOU THINK OF STARTING A NEW ADVENTURE IN THE MIDDLE OF THE LAKE?
YES!!!
LAST ONE IN'S A ROTTEN EGG!

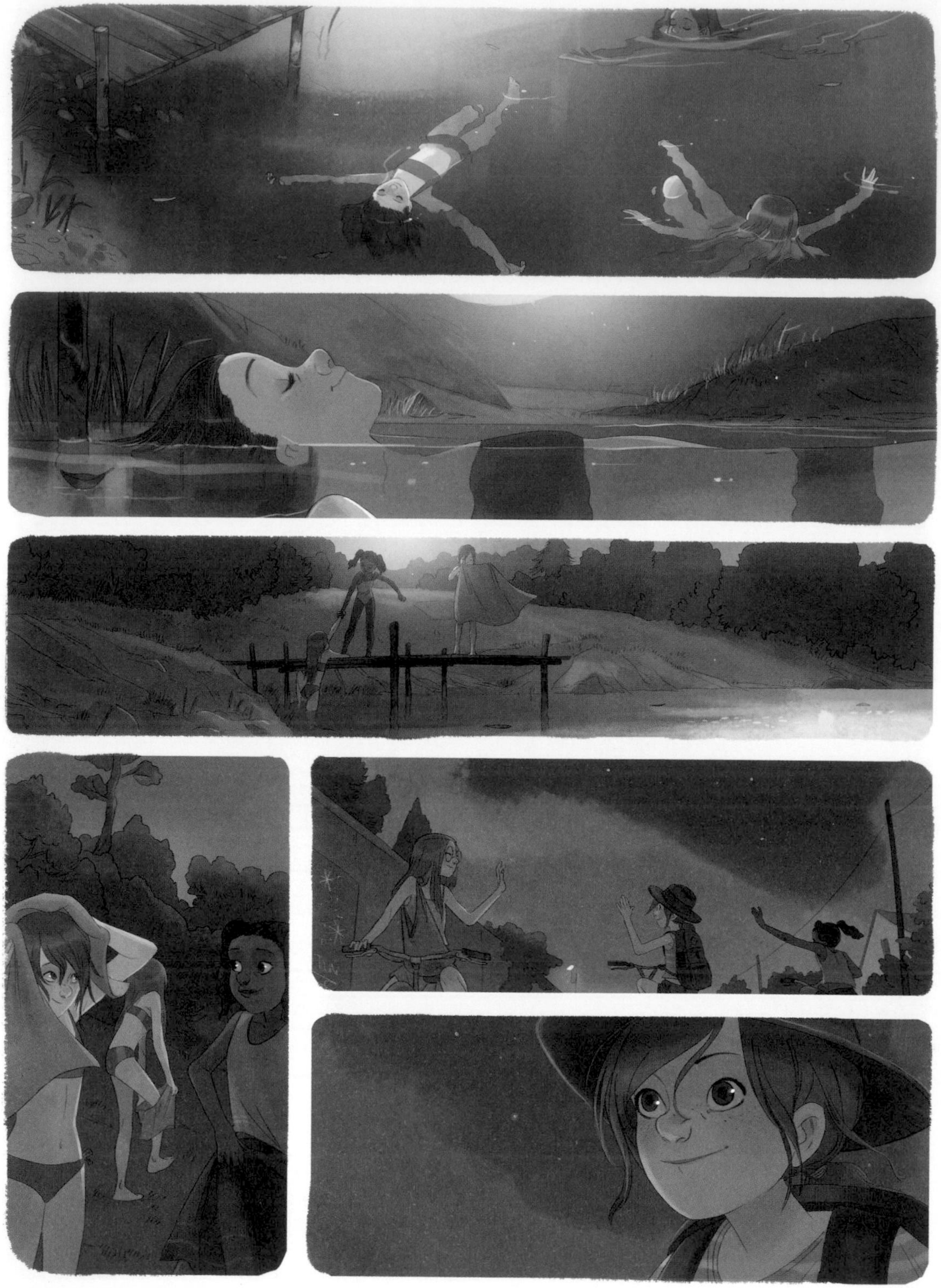

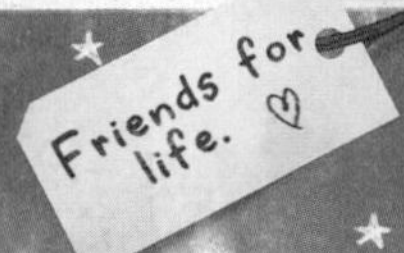
Friends for life.

A few days after our day at the lake, the girls and I met up in our treehouse. They gave me a compass so I can always find them again, no matter where I am.

Lena is going to spend Christmas vacation in London. Maybe we'll be there at the same time! She's signed up for the photography club next year. She's going to learn a ton of new stuff! She promised to send me some of her best shots.

Erica gave me an update about Marvin. They've been texting each other all summer! I still can't believe that she's got a boyfriend!

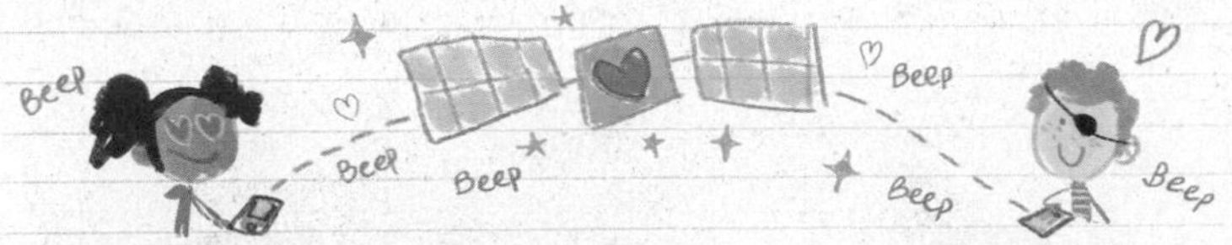
Beep
Beep
Beep
Beep
Beep
Beep

Next spring, she'll go to French Guiana to see her cousins. Maybe I'll get to see her there too!

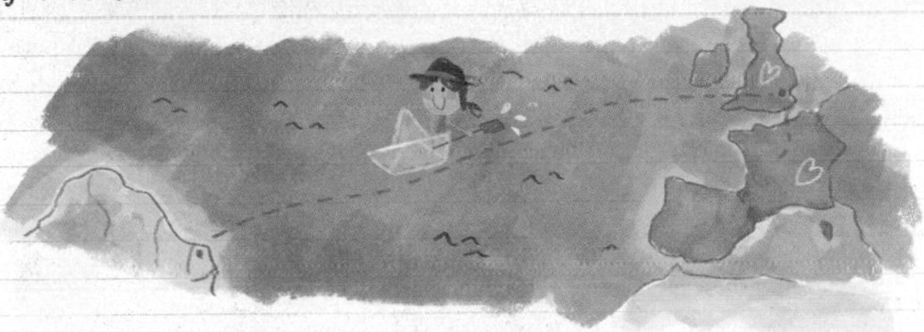

I'm going to miss them both so much!

As for me . . . I'll be a real globe-trotter! I just realized that by going on a world tour, I'll be walking in Mrs. Flores's footsteps! I wonder if I'll run into her again someday too.

I hope so, with all my heart.

So—there you have it. I've finished my investigation. I've unraveled the mystery of the central character and helped her—that is, helped me—through a difficult time. This investigation has been the hardest one of all, but also the most rewarding. I don't know when or if I'll open a new one—only time will tell.

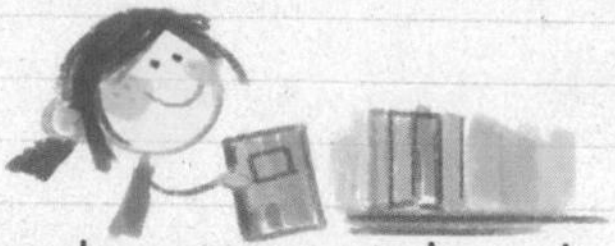

It seems that everyone has a secret deep down inside—a secret they never talk about, but one that makes them who they are. Here's what I've learned about myself:

Cici

I lost my father when I was very little.

I never realized how much pain that caused me. But, with a lot of love from my family and friends, I've begun to heal at last.

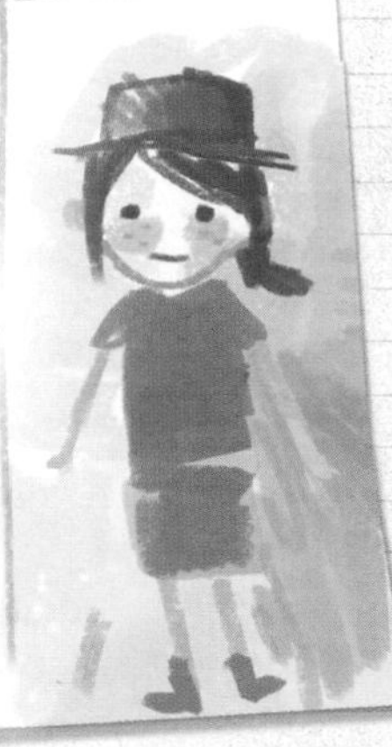

I've learned that forgiving people doesn't mean ignoring what they did. Instead, it means, "What has happened to me can't stop me from being happy."

Now I know who I am and I'm ready to make the most of my future!

I can't wait to take my first step . . .

It's August, and Poppa says the Perseid meteor shower begins tonight. I'm staying up late to watch it with the girls.

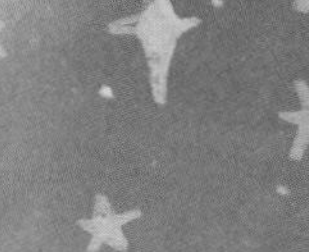

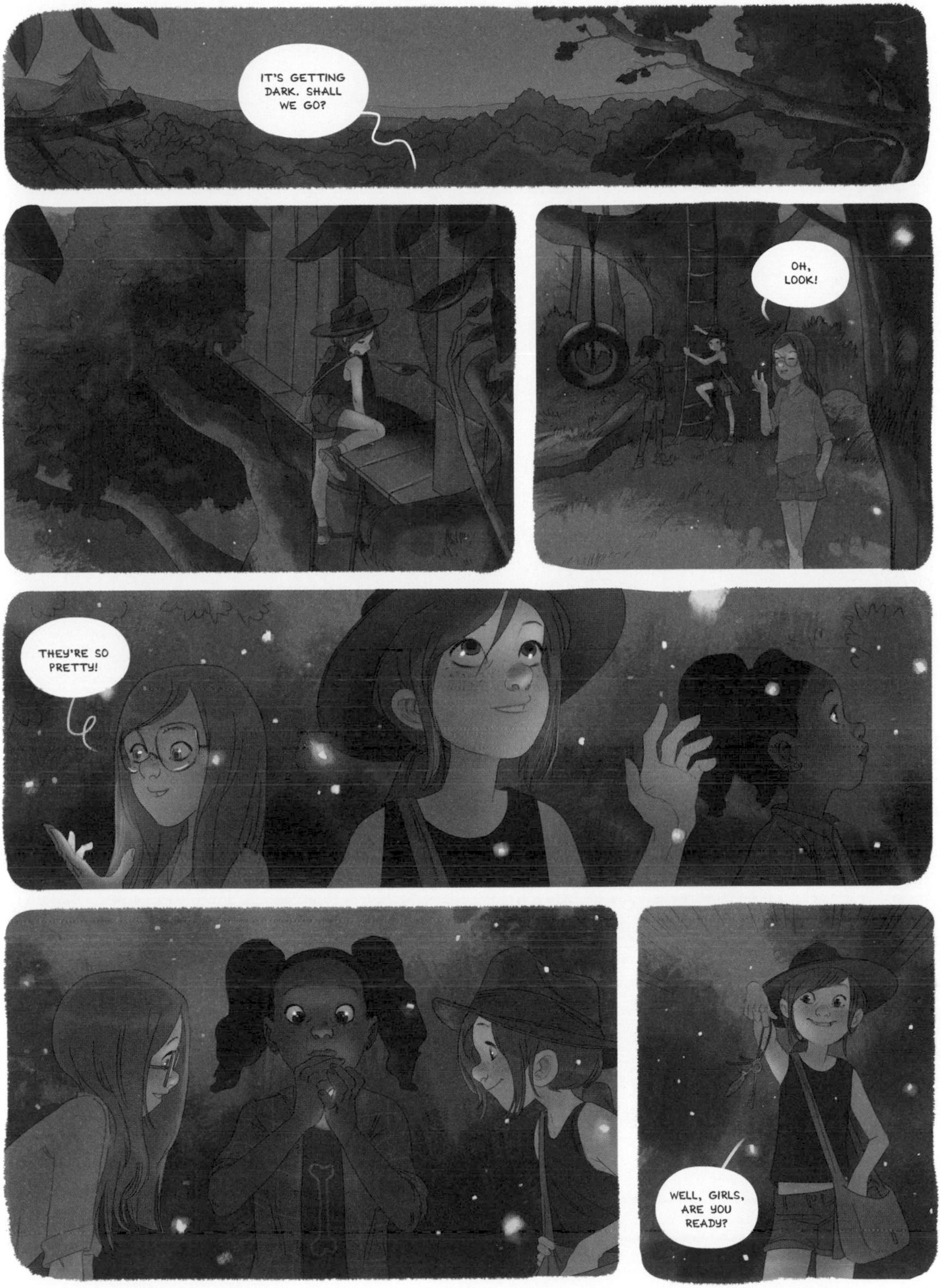
IT'S GETTING DARK. SHALL WE GO?
OH, LOOK!
THEY'RE SO PRETTY!
WELL, GIRLS, ARE YOU READY?

IT'S A SHAME THERE'S NO TRAIL OF PAINT DROPS TO HELP US FIND OUR WAY!

NO PROBLEM. WE KNOW THE WAY BY HEART . . .

WOW!

LOOK AT THAT! THE ZOO IS EVEN MORE MAGICAL AT NIGHT!

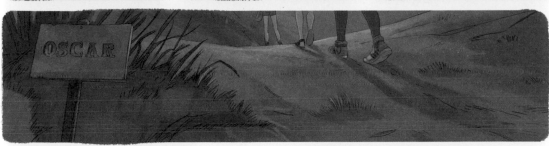

DO YOU THINK ANYONE ELSE IS GAZING AT THE SKY TONIGHT?

I HOPE SO.

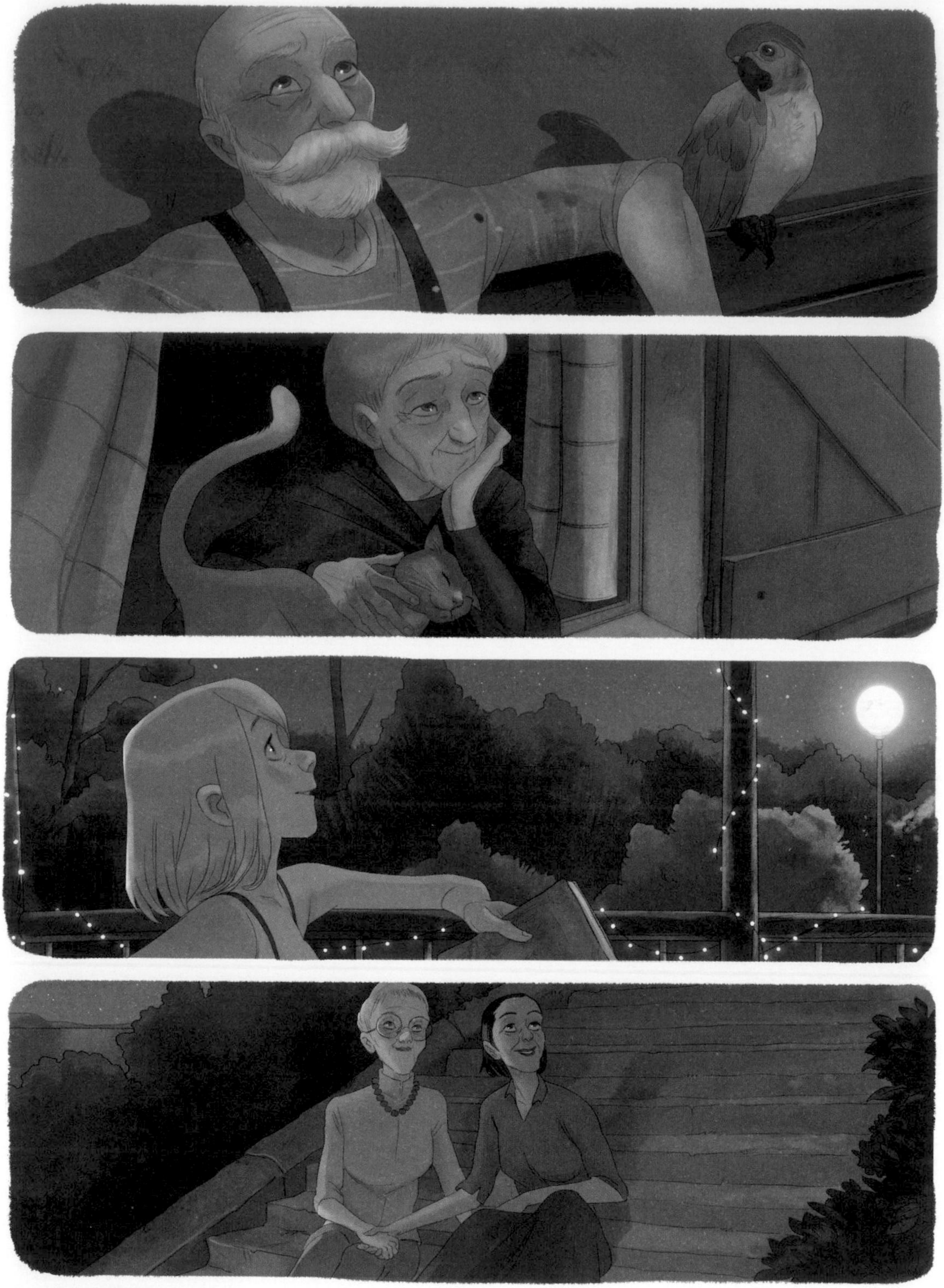

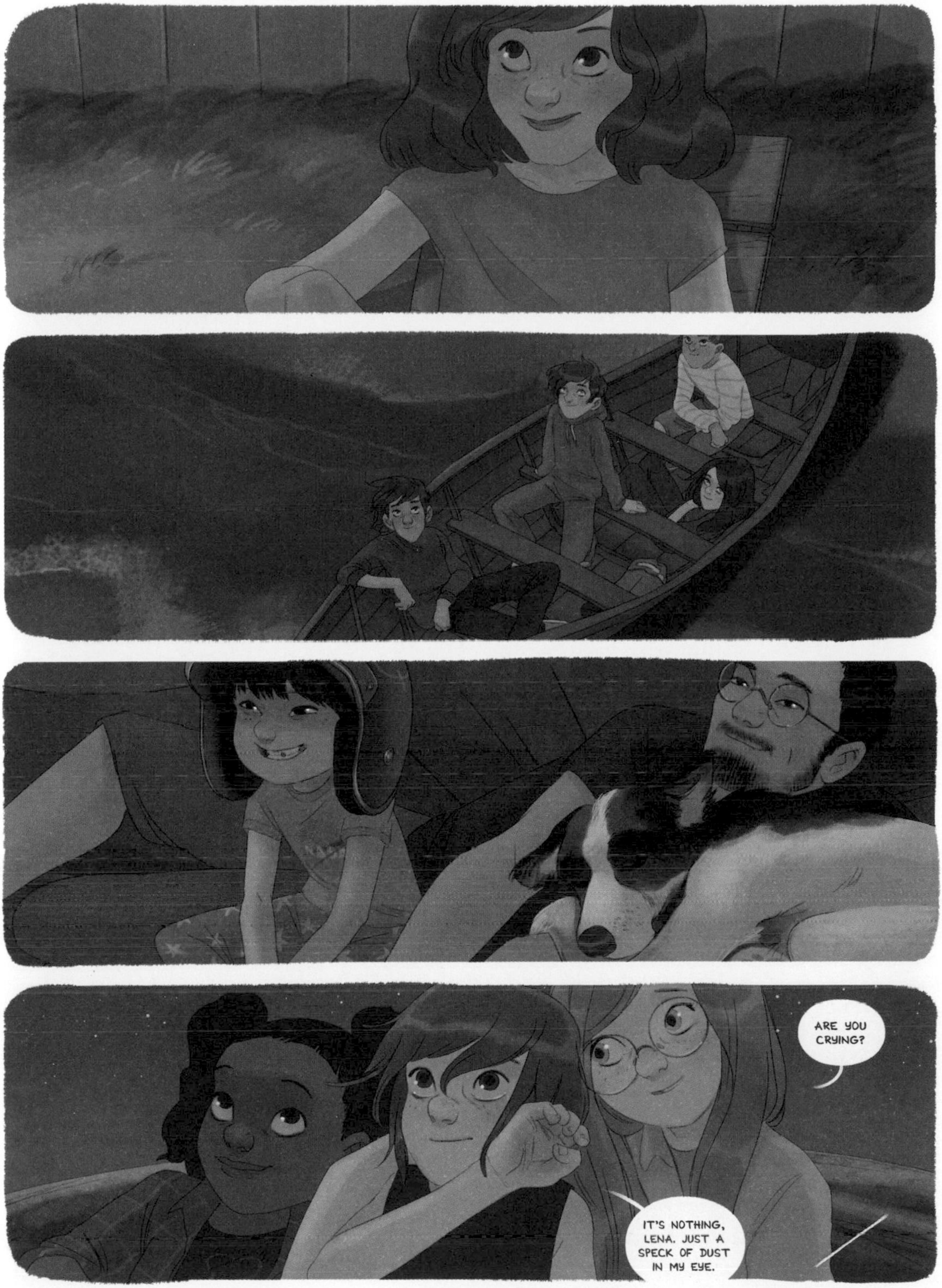
ARE YOU CRYING?
IT'S NOTHING, LENA. JUST A SPECK OF DUST IN MY EYE.

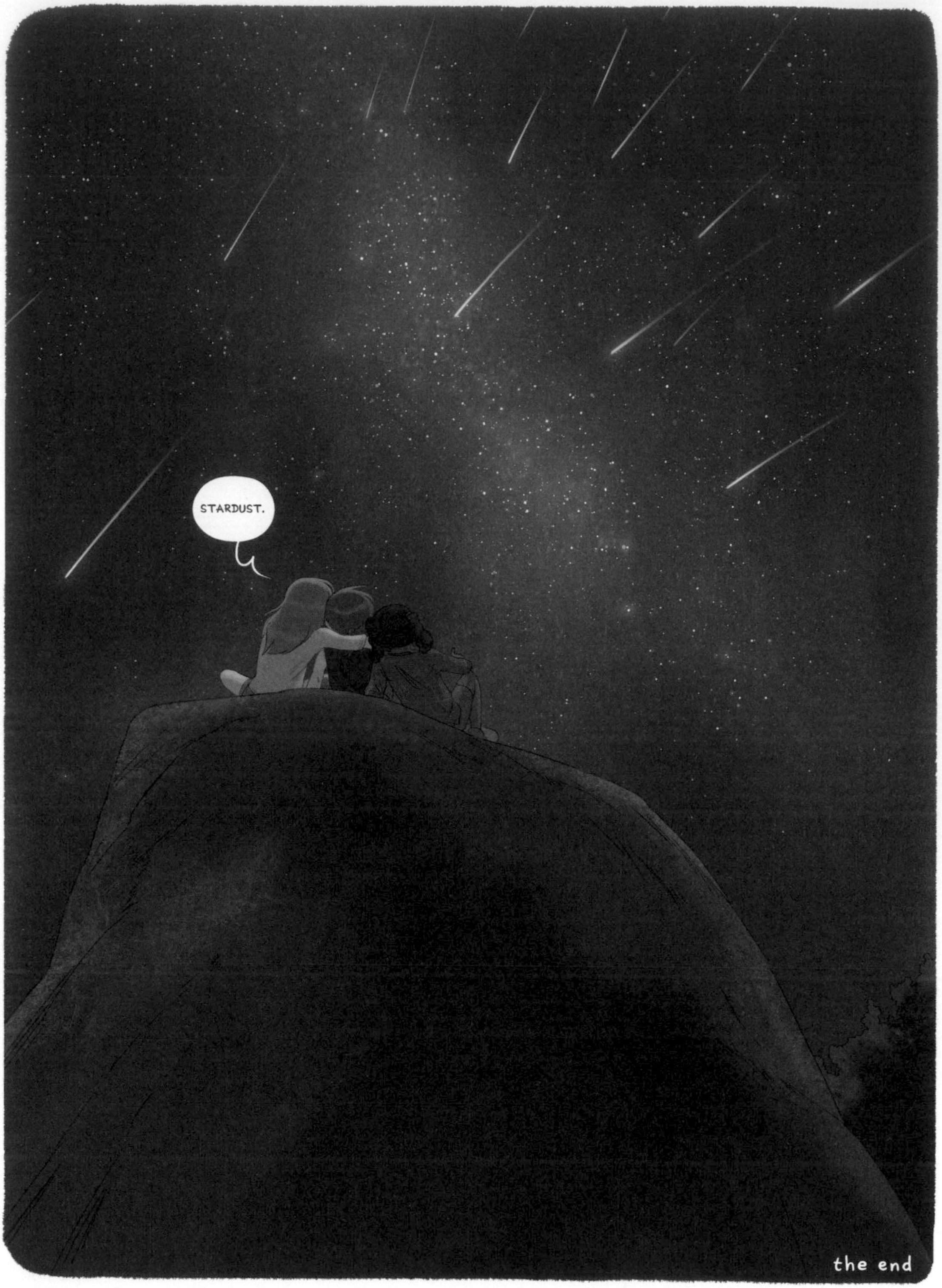
STARDUST.
the end